SISTER S

Not content with her hectic job running
the women's surgical ward at Thames
Vale hospital, Sister Stephanie Driscoll
gets involved in the Christmas pantomime, too. And can there be anyone
better suited to play the wolf to her
Red Riding Hood than moody Mr Guy
Atherstone, surgeon and bane of her
life?

*Books you will enjoy
in our Doctor Nurse series*

A NAVAL ENGAGEMENT by Elspeth O'Brien
MATCHMAKER NURSE by Betty Beaty
STAFF NURSE ON GLANELLY WARD by Janet Ferguson
DR PILGRIM'S PROGRESS by Anne Vinton
HEARTACHE IN HARLEY STREET by Sonia Deane
DOCTOR ON THE NIGHT TRAIN by Elizabeth Petty
LOVE ME AGAIN by Alexandra Scott
A MODEL NURSE by Sarah Franklin
NURSE ON THE SCENE by Lindsay Hicks
ISLAND DOCTOR by Clare Lavenham
TABITHA IN MOONLIGHT by Betty Neels
MARINA'S SISTER by Barbara Perkins
EXAMINE MY HEART, DOCTOR by Lisa Cooper
INTENSIVE AFFAIR by Ann Jennings
NURSE IN DOUBT by Denise Robertson
ITALIAN NURSE by Lydia Balmain
PRODIGAL DOCTOR by Lynne Collins
THE HEALING PROCESS by Grace Read
DREAMS ARE FOR TOMORROW by Frances Crowne
LIFE LINES by Meg Wisgate
SISTER IN HONG KONG by Margaret Barker
DOCTOR MATTHEW by Hazel Fisher
NURSE FROM THE GLENS by Elisabeth Scott

SISTER STEPHANIE'S WARD

BY

HELEN UPSHALL

MILLS & BOON LIMITED
15–16 BROOK'S MEWS
LONDON W1A 1DR

*First published in Great Britain 1984
by Mills & Boon Limited*

© Helen Upshall 1984

*Australian copyright 1984
Philippine copyright 1984*

ISBN 0 263 74845 6

Set in 11 on 12½ pt Linotron Times
03–0984–45,000

*Photoset by Rowland Phototypesetting Ltd
Bury St Edmunds, Suffolk
Made and printed in Great Britain by
Richard Clay (The Chaucer Press) Ltd
Bungay, Suffolk*

CHAPTER ONE

STEPHANIE read through the names of the patients on the list again. She supposed she would get used to a ward of thirty women instead of twenty men. It was quite a challenge to be in charge of a surgical ward after the quieter men's medical ward.

'Good morning, Sister.'

'Mm? Formal this morning aren't we?' she replied vaguely, glancing up slowly in anticipation of seeing the surgical registrar, Pete Burnley. Instead a pair of deep, navy blue eyes glared down at her harshly.

Stephanie was glad that she was sitting down. At least his first impression would be that she was of average height, but she realised that when she stood up her five feet two inches would be diminutive in comparison to Mr Guy Atherstone's six feet three inches!

She knew she had paled. Reputations spread around a hospital like poisoned ivy and she had been at Thames Vale hospital long enough to have heard of the tyrant of general surgery.

'Good morning, Mr Atherstone,' she said brightly in spite of trembling knees which refused to allow her to stand. 'I'm sorry, I thought you were Pete.'

'I'm not here to do a round, Sister,' he explained, ignoring her apology, 'but to confirm that you have a decent one-bedded ward prepared for a special case.'

'Yes.' Stephanie began to fumble with various reports on her desk and in confusion some of them wafted to the floor.

Without looking at the invincible consultant she knew that he was irritated by her lack of discipline.

'I've just taken over this ward,' she clarified. 'I'm trying to get acquainted with my patients.'

'Then I sincerely hope you'll be successful, Sister.'

She thought by the mocking tone that he might leave and come back later, but he was still leaning heavily on her desk, contributing to her feeling of inadequacy. It was no use. Common sense prevailed at last. She might just as well let him see from the start her inadequate size, so she stood up and hastened to retrieve the papers from the floor.

'I thought 2B would be suitable for Miss de Souza. Would you like to see it?' she offered.

She only remembered the name because of its distinguishable sound, and suddenly she felt like a hotel receptionist instead of a ward sister.

'I'm sure your choice will be excellent, Sister,' he said loftily. 'I understand she'll be coming in later today, so I'll look in when my afternoon clinic is through.' He turned and walked briskly into the ward. Stephanie followed him hesitantly—after all, hadn't he just told her that he wasn't here to do a round?

Guy Atherstone was certainly a cut above the average hospital consultant. His broad shoulders were made to appear less muscular by the style and perfect fit of his dark blue suit, but inside it his body flexed intimately, exaggerating his proud swagger. As he strolled nonchalantly from each cubicle of four beds to the next, Stephanie had time to appraise the length of his long legs and the size of his feet, elegantly encased in smooth, black leather, casual-styled shoes. She had seen him many times before from a distance, glad that they were not working colleagues, and now she doubted the wisdom of her decision to apply for the post of sister of women's surgical.

She trailed behind him just in case he needed to consult her but as each patient responded coyly to his interest Stephanie realised that his reputation was not without foundation. He was, or appeared to be, attracted to every female patient—just as rumour claimed. Little did the women know that his square jaw denoted his quicksilver temper which, she supposed, was the reason for his reputedly stormy marriage. His hair was dark, yet now, gazing up at the back of his neck, Stephanie noticed that it was lightly streaked with silver which enhanced his elegance.

She was lost in her appraisal of the surgeon until Pete's familiar voice greeted her.

'Hi, Stevie,' he said cheerily. Then Mr Atherstone turned and Pete hurried on to explain to him that a patient's test results were not yet available. But the consultant appeared not to be perturbed by the news, for instead he was gazing down at Stephanie as if noting her size. She shrank from his intense stare, realising that the glimmer of a smile which was reflected in his eyes was not meant for her, but rather a left-over from the patient he had been conversing with.

So she was short, she thought, without visibly shrugging. It didn't warrant such rude assessment! She felt her cheeks begin to glow. This evidently amused him, and the hard line of his lips actually relaxed in what seemed to be more of a smirk than a grin.

Stephanie felt discomfort creeping up from her toes until every muscle was rigid. She glanced helplessly at Pete, who seemed to be mesmerised by Guy Atherstone's attitude, and then suddenly the consultant reacted to what Pete had said.

'Tell them I want it in ten minutes,' he announced gruffly, and any sign of familiarity disappeared immediately.

Pete raised his shoulders in a negative gesture and went off down the ward to retrace his steps to the path lab.

Mr Atherstone exchanged a few words with his two remaining patients, then he, too, turned towards the door. Stephanie was at a loss for anything to say but she considered she must accompany him to the corridor, as protocol demanded. Once outside the ward the big man paused and looked down at her critically. Stephanie noticed that his silver threads were much more prominent in his sideburns, and she hoped she wasn't going to have to look up at him too long or she would lose her cap. The light from the huge windows reflected in his eyes, making them seem momentarily less dark and intense. He couldn't be smiling again! She had been warned not to expect any such human expression from him. She felt her eyes burning as his gaze swept and searched impudently over her.

'You hardly seem like a "Stevie" to me,' he said in a low, mellow voice, a tone she was wholly unprepared for. 'I suppose it's got to be short for something, Sister—?' He placed a steady finger under her name-brooch, tilting it so that he could read her surname. '*Driscoll*,' he added.

'I prefer Stephanie,' she said quietly, at which he raised his eyebrows significantly. 'I mean,' she added in confusion, 'to having it shortened.'

Now her cheeks were flushed dark red. It wasn't what she had said, but his reaction to it which made her realise that it sounded as if she were asking him to call her by her Christian name.

'Stephanie it shall be,' he replied smoothly, 'though I suppose the shortened version fits your size. Of Lilliputian or pygmy descent?'

'Neither,' she managed to say coolly just as she felt her cap free itself from the clips which seldom stayed put in her wiry, golden-brown hair. She put her hand up to catch it and Guy Atherstone strode away down the corridor without another word.

Mm, Stephanie thought drily, that wasn't too bad a confrontation to start with. He had been reasonably affable, which was better than she had been led to expect.

She went back to her desk, pondering over the

tales which circulated Thames Vale hospital frequently. In theatre he was viewed with much fear, renowned for shouting abuse at anyone from the most junior nurse to sister if something was not to his liking. It was whispered that on one occasion he had reduced the theatre sister to tears, yet apparently she still adored him. Stephanie sighed and wished longingly that she was as stunningly beautiful, slim and curvaceous as theatre sister, who was a silvery blonde with sparkling turquoise eyes, flawless creamy skin and a teasing smile to bewitch the most diffident of men.

In her mind's mirrored view of herself, Stephanie tried to imagine how perfectly silly she must have looked by the side of so tall a man as Mr Atherstone. But she was passable when sitting down. She had similar hair to her mother's, about which her father had always teased them. The colour was really brown, but in certain lights it had a golden sheen on it, and bright sunlight set it on fire so that they almost became redheads. Stephanie's complexion was paler than her mother's but both of them had oval-shaped faces with high cheek-bones and large emerald green eyes. Her father, she could see him now, gazing at his 'two girls' with affectionate admiration, had laughingly placated their lack of inches by assuring them that small was beautiful.

Oh, why did life have to be so cruel? she wondered. They'd been such a contented and happy family, not asking much except to have each other, and then she had almost lost both parents at once.

A runaway lorry had just come out of an industrial site straight at them, the sudden impact causing a dreadful fire in which her father had died still strapped in his seat. Stephanie had ceased to see the names of her patients in the report book. Instead she saw her mother, petite and chic; in Stephanie's eyes still lovely to look at, despite the scars usually hidden by a dainty chiffon scarf at her neck.

Stephanie thanked God for her mother's courage. She had fought back after the tragedy, determined to make something of her life. It would have been so easy for her to sell up her home and go to live in Maidstone with her parents, who were still only in their late sixties, or her in-laws who were a little older and might have been glad to have her near to share a grief which devastated them. Instead, after the shock had diminished and she was attending the burns unit at a London hospital, she had announced that she wanted to remain in the home that she and Stephanie's father had lovingly built together.

Even now, two years later, Stephanie could find no easy remedy for the pain. The anguish of losing her father, and the compassion she felt for her mother.

Then she had been twenty-four and qualified. After working on a gynae ward at the same London hospital her mother attended, she had come to Thames Vale hospital outside Reading to take up her first post as junior sister of the men's medical ward. It had been a stepping-stone, a much needed one in her career to offset her personal tragedy. In spite of the family closeness Stephanie had been brought up to be independent, and although she had offered to go home to live with her mother in Windsor, Pam Driscoll had firmly refused to have her.

'Your dad was proud of you, Stephanie,' her mother had said. 'He believed we'd brought you up to be straight and honest, to know the difference between right and wrong, and it was his challenge to you to see that you don't make a mess of your life. Don't let him down.'

The neatly written words on the page cleared as she came down to earth, glad of her go-ahead parents' challenge, which she had readily accepted. Not that the past two years hadn't added more misery. No, she reprimanded her self-pitying thoughts. It hadn't all been bad. For one thing she loved her work, and Graham Porter had been a compatible colleague and ally to have on the ward. He was a most competent charge-nurse and when Stephanie had come to Thames Vale hospital he had helped her through the first difficult months in new surroundings as well as a more responsible position in her career.

They had quickly become more than working colleagues and Stephanie realised now how easily she had taken him for granted. She hadn't sat down and estimated the growing strength of their relationship, yet she had assumed that it meant as much to Graham as it did to her. He'd been a frequent visitor to her two-roomed flat and she'd had no conscience about him staying overnight in a sleeping-bag on the couch.

She sighed aloud and felt her cheek-muscles tighten as she remembered the very last time Graham had taken her out for a meal after an extravagant shopping expedition a few months ago. She had become so relaxed in his company, so sure of him, that his sudden demand had shaken her to the core.

Up to that time she hadn't considered her potential as a fighter. But the realisation that she did not love Graham enough to be carried away emotionally gave her the courage to hold her own in the verbal battle which followed. Even now she could hear her own shrill voice accusing him of wanting her just for his own sexual pleasure. Marriage was never mentioned yet, deep inside, Stephanie knew that she had presumed that to be the ultimate goal as far as her own future was concerned. Strangely, though, she felt relief now that the affair was over.

Graham was good-looking and had no difficulty in finding the type of casual friends he obviously preferred. He evidently didn't love Stephanie enough to want to spend the rest of his days tied to her. She hadn't loved him enough merely to be a sleeping partner.

She supposed she had been naive. She looked only for the good in a man and expected them all to be of her father's calibre. The denouement had left her drained, but after discussing it briefly with her mother she had pulled herself together, faced

Graham with confidence and continued working as if nothing had happened.

Stephanie suspected that his next affair ended similarly when he asked her for a date less than two months later, but she had met his gaze stoically and told him that the past was over and done with, buried with no recriminations. It would have been easier to apply for a move to another ward then, but Stephanie had her pride, and to everyone's astonishment it was Graham who transferred to a special ward for the terminally ill, mostly cancer cases.

Stephanie never doubted Graham's devotion to his profession, even if she doubted his integrity, but now when they met she was forced to wonder whether he was losing his prestige as a lover. He seemed to lack the sparkle he had once had and female interest was less important to him. He still sought her company on occasion in the canteen, but usually the conversation trod the well-known path of concern over his patients and Stephanie was dedicated enough to be a willing listener. Perhaps that particular ward had changed Graham. Perhaps he was giving more serious thought to his personal life and future . . .

Stephanie went to join Staff Nurse Liz Rushden who was doing the medicine round. After just two days she was beginning to associate patients with their names and treatments, and the patients in turn were beginning to view the sister of the ward with less reserve.

'Feeling more comfortable today, Mrs Dalby?'

she greeted the middle-aged woman who gulped down the small glassful of liquid Liz had given her and made a face.

'I will when I can soak in a nice hot bath,' she said with a smile.

'Bit soon for that, but I'll get one of the nurses to take you along for a shower later. You can get up in time for lunch, but don't overdo it.'

'Thank you, Sister. I don't know about lunch though. I'll be terrified I'm going to start vomiting again.'

'Just a light lunch. It's the anaesthetic which causes the vomiting. You should be over that now. You've got more colour today so you're on the turn, I'm sure.'

Mrs Dalby responded to Stephanie's light-hearted chat, and Stephanie moved on to the next cubicle of four beds.

It hadn't taken her long to appreciate why this particular set of four patients had been selected to be companions in one cubicle. They were of differing ages, ranging from Carol, who was in her thirties and had had an emergency appendicectomy, to Mrs Hadley who was in her early fifties and recovering after a hernia operation, to young Amelia, a teenager who had needed exploratory surgery for an as yet undiagnosed stomach disorder. The last of the four was Mrs Davis, a sixty-year-old widow who had had gallstones removed.

Apart from the fact that they had undergone surgery within days of each other, they appeared to be compatible and it was evident they had done much to help each other. Stephanie and Liz joined them now to the sound of their frivolous laughter.

'We'll have to get rid of this lot soon, Sister,' Liz said. 'They're getting out of hand!'

'Give them an extra-strong dose of castor oil then, Staff Nurse,' Stephanie suggested with a grin.

'Sister! You wouldn't!' Mrs Davis pleaded, wiping her eyes as she recovered from the hilarity.

'What's the joke, anyway?' Stephanie asked. 'Can't we all share it?'

The patients looked at each other, wondering which of them would be the spokeswoman.

'Depends on your opinion of *Sir*,' Mrs Hadley said drily.

'You mean Mr Atherstone?' Stephanie asked hesitantly.

'He's so—so—' Carol began dreamily.

'She's off again,' Amelia cut in with a scornful look at Carol, then added, 'I don't know who was the most embarrassed when he came in just now, Mrs Hadley or Mr Atherstone.'

Stephanie and Liz waited patiently for an explanation.

'I was out of bed looking for my slippers,' Mrs Hadley explained. 'You could say he caught me bending, and this nightie doesn't leave much to the imagination.'

'And she didn't hear Mr Atherstone come in, so she carried on grumbling about having tubes in unmentionable parts of her anatomy and he just stood there watching her, mesmerised,' Amelia put in. 'I don't know which of their faces was the reddest when she finally turned round to find him standing behind her!'

'I expect he was amused rather than embarrassed,' Stephanie said.

'And he's not often amused,' Liz said tartly with sarcasm.

'I don't know why you nurses don't like him,' Mrs Davis said. 'He's got charm. He's tall and handsome.'

'And he's got a reputation,' Liz added primly.

'People always speculate when they don't really know the truth about someone,' Stephanie intervened. 'He's a competent surgeon, and the patients like him, so who are we to complain?'

'Tell me, Sister,' Mrs Hadley asked seriously, 'do you meet socially? I mean nurses from all the wards with the doctors?'

'Like any other profession or job, Mrs Hadley,' Stephanie said, 'you get to know the people you work closely with best, then you move on and become friends with the next lot. Most of the doctors are married except the younger and newer housemen.'

'And not enough to go round for all you girls?' Mrs Davis commented sympathetically.

'I'm told the female population outdoes the male one anyway, so some of us have to dedicate our lives to looking after other people.'

'I thought Mr Atherstone looked at you—well, as if there was something between you,' Amelia said with a giggle.

'We're hardly acquainted yet,' Stephanie said. 'I've managed to keep well out of his way up to now.'

Liz laughed. 'You can hardly do that in your present position. He only acknowledges the sister of any ward, and he expects top priority whenever he graces *us* with his presence.'

'Which, if we're lucky, will only be about twice a week,' Stephanie predicted.

'Don't kid yourself, Sister,' Liz said, 'he drops in at all hours of the day and night.'

'Let's hope it's night rather than day, then.'

'Rumour has it that he has a soft spot for night sister, so he often appears late evening,' Carol said.

'There's theatre sister too,' Stephanie laughed. 'Apparently she's carrying a torch for him and quite a few others besides—never mind about his poor wife!'

'Unhappily married, so I heard,' Mrs Hadley said. 'It's a rotten shame, I think he's gorgeous. He's a bit too young for me though—still, you never know, he might prefer older women. How old do you reckon he is, Sister?'

Stephanie raised her eyebrows. 'I've really no idea, Mrs Hadley. I've never even thought about it.'

'Thirty-six, my mum said,' Amelia announced confidently. 'My mum knows someone who knows a friend of his.' She slid her soft brown eyes in Stephanie's direction. 'He was certainly giving you the once-over, Sister,' she went on. 'Looking you up and down—'

'Probably unable to believe I could possibly qualify, on account of my size,' Stephanie commented drily. 'Most men consider small women insignificant and inadequate.'

'That's only your opinion, my dear,' Mrs Davis said. 'I wasn't going to mention it, I don't want to embarrass you. But as Amelia says, he did look at you with a gleam in his eye.'

Stephanie laughed in an effort to hide her confusion.

'He did seem amused,' she agreed, 'but that was because I'd just dropped a sheaf of papers on the floor. He probably couldn't believe that the new sister could be so utterly disorganised.'

'I thought he looked down at you with a lovely warm expression, just as if he wished he could pick you up and put you in his pocket.'

'Not the pocket of that immaculate suit!' Stephanie tut-tutted, and was relieved that Liz was already moving on to the next cubicle.

'I'll expect you all up for lunch,' Stephanie added as she followed Liz, who had paused by the door to the day-room.

'They don't miss much do they?' Liz whispered.

'What vivid imagination, seeing things which aren't there!'

'No need to be embarrassed, Sister,' Liz said. 'I've been on this ward over a year now and he did seem in a most unusually perceptive mood this morning. I've never known him show the slightest interest in any of the nursing staff.'

'Ah, that's because he has a special case coming

in today. A Miss de Souza. All he called this morning for was to make sure we had a special ward ready for her.'

'What's she in for?'

'I haven't received any notes yet. Can't be one of his lady-friends, that wouldn't be ethical.'

Liz snorted her disapproval. 'Mr Atherstone wouldn't worry about ethics, Sister.'

Stephanie sighed. 'Guess we'll just have to wait and see. Whoever Miss de Souza is, she's someone pretty special to him.'

Stephanie tried not to dwell on the expected patient. It was always off-putting to have a consultant's special case on a ward and knowing so little of Guy Atherstone gave him the advantage.

It was early evening when the consultant strode into Stephanie's office. She was absorbed with writing a report and didn't notice the approaching footsteps.

'Which room is Miss de Souza in?' His tone was short.

'She will be in 2B when she arrives, but so far she hasn't turned up,' Stephanie said, meeting his dark frown as coolly as she could.

'Not arrived?' he questioned with disbelief.

'No, Mr Atherstone.'

He turned, tight-lipped and, she suspected, on the verge of gnashing his teeth. He swayed in the doorway and looked back to glare at Stephanie.

'You—you've been on duty all day?'

'Except for early afternoon, yes.'

Surely he didn't imagine that a patient would be admitted without her knowledge?

'Well, shouldn't you have made enquiries by this time?' he thundered, unable to hide his impatience.

Stephanie was momentarily speechless, then she said calmly, 'Enquiries, sir? Where do you suggest I should begin?'

'Don't be impertinent, Sister Driscoll.' With one long stride he was at the side of her desk, the deepening frown transforming his usually handsome features to an expression of brooding contempt.

'Coming into hospital is a traumatic event in most patients' lives. We seem to have lost not only discipline in our hospitals but human understanding as well. Sympathy and compassion, Sister,' he lowered his face closer to hers to stress the point, 'are top priority on *my* ward, so you'd better forget any preconceived ideas you have of nursing being a glamorous profession. As well as the surgical, scientific and technical side of the job, it's all about human relationships. So perhaps you'd better start studying again.'

He turned and left her office, leaving an icy draught in his wake.

CHAPTER TWO

KEEP CALM, keep a hold on yourself, Stephanie told herself as she tightened the grip on her pen. She ought to have been prepared. She had been warned, but after his pleasant approach earlier in the day she had imagined that the rumours were unfounded. Now she had experience of his unpredictability.

For several minutes her eyes refused to focus as she felt anger rising within her. How dare he talk to her as if she was an inexperienced student nurse? He was the one who needed a lesson in human relationships! Now she realised that all the stories which circulated so readily about the great Guy Atherstone were probably true.

Stephanie lifted the paperweight on her now tidy desk and retrieved the form which informed her of Miss de Souza's impending admission. How could she chase a patient about whom she knew so little, not even a telephone number? The administrative offices were all closed so she was virtually helpless in her search for someone whom as yet she hadn't even met.

If *he* was so concerned, let him do the worrying and searching, she decided, though it nagged at her that she had been accused of lack of interest. Compassion was something she had first-hand knowledge of, but such an arrogant consultant wouldn't bother his head about the staff's personal traumas.

Her pen ripped across the page with finality as she finished her report—just as the shuffle of footsteps echoed in the corridor and warned her of the night staff's arrival.

'One missing patient found, Sister.'

Stephanie could hardly believe that the smiling blue eyes were the same as those which had held such reproof less than half an hour before. Guy Atherstone stood etched in the shadow of the doorway behind a tall, slim woman. His face seemed to be framed above the woman's shoulder, slightly rugged, appealing, wearing a smug smile, in contrast to the delicately pale, apprehensive features of his companion.

Stephanie stood up and accepted the hand extended by Miss de Souza.

'Sister Driscoll, darling,' the consultant introduced them. 'She was beginning to think you'd taken a slow boat to China.'

Stephanie had to bite her lower lip to prevent herself from setting this patient straight about a few things. She took the necessary form from her desk drawer and sat down again.

'Most patients like to come in early to get the formalities over and done with,' she explained. 'I'll just take your particulars, Miss de Souza, then leave you in the capable hands of the night staff.'

Stephanie indicated the vacant chair. Perhaps now Mr Atherstone would go away and leave her to it. But he wandered casually behind them, going to the window, hands deep in his pockets, jingling coins and keys as he listened to Stephanie asking the questions and Miss de Souza replying in a quiet, sometimes faltering voice—until she was asked what religion she was, and then her eyes flashed with indignation.

'I don't know what that's got to do with anything,' she retorted testily, 'or anyone.'

'C of E.' The masculine voice rang out decisively behind Stephanie, who wrote it down on the form.

'No, Guy. I'm not a child you know! I'm quite capable of making up my own mind about religion or anything else for that matter. Atheist, Sister Driscoll.'

Stephanie crossed out the C of E and wrote as the patient requested, but she recognised this as some sign of protest rather than that Miss de Souza actually believed there was no God. Stephanie also sensed Guy Atherstone tightening his muscles, so she was not surprised when he turned, snatched the pen out of her hand, tore the form into shreds and demanded, 'Begin again, and stop being militant, Andrea.'

Stephanie sighed with annoyance. He was the militant, she decided as she reached in the drawer for a clean form.

'Just leave religion a blank,' he ordered crisply.

'If you hadn't torn up the first form I could have crossed it through,' Stephanie said, half to herself. 'Now I have to ask all the same questions again, Miss de Souza.'

'Name—Andrea de Souza. Address—Flat 3C, Curzon Court, Reedway Square, Thames Vale. Age—twenty-seven. Eyes—green. Hair—chestnut. Do you need vital statistics as well?' he asked sarcastically, tapping the form with one long, aggressive finger.

Stephanie paused, her own fingers trembling. She glanced over her shoulder to discover Guy Atherstone's face almost on a parallel with her own.

'I'm asking the questions, Mr Atherstone,' she said in a cool, patient, indulgent tone. 'I'm sure you must have something else more constructive to do than helping me.'

She knew by the indrawing of his breath that she had incensed him.

'I'm doing my best to get a patient admitted before I go home,' he said sharply.

Stephanie rounded on him, finally giving way to her own agitation.

'That's my job—*sir*,' she said fiercely, 'and I'd like to be given the opportunity to get on with it before *I* go off duty.'

His blue eyes were emitting lightning sparks. He looked down at her as if he would like to have slapped her across the face, but with an attempt to retain his pride he slowly pulled himself up to his full height and walked out of the office and down the corridor with a firm tread.

Stephanie looked across at Miss de Souza. 'Now, let's do it properly,' she pleaded.

Miss de Souza laughed nervously. 'Andrea de

Souza, and you can call me Andrea. I'm terribly sorry. Poor Guy, he was only trying to be helpful. Just to please him you'd better classify me as C of E, even though—oh, well,' she shrugged. 'In case I don't come round, better to be safe than sorry,' she added with a hint of frivolity.

Stephanie wasn't amused and felt like telling this patient that it was no laughing matter. But she guessed that she was feeling tense, perhaps even terrified of whatever ordeal she was about to experience, and Stephanie's job was to try to put her at her ease.

'You'd better come round,' she quipped. 'I wouldn't like to be on the receiving end of Mr Atherstone's wrath if you let us down.'

Stephanie heard the long intake of breath but ignored it. This girl was so uptight she hardly seemed to know what she was saying, but they managed to complete the form successfully.

'I don't have any notes or information to go on yet, Andrea, but I presume you're in for surgery, so there'll be one or two tests to be carried out, and a check by the anaesthetist.'

'I . . . I can't bear the thought of being put to sleep,' Andrea stuttered. 'I've chickened out a couple of times in the past, that's why Guy is getting short with me. I don't know why he bothers. I keep telling myself that it will all be worth it in the end, but then I argue that the decision is mine. I can go home and refuse to have the operation. I don't know why I don't. I don't know why I allowed myself to be persuaded.'

'I'm sure Mr Atherstone has given you the best possible advice, and you'll be in expert hands, Andrea,' Stephanie consoled gently.

'But Guy can't do the op. I'm not his patient. We . . . we're too close for that, so Mr Perry is doing it. I feel so unsure, Sister. I think they're too eager to cut people up these days, but Guy seems to think I owe it to him to have it done.' Her voice faded and her lips trembled, then she looked directly at Stephanie, a slight flush in her cheeks. 'You obviously don't like him. He isn't easy to get on with, but he's always surrounded by admiring women, you know.'

Stephanie lowered her gaze to the completed form.

'I'm not in a position to comment, Andrea. I've only recently been transferred to this ward, so I've never worked with Mr Atherstone before. It always takes a little time to get used to the differing methods used by the various doctors. Now, I'll take you along to your room.'

Stephanie stood up, and as she led the way along the corridor to the single room she noticed Guy Atherstone in the middle distance. He was on the landing, in deep conversation with night sister. The staff nurse and two other nurses who were the night staff on the women's surgical ward were coming along.

'I'll be with you in a moment,' Stephanie called to them, and opened the door of 2B. 'Here we are then, Andrea. I think you'll find it comfortable, though if you should be lonely at any time we can always move you into the main ward.'

'She won't be lonely. I shall see to that, Sister.' Guy Atherstone had followed them in and then went on to introduce night sister to Andrea.

'If you'll excuse me then,' Stephanie said, 'I'll go to give my report.'

'All right, Stevie, I'll see to things here,' Vicky Mounsden said, and Stephanie was glad to escape. She was welcome to him and his girl-friend, Stephanie declared silently as she returned to the office where Staff Nurse Jill Fox was hanging up her cape.

'Last minute panic, Sister?' she asked.

'Not really. Just the VIP being admitted.'

'Bit late, isn't she?'

'Apparently I should have gone out looking for her,' Stephanie said crossly. 'I don't have any notes about her condition. It seems she's Mr Perry's patient, so you'd better see if you can contact one of the housemen and chase up some information about her. I can feel it in my bones that she's going to be trouble.'

'Just because she's the heart-throb's girl friend— or one of his harem?'

'No. I have no idea what she is to him except special in some way, but I think she needs watching. She didn't really want to come in, she doesn't like the idea of surgery and she wouldn't be above packing her bags and making off in the middle of the night. Unless,' Stephanie paused, holding up her forefinger significantly, 'it's all a big dramatic game to gain our attention, *and* Mr Atherstone's.'

'Looks as if night sister will be giving her pre-ferential treatment, anyway,' Jill said, 'so I'll leave her to it. As long as Mr Atherstone frequently graces us with his presence, I'll be quite happy.'

'Not you, too? Let me get off duty,' Stephanie groaned.

By the time the change-over had taken place she was quite late leaving the ward, and she had reached ground level when she ran into Graham Porter.

'Just the girl I'm looking for,' he announced as he fell in step beside her.

'I'm not in the best of moods,' she said hoping he would go away.

'I've taken rejection before, I can do so again,' he laughed.

'I'm in a hurry to get home.' Stephanie tried again but unsuccessfully.

'I'll treat you to supper if you'll come to the canteen with me, Stevie.'

'I don't eat here any more than I have to since I moved, as you well know,' she told him.

'I want to discuss the drama group with you—and I know it's no use suggesting we meet anywhere but in the canteen, for obvious reasons,' he said raising his eyebrows hopefully.

'Oh, the drama group. I'd forgotten about that.'

'We need you, Stevie, and surely we can work together again? We need a committee meeting, we ought to get some ideas sorted out so that we can make a start.'

'How did I get into this?' bemoaned Stephanie.

'You're a natural director and producer and you're too good to lose. Just because I blotted my copy-book once doesn't mean that I shall ever try anything on again.'

'You'd better not,' she snapped.

'Come on, Stevie. What have you got to go home to? An empty, cold house? No supper?'

'I know it's not that warm for August but it's not mid-winter and I can soon cook some supper,' she argued.

'But there are some good cheese dishes in the canteen on a Tuesday. Can't you be persuaded? No—of course, you're the one girl who says no and means it.'

'All right—but only for as long as it takes to eat supper,' she agreed.

Graham put his arm round her shoulder as they turned to the lift.

'To tell you the truth, Graham,' she admitted, 'I don't feel like cooking and I don't particularly relish the thought of my own company tonight.'

'Had one of those days? I was surprised to hear that you'd chosen women's surgical of all wards.'

'I was too familiar with everything on men's medical' she said. 'I liked it, but then I'd like my work wherever it was! No, it got too humdrum and I felt I needed a challenge. It was only by the merest chance that Vicky Mounsden mentioned about women's surgical. It's busier, different in so many ways.'

'But today hasn't been that good?' he queried.

'Mr Atherstone is not the easiest of men—I

mean, he's so unpredictable! He *would* have this special case expected just as I take over the ward, and he blamed me for her not coming in early.'

'What's she in for?'

Stephanie shrugged as she stepped out of the lift on the fourth floor. 'Don't know. The whole situation is shrouded in mystery.'

'Abortion?' Graham suggested.

'Not *that*! Not here at Thames Vale, in a hospital where the great man is so respected.'

'Sounds as if you've taken an instant dislike to him, Stevie.'

'First thing this morning he was quite pleasant—just to give me a false sense of security, I suppose. Now he'll be looking for the slightest indiscretion. He obviously isn't used to anyone arguing with him or matching his sarcasm with sarcasm, and I'm guilty of both.'

'Doesn't sound like our sweet-natured Stevie!'

Stephanie related the incident in detail to get it out of her system.

'We were such a happy crowd on men's medical. The patients were all nice men, apart from the occasional misfit, and the staff, doctors and nurses alike, got on so well.'

'Just like a happy, family, till I—'

'Oh, forget that, Graham, for heaven's sake! I'm not one to bear grudges.'

'You mean I'm forgiven?' He swung her round and took her hands in his, in the deserted corridor. Stephanie smiled up at him. Graham at this moment was a calming influence, familiar, pleasant, a friend, which she needed more than food tonight.

'There was nothing to forgive, you idiot,' she said screwing up her eyes at him.

Graham pursed his lips in a doubtful expression.

'I wish I could believe you meant that, but,' he sighed, 'that's not the way it sounded to me before.'

'You know the score now. You caught me by surprise—I wasn't prepared.'

'Then you'd better be prepared next time, my girl,' he said forcibly.

'There won't be a next time—promise?' she urged.

Graham shook his head. 'Some of you girls are so naive! Stevie, I get the message! You don't, and didn't, care enough for me to get physical. A few kisses, some horseplay, a lot of laughs—where the hell do you think that was leading? I'm not made of stone, for God's sake! And neither will the next guy be. For your own sake don't lead a fellow on if you're going to cry off at the last minute.'

'I didn't lead you on,' she denied hotly, the colour rushing into her cheeks. 'You don't need any leading.'

'Exactly. That's what I'm trying to tell you, Stevie. Men are supposed to be the leaders, the pursuers, the wooers.'

'There's such a thing as Women's Lib and I like everything on a fifty-fifty basis. When I meet someone who is extra-special I'll know, and I'll react accordingly.'

Graham laughed scornfully. 'If I didn't think you were some hell of a girl I'd throw you off the roof of this hospital,' he vowed. 'You're all creased up inside—you know that? Oh, I know the sob-story and I agree life has been cruel, but men are men, relationships develop, love *grows*, Stevie.'

'Thanks for the lecture. So, I don't know what love is—yet. Isn't that what *I* tried to tell *you*? You don't either. You only wanted a sexual relationship, not love and marriage.'

'We might not have been compatible and now we'll never know. But you just watch yourself. The next man might not be so understanding.'

'And what makes you think you're understanding?'

Stephanie turned from his grasp and pushed open the swing-doors to the canteen. Immediately they were caught up in a hubbub of voices and laughter, but after being served with a supper of lasagne and coffee they found a vacant table. They ate in comparative silence, Graham's strong words only adding to Stephanie's already harassed mind, but when the pangs of hunger had been satisfied she looked across at him in a more relaxed mood.

'This is good. I don't suppose it's like you'd get in Italy, but it's tasty, with plenty of meat.' Stephanie was glad she'd agreed to come.

'You won't sleep tonight,' Graham joked.

'I won't anyway.'

'Sorry, Stevie. I didn't mean to be ruthless but it had to be said. Your mother worries about you.'

Stephanie faced him sternly. 'When have you seen Mum?'

'The last time she came over on your day off.

About two weeks ago? You dropped her off in Reading and you came on duty. She did some shopping to kill time till her next train back to Windsor. I met her in the shopping precinct, so we had a cup of tea and a chat.'

'Parents don't arrange marriages any more, Graham.'

'I have never mentioned marriage,' he reminded her sharply.

Stephanie felt humiliated. 'Sorry,' she muttered. Then, 'I told you I was in a rotten mood.'

'A self-pitying one, so snap out of it. I asked you here to talk about the drama group.'

'So?' Stephanie tossed her head defiantly.

'So, we'll get all this over with first. Your mother didn't know the real reason why we had split up and naturally she was concerned.'

'You didn't—' Stephanie began.

'There you go again! You're twenty-six, Stevie, and your mother doesn't expect you to go on being a virgin for the rest of your life.'

'Don't be so personal,' Stephanie snapped.

'You don't have to hide anything from her, she knows the score.'

'Thank you very much!' Stephanie stormed.

'And I expect the whole hospital does, too. Your innocent expression gives you away and your self-righteous attitude. If you want everyone to think we're just good friends then behave like it.'

'Find someone else to help you with the drama club. I'll give you my resignation in writing to make it official.'

'I'll tear it up,' he said lightly.

'Go to hell!'

Graham laughed and suddenly Stephanie was laughing with him, though the tears which escaped were of insecurity.

'That's better,' Graham consoled gently. 'Now I know you can stand up for yourself I'll leave you to your own personal devices. Just remember, though, to spare a thought for a man's feelings. You can physically hurt a chap and he'll keep coming back for more, but his emotions are more sensitive than a woman's.'

'Are you trying to tell me I hurt you?' Stephanie's big green eyes opened wider in challenge. 'Only your darned pride, Graham Porter, so let's get on with the drama club.'

They had refills of coffee twice over and it was late, the dining-room almost empty when Stephanie finally picked up her bag.

'I can't get in the mood for a pantomime in August,' she said, 'but see what the other committee members can come up with.'

'Can I run you home?' he offered.

'I've got my car—silly,' she retorted.

Outside in the corridor he danced her frivolously all the way to the lift. He had wiped the slate clean as well as helped her to forget the rigours of a trying day. In the lift he kissed her in spite of her protests, and during the light-hearted struggle they didn't realise that they had come to a stop on the second floor. A passenger stepped in and the doors closed again before either of them appreciated that Mr

Guy Atherstone was their scowling companion.

'Which floor?' he snarled.

'Ground floor, sir,' Graham replied politely, with egg on his face.

Stephanie hoped she hadn't been identified. She tried to dissolve into the corner and seconds later the doors slid apart.

Guy Atherstone paused and turned to stare first at Graham, then at Stephanie.

'Goodnight. I hope you'll find your way to the kindergarten successfully.'

Stephanie wished she could fade into oblivion. 'Graham—how awful!' she breathed.

He pulled her out of the lift and they watched as the consultant's long legs took him across the reception hall to the exit.

'That hasn't done me much good,' Stephanie said penitently.

'We are off duty—and by all accounts he's no angel. Brace yourself and meet force with force.'

'Oh, Graham, that's easy to say. He is a formidable character, and I've got to work with him.'

'So have I on occasion, and I bet he'll have a laugh at my expense tomorrow.'

Graham did his best to comfort Stephanie as he walked her across the car park, but she wasn't proud of their behaviour.

'Anyone would think we were a couple of kids,' she said bitterly.

'So we are, at heart. Don't let it worry you, Stevie. Tomorrow is another day.'

'That's no consolation,' she muttered miserably.

Graham held her fast and kissed her lightly.

'Take care, give me three rings when you get in. I feel I ought to see you home really. At least at the flat there were other people around. Your new house must seem very isolated.'

'I'll be OK. It's main road most of the way and I've got good neighbours.'

She secured her safety-belt and started up the engine. It wasn't really late or particularly dark, just gloomy. As she encircled the hospital on the one-way system she realised that a large car had come up behind her, a lone figure at the wheel.

She tried not to keep looking in the driving-mirror but it soon became evident that she was being shadowed. At the main road junction she had time to study the reflection more closely and recognised the figure as being Guy Atherstone.

Was it coincidence that he was travelling in the same direction as her, or was he seeking a confrontation?

She tried to keep level-headed as she continued on through the small suburban town of Reedway, and as she swung off to the more rural area leading to the new housing estate she slowed down and prayed that the large car behind had continued on the main highway. But to her dismay it turned the corner and was soon on her tail.

Well, at least he was someone connected with the hospital, someone she knew—or did she? She indicated her left turn and ran up into the carport, only

to discover that the highly-polished TR7 had pulled
into the kerbside, and Guy Atherstone was getting
out.

CHAPTER THREE

STEPHANIE wasn't really scared, but prepared to do battle with the man whom everyone loved to talk about. He walked briskly up to where she was locking her car door.

'Don't be alarmed, Stephanie,' Guy began. 'I'm not chasing after you with an ulterior motive, just to warn you that you've only got one rear light in action. I believe the police are on the look out for such offences now that the evenings are beginning to draw in. I would have tried to attract your attention at the lights, but no doubt you'd have thought I was out to assault or rape you.'

She felt the colour rush to her cheeks and was glad it was dark and she was standing in the shadow of the carport.

'I'm terribly sorry if you've come out of your way to tell me, but it's very kind,' she acknowledged. 'I always carry spares, so I'll check them in the morning and see that they're all in working order.'

'Before work?' he asked.

'I'm not on duty until mid-morning so I'll make that top priority. Thank you very much. I'm really sorry you've had to come all this way.'

'Doesn't your boyfriend see you home?' he changed tack suddenly.

'Graham isn't my boyfriend, not in that context,

just a friend.' She turned and fitted the key in the lock of the front door. 'I mustn't keep you—your wife—'

'I thought I might get a cup of coffee if I saw you safely in, or would we be waking anyone up?'

'No—I—' She decided against telling him that she lived alone. With a shrug she pushed open the door and switched on the light. 'I'll put the kettle on,' she said, while she worried about what he was going to think of her humble domain. She'd been able to buy the house more reasonably because it had been the show house for the builders, and it was all fitted out with fixtures, fittings, carpets and some furniture. She had also been granted a good mortgage, which had helped, but there were lots of things she wanted to do in the house and as yet it lacked the personality she felt it needed.

She opened the kitchen door and flooded the place with light so that she could see to fill the kettle.

'The lounge is across the apology for a hall,' she laughed, opening the door opposite, switching on more lights and drawing the curtains across the double-glazed patio doors.

'Do please sit down,' she said. 'How do you like your coffee?'

'White, if you have sufficient milk, please.'

'That's one thing I do keep plenty of in the fridge,' she said going to the cupboard, taking out a small saucepan and pouring a mugful of milk in it. At the touch of a button the front burner glowed vigorously—and then the telephone rang.

'Oh, excuse me, and do sit down,' she apologised again as she squeezed past him in the kitchen doorway.

'I'll watch the milk,' he offered.

Stephanie picked up the telephone and gave her number breathlessly.

'Stevie? Are you OK?' Graham's distant voice asked.

'Yes, why shouldn't I be?' she said, puzzled.

'You sound strange. I thought you were going to give me three rings, what took you so long?'

'Well—um—actually, Mr Atherstone caught up with me to tell me that one of my rear lights isn't working.' There was a long pause.

'And he's with you now,' Graham stated flatly.

'Mm—ye—es.' Stephanie drew it out, knowing that Guy Atherstone would hear every word she was saying.

'I actually rang to tell you the same thing. I did yell after you, but you went like a bat out of hell. Shall I come round tomorrow and see to it for you?'

'No. I'm not on early shift so I'll have time to see to it in the morning.'

'Get rid of him—and fast.' Graham's voice was unmistakably riddled with annoyance.

'Thanks very much all the same,' Stephanie said non-committally. 'See you, goodnight, Graham.'

She hesitated before putting the phone down and just caught Graham's growled, 'You bet you will.'

Guy came in with a tray of steaming mugs.

'I meant to get cups and saucers out,' Stephanie said, somewhat confused. 'I'm sure you don't usually drink from a mug.'

'I frequently drink from a mug at home. It saves the bother of refilling. I hope you don't mind but I looked in your cupboard to find the coffee and sugar.'

'Sorry about that,' Stephanie apologised, waving a hand towards the telephone on the low teak coffee-table. 'Graham noticed my lights too, so he rang to tell me.'

'And to make sure you'd reached home safely. You evidently live alone and I feel sure he noticed me tearing after you.'

'It was very kind of you.'

'So, it was kind of me! I'd do it for any member of the hospital staff. Sit down and relax. You don't need to be tense with me.'

She laughed awkwardly and perched on the edge of a chair, mumbling an offer of biscuits or a sandwich, and when she found the courage to glance in his direction she saw that he had lounged back on the settee, one arm stretched lazily across the back, his long legs sprawled out in front of him in an easy, homely manner. But the most unnerving thing about him was the smile that danced wickedly round his mouth and sparkled mischievously from his blue eyes. He knew that she felt nervous and he was revelling in her discomfort.

'It's late, Stephanie, so nothing to eat, thanks. I expect you're wanting to get out of your uniform and do whatever you have to do before you go to bed, but I must say I find it pleasant to see you on home ground. I like to know my staff intimately, it helps in the understanding of our patients. I also like things to run smoothly, and I don't accept that in our profession there is room for mistakes.'

'I like my ward to be run efficiently, Mr Atherstone,' she said, a hint defensively.

His smile was diverting and she quickly forgot the need to keep her wits about her when he said in a low, sexy voice, '*Guy*. Please call me Guy when we're off duty. I'm sure that when you've succeeded in becoming confident on my ward we shall work together in harmony, Stephanie.'

She held her mug of coffee between both hands, trying to steady her quickening reflexes. He had a persuasive charm which she found difficult to disregard while she was bent on making a positive stand as ward sister. He claimed it was his ward, she regarded it as hers.

She drank from her mug and then, choosing her words carefully, said, 'I find it disconcerting to have a patient come on to the ward about whom I know virtually nothing.'

He drummed his fingers on the back of the settee. He looked so comfortable, so at ease, that she felt as if she were the visitor in her own home. But as he gazed at her intently, Stephanie watched all traces of good humour vanish from his expression.

'Andrea.' Stephanie couldn't determine what lay behind the emphasis on the single word. He stood up so suddenly that she slopped her drink as she hastily put her mug down on the tray. Guy drained his coffee in one long gulp.

She felt so small beside the tall, elegant doctor, and when he glanced down at her he seemed to find the difference in their heights amusing all over again.

'Don't you find being so tiny a disadvantage?'

She shook her head decisively. 'Not at all. Except, of course, when it comes to reaching things on high shelves in supermarkets, and the fact that some people seem to think that if you're small you're retarded, mentally.'

He laughed readily and caught her neck in his warm hand, squeezing gently so that she felt a chill run down her spine.

'With high heels and your frilly cap you can walk as tall as anyone else. I didn't mean to belittle you, Stephanie.' One tantalisingly smooth fingertip caressed her jaw-bone. 'It's just as disadvantageous to be over six feet tall, you know. I find it difficult to hide.'

She looked up at him confidently then, and with a daring grin retorted, 'You don't seem the sort of person to me who would want to hide.'

'There are times,' he began, gently urging her forward, allowing his hand to stroke the length of her back and ending with a familiar pat on her bottom. 'I've enjoyed having a friendly chat with you, Stephanie. Andrea de Souza is not my case, therefore I shouldn't discuss her condition with you, but at some time in the future maybe we'll discuss her psychological hang-ups. I hope she won't be too difficult for you to handle. I feel there is a need for me to keep a close watch on her.'

'She's afraid of being anaesthetised. She admits she's chickened out in the past and that she doesn't really want surgery. I didn't know how to answer as I don't have a case history as yet, except to say that I felt sure you had given her the best advice possible.'

Guy looked down at her with an 'I'm not telling you anything' kind of look and again ran his hand across her back. 'Goodnight, Stephanie. Thanks for the coffee, and don't forget to get that rear light fixed.'

At the front door he turned. 'I hope you'll invite me again sometime. I like the design of your house. Next time you can give me a conducted tour.'

Later, when she was in her bedroom, she peeled off her clothes and slipped on a fleecy jumpsuit, then she went downstairs and put the television on. The late news was on but she didn't really absorb that the pound was falling again, inflation and unemployment rising. She curled her toes beneath her and snuggled up cosily on the settee where Guy Atherstone had sat a short while ago. She felt his presence still in the room. There was some very strong influence lingering and she could only sit still and ponder over his visit.

He had two very different faces. Nothing could ever alter the fact that he was handsome. His deep blue suit complemented his dark, sleek hair, but his moods were evident. He could look almost wickedly sensual when his blue eyes sparkled invitingly, but in a flash they could harden, and then the wrinkles at their corners became aggressive furrows of anger. His face was long, with a firm square jaw, but his forehead high and wide. There was the merest hint of a dimple somewhere in his chin but he preferred to keep that concealed most of the time.

She went over in her mind all that had passed between them from the moment they'd met this morning. She realised she couldn't have appeared to be that confident and she guessed that on account of her size he was underestimating her competence as ward sister. She'd show him what she was made of! No one had complained before, so she was sure she could handle the work as efficiently as her predecessor. Whether she could handle Guy Atherstone was another matter.

She tried to remember things rumoured about him, but she'd never taken much interest. He was one of those men at the top whose domain was mostly in the theatre block, and if you did by chance meet him anywhere you simply made yourself small enough not to be noticed. And he didn't notice anyone unless they happened to directly cross his path, or, so she'd been told, unless they happened to be exquisitely beautiful.

She had crossed his path by becoming sister in charge of the women's surgical ward; she wasn't beautiful, so he *must* have chased after her because of her broken rear light. But why had he invited himself in? Curiosity about the new ward sister? Stephanie knew that she could be taken for younger than her twenty-six years because she was petite with a youngish type of face.

Or had he really wanted to discuss Andrea de Souza? That was nearest the truth she decided, and then, given the opportunity he'd funked it. Why? Did he want Stephanie to believe that the lovely young woman patient meant something special to him—or that she was not so special?

The television closed down, but Stephanie didn't even notice. She remained motionless, trying to unravel the mystery surrounding Guy Atherstone and Andrea de Souza.

She urged her memory to recall everything she'd ever heard, and into her mind came a long-forgotten and somewhat hazy picture of the much talked about surgeon with a beautiful blonde woman on his arm. It had been Stephanie's first Christmas at Thames Vale. She was still in a state of shock over her parents' accident and the death of her father, so all the new people she met were just names to her. The patients in her care were treated to an almost obsessive sympathy, but otherwise she chose not to bother her head about the hospital's staff—until Graham had taken her under his wing and helped to lift her out of her despair. Guy Atherstone had attended the Christmas carol service with his wife—it had been a talking point for almost every member of the staff because earlier it had been reported by the scandalmongers that a divorce seemed likely.

Stephanie remembered the delicate beauty of the woman she supposed was his wife. Everything about her features was perfect—strong, emerald green eyes and silky, sunlit hair. Her smile had been wide and eager as if she felt proud of her tall, handsome doctor husband. Stephanie recalled thinking what a striking couple they made and refused to listen to the grapevine tittle-tattle that hinted at divorce and Guy Atherstone's harem of gorgeous women. But now, she supposed there was evidence of it being true. He'd said that he lived further on in the country. And he'd cut her short when she mentioned 'wife'.

For some inexplicable reason she wanted to think nothing but good about him. Maybe Andrea was a long-lost cousin or something and right now, at this minute, he was embracing that attractive wife of his. Oh, she *did* hope so—but then she remembered him calling Andrea 'darling', and that put paid to her loyal thoughts. She uncoiled her legs and switched off the television disconsolately before wearily going upstairs to bed.

The ward was in a state of mild chaos when she went on duty next day. Staff Nurse Liz Rushden was supervising Mr Atherstone's theatre list. Already the first two patients were in the recovery room and the third was in the theatre.

'Mrs Penny's next and she's a colostomy, so that will last until lunch-time I should think,' Liz said. 'After that there's Miss Barrett for haemorrhoids and Mrs Hall for obstruction. Craig's written up all the pre-meds.'

'How's everyone else?' Stephanie asked. 'Any

problems before you go off to the canteen?' She was reading down the night report. 'Miss de Souza settled in OK?'

'Fine, it seems, at present,' Liz said. 'She didn't sleep too well according to Jill, but she seems quite calm this morning and Craig came up with her notes, so there's quite a bit there for you to digest.'

'Under Mr Perry, I believe?'

'Mm—but Craig says he's not too keen to operate.'

'That should please Miss de Souza. According to her it's Mr Atherstone who's in favour of surgery—what for, I wonder?'

'You'd better study her notes. All right if I go for a quick break?'

Stephanie affirmed that it was by raising a hand. She was dying to read the case history of Andrea de Souza but there were more urgent things to attend to first. She bent low over the white-gowned patient in bed four.

'Feeling drowsy, Mrs Penny?'

With some difficulty the patient opened her eyes slightly, but she seemed none too sure of who was speaking.

'Dry,' Mrs Penny managed in a whisper.

'Won't be long now, then you can have a nice long sleep.'

Stephanie took and held the middle-aged woman's hand, patting it gently. She knew that Mrs Penny was awake but only in a hazy, dreamy kind of world. It was these last waiting moments which were the most traumatic. Part of her would be wishing she could get up and go home, the other part desperately wanting things to start happening. Every minute seemed like an hour, yet to the busy nursing staff patients usually returned before they could look round.

'You'll be all right, Mrs Penny,' Stephanie comforted. 'Just try to doze until they're ready for you.'

Mrs Penny squeezed Stephanie's hand and did her best to smile, so Stephanie moved on to bed number five where Miss Barrett, who had only just received her pre-medication injection, was still very alert.

'How long before I go to theatre, Sister?' she asked irritably.

'Not for a while yet, Miss Barrett, but there's nothing to worry about. You'll find yourself getting drowsy and you'll feel a bit dry but your turn will come soon enough.'

'Fool, I was,' Miss Barrett grumbled. 'Should have put up with the discomfort. Better than going through all this performance. Like a blessed conveyor belt in a factory. Dressed up like mummies and wheeled away! I don't wonder some of them don't come back, it's enough to frighten anyone to death.'

'Only because you're a little uncertain of what's going to happen, Miss Barrett.'

'I know what's going to happen all right,' she returned sharply. 'Mr Atherstone took great pains to give me all the gory details. Still, I must say that's better than being kept in the dark. Just hope he's up to his task this morning. Don't want any mistakes—not on me, anyway.'

'Mr Atherstone doesn't make mistakes and doesn't expect anyone else to make any either,' Stephanie said with a knowing wink.

Miss Barrett's thin, scraggy face widened in a rare smile. 'Bit of a devil isn't he, in more ways than one?'

'He's a very clever surgeon.'

'That's not what I meant and you know it. You only have to watch his patients come out of his consulting room to see that he's one for the women. That sort usually go for gynaecology.'

'Mr Atherstone is just as popular with the men, Miss Barrett.'

'How would you know? Chit of a girl hardly out of navy blue knickers,' Miss Barrett snorted.

Stephanie laughed. 'They're a thing of the past, and I happen to have been sister of men's medical ward before I came to women's surgical, so I was used to hearing the men talk about Mr Atherstone. He was involved in cases where surgery had been considered but for one reason and another the patient wasn't suitable.'

'Too old or too ill, you mean. Well, I don't care what sort of chap Mr Atherstone is as long as he knows his job.'

'I think you can be sure he does,' Stephanie assured her and moved on to the next bed.

'How are you feeling, Mrs Hall?'

'Nervous, though I shouldn't complain. At least I haven't had weeks of waiting like some of those others. I feel guilty, Sister, as if I'm jumping the queue.'

'In a case like yours when we don't know what the obstruction is, it's better to be investigated fairly quickly, and that's all Mr Atherstone may need to do today.'

'Today?' Mrs Hall looked alarmed. 'I hope you don't mean I might need another operation later?'

'Highly unlikely, Mrs Hall, but now that you're here, Mr Atherstone will want to get to the bottom of things.' Stephanie smiled reassurance. 'Why don't you go for a walk round the ward and chat to someone who's up and about. It'll help pass the time. Nothing to eat or drink, of course, and Staff Nurse will come and find you when she's back from her coffee-break.'

'If I'm last on the list that means it'll be late afternoon or evening, I suppose, before I go to theatre?'

Stephanie shook her head. 'Shouldn't be too long after lunch. You're the last on our list but there's men's surgical to go after you.'

'It's a horrible job. I can't imagine why nice people want to be surgeons.'

'Someone has to do it, Mrs Hall, and you're lucky in being under Mr Atherstone.'

Stephanie helped Mrs Hall put on her dressing-gown and as she went to visit all the rest of her patients she wondered why she was so quick to defend Guy Atherstone. His reputation as a surgeon was of the highest order, she reminded herself as she went into the day-room to see the women who were making good recoveries, most of them up and dressed.

'All in good practice for going home?' she greeted them cheerily.

'When does Mr Atherstone come round to tell us?' Carol asked.

'Tomorrow I expect, so be prepared.'

She hated hurrying away, but everyone seemed happy enough so she returned to her desk. She had started to read the notes on Andrea de Souza when the bell rang, advising her of the next patient's turn for theatre. With a sigh she got up as the porter arrived to fetch Mrs Penny. A student nurse, already detailed to accompany Mrs Penny, helped move the patient onto the trolley and Stephanie went as far as the lift with her. Then she went back to her desk and became absorbed in Andrea de Souza's case history.

It made interesting reading, for she learned that Andrea had helped to nurse her sister who had died of a rare type of cancer. Now Andrea was convinced she was suffering from the same disease. Tests were all negative but this had not satisfied Andrea so she had been admitted for further screening and possibly an exploratory operation— though this was not advised by Mr Perry, the senior consultant whose patient she was.

Stephanie closed the folder and sat looking at it for several minutes. Why was Guy Atherstone keen for Andrea to undergo surgery if there was no evidence of any disease? She tried to recall her previous conversation with Andrea, who had admitted to being scared of being put to sleep as well as having misgivings about surgery generally. If Andrea and Mr Perry were in agreement over this, what did it have to do with Guy Atherstone? Was he divorced? Did he want to marry Andrea but was insisting on a clean bill of health for his future bride?

Stephanie's imagination was taking off in all directions. But it was only speculation so she tried to calm herself and reserve judgment until she had spoken again with Andrea and heard Mr Perry's opinion, if only through his houseman Craig Stewart.

She couldn't help remembering the unkind things which circulated about Guy Atherstone and his private life. People were so quick to judge, yet as far as Stephanie could see he left himself open to criticism by his attitude to women. Underneath all that charm could he really be as cold and calculating as she supposed?

She'd wanted to think good of him because she had to admit to being flattered by his attention, but at the back of her mind conflicting thoughts raged like savage winds in a tornado.

It was kind of him to tell her about her failing rear light, but why had he been so eager to be her guest when rumour had it that he was never short of female hospitality?

CHAPTER FOUR

THERE WAS just time before lunch to visit Andrea de Souza, so Stephanie went along to her room and found her lying in bed, staring into space. After a brief greeting Stephanie went to the window.

'Quite a nice view from up here,' she said. 'It's a lovely day, so I think it's time you were up.' She turned and smiled at Andrea, whose eyes seemed to be deep-set with an expression of fear in them.

'I thought I ought to be in bed in case Mr Perry comes,' she said huskily.

'I think he'd be better pleased to find you up and dressed. He's a very go-ahead man and hates to see patients remain in nightclothes and dressing-gowns a moment longer than necessary.' Stephanie studied the temperature chart hanging at the foot of the bed. 'And if this is anything to go by, there's no reason why you shouldn't be up for some exercise.'

'Guy's operating today, isn't he?'

'Yes.' Stephanie pulled a face, quickly followed by a cheery smile. 'One of our busiest days, but, thank goodness, the list isn't too awful. The last one before lunch is in theatre now, so there's just time for you to freshen yourself up and then I'll get one of the nurses to take you along to the day-room for lunch.'

'Can't I stay here?'

'It's easier on a busy day if we can serve everyone who's up together. Come on, I'm sure you've got something pretty to wear to impress Mr Perry.'

'I didn't come in here to impress anyone,' Andrea replied shortly.

'You're a woman, and a most attractive one, and I'm sure you want Mr Perry to see you at your best.'

'It might be better for him to see me at my worst.'

'Hasn't he done that already? Isn't that why you're here?'

'Mr Perry doesn't believe that there's anything wrong with me.' Andrea laughed briefly and her eyes shone with a self-satisfied look. 'He and Guy are in total conflict over my case.'

'From your notes I understand you're here mainly for observation, so there's no reason for you to need bed-rest at this stage. In fact, Andrea, tests are usually more reliable when a patient is continuing a normal routine, so please get dressed at once. I'll send a nurse along to help you in ten minutes as lunch will be ready for twelve-thirty.'

'I don't think I'm supposed to eat anything.'

'Oh? Why's that?'

'In case I have to have surgery.'

'But there's no question of surgery for the present, certainly not today,' Stephanie assured her. 'I'm afraid we don't have the menu system here which they do in some hospitals. We believe we know what's best for our patients, so there's a choice of fish or meat and some very appetising sweets.'

'I wouldn't like to be at lunch when Mr Perry comes,' Andrea said doubtfully.

'I'm afraid I've no idea when that will be, but I do assure you that he'll see you here, and we'll find you, don't worry. We have other patients of his on the ward, so we'll give you time to prepare yourself.'

Stephanie opened the small wardrobe door noticing that three or four light summer dresses were hung up inside. Andrea evidently came prepared for a reasonable stay, but unless surgery was decided upon it was likely to be less than a week.

One of the junior nurses was detailed to help her dress and take her along to the day-room, where she was introduced to some of the other patients. Stephanie had just started to dish up lunches from the huge trolley when the theatre bell rang.

'That'll be Mrs Penny. Nurse Bingham, will you ask Staff Nurse Rushden to supervise Mrs Penny's return to bed, please.'

The pupil nurse went away and as soon as all the patients in the ward had been served with the first course Stephanie went to the cubicle where Liz was watching over Mrs Penny.

'How is she?' Stephanie asked.

'Pulse rather weak, otherwise as expected.'

'Let's hope she's one of the lucky ones, and will have no further trouble. It's time Mrs Hall had her pre-med, Liz, so I'll leave that to you. Keep an eye on Miss Barrett, who's to go next, and be here when Mrs Penny comes round. I'd better check that Andrea has eaten something, then I'll finish sweets and we'll get lunches over before theatre starts again.'

When Stephanie looked in on her patients in the day-room she noticed at once that Andrea looked brighter, with more colour in her cheeks. It was obvious that she was amused by some of the chatter, but she was holding back from joining in. It was a pity that the Frivolous Four, as they'd become known, were due to be discharged within the next couple of days, for Stephanie felt that their light-hearted approach would be good for her.

'Did you enjoy your lunch, Andrea?' she asked with a smile. 'I see you have an empty plate.'

Andrea's expression was definitely more alert as she said, 'I really did enjoy it. Some sort of fish pie—it was tasty, Sister.'

'Good. How about a sweet? There's milk pudding, jelly and custard, or fruit.'

'Milk pudding would be too stodgy,' Andrea replied thoughtfully. 'What sort of fruit?'

'How about fruit salad?'

'Mm—sounds lovely.'

Stephanie went away smiling secretly. According to her notes Andrea had shown signs of colitis which Mr Perry considered was the result of nervous reaction following the death of her sister. Fruit was not really advisable but Mr Perry wanted to observe the patient's behaviour under hospital conditions. And in just the hour since she had been persuaded to get up, there was a marked difference. The Frivolous Four wouldn't allow anyone in their company to be depressed. They had helped each other very satisfactorily, so Stephanie hoped she was being diplomatic in allowing them to influence Guy Atherstone's special case.

The theatre bell sounded before all the sweets had been served and a second year nurse was detailed to accompany Miss Barrett to the theatre suite on the floor above, even though she was already asleep.

'Does he usually have so short a lunch-hour?' Stephanie asked Liz, who was more acquainted with Guy Atherstone's methods than she.

'This does seem a bit quick, but on occasion he hasn't even stopped for lunch. We have to be prepared for anything where he's concerned. Theatre sister says that if he's in a foul mood he doesn't stop for lunch. They reckon they can tell his moods by his eyebrows. When he's feeling happy they're smooth and silky, when he's cross they're ruffled.'

Stephanie laughed. 'Thanks for the tip. I'll take special note of his eyebrows next time he comes. Is that likely to be later? Does he usually check on his cases after surgery?'

'Not usually,' Liz shook her head. 'But he does get mad if either Pete or one of the housemen don't keep a close watch.'

'He'll probably come to see Andrea later. I know it's early days yet, but I'm inclined to agree with Mr Perry that she's suffering from cancer phobia. Since she's been in the day-room with the others she seems brighter already.'

Liz paused in her task of drawing up Mrs Hall's

pre-medication injection and raised her eyebrows. 'You're pushing your luck,' she said. 'Sir doesn't like his special cases mixing with the riff-raff.'

'Riff-raff be blowed,' Stephanie said indignantly. 'My patients are all of equal importance to me—and, for the record, Andrea de Souza is a special friend of Mr Atherstone's, *not* his patient. They're too close for him to treat her, or so she told me.'

'Lucky Andrea. By the way, have you met Mr Perry before?'

'Only in passing. We had a case on men's medical once that interested him, but he only called in a couple of times.'

'He's a super man. Quiet and unassuming, but he likes you to do the talking and you get far more out of him if you elucidate in great detail about the patient. He's a bit shy, I suppose, but once he realises you know what you're talking about he responds—I find him charming.'

'Oh you do, do you? Well I hope he comes while I'm on duty so that I can assess your judgment. Next time *you* can have him,' Stephanie laughed, her green eyes sparkling mischievously.

'He's old enough to be my father,' Liz protested, 'and anyway, Mark wouldn't like it!'

'You make sure you keep that husband of yours happy or there's plenty of us who will oblige.'

Liz threw a mock punch. 'There was a time when we all thought you and Graham Porter were going to get hitched.'

Stephanie sighed. 'Maybe I thought so too. We're just good friends now.'

Liz pulled a face and groaned disbelievingly. 'I seem to have heard that story a hundred times before.'

'Happens to be true. So you can scotch any rumours to the contrary just because we may have been seen at supper together. We're planning the usual pantomime, but we need to write some sketches about the staff and it's difficult to get good original material. Graham's touting for ideas.'

'And who is Graham?'

Both girls turned in surprise at the sound of an unfamiliar voice. Andrea de Souza was propped up against the door jamb. Stephanie experienced strange misgivings and she wondered how long Andrea had been listening to their conversation.

'A colleague,' she said, and Liz hurried away to Mrs Hall's cubicle.

'We're both on the entertainments committee. Sometimes we put on a show, old-time music-hall stuff or a play, and at Christmas a pantomime.'

'How ambitious,' Andrea said.

'Not really as out of character as you'd think,' Stephanie explained. 'There's a large staff at a hospital this size, so there's no shortage of talent.'

'And what particular talent are you noted for?'

'I'm not noted for any, but I've always loved amateur dramatics. Though since I've been here I've been more on the production side, and I enjoy it.' Andrea fell in step beside Stephanie as she returned to her office.

'My sister was a singer and I was her manager.'

'How marvellous,' Stephanie said. 'What kind of singer?'

'A trained opera singer, but of the minor part and chorus variety, so she went solo. Well, to be honest, we formed a singing partnership first. Did some of the forties songs as well as popular music from shows. We were quite good and had begun to gain recognition touring abroad and so on until—'

'Your sister was taken ill? How very sad,' Stephanie sympathised, glad that Andrea was talking openly, which had to be a good sign.

'Well, yes—that too—but she,' Andrea shrugged, 'messed up her life. I opted out of the partnership. For one thing she was too good not to be a star in her own right, but her husband didn't approve. Not that he was in any way to blame, far from it, but Claudine, being the beauty she was, couldn't be blamed either if every man who set eyes on her was bewitched. Of course, when she was taken ill in Australia it all came to an abrupt end and we flew home. But that's all in the past. If I can help in any way—I've got loads of unpublished songs. I've done a bit of song-writing in the past, but,' she shrugged, 'after Claudine died, the enthusiasm died too.'

'We're always glad to have professional help. I'm sure Graham would be pleased with any suggestions. We usually use *Aladdin* or *Cinderella*, but then topical and personal lyrics have to be written in. I'll mention it to Graham. By the way, did you want me, Andrea? Were you looking for me?'

'Only to ask how the theatre list is going and if Guy is likely to be around.'

'We've one more to go, but I'm afraid there are probably as many men still waiting. I expect he'll visit you this evening before he goes home.'

Stephanie persuaded Andrea to have a short rest before returning to the day-room to watch television, and while she was busy at her desk a visitor arrived.

'I know it's theatre day,' Graham said, 'but have you got five minutes?'

'Five seconds—something wrong?'

'I hope not, but I feel I should warn you—you're looking for trouble if you start entertaining Guy Atherstone at your home.'

Stephanie tapped her chin with her pen and narrowed her eyes against Graham's intense stare. 'He followed me to tell me about my light. *He* suggested coffee, and it was the least I could do. I suppose he was only in the house twenty to thirty minutes. But who I entertain can't really be of any interest to you, Graham.'

'Of course I'm concerned! I don't want to see you make an idiot of yourself.'

Stephanie faced Graham aggressively. 'I'm not in the habit of making an idiot of myself, and perhaps this is a good moment to remind you that I can take care of myself.' Graham turned aside as if to leave, but changed his mind.

'That was uncalled for. Get involved and see if I care!' he grunted.

Stephanie realised that she had been rather

cruel, but Graham did not own her and if they were going to remain on speaking terms she knew she'd have to keep up her independence.

'Just giving someone a coffee isn't getting involved,' she said. 'Besides, Graham, the great man is involved with someone far more sophisticated than I am. Which reminds me, she's just shown some interest in our pantomime. She and her sister were in show business and Andrea has done some song-writing. Perhaps you'd like to meet her.'

Graham's face lit up with enthusiasm. 'Lead me to her—please.'

They went along to the day-room together but Andrea was not with the Frivolous Four and Stephanie led the way back to the single room. The door was tightly closed. Stephanie knocked gently and opened it. Andrea was at the wash basin wearing only a pair of lacy panties, which were rather brief.

Stephanie motioned to Graham to stay outside.

'I've brought someone to see you, Andrea.' Andrea grabbed a towel and began to pat her cheeks dry.

'Mr Perry?' she asked brightly. 'Guy?'

'No, a colleague. Graham Porter. The producer of the panto, but he can hardly see you like that.'

'I'm preparing to see Mr Perry,' Andrea said with a disappointed expression.

'Andrea, you had a shower this morning. There was no need to undress to wash your face. Mr Perry would much prefer you to be up and dressed. If he wishes to examine you he'll tell me in good time.'

'I thought he'd expect me to be in bed.'

Stephanie shook her head. 'No, Andrea, not for the moment. Can you pop some clothes on and be ready in five minutes? Graham will wait outside until you're respectable.'

Stephanie noticed Andrea's disappointed expression as she retreated to the door and added cheerfully, 'We need all the help we can get. You'll find Graham a willing listener. Just give him a call when you're ready.'

With little modesty in evidence, Andrea hung up her towel and went to the wardrobe. Her eyes sparkled impishly as she met Stephanie's gaze. 'Is he—um—safe to entertain in my room without a chaperon?'

Stephanie laughed. 'No, but you can leave the door open.' Outside in the corridor she invited Graham back to her office in sign language.

'She's going to be quite a handful,' she said, 'so your pantomime might be just the thing to keep her mind occupied. I've just encountered a different side to Andrea de Souza. I thought she was devoted to Mr Atherstone but I have the feeling that she finds any eligible male worthy of seduction, so leave the door open,' Stephanie warned.

Graham raised his eyebrows. 'Is she? Does she? I mean—am I likely to fancy her?'

'You would in the state of undress in which I found her. She is stunning. But isn't that what you'd expect of Guy Atherstone's friends?'

Graham tapped his brow with one finger. 'Keep your mind on the pantomime, Porter,' he advised himself. 'Remember she is the property of Guy Atherstone! Can I go in now or would I be an embarrassment to her—or myself?'

Stephanie laughed. 'Neither probably—she should be dressed again. I hope you can use some influence to take her mind off her condition. Until I've talked with Mr Perry I'm not qualified to judge, but so far all tests have proved negative. There's every indication that she's suffering from cancer phobia, so we have to be extra thoughtful but firm and diplomatic.'

Graham's face sobered as he sighed. 'She should come and see the real thing on my ward,' he said seriously.

'She nursed her sister, so it's not as if she hasn't seen the real thing. It's probably the grief which is causing her phobia—the big problem is that Mr Perry and Mr Atherstone have differing views about exploratory surgery.'

'So what line do I take?' Graham asked, puzzled.

'Give her something else to think about and play it down for the present.'

Stephanie left Graham while she checked on all the post-operative cases, then she went back to her paperwork. Liz was due to go off duty after tea and Stephanie wanted to keep ahead so that she would be free to give special attention to Miss Barrett, Mrs Hall and any of the other women who might not feel well as the effects of the anaesthetic wore off.

She was engrossed in her report when voices attracted her attention. Masculine voices, which drew nearer—and then Graham preceded Mr Perry into the office.

'This is Sister Driscoll, sir,' Graham introduced them and then left as Stephanie stood up, dwarfed by the tall, stately gentleman who smiled down in recognition.

'Ah, I remember—you were on men's medical, weren't you, Sister? I'm afraid the name was unfamiliar.'

'You've come to see Miss de Souza I expect?' Stephanie answered with a smile.

'That's right, but please sit down. I'd like you to tell me about her first.'

Stephanie knew instantly that she was going to like Mr Perry. A kind, fatherly figure with a totally different approach from the arrogant and self-opinionated Guy Atherstone!

Stephanie brushed her skirt down at the back before sitting again.

'Does Miss de Souza know you're here, Mr Perry?' she asked.

'No. I made straight for your office and met Graham in the corridor.' He beamed suddenly, the kind of relaxing expression which lit up his wrinkled face. 'I rather think Graham wished he'd got here first.'

In spite of her feeling at ease with Mr Perry, his suggestion brought a faint flush to her cheeks, so she went on to explain about the pantomime. Mr Perry listened attentively.

'You seem to have the right idea, Sister. In a case like Andrea's the problem is a very real and fright-

ening one, but so far all the tests have proved
negative. I can find no legitimate reason for
surgery, other than putting the patient's mind at
rest. If, indeed, we were successful in doing so.
Personally, I feel time alone will prove to Andrea
that she is a very healthy young woman. She's a
rather lonely person and your idea of interesting
her in the pantomime is a splendid one.'

'I'm only one member of the committee so I can't
speak for anyone but myself. I don't know how the
others would feel about an outsider being in on it,'
Stephanie said cautiously.

'I'm sure that with your charm, Sister, you can
win them round,' Mr Perry smiled.

Stephanie responded to his gentle flattery with a
shy, wistful look. 'Everyone's always complaining
about lack of time so I think we might all welcome
some professional help, even just interest, to get us
started. I suppose Andrea will be returning to work
eventually? Isn't that the best cure for her phobia?'

'Therein lies the problem, my dear. She managed her sister in her career, nursed her devotedly
through her illness, and now her sister has gone
Andrea's job has gone too. Delightful though she
may be, she doesn't have much in the way of
qualifications to help her do anything else.' Mr
Perry sighed with an expression of despondency.
'She ought to be married, of course, but I believe
there are problems there, too. However, we must
do all we can to help her take an interest in life
again. This is a good ward for that. Plenty going on,
and she should be persuaded to meet other patients

with genuine problems. Then, in a few days time, I hope she'll be ready to go home and start thinking positive.' He stood up, indicating that it was time he saw the patient.

A few final tests were to be carried out, but no mention of surgery was made. Stephanie was surprised at the firmness with which Mr Perry handled the situation. Andrea was frightened and was seemingly begging the consultant to find evidence of some disease, but he remained adamant that no such evidence existed.

'Sister Driscoll is highly trained, Andrea,' he finally explained, 'and I want you to co-operate with her so that she can give me a good report in three or four days' time. I have many extremely ill patients who need my attention, but meanwhile I'll arrange for the final set of tests to be carried out over the next few days.'

He paused to chat briefly with Andrea on a more personal level and then Stephanie walked with him to the end of the corridor. When she retraced her steps to Ward 2B she found Andrea de Souza pacing the floor and blowing short puffs of smoke from the cigarette she had between her lips.

'Oh, come on now, Andrea,' Stephanie reprimanded kindly, 'that isn't going to help anyone.'

Andrea rounded on her aggressively. 'That idiot doesn't understand my case. He can't know what he's talking about, let alone learn anything from tests!'

'Andrea! I really can't allow you to make such accusations against one of our senior consultants.

He's a very experienced surgeon. He's most concerned about helping you, but you aren't helping yourself. We don't allow smoking in the wards, so please put that cigarette out—for your own good as well as ours.'

'*Allow! Allow!* All I hear is what I'm *allowed* to do!' She was crimson with rage, but she did stub out the offending cigarette. 'I want to see Guy,' she said angrily. '*He'll* have to operate if Perry won't.'

'It would be most improper for anyone to operate without just cause.'

'And *you* don't think there's cause, just or otherwise!' she shrieked at Stephanie.

'I think you'd better get to bed now, Andrea,' Stephanie said calmly. 'It's been a difficult day for you and the drinks trolley will be round in a short while.'

'Like gin and tonic, or vodka and lime? Oh, you sanctimonious creatures make my blood boil! Warm milk I suppose, to calm my nerves!'

'A good smack across the face might prove more effective in a case of hysteria.' Stephanie was outraged at Andrea's behaviour and then just as suddenly vexed as the beautiful girl collapsed in a heap, crying uncontrollably.

Stephanie hurried quietly away, thankful that the drinks trolley was all prepared in the kitchen. She poured two cups of tea and carried them to Andrea's room.

CHAPTER FIVE

STEPHANIE wasn't proud of the way she'd reacted to Andrea's outburst and she knew she was going to find it difficult to be as sympathetic as she ought. She'd had aggressive patients before, as well as moaning miseries, but on the men's medical ward she'd found them easier to cajole than Andrea.

'Come on, Andrea,' she said now, persuasively, 'let's have a cuppa.'

Andrea blew her nose, and as she turned and sat cross-legged on the bed she pushed her wavy, tawny-coloured hair away from her eyes.

'Forgive me, Sister,' she pleaded with a trembling voice. Then, with self-reproach, 'Behaving like a spoilt brat, being so damned selfish when you've got a ward full of really ill patients . . .'

Stephanie patted her shoulder gently as she handed her the tea. 'Cure for all our ills, this,' she laughed. 'This is one profession where a single term of night duty teaches you to consume gallons of it. Cheer up, Andrea, you won't get me down, we nurses have to be made of sterner stuff. I do understand how you feel—honestly. Grief affects us all in different ways. My father was killed in a car crash not too long ago, my mother badly burnt, but she came back fighting and she's taught me so much. I reckon I've been pretty selfish one way and another. Their only daughter, living away from home, going my own way, doing my own thing with little consideration for their feelings.'

'But you're a trained nursing sister, which must have made them very proud.'

'It did, it does. Mum wouldn't want me to give it all up except to get married, and isn't that what every woman wants for her daughter, or son, come to that? I've been so lucky, Andrea. My parents were so selfless in bringing me up to be independent, but now Mum and I are like two sisters, we're really good friends.'

'Then you *are* lucky. Perhaps she'll marry again—would you mind?'

Stephanie pursed her lips thoughtfully as she gazed down into the weak tea in her cup.

'Guess I would, in some ways. I'd be hurt for Dad, which is silly—and me being self-centred again. A friend of mine once said that it's a compliment to the first marriage to want to get married a second time. They were devoted, they did enjoy their marriage, yet I find it hard to imagine Mum with someone else. On the other hand I know that at forty-six she could do with companionship—but that's *her* life, not mine.'

'And what about yours? Graham seems pretty fond of you.'

'Oh? What's he been saying?'

'Nothing, but I gathered you are, or were, close.'

'*Were*. He's been kind to me in the past. When I first came here and I was the new girl, I valued his friendship. Life had seemed pretty cruel, just as it must seem to you now. Losing someone you love, well—there's no way to describe how you feel, is there? We tend to think no one understands, but most people do, especially those who have suffered similarly. Others want to sympathise, try to understand, but they're just as lost as you, and you begin to feel isolated. And because you've become isolated, Andrea, you've made yourself ill.' Stephanie smiled compassionately. 'You need more to occupy your mind.'

'But I *am* ill. Sometimes I feel terrible and in such pain, which is why Guy wants me to have an operation.'

'To do what, Andrea? The tests we do these days are really sophisticated and tell the doctors so much—and if these next tests prove negative what's the point of going through all the discomfort of surgery, which won't tell them any more?'

'You don't think I should listen to Guy then?' she pouted.

'Oh, I didn't say that. I think you should talk things over with him very seriously, but in the end it will be up to Mr Perry.'

'Unless I insist.'

'I thought you didn't want to be put to sleep?'

Andrea put her empty cup down on her locker and buried her face in her hands. 'How can I be sure I haven't the same as Claudine? She started by being listless, stomach pains, losing weight.'

'But you *will* lose weight if you don't eat, Andrea. Look, the best way to discover for yourself, find out how much you can cope with, is to occupy your mind. We do need help with this pantomime if we're to get it in production—would you like to be co-producer?'

Andrea's eyes brightened with interest. 'Yes, yes I would. If I can keep well enough and don't need surgery, I'd love to help.'

'If Mr Perry doesn't advise surgery then I wouldn't give it another thought. Now, I must go to check on my post-operative cases and I expect you'd like to tidy yourself in case Mr Atherstone visits you.'

As Stephanie returned the cups to the kitchen she realised how difficult it was going to be to convince Andrea that she was not suffering from the same disease as her sister. She ought to be on a medical ward, Stephanie thought, where the nursing staff would have more time to talk to her. A busy surgical ward just didn't provide such opportunities. As she made her way from cubicle to cubicle Pete Burnley, the registrar, joined her.

'Had a long list?' Stephanie enquired.

'Too long—as always.'

'Problems?'

Pete shook his head. 'No more than usual. Everyone all right in this department?'

'Seems like it. What about Mrs Hall's obstruction?'

Together they went to the foot of the patient's bed and Pete consulted his notes. 'Um—as we suspected, coil of gut twisted. It was necessary to remove the affected piece but it should be satisfactory as she was admitted in time. Miss Barrett will

be decidedly uncomfortable for the next few days—
the first dressing will need to be done under anaesthetic. And Mrs Penny. Mm—not good I'm
afraid, she'll need careful watching. I'll be on call
overnight, but I'll pop in and out anyway. Keep an
eye on all these drips.'

All the post-operative cases had come round
from the anaesthetic and had been given pethidine
and an anti-emetic to make them more comfortable
and ensure sleep for several hours. Stephanie was
glad when eight o'clock arrived and visitors left,
even though so many wanted to talk to her, making
enquiries about their relatives, concerned, but
anxious to have them home again. In between
seeing patients and their visitors the telephone kept
up a non-stop intrusion, mostly enquiries about the
patients who had undergone surgery earlier in the
day. At this stage there was little she could tell the
callers except that their relatives were round from
the anaesthetic and as comfortable as possible.

As the evening drew in Mrs Penny, Miss Barrett
and Mrs Hall became increasingly restive. Mrs
Penny was in a serious condition after a colostomy
and close watch needed to be maintained in case of
bleeding. Miss Barrett, an elderly spinster, was
confused as well as being uncomfortable and, in
spite of frequently being turned from one side to
the other, she made several attempts at getting out
of bed and at one stage was quite violent with the
nursing staff. Stephanie didn't have time to go for
supper and she knew she wouldn't be sorry when
the night staff arrived. She had just given Miss

Barrett a further injection, prescribed by Pete, when the ward seemed to fill with an aggressive phenomenon. Mr Atherstone hadn't made any sound as he approached her and at first he didn't speak—but his expression said everything.

Stephanie was already flushed from dealing with Miss Barrett and now Guy Atherstone's ruffled eyebrows sent the blood draining away from her taut cheek-muscles. His face was furrowed with what seemed to Stephanie like a million angry creases, but in little more than a whisper he said, 'Can I see you in your office, Sister?'

Stephanie handed the kidney dish to Nurse Bingham to dispose of while she led the way to the corridor and her office. The slam of the door behind her made her jump and she reeled quickly round to face the consultant.

'Don't ever do that again or I'll bodily lift you out of this hospital, and you'll stay out!' he yelled aggressively.

Stephanie blinked. Was she having a nightmare? What was he on about!

'And you needn't look so innocent, young lady.'

Colour flooded back into her face at last. An angry, spirited flush as she lifted her chin defiantly.

'What *have* I done?' she asked with a hint of sarcasm.

'Setting one consultant against another, no less. A crime I've never encountered in all my years as a surgeon.'

'If you'd just calm down, Mr Atherstone,' she

began in a polite, placating tone, indicating the visitor's chair.

'Calm down?' he thundered. 'Don't you realise the harm you've done? Just when I was finding a way of putting Andrea's mind at rest, *you* fill her head with all this nonsense of helping with the hospital theatricals. It's an insult,' he stormed, 'she's a professional artiste!'

'And I am a qualified nurse. I strongly object to your attitude, Mr Atherstone, and the inference that I have deliberately set out to play off one surgeon against another. Miss de Souza is not your patient I understand, therefore I regard you as a visiting relative or friend, and I must tell you that Mr Perry is all for the idea.'

Hostility transmitted itself silently from one to the other across the short space dividing them, threatening an explosion.

Stephanie had remained standing, confronting her adversary with little consideration for the difference in their heights as he stood like a monster ready to devour her, but she would not be victimised.

'Don't insult me,' he ground out accusingly.

'I think you're the one who has insulted *me*,' she replied with equal indignation.

'If you go on this way you won't last long on my ward,' he warned.

'*My* ward, Mr Atherstone,' she argued. 'I have patients here under other consultants, Mr Perry being one of them, and from what I understand of this case, though I suspect I haven't been fully informed, Miss de Souza is as healthy as me. All she needs is some reassurance and the best way we can help her is to give her something else to think about.'

'I'm very well aware of Miss de Souza's state of health, Miss Know-it-all! What I'm concerned about is her state of mind. A simple exploratory examination under anaesthetic would suffice.'

'Mr Atherstone, you wrongly accused me of setting one consultant against another. That's a pretty damaging conclusion to have reached against a colleague, but I'm not here to take sides, nor do I worry what you think of me. But that same allegation could be made of the patient. I've made a point of ignoring it as it didn't take me long to realise that anything Miss de Souza does is to gain attention. She has nothing to do but think about herself.'

'You're a heartless little nobody. I'll discuss Andrea's condition in future with George Perry.'

He slammed the door so violently that the place shook. Stephanie sat down at her desk exhausted. What had she done? What had she said?

The telephone rang. 'Sister Driscoll speaking,' she announced in a slightly unsteady voice while she fought to control her temper.

'Is that the little Sister? The pretty, fair one?'

'Who is this please?' The familiarity of the tone at the other end of the telephone angered her still further.

'It's Ted Barrett, Sister. I just wanted to know

how our Hilda is after her operation.'

'Oh, Mr Barrett—yes, well, Miss Barrett is as comfortable as can be expected. She'll be better after a good night's sleep. Perhaps you could ring tomorrow morning, then we can tell you when you can visit.'

'Thanks ever so much, Sister. I hope she's not being a bother—bit bossy is our Hilda.'

The soft apology in Miss Barrett's brother's voice helped Stephanie to relax and she smiled in acknowledgement of his appraisal of his sister.

'I don't think she'll feel much like bossing anyone for a few days. When she does we'll know she's on the mend, Mr Barrett.'

'That's right, Sister, but you keep her in her place! Give her my love. Ta ever so much, I'll ring again tomorrow. Goodnight.'

Stephanie rubbed her eyes. Dear, down to earth Miss Barrett and her brother! She'd had her own views of the consultant, Stephanie recalled, though she'd also considered Stephanie a chit of a girl, hardly out of navy blue knickers! Stephanie sighed dismally. Would no one ever take her for a sensible, mature woman? There were times when it was fun to be thought of as little more than a teenager, but when it affected your work it was different. It hadn't before—not until now, when she seemed to be at loggerheads with the most prominent surgeon at Thames Vale hospital.

She pushed back her chair, smoothed her apron and went back to her post-operative patients to pass on Mr Barrett's message to his sister, who was dozing fitfully. Nurse Bingham raised her eyebrows doubtfully.

'Your brother's just telephoned, Miss Barrett,' Stephanie said in a fairly loud voice, close to the patient's ear. 'Sends you his love, and if you're a good girl he'll be able to come and see you tomorrow.'

Miss Barrett flung one arm wide. Stephanie took her hand, stroking it gently as she soothed her with a few comforting words.

'Don't want 'im 'ere, causing trouble,' Miss Barrett muttered before she quietened down again.

Stephanie tucked the patient's arm inside the sheets and met Nurse Bingham's harassed expression with a grin. 'Cheer up, Nurse, tomorrow she'll be ordering everyone around and would strongly deny giving anyone any trouble. It's nearly time for the night staff to take over, so get yourself a chair and sit by Miss Barrett till then. The injection should soon take effect. It's taken a long time because she's the fighting sort.'

'I found that out, Sister,' Nurse Bingham said drily and Stephanie returned to her office commiserating with the young pupil nurse, who couldn't know about her own recent fight with Mr Atherstone.

As long as Stephanie remained on duty she tried to put it out of her mind, but once she reached her own domain she gave way to a moment of self-pity. He thought her heartless and cruel. He'd already given her a lecture on compassion, sympathy and understanding, but, she decided, he didn't seem too well endowed in those emotions himself. At present he was concerned with only one person and that was Andrea de Souza who, it seemed, had him just where she wanted him!

He must be pretty besotted with her. What doctor in his right mind would persuade anyone to have surgery, however minor, if there was no need? And the more Stephanie involved herself with Andrea de Souza, the more positive she became that the girl was a hypochondriac. But, of course, I would think that, Stephanie said to herself, because I'm a heartless little nobody. Well, that was telling me all right!

She went to put the kettle on and tried not to listen to the echo of his words, and when she'd made a pot of tea she sat on a stool near the kitchen window gazing out, letting her imagination create visions—visions of a highly-polished, slinky TR7 which had trailed her home only twenty hours or so ago. Mischievous, dark blue intense eyes taunted her. It was almost impossible to believe that they belonged to the same man who had recently called her a few unkind things. She had told him she didn't care what he thought of her, but that wasn't true. She cared probably a great deal too much because she had been brought up to believe that her character and reputation were the reflection of the real Stephanie Driscoll.

All her life she had been mindful of being a credit to her parents, though sadly she recalled that on many occasions she had wilfully gone her own way, sometimes making mistakes—as she had done with Graham Porter. Her father's philosophy had been to learn by one's mistakes. Had she learnt anything by not giving in to his sexual demands? Yes, she had learnt that she didn't really love him. But love grows, he had said. Had she thrown away the chance of happiness? Would her feelings for him have become deeper with more time, more experience?

The street lamp outside suddenly flashed on. It was getting dark earlier every night and she shivered in the gloom. Not too many weeks to go before the clocks changed again, and then winter would envelop the countryside for several months ahead. But there was autumn to enjoy first. At least a few more warm, sunny days she hoped.

Stephanie snapped on the fluorescent light in the kitchen and lowered the colourful blind. She stood looking at it for several seconds as she so often did, admiring the artist's impression of the four seasons of the year in a huge tree with spring buds bursting into life at the tip, and falling leaves midst snowflakes at the lower branches.

Like me, she thought. I'm past the spring stage and supposed to be in full bloom of summer. Sentimental fool, she chided herself, you've got the best years ahead. And then for some unknown reason unshed tears pricked her eyes and her expression saddened with sympathy for Andrea de Souza. Or was she feeling just a little bit guilty? No! Why should she feel guilty at trying to boost a patient's morale? There was no reason for Andrea to imagine that she had the same disease as her sister. Stephanie found herself wondering about the sister. Andrea said she had messed up her life, but she hadn't deserved to die so young. Even if she was older than Andrea she couldn't have been more than about thirty. Andrea was lonely and grieving.

Stephanie acknowledged that she was going through a difficult time but that did not excuse her causing trouble between Guy Atherstone and Mr Perry. Would Guy Atherstone talk to Mr Perry as he had done to her? Stephanie doubted it. Even *he* would have to show some respect to the senior consultant, and Mr Perry wasn't the type of man you could quarrel with. Whatever the outcome of Andrea's case, women's surgical was *not* Guy Atherstone's ward and Stephanie remained adamant that she would retain the right to call it hers.

She was slapping butter on some wholemeal bread when the telephone rang, and at once she brightened up at the sound of her mother's voice.

'How's your day been?' she asked her mother.

'Quite busy. Tailing off a bit now as the children get ready to go back to school.'

Pam Driscoll had been fortunate enough to find a part-time job in a craft shop in Windsor, not too far from where she lived. It had started off as three mornings a week, but gradually over the past few months the proprietors had persuaded her to go as often as she could.

'Still a fair few tourists about though, I should think?' Stephanie suggested. 'Will Mr and Mrs Kane still want you through the winter?'

Pam Driscoll laughed. 'As often as I can manage it by the sound of things! There's the Christmas trade to prepare for after the tourists, and people settle down to needlework in the dark evenings.'

'Yes, I suppose it's an all year round trade, really. You aren't over-doing it, are you?'

'Don't you start! I telephoned your grandparents in Maidstone and got a lecture from Mum, probably because I haven't been to see them lately.'

'You should go, Mum. They are your parents and they're getting on.'

'Late sixties isn't old, Stephanie, or at least, we won't think so when we reach that age. Dad's still able to drive, so they thought they'd come to Windsor for a few days before the evenings get too dark. Any chance of you popping over?'

'I'll try. Better still, why not come to me? I'd like them to see my house. After all, Grandad did help me with the legal side of things.'

'They're coming on Thursday until about next Tuesday but you don't have the weekend off, do you?'

'No, not this weekend, but I can have Monday afternoon off, it's not a theatre day.'

'That should be fine. I know you were hoping we'd get away for a holiday together, Stephanie, but I haven't been at the shop long enough to ask for time off—well, not a whole week. I'm having Thursday and Monday off, and I'm only working Friday and Saturday mornings so that I can spend some time with Mum and Dad.'

'That'll be nice! I'll expect you for lunch on

Monday, then. You've got a key and I'll leave everything ready, but I'll ring you over the weekend anyway. I ought to try to telephone the other grandparents in Oxford but I haven't had time. Are they OK?'

Stephanie's mother didn't answer at once. Then she said quietly, 'Yes, they're coping. Your gran had a funny turn last week, giddiness and bad headaches, and your grandad fell in the garden. I rang Auntie Pat and she said they'd had the doctor but it was nothing serious. Still suffering from the shock of your dad being killed. It's certainly aged them. I want to visit, but it upsets them so much.'

'I promise I will telephone, and on my next weekend, Mum, we'll drive up to see them, even if we only go for the day.'

'It's a tidy old way doing the two journeys on the same day,' her mother warned.

'I can manage that, Mum, it's not really far and if we go on a Sunday there won't be so much traffic.'

'It's good of you to give up your time, love, but we must help them all we can. I don't think they'll ever get over it, you know.'

Stephanie sighed. 'It isn't easy for any of us, and worse for you. Grief does strange things to people. I've got a problem patient in at the moment. Her sister died a few months ago, only about thirtyish.'

Stephanie was back to Andrea de Souza again, but at least her mother's sympathies lessened her own pain for a short while.

They chatted on for some time. Stephanie explained about the proposed pantomime, suggesting that they had better do all their visiting soon or she would be too tied up with the project.

Theatricals, Guy Atherstone had called it, obviously disapproving of Andrea having anything to with it. But Mr Perry *did* approve, and Andrea was his patient, so Stephanie was justified in doing all she could to keep Andrea interested.

CHAPTER SIX

STEPHANIE arrived at Thames Vale hospital soon after seven thirty the next morning. She hurried to the ward, anxious on behalf of the post-operative cases. As she expected, the night had not passed without some incidents, the main cause for concern being Mrs Penny, who had suffered some slight bleeding. But it had been stopped by the application of a small pad of gauze soaked in adrenaline to the wound. A firm dressing had since been sufficient and the patient was now sleeping peacefully. Miss Barrett had also given the night staff a fair bit of excitement in the early hours, but at last was quieter and more subdued. Throughout the day Stephanie saw that her position was changed frequently to aid her comfort.

Mrs Hall was greatly relieved by the cause of her obstruction being removed. She was appreciative of all that was done for her and Stephanie had little doubt that she would soon be well on the road to recovery.

Andrea spent much of the morning in the X-ray department where tests were carried out, but she was back in the ward in time for lunch before Stephanie went off duty for four hours. On her way home she stopped off at the supermarket and bought some good-sized pork chops and other groceries in preparation for her grandparents' visit. She liked to be organised well in advance, and with Mr Atherstone's second operating day of the week being Friday she would be too busy to give much thought to her own needs at the weekend. She was still smarting from her last altercation with him and wondered how she should react when he came to do his round the following morning. Be as calm as she could, she supposed; polite, at least. Because of her bad conscience, even though she refused to admit that she was to blame, she tended all her patients with extra-special attention so that he could not find fault with her post-operative care.

The latter half of the day passed reasonably well. Andrea seemed subdued but during early evening she went along to the day-room with the Frivolous Four to watch television.

Stephanie had allowed only a half-hour visiting time for Mrs Penny, Miss Barrett and Mrs Hall. The relatives took up a considerable amount of time enquiring about the condition of each of the patients, and she was glad to get back to finishing her report and working out the day staff's duty rota for the next month when Liz burst in to her office.

'Mrs Penny, bleeding profusely,' she announced.

Stephanie picked up the phone and asked for an urgent call to be put out for one of the doctors on Guy Atherstone's team before she hurried to Mrs Penny's bed, where everything possible was being done to arrest the flow of blood. A firm dressing was being held in place and when no houseman or

Pete Burnley, the registrar, appeared, Stephanie went back to her office to repeat the call.

To her surprise she saw the back of Guy Atherstone striding away down the corridor. Her first thought was to prevent him from getting away, but she knew that unless she raced, he would reach the lift and be gone before she could catch up with him—so she called his name. Fortunately the corridor was empty, for all visitors had left the wards nearly an hour earlier, but Guy Atherstone turned the corner out of sight as Stephanie tore after him. She heard the lift doors open when he reached the corner so she yelled his name again. Breathlessly she came to an abrupt stop in front of him. He kept his finger on the 'door hold' button and the length of him seemed to be skyscraper high as Stephanie's gaze travelled upwards to meet his.

'I didn't know you were on our floor,' she managed to say. 'I've put out a call—it's Mrs Penny, she's bleeding.'

Guy Atherstone made no reply and Stephanie cringed under his cold scrutiny. She expected contempt, and there were disapproving lines in his expression, but his eyes were so . . . so *angelically* blue. She couldn't think of a more apt description as he stared down at her and her moment of urgency faded into what seemed like a suspended sentence of submission. She blinked in an effort to see him as he really was. Unrelenting, conceited at the very least, but his eyes appeared to contain an element of reprieve in them.

'I put out a call for anyone on your team,' she

said again, convinced that she was not seeing anything remotely like friendliness in his regard of her.

He let the lift-button go and with one hand on Stephanie's shoulder turned her round, guiding her back through the long, clinical corridor.

'Chasing after me, Stephanie?' he mocked in a soft voice. 'Isn't that against the rules?'

'It didn't occur to me that you might be with Miss de Souza. After all, visiting time is over and I think you might have had the courtesy to let me know you were with her.' They both seemed unaware of the emergency in the ward.

His hand was warm as he drew it across her back and then up to her neck. His fingers pinched gently, but in confusion Stephanie twisted out of his grasp.

'I don't need a collar and lead,' she said icily and, daring to look up into his face, saw that he was trying to suppress a laugh.

Amused because I'm so blessed tiny up against him, she thought bitterly. She felt inadequate beside such a monster and wished she could stop feeling embarrassed.

'I shall see Andrea most evenings,' he said in a low voice. 'Why else do you think I wanted her in a special room?'

'It might be less embarrassing for you if you advise me of your arrival then,' she replied haughtily.

His fingers closed round her bare arm just below her gathered arm-band. 'I never get embarrassed, Stephanie, so I don't intend to keep you informed of my comings and goings in my own ward.'

'I'm responsible for *my* patients,' Stephanie informed him.

They had reached her office. Guy placed his leather brief-case down behind the door and took his jacket off while Stephanie lifted down a white coat from the back of the door. He bent his knees slightly to enable her to reach his shoulders better and she pulled the white coat over his broad back. His suit was a kind of donkey brown colour with a light stripe in the weave, and his shirt was cream.

As she covered it up Stephanie felt a funny, prickly sensation run up her spine. She couldn't help but admire his masculinity, even though she tried desperately to ignore it. But as she followed him to Mrs Penny's bedside such disturbing thoughts were swept aside.

He spoke calmly and gently to Mrs Penny.

'My dear, I'm so sorry about this,' he apologised. 'One of the minor complications of such an operation as you've had, but I do assure you you'll be all right.' He turned to Stephanie. 'Alert theatre two and someone from my team. I thought you said you'd put a call out.'

'I did—but I'll do it again.'

A stitch was all that was required, a seemingly routine event to the medical staff, but both Stephanie and Guy Atherstone knew the effect it could have on Mrs Penny. She had lost a fair amount of blood so her saline drip was changed to blood on her return to the ward.

By this time the night staff were on duty, so

Stephanie got ready to leave while Guy sat at her desk reporting the incident on Mrs Penny's notes. He had returned to the ward primarily to fetch his jacket; now he closed the folder and slowly screwed the top of his pen back on.

Stephanie wished he would hurry up and go so that she could leave, but he seemed in no rush to get away. Evidently there was no immediate desire to go home to his wife. His profession would cloak such reasons for lateness as visiting Andrea de Souza, but, she chided herself, it was fortunate that he had still been around. Pete Burnley had already been called to a similar crisis on men's surgical, which accounted for his lack of response to her calls. But now the crises were over and everyone could go home—if only *he* would move himself!

Stephanie stood with her back against the cold radiator, studying Guy Atherstone's neck. It was well-proportioned in relation to his long head and as she viewed his smooth skin she felt prickles again round her own neck. He turned suddenly.

'Another day done,' he observed with a lopsided grin. 'Checked your car over satisfactorily?'

She nodded in a distant way. She did hope he wasn't going to embark on a long session of small talk.

'Andrea tells me that you help to produce the hospital shows?'

'I . . . well, I'm just on the committee,' she said.

'You're fond of music?'

'Very much so.'

'We must chat about it some time.'

Heavens above, she thought, why would *we* want to chat about music?

He stood up and she reached for his jacket at the same time as he did. He waved aside her help.

'Can't have you overreaching, can we?' He was openly sending her up and she wanted to feel indignant—but something in his wicked eyes made her relax and respond.

'I'll try to get a step-ladder from the stores,' she said, and in spite of her resentment of him she found herself fluttering her golden-brown eyelashes at him. He dug his hands deep into his pockets and his open jacket revealed his elegant brown silk tie, which just lapped over the waist-band of his trousers. Somehow, one would expect a man of his size to have a tyre of flab around his waist, but his belt seemed quite slack, indicating a firm, lean torso. For goodness sake, Stephanie reprimanded herself, you sound like an advertisement for a model agency!

Guy sat back on the edge of the desk and folded his arms. 'I'll be round to see them all tomorrow morning, Stephanie. Will you be on duty?'

'Yes, but if I'm not here Liz will be,' she said smoothly.

Guy inclined his head and gave a slight nod. It might almost have meant that he'd prefer Stephanie to be there, but of course he couldn't possibly have indicated any such thing.

'Right then,' he said, again with only the hint of a smile, 'we'll be on our way.'

Stephanie hedged. She wasn't going to get caught with him again.

'I'll have to check with Vicky,' she explained, 'you carry on.' Her voice trailed to a hesitant whisper, almost as if she were apologising for not being ready, but in reality she meant to sound officious, she wanted him to go. As if he sensed her rejection he nodded, and with a lazy grin picked up his brief-case and went on his way.

Stephanie, her cheeks pink, though she couldn't imagine why, hurried into the ward where she found Vicky chatting to the Frivolous Four.

'I'm off, then,' she said. 'You've taken the report from Liz?'

'Yes, we'll manage with your problems, don't worry.'

'The only problem Sister Driscoll's got is with that dishy Mr Atherstone,' Carol commented drily.

'You can say that again,' Stephanie retorted, 'and you'd better all be on your best behaviour in the morning because he's coming round, hopefully to get rid of you lot.'

'You don't really mean that, Sister,' Amelia said. 'You know you've enjoyed having us livening up your ward.'

'The ward won't be the same without you, I grant you that,' Stephanie laughed. She said goodnight to them all and headed for the car park.

She was unlocking the door of her bright yellow car when she heard someone call her name.

'Hang on a minute, Stevie!' It was Graham, and inwardly Stephanie groaned.

'Are you in a hurry?' he asked.

'Yes. I've had a long day and I want to get home.'

'Committee meeting on Monday evening,' Graham informed her.

'Sorry—I've got a half-day and my grandparents are coming over with Mum, but you can make my apologies. Right now, I'm tired, and I want to have an early night.' She sounded sharper than she'd intended.

Graham gave her a funny look but he pushed a folder into her hands.

'OK. I'm sorry, but I thought you'd like to see these in advance of Monday. I'd rather you were going to be at the committee meeting, but if everyone agrees, we're going to start rehearsals first week in September.'

'But that's only days away!' she protested.

'I sent off for panto scripts and there's a rare *Red Riding Hood* one which I like,' Graham explained. 'At least it'll be a change from the usual ones, and the "wolf in bed" scene will provide a good opportunity for hospital jokes. Andrea's a nice girl and from what she tells me she has experience and talent. We could use her and in turn be doing her a favour. It's what she needs, you said so yourself.'

Stephanie made a face, put her bag and the folder on the passenger seat and strapped herself into the driver's seat while Graham stood by, holding the door.

'Women's surgical getting you down?' he ventured to suggest.

'No, of course not, but we just had a minor crisis.

An elderly patient who I'm concerned about. A colostomy, so you know all the implications.'

'Leave your worries here, Stevie,' Graham advised.

'Can *you*?' she asked quickly.

Graham pursed his lips, then smiled a little too intimately at her as he leaned closer. 'I could do if I had a nice girl to go home to.'

'Then I hope you soon find her,' Stephanie quipped and pushed him out of the way, but before Graham closed the door he reached in to ruffle her hair and while she was busy protesting he stole a kiss.

'Graham!' she remonstrated heatedly, and with a gleeful laugh he closed her door and waved her on.

Stephanie felt downcast as she travelled home. The kind of feeling that steals over you for no apparent reason. Perhaps it was concern for Mrs Penny, who seemed so frail. Stephanie suspected that her heart might not be up to the strain of the major surgery she'd undergone, but lurking at the back of her mind was the image of Guy Atherstone. He hadn't treated her in the hostile way she had expected after their confrontation of the day before. Perhaps he had seen Mr Perry and was ready to acknowledge that there was no need for Andrea to have surgery, after all.

As she pulled into her carport a deeper depression settled over her. Could it be disappointment that the TR7 was not standing at the kerbside? She chided herself for such vain imaginings and then recalled Graham's words. It *would* be nice to have someone at home waiting for her after a hard day's work. But that someone could never be Graham Porter, she decided.

After her bath Stephanie made an omelette, which she enjoyed with tomatoes, cheese and mushrooms, and then she curled up on the settee in her favourite place and with reluctance browsed through the typewritten script for the pantomime.

At first she found it difficult to concentrate. Visions of the TR7 persisted, visions of Guy Atherstone, which in turn brought to mind a vivid picture of Andrea de Souza. Just what were they to each other? Somehow it didn't all seem to knit together tidily. Stephanie felt that Guy showed signs of impatience with Andrea on occasion, yet it didn't seem to worry Andrea unduly. No one else had visited her, so Andrea was evidently in this area because of Guy, Stephanie supposed.

Maybe all this conjecture about his private life was close to the truth. A divorce in the offing, and then he and Andrea would marry. The sooner the better, Stephanie decided, then Andrea might stop worrying about herself.

Stephanie's gaze had settled on the bare wall above the fireplace. I need a picture there, she thought absent-mindedly, but she quickly turned back to the pantomime script and began studying it in earnest.

Soon she was absorbed in it, seeing the stage and characters in her mind's eye, and most of all loving the musical part of it. She looked forward to playing the tunes on her piano, a much valued present given to her on her eighteenth birthday by her parents. She loved to play and sing for her own amusement. Her emotions ran deeper than she cared to show the outside world, and when things on the ward went badly or depression crept up unbidden, bringing back memories of the past, she could lose herself in whatever melody fitted her mood.

When she went to bed she was unable to sleep. The new interest stimulated her brain, and she found herself sifting through the hospital staff to find people suitable to play Red Riding Hood and the wolf.

With a touch of irony she saw Guy Atherstone in that role, herself as Red Riding Hood, and she smiled at such a impossible casting, even if he did have a tendency to devour her whenever he visited the ward. Consultants didn't take part in hospital theatricals and neither did she any more. She had enjoyed showing off her talent as a junior nurse, but no one at Thames Vale need ever know about it now that she co-produced with Graham.

In spite of her restless night Stephanie reached her ward next morning on time. She learnt from Vicky, the night sister, that Mrs Penny had slept reasonably well and seemed to be brighter on waking.

'Definite air of jubilation in the Frivolous Four's ward,' Vicky said. 'Not sure whether it's because they'll probably be going home or because Mr Atherstone will be visiting them.'

'A bit of both, I expect.' Stephanie laughed

and continued to hear the full report on all the patients.

'A new admission,' Vicky said lastly, 'Sharon White, motor cycle accident. Her boyfriend is in intensive care. Sharon has various contusions and has had a splenectomy. Mr Atherstone was called in as Pete was off, just after midnight. She's in shock, but fairly comfortable now.'

'How does that suit us for beds?' Stephanie pointed to a list on the wall. 'Six coming in for Friday's list. We could do with Andrea's room couldn't we? As it is we shall have to squeeze an extra bed into the cubicle, which we hope will become vacant today if the Frivolous Four go, unless Mrs Dalby goes out as well.'

'It's always a nuisance when 2B is in use. It's better kept for any overnight emergency,' Vicky grumbled. 'But we can't offend *Sir*, can we?'

Stephanie pulled a face. 'You may not want to, I'm game. Andrea's had her tests, she could go home now and come in to see Mr Perry as an outpatient. I'll have to tell Mr Atherstone the position.'

'Rather you than me,' Vicky said, putting on her coat.

'I suppose it'll be a late round if he was called out for the new admission.'

'Don't bank on it. He's unpredictable, but for once I'm quite happy to leave him to you.'

'Thanks very much,' Stephanie said. 'Isn't he very good-tempered in the middle of the night? Or was theatre sister on duty?'

'He's usually at his most charming at night, and Meg Welford was on duty last night, but I've had enough of him and everyone else for now. I'm off for three nights. By the way, I saw the poster in the canteen for the pantomime. *Red Riding Hood* is a bit different.'

'We shall have to audition, mainly for singers. Can you sing? I've read through the score and lyrics and I like them, but we need a really stunning Red Riding Hood.'

'I can't sing a note but Meg Welford can. Before she became a sister she used to do solo spots at concerts.'

'Thanks for the tip, I'll tell Graham.'

At the sound of shuffling feet Vicky put her head round the door. 'Hope you're prepared, Stevie, he's on his way—with what looks more like a delegation!'

'Not this early!' Stephanie could hardly believe it. 'He can't have been to bed.'

'Probably popped into someone else's for a couple of hours, but it wasn't Andrea's, I can assure you.' She disappeared after her whispered suggestion.

Vicky met up with Guy Atherstone just beyond the office door and Stephanie could hear them discussing the new admission. He then gave a brief résumé of what he had done, to several medical students he had in tow, which gave Stephanie time to gather her wits and glance in the mirror on the back of the door to check that she was presentable. Not that there was much time to carry out any repairs to her hastily applied make-up, which she regretted, for she felt that she wasn't at her best and her eyes still carried the shadows of sleep. But mentally she was wide awake and ready for any aggravation the surgeon might offer if he, too, was suffering from lack of sleep.

He strolled nonchalantly into the office moments later and at once Stephanie was impressed with his immaculate image. He was wearing a dark blue suit and a pale blue shirt with quite a colourful tie in complementary colours, which all suited him perfectly.

'Good morning, Sister Stephanie.'

Stephanie pinked slightly at the guarded familiarity.

'Good morning, Mr Atherstone.' She met his gaze conservatively and noticed that he was looking particularly bright, with an easy smile. The eyebrows were smooth and well-groomed, she observed, which augured well for this time of day.

'You've gained one patient overnight, but you'll be losing several others, I believe,' he said. Unlike many men who seem to be at a loss to know what to do with their hands so resort to rubbing them or putting them in their pockets, Guy Atherstone's long arms didn't look the least bit out of place just hanging leisurely at his sides as he waited for Stephanie to respond.

'I rather hope you'll be sending as many as possible home,' she replied, 'as we've six admissions for your list on Friday.'

'I've done my homework, Sister, and I agree entirely with that, so let's go and see what we can do. I hope you're up to strength this morning. I've brought along some students.'

'So I see. Perhaps you don't really need me then?' she ventured hopefully.

He had a funny way of twisting his lips when he appeared to be suppressing a laugh. 'On the contrary, Sister, we couldn't do without *you*.' Sarcastic devil, she thought.

He stood aside to let Stephanie pass and Pete Burnley raised his eyebrows at Stephanie meaningfully. She wondered if he realised the implication behind those words.

As usual Guy visited all the more recent cases first, starting with the new admission who was comfortable but sleepy. He went into great detail about Sharon White's injuries before moving on to the next cubicle, where Mrs Penny was sitting up looking much brighter and with a healthier colour. As was his usual custom, Guy went to each patient's bedside where he held a semi-private conversation to start with. Stephanie and Pete remained at the foot of the bed until he chose to include them, and Stephanie admired the consultant surgeon for this practice. She knew if she were a patient she would find it embarrassing to have to talk to a sea of faces. Sick people were often weepy and appreciated the chance of speaking to the doctor alone. Guy would never be hurried on these occasions and after each consultation he stood away, out of the patient's hearing, to discuss the technicalities of every case with his registrar, the housemen on his team and, today, the additional students.

Meanwhile, Stephanie had to try to keep her eye on the rest of the ward, though she was fortunate enough to have a good staff nurse in Liz and conscientious qualified and pupil nurses. But the minutes ticked by and she thought this round was going to take forever.

Mrs Dalby, Miss Barrett and Mrs Hall were all making satisfactory progress but Mrs Penny still needed careful nursing with more than the usual degree of sympathetic understanding and medical attention.

Stephanie had hoped that Mrs Dalby might have been allowed to go home but Guy made no such suggestion, so they moved on to the Frivolous Four. Stephanie was getting agitated. He'd been on the ward all morning; soon it would be time to serve lunches and no one had even had coffee. His students were getting fidgety, but if Guy Atherstone noticed this he made no comment—if anything, he held longer conversations with those last four patients than the others. Thankfully, as he turned away from each one he indicated that they could be discharged, leaving Stephanie to make the arrangements. Then, just as the retinue began to move towards the corridor, Mrs Hadley called Guy back.

Inwardly Stephanie groaned and exchanged an impatient sigh with Pete.

'I know you're a very busy man, Mr Atherstone, and I hope you won't be embarrassed,' Mrs Hadley began.

Oh, heavens! thought Stephanie, what on earth had these four hatched between them now? And as she turned she saw Amelia nipping out of bed. Didn't she know—didn't *they* know this sort of thing just wasn't done during a consultant's round!

'I'm never embarrassed, Mrs Hadley,' Guy said genially, returning to her bedside with an un-concerned air and a curious smile.

'Well, you see, everyone's been so kind here,' Mrs Hadley went on. 'You and the other doctors have been very understanding, *and* our little Sister there, so, as there's four of us and we argued as to who should make the presentation, we wondered if we could give this token of our appreciation to you—I think it's too big for Sister Driscoll to handle.'

Amelia, Carol and Mrs Davis were out of bed, in slippers and dressing-gowns, pointing to a beautiful, standing multi-plant holder. Mrs Hadley handed him a large spray of cut flowers in cellophane with a bow of golden-coloured ribbon, to which was attached a card signed by the Frivolous Four.

'For Sister,' Mrs Hadley explained. 'She's been sweet and lovely, and I hope will forgive us for all the trouble we've caused.'

Stephanie was speechless. Even Guy was, too, for a moment—then he pulled Stephanie to him, encircling her in his arm as he held the flowers closer for her inspection.

Stephanie realised that she was expected to say something so she opened her mouth, but Guy forestalled her.

'Should I do this properly?' he asked of the Frivolous Four with a wicked gleam of satisfaction in his blue eyes.

Something urged Stephanie to escape and run, but Guy was holding her too firmly for evasion and as he bent to kiss her she turned her head to one side. It was of necessity a quick peck but it was enough to start everyone clapping, and then to Stephanie's mortification he placed the bouquet of flowers on Mrs Hadley's bed, held Stephanie's chin very firmly between his fingers, and kissed her decisively on her lips.

CHAPTER SEVEN

STEPHANIE wished she could swoon right away into oblivion but, in spite of her indignation building up aggressively, she was forced to smile and in a croaky voice thanked the women for their generous thought. Then Guy led her to look closer at the tall, standing plant-pot holder, a profusion of colour with geraniums, fuchsias, begonias, a fern and bright yellow calceolarias.

'I'm sure you'll know the best spot to have this, Stephanie,' Guy said. 'Somewhere to remind you of—' he paused and she looked up into his devilish eyes, daring him to continue.

'I won't really need anything to remind me of those four,' she said, hurriedly forestalling him. 'I think we'll have it in here while they're still with us, then perhaps it would look nice at the entrance to the ward.'

The students were idling their way towards the swing-doors.

'All right—it is nearly lunch time. Men's surgical in an hour,' Guy called after them. Then he picked up the bouquet again and placed it on top of the pile of folders Stephanie was carrying. He changed his mind and took the folders from her so that she could hold the flowers more gracefully.

'She'll make a lovely blushing bride,' he

observed, for the patients' benefit. 'You'll need a small bouquet when you get married, Stephanie,' he added in a more intimate tone, 'a big one would hide you.'

'If I'm ever silly enough to get married,' she retorted, 'I'll probably want to hide.' She started off down the corridor with Guy in close pursuit.

'A bit cynical aren't you? What's wrong with marriage?'

Before Stephanie could answer Andrea de Souza appeared at the door of her room and, with her hand to her mouth, pretended she was playing a trumpet to the tune of 'Here comes the Bride'.

'Darling—how very charming,' she gushed, coming to meet Guy. 'Such a handsome couple!'

'I'm glad you think so, but perhaps you can change Stephanie's mind about marriage. She sounds rather cynical and not in favour of the idea.'

'Ah—that's because your name isn't Graham. Did he send you that gorgeous bouquet?'

'No, he didn't.' Guy's voice was impatiently curt. 'Grateful patients gave it to her.' He glowered down at Stephanie as if she were at fault in some way and then, with eyes that had turned to ice, he said, 'I'll give you half an hour to serve lunches, and then we'll continue our discussion about my patients.'

He strode off down the corridor, completely ignoring Andrea who followed Stephanie into the office.

'Mm . . . *Stephanie* is it? I thought hospital staff weren't that familiar? Well not with consultants.'

'This was a less formal few minutes,' Stephanie explained. 'Shouldn't you be in the day-room for lunch?'

Andrea sighed. 'Mm—if you say so.' She giggled childishly. 'You're all red—and just because I mentioned Graham's name! Big secret, is it?'

'It's no secret, Andrea, that there's nothing between Graham Porter and myself,' Stephanie fought hard to stay calm.

'Good, then I can make a play for him.' Andrea's remark threw Stephanie.

'But surely—'

'You thought he wasn't my type?' Andrea giggled like a schoolgirl. 'Any man is my type,' she said and turned to go down the corridor to the day-room.

Stephanie stood at her desk feeling ready to burst. Andrea de Souza is twenty-seven, she thought irritably, yet she behaves like a seventeen-year-old!

Liz was getting on with serving lunches and Stephanie was relieved when everyone had finished and she could sit down to a much-needed cup of coffee. It was all right for Guy Atherstone she reflected, he could go off and have his lunch whenever he chose, but now she would have to go late. She listed the discharges and balanced them against the admissions, but nothing could alter the fact that they were one bed short, and that this would mean putting an extra patient in one of the cubicles.

After she had finished her coffee she went along

to the Frivolous Four's cubicle and suggested that they all telephoned home to arrange transport. When she returned to her office Guy was sitting in her chair at the desk. He looked pointedly at his watch as she entered.

'I said half an hour and I've allowed you forty minutes,' he said sarcastically.

'Thank you,' she returned with the same amount of sarcasm. 'I was here until a moment ago, when I went to tell the discharged patients to telephone home.'

'So you haven't had lunch?' he asked.

Stephanie shook her head and muttered, 'No.'

'Then let's get started.'

She refrained from reminding him that he was sitting in her chair, but at least it was easier to stand beside him than having to hold her head back to look up at him.

'You were saying that we need six beds and I've discharged four patients.'

'We had two empty beds, one of which Sharon White is in, so we're still one short.'

'Mm—*your* problem, I believe.' He sat back and glanced up at her, dark blue eyes riveted on her face, evidently hoping to antagonise her.

'Of course,' she agreed sweetly. 'I had hoped Mrs Dalby—'

'No, Stephanie, her home circumstances aren't suitable. The social people will be getting in touch with you—I hope to get her moved to a convalescent home to ensure she continues to rest. She has a daughter and three young children staying at her home waiting to be rehoused after a breakdown in the marriage, and from the reports we've had, Mrs Dalby has been doing all the work. It's been too much strain on her.'

'Yes, I do realise her home conditions are far from ideal.' She paused. 'I understand 2B was usually kept for emergencies until—'

'I needed it for Andrea,' he finished for her.

'She's had all her tests now. Couldn't she see Mr Perry in out-patients?'

There was a long, uncomfortable silence. Then Guy placed two hands on the desk and stood up.

'She could,' he said. Then, as he guided Stephanie to take the chair, he added with finality, 'but she's not my case.' He drew his hand across Stephanie's back and tapped lightly on her shoulder before leaving her feeling totally defeated.

A fat lot of help he's been, she thought defiantly and remembered that he had said much the same to her over Andrea de Souza. He had a grudge because Mr Perry saw no reason for exploratory surgery on Andrea, she supposed, so suddenly today *she* was responsible for the ward!

Liz returned from lunch at that moment with three other nurses. 'We're back,' she reported, 'and it looks as if you need a stiff drink. *Sir* was striding down the passage as if he's about to murder someone.'

'He'd like to murder me,' Stephanie mumbled.

'Oh, not after that delectable kiss!'

Stephanie covered her face with her hands.

'Don't remind me,' she groaned. 'The most embarrassing moment of my life, but I love the plant-holder and those flowers are gorgeous. Get one of the nurses to put them in vases.'

'I'll get a bucket to stand them in until you go home.'

'No, they're for everyone.'

Liz shook her head. 'Definitely yours, and rightly so.'

'That's not fair. I haven't done nearly as much as the more junior staff—besides, I haven't been on the ward that long.'

'We get tons more flowers than we can use, so you take the bouquet home and on your day off think of us slaving away. I bet you find this ward hectic after men's medical, don't you?' Liz sounded mildly sympathetic.

'It's vastly different, but the days slip by much more quickly and I think I'm going to like it, although I could do without Mr Atherstone.'

'You'll get used to him, he's not so bad really.'

'I'll take a rain-check on that opinion,' Stephanie stated flatly. 'While I'm at lunch get someone to help the four discharges pack up. The beds can be stripped and remade, then we'll have to get an extra bed put up in that cubicle.'

Stephanie was quite hungry but settled for ham and cheese salad which would be easier to work on, she decided. The canteen was almost empty so she took her tray to a far corner in the sun where she could relax. Not that she was really uptight. She felt she had enough spirit to cope with the likes of

Guy Atherstone. She admired him as a surgeon and she did enjoy her work, even if he was a bit unpredictable.

Unpredictable? Golly—fancy kissing her like that in front of patients, students, nurses! She felt herself go hot all over again. Now that she had time to collect her thoughts she could relive the incident more slowly. She remembered the last second of panic as his rugged, mischievous face had come close to hers, and her precision timing as she turned her head so that his lips made contact with her cheek. She thought she had cleverly averted an awkward incident, but she'd never be clever enough for him!

She stared out of the window, pausing momentarily from her salad, as she felt the sheer ecstasy of his kiss. She had never before experienced such bliss. Did Andrea not realise how lucky she was? Apparently not, if she set out to capture any man who came within chasing distance. Although she saw Guy as a womaniser, Stephanie found it hard to believe that he could be attracted to Andrea. Could her behaviour be attributed to her show business experiences, she wondered? There was a common side to her which didn't fit with Guy's image.

No matter how much they disagreed on professional matters, Stephanie had to acknowledge that he was a man of distinction. Even that kiss had contained a reflection of the man's quality and polish. She went on eating, finishing her meal with coffee ice-cream and a cup of tea.

There were joyful goodbyes later that day as the

Frivolous Four's relatives came to fetch them, and in a way Stephanie was sorry to see them go. She was at her desk at about five-thirty before going off duty when Guy appeared at the door.

'Still here?' he commented.

'I'm going in a few minutes,' she said.

He came closer to the desk, leaning heavily on one end of it so that she could feel his warm breath wafting across her forehead. She experienced a waver of confidence. He was beginning to influence her in a way which she found disconcerting.

'Sorted out the beds satisfactorily?' he asked.

She explained about putting an extra one up. 'It seems unfair to the others to make it so cramped,' she said.

'The cubicles were designed to take four when we can afford to be generous, six in more usual times, and unless Liz has been deliberately misleading you there are usually six to a cubicle. I agreed to my female list being shorter for the past couple of weeks to allow for the change-over to you—so that you can get used to the ward—and me.'

'I doubt if I shall ever be that.' The words were out before she realised what she had said.

'Get used to the ward—or me?' he queried.

'I think I'm getting familiar with the ward routine.'

'But not familiar with me? Oh, come now, Stephanie, you disappoint me! I thought I had gone to great lengths to initiate you to my methods.'

She looked at him intently. He was being light-hearted, but how far dared she go?

'You look ravishing when you're embarrassed,' he whispered. 'So tiny and defenceless.' He took her chin in his hand just as a cutting female voice echoed from the doorway.

'You two at it *again*!'

Guy's eyes were alight with madcap daring as he peered closer into Stephanie's face, pulling down one of her lower lids with his left hand. 'Sister Driscoll has something in her eye.' He deliberately rubbed her upper lid with his thumb so that her eye smarted, and she jerked her head backwards.

But now Guy transferred his immediate attention to Andrea. 'I just came to report to Sister that I'm visiting you, darling,' he said and, putting his arm around her waist, led her back to her room.

Stephanie's eye watered badly for about a minute. Rotten so-and-so, she thought crossly as she dabbed at it with her handkerchief. Mustn't let the girlfriend be jealous, I suppose. And with that she packed up her written work and handed over to Liz.

There seemed little spare time for anything over the next few days. The new admissions arrived, were allocated their beds and were examined by Pete Burnley before being checked over by Jason Nye, the anaesthetist.

He was a good-looking young man, aged about thirty-two, of medium height and build but with the type of youthful features which were near-perfect, Stephanie considered. Dark brown hair with large, appealing eyes to match, silky smooth brows and lashes and a short, straight nose to complement his peaches and cream complexion, which was clean shaven. He hadn't been at Thames Vale long, only about four months, and rumours were rife about him and Meg Welford, theatre sister. Now, as he moved away from the last of the six patients on the theatre list, he shoved his stethoscope into the pocket of his white coat.

'That's the second one with a dicey heart for tomorrow,' he said in a low voice.

'Anything to be concerned about?' Stephanie asked.

Jason consulted the notes and raised one eyebrow. 'Not unduly, but you can never be certain how these people will react on the day. Up to now it's only been a minor murmur which her GP decided not to alarm her about. Strictly speaking her family should be warned, but that was really his job. We've got a patient in men's surgical in much the same condition, though his chances are slight anyway, as he's got cancer. Mrs Blanchard being in for partial thyroidectomy will require particular care, especially afterwards. But I expect you're well informed even though this is a new ward for you.'

He smiled amicably at Stephanie and she decided he was one of the nicest men she knew, although they were not that well-acquainted as yet. 'How are you liking it here?' he asked.

'Very different from men's medical,' she said, 'but I feel as if I've been here for ages. It's that kind of ward isn't it? All go, and a fairly quick turn round of patients.'

'Certainly no time for boredom to set in, especially with a man like Guy Atherstone in command. By the way, I believe you're on the committee that's trying to produce this pantomime?'

'Not trying to, we *are* going to produce it. Think positive! Are you interested in taking part?'

'I'd love to. Singing is my forté, if you like. Sometimes I think I should have persevered with an operatic career, but that's only on the bad days. I love medicine more, but with singing a close second. Will you soon be auditioning?'

'There's a committee meeting on Monday which I'm unable to attend. But see Graham Porter, he'll know when the auditions are to be held. It'll be a change to have a willing male voice.'

'Meg's interested too, so we'll go along together.' He smiled again before hurrying off. He and Meg would be ideal for the main parts in the show; ideal for each other too. Lucky Meg, Stephanie concluded. But how would Guy Atherstone react to their friendship?

Stephanie had no further opportunity to discuss the show with anyone as Friday and Saturday were hectic days, with Mrs Blanchard suffering a mild crisis after surgery. Fortunately, it had been anticipated owing to the patient's previous degree of toxicity. The nurse keeping a careful watch on all post-operative cases reported to Stephanie that Mrs Blanchard had begun to sweat profusely and her pulse was racing. Stephanie went into immediate action by administering oxygen and sponging the patient with tepid water, and Guy answered his bleeper to write up for a morphine injection. Mrs Blanchard responded well and settled quietly. Guy returned to theatre after discussing the case with Stephanie. At least they were working together now in better harmony, as long as Andrea's condition wasn't mentioned. Mr Perry called to visit his two or three patients on Saturday morning and spent a short time with Andrea, though made no mention of her leaving Thames Vale hospital.

'I'm deliberately keeping her in suspense about the test results, Sister,' Mr Perry explained later in the office. 'It's a case of being cruel to be kind but, as you've observed, she likes plenty of attention and only becomes depressed when she's left to her own devices for any length of time. It's sad that a young woman should find herself in such a situation, but Guy Atherstone and I are seeking the help of a psychiatrist as there is nothing physically wrong with Andrea. When we feel the time is right we shall confront her with our findings. I'm hoping this pantomime will really interest her—then we can tell her that she can only take an active part if she's been discharged.'

'I'll do all I can to help her,' Stephanie assured him.

'I think you've made quite an impression on her already, my dear. I came in for a few minutes late one evening after you'd gone off duty and she told me that disease and ill-health seemed to be viewed quite differently here from what she expected. She's confused, you see. She associates hospitals with her sister's illness and subsequent death and her own grief. Here she seems to have found a certain amount of—well, happiness, for the want of a better word. But we mustn't forget that her loss was a very real tragedy to her.'

'We have a lot to be happy about, Mr Perry, when we send people home in a better condition than when they come in. I find this ward very rewarding from that point of view.'

'Keep up the good work, Sister, and persevere with Andrea. I know Guy Atherstone will be eternally grateful.'

Stephanie felt a little pessimistic about that! He seemed to do everything to influence Andrea into believing that she was really ill, which made the situation somewhat difficult. But Andrea was his girlfriend, so maybe he was over-concerned for her.

By the time Stephanie went off duty at midday on Monday, four more patients had been discharged and a further four admitted for Tuesday's list. Today, though, she put all thoughts of them out of her mind as she greeted her mother and grand-parents when she arrived home.

'We should have met you in town and taken you out to lunch,' her grandfather said, hugging her.

'But this is a family house-warming,' Stephanie insisted, 'so it wouldn't be the same if I hadn't cooked lunch. Well, Mum saw to it all really—was everything OK, Mum?'

'It's all ready for dishing up, love. Bit extra-vagant aren't you? Roast beef and Yorkshires?'

'Special occasion! Wish I could have had the whole day off. Sorry you had to come and work in the kitchen,' Stephanie laughed.

'I've only supervised what you had put ready to come on. I'll see to the dishing-up if you like—you show Mum and Dad over the house.'

Suddenly, with people in it, her two-bedroomed house seemed like a proper home. Her grandparents were impressed, though Stephanie knew that they considered an older type of property a better buy. They didn't care for the newer, open-plan, estate-type surroundings, but they did approve of her home and the design of the house, where not one inch of space was wasted anywhere.

There was a small patio outside the double-glazed, sliding french windows, and the tiny garden was well planned with paving stones and neat circular flower-beds, which helped to make it look spacious.

'I'd have loved a lawn,' Stephanie said as they sat outside on the patio, 'but being the builders' show house the garden was already landscaped. The soil is a bit like clay and rather wet, being near the river, so my neighbours tell me I'm lucky.'

Her mother's parents were still young at heart, although past retiring age, and loved to hear all about Stephanie's work-filled days as well as her activities outside the hospital. The time passed all too quickly though, and they started the drive back to Windsor before darkness fell, which gave Stephanie the opportunity to have a bath and wash her hair ready for duty next day.

It was another theatre day, which meant that she lost out on some of her off duty. But during her tea break Graham met up with her in the canteen.

'You're very elusive these days, Stevie. I thought you'd want to know how the meeting went.'

Stephanie sipped her much-needed cup of tea. 'So, how did the meeting go, Graham?'

'On till midnight. You could have came late couldn't you?'

'I told you, I had company. Besides, the reason we have a large committee is so that each job is doubled up.'

'The idea being to make it less of a hassle if people can't get off duty, yes, but like last year's pantomime it always falls to the faithful few like you and me to see the thing through,' Graham complained.

'Then it's up to us this time to see that the others do their share,' Stephanie retorted.

'I think they will. Everyone seems over the moon with the idea—what did you think about the script and score? Or haven't you bothered to look at it?' Graham surveyed her with a hesitant look of disdain.

'Yes, I found it good—it kept me up very late to finish it. Have you seen Jason Nye lately? He wants to audition.'

'Good. Yes, he rang me on the ward and says that Meg is interested too—but—I hate to say this, Stevie, aren't they a bit old to play leading parts?'

'Aren't we all a bit past doing this sort of thing?' she laughed.

'No. You wouldn't think twice about taking a straight part in a play would you? Mature people do have good voices sometimes, but we need to encourage the younger element,' Graham said.

'I suggest we wait and see what comes along. The untrained staff have difficulty in getting to rehearsals if they're moving around and studying for exams. When's the auditioning to start?'

'Sunday morning and evening, and Monday evening. All the committee are hoping to sit in at each session.'

'Did you tell the committee about Andrea de Souza?'

'Yes, and they all liked the idea of her helping. Midwife Kate Allday is going to do the choreography for us as usual.'

'It's a bigger job than we've done before,' Stephanie said. 'A much larger chorus for one thing. Shouldn't she have help?'

'Yes, if we can find someone with either similar talent or experience.'

'You're pretty good yourself, Graham. I mean, you're an expert dancer and you're full of ideas.'

Graham spluttered over his tea. '*That*—coming from you, is a compliment. Actually Katie's very experienced. She came into nursing late after being a Bluebell girl or whatever.'

'I'll try to go over the music on my piano this week. We're mad!' Stephanie looked at Graham and laughed. 'I always think how mad I am to get involved in hospital *theatricals*, as Guy Atherstone calls them. There's always a panic on at the last minute *and* it's Christmas. You'd think we didn't have anything else to do in our spare time! We'll never have a minute to ourselves.'

She reiterated this many times during the following days and weeks, but the hospital seemed to reverberate with enthusiasm for this particular pantomime, which became an instant hit with the members of the cast. Stephanie found it easy to learn, and often late at night she would play the songs softly on her piano. She loved music of most types and these songs were different. She almost wished she had auditioned for a part herself but she felt safer keeping behind the scenes, although she had been persuaded to understudy Meg.

Initially it had brought her and Graham closer together, just as Meg and Jason were, and not only in their roles of Red Riding Hood and the wolf. It was evident that they were becoming totally engrossed in each other and Stephanie wondered frequently how Meg's relationship with Jason affected Guy Atherstone. But didn't he have his attractive wife tucked away somewhere?

At that, Stephanie's thoughts turned to Andrea and her problems. She had had a series of consultations with a psychiatrist and attended remedial sessions before being discharged only a day or so ago.

'I shall miss this place,' she said to Stephanie as she fastened her case. 'You've all been so kind and there's this exclusive atmosphere in hospital that can't be found in any other profession. Well,' she said pursing her lips in contemplation, 'I said

kind—but there have been times when you've been
. . . oh, Stephanie,' she whispered in a faltering
voice, suddenly hugging Stephanie, 'You've been
an officious bitch on occasion, but I know I've been
very trying at times. How am I going to cope once
I'm home?' she pleaded with tears in her eyes.

'You're going to be fine,' Stephanie assured her.
'We shall look forward to seeing you at every
rehearsal—we're depending on you, Andrea. We
could never have done it without you, and I have a
feeling about this show—it's going to be a great
success, even if it is only an amateur production.'

'Stephanie, forgive me, perhaps I shouldn't say
this, but you should be taking the lead, you know!
You have a super singing voice and when you're out
in front, ordering everyone around when they don't
emphasise in the right place or something, it's plain
to see you're a born natural! At least Graham
persuaded you to be Meg's understudy. That's
something, I suppose.'

'A born natural—doing what?' a masculine voice
demanded.

'Hullo, Guy, darling.' Andrea wiped away a
tear. 'Oh, we're saying horrid goodbyes,' she said,
'but I've been telling Stephanie she ought to be
playing the lead—the part was made for her, wasn't
it?'

Guy's face was a mixture of pain and fury.

'How would I know?' he demanded between
gritted teeth. 'And you can stop filling her head
with ideas of instant stardom. We both know what
that can do to a person, don't we, Andrea?'

Stephanie felt insignificant standing so small between them. She was puzzled at the electric arc, which almost hissed with heat, spanning the distance between Guy and Andrea. Guy's eyes were like blades of steel while Andrea's expression was one of painful submission. In that moment Stephanie realised that there was a great deal more to their relationship than she would ever know about. The tension hung in the air.

It was like standing at the ringside waiting for a 'box-on' command, so she switched off the current by saying, 'I can only tell other people how I like to see it done, Andrea. It's probably not at all professional.'

'It hadn't better be,' Guy growled down at her. 'You're a trained nurse, and *that* should occupy seventy-five per cent of your life. I hope this confounded show isn't going to dominate this hospital. If it does I shall put a stop to it.' He picked up Andrea's suitcase and left the room.

Andrea kissed Stephanie's cheek. 'Ouch! What have I done? Sorry, darling, but don't worry, I'll placate him. He doesn't realise that I know just how to manage him. This isn't really goodbye as I'll see you soon at rehearsal.' As they went out into the corridor Andrea said in a louder voice, 'I should have asked Guy to bring in flowers and chocolates for you all—there must be some way I can show my appreciation.'

'There is,' Guy snapped, 'by keeping fit and well. It's their job to care for the sick.' And with that he marched Andrea off.

CHAPTER EIGHT

STEPHANIE watched them walking side by side down the corridor in disbelief. He was a brute, and *he* had been the one to give her a lecture about the ethics of nursing! She was about to go into her office when she noticed Guy and Andrea turn to look at one another, simultaneously moving closer together. Guy put his arm round Andrea's waist and even from this distance Stephanie could see that they were laughing happily. Then Guy planted a kiss on Andrea's cheek.

Stephanie just stood and stared at them as they disappeared round the corner on their way to the lifts area. Evidently Andrea did know him intimately and was an expert at winning him round. He should show an interest in the show, if only for Andrea's sake, Stephanie thought. She remembered that he had suggested they should discuss music some time but today he didn't sound like a music-lover. Or was it performers, perhaps, against whom he had a conviction?

That must be it, she decided as she sat at her desk, looking vaguely into space. Perhaps Andrea wanted to get back into show business, and why shouldn't she? Helping with the hospital entertainment wasn't going to earn her any money or put her back in the public eye. Her sister, the supposedly lovely Claudine, may have gone solo as a star in her own right, but they had been a partnership originally—so why couldn't Andrea now go on to do her own thing? She was beautiful and she had talent. Then Stephanie recalled all the reasons for her being in hospital and the fact that Claudine's marriage had broken up because of show business. Obviously Guy Atherstone was aware of this, and if he was anticipating marrying Andrea at some stage in the future he wouldn't want history repeating itself.

Stephanie was beginning to find the pressures of such a busy ward and her spare-time task of directing and producing the pantomime conflicting in some ways, but she tried desperately to keep the two things separate. Another colostomy case came in and so she took the new patient, Mrs Ryder, to meet Mrs Penny, who was still maintaining steady progress but needed plenty of reassurance.

When Guy Atherstone came round unexpectedly one morning to visit all his patients, Stephanie's head was still buzzing with all that had taken place at the previous evening's rehearsal. Everyone had fed Andrea bits of information and gossip about prominent members of the hospital staff, from senior consultants down to the canteen and domestic staff, so she and Graham had been very busy re-writing some of the words of the comedy songs and sketches to send up as many people as they could. Even in the bedroom scene when Red Riding Hood visits her grandmother there were certain implications about a tiny nurse and a very tall doctor. Rehearsals were pretty chaotic because the script was getting funnier each day as Andrea and Graham got carried away with enthusiasm, causing a great deal of hilarity and making Stephanie's job of directing almost impossible. She was trying to recall the send-up in that sketch—was it applicable to herself and Guy Atherstone . . .

'*I said—*'

Stephanie fluttered her golden lashes and returned to her job of escorting Guy on a round of the ward. 'Sorry,' she muttered in embarrassment. 'You were saying?'

'That we hope Mrs Penny is going to be a help to Mrs Ryder, don't we? Especially after surgery.'

Stephanie smiled at Mrs Penny. 'She's already been very helpful in telling Mrs Ryder a little of what to expect, haven't you, Mrs Penny?'

'Some of what I can remember. It all seems so long ago now. I thought I'd have gone home long before this, Mr Atherstone.'

'All in good time, Mrs Penny. I expect Sister wishes she had a whole ward full of patients as good as you've been. Isn't that right, Sister?' he said gently.

'It is indeed,' Stephanie agreed. 'We're reluctant to send you home, Mrs Penny.'

As they walked away Guy said in a low voice, 'Thank you for eventually taking an interest.'

'I'm sorry,' Stephanie said tartly, looking up at him fearlessly. 'I know you like your conversation with the patients to be private so I try not to intrude.'

'You mean your mind was wandering,' he accused acidly. 'On this wretched show again I suppose. You're looking weary so I take it that it's all too much for you?' He didn't give her a chance to repudiate his officious statement, but went on, 'It needn't be if you're sensible. Just keep hospital routine your number one priority and reserve the entertainment projects for off duty.'

'I hope I do, Mr Atherstone, only this time it's been a little different with Andrea helping. I would have thought you'd be delighted at her reaction to it all. She's being a tremendous help to us and maybe it'll help her to revive her singing and showbiz talents. That's what she needs, don't you agree?'

'Frankly, I couldn't care a damn. I just like my nursing staff to be on the ball in their profession.'

Stephanie stood by his side, swaying slightly to and fro with the pile of folders in her arms. Was she beginning to feel a little too cocksure of herself now with the great consultant? She hoped she wasn't being impertinent when she said, a trifle haughtily, 'Do I take it you're complaining?'

She was fluttering her eyelashes at him again, for some reason trying to be provocative in view of the fact that his eyebrows were elegantly smooth. He glanced down at her. There was so much space between his face and hers, but it didn't dissuade her and she could almost believe there was laughter in his eyes—not the usual ice-cold blue glare but warmth, like a summer-blue sky.

'If I were complaining, young lady, you would

not need to ask that question. I'd make it very obvious.'

She began to colour slightly under his intense scrutiny and she felt embarrassed when various members of the nursing staff eyed them circumspectly as they went about their duties.

'Keep your mind on your work and don't get carried away with that wretched pantomime,' he advised.

'I don't intend to do either,' she said confidently, 'I'm off for the weekend.'

'Then make sure you have a real break.' He sighed. 'I suppose you'll still rehearse all weekend?'

'Actually, no.'

'You're spending the weekend cleaning, washing, tidying the garden, doing whatever bachelor girls like to do?'

Stephanie smiled sweetly. 'I'm having company for the weekend,' she told him. He inclined his head and by his smouldering expression she knew she had given him the wrong impression.

'Then have a good time. Pointless though, my telling you to come back refreshed,' he added.

He left her and she wondered why she had wanted him to think she was entertaining someone special. Her mother was special—to her—and she might just as well have told him the truth. She had sounded cynical about marriage on a previous occasion, now she supposed in her sub-conscious she was trying to amend that. Why? And what could it possibly mean to Guy Atherstone? She felt annoyed with herself, but then put the whole matter out of her mind as Jason Nye came to see the patients on Guy's list for the next day.

September had been a lovely month with warm sunshine almost every day. It had continued into early October, though the evenings were chilly and dusk came down early. Stephanie really had put ward matters and all thoughts of the pantomime out of her mind once she reached her house on Friday evening. She cleaned and cooked in readiness for her weekend guest. Although she had offered to drive to Windsor to fetch her mother, Pam Driscoll insisted on travelling to Reading by bus, so on Saturday morning Stephanie parked her car in the nearby multi-storey car park and was at the bus station to meet her mother.

They had coffee first, chatted and shopped; had lunch and chatted and shopped some more before finally making for the estate where Stephanie lived in the late afternoon.

They were happy in each others' company, more like sisters than mother and daughter as they exchanged news and gossip, often laughing helplessly over some trivial incident. There was only one subject which was taboo, and that was Graham Porter. Stephanie had found it necessary to keep quiet about her mother's visit as Graham would have suggested coming round in order to see her again, and that might have given her mother ideas. Ideas which would have been without foundation, however hard Graham tried to please Stephanie and would like to have started something meaningful between them.

So, Stephanie and her mother ate toast and pâté for tea as they watched television. They sat up late, never short of a topic of conversation and Sunday morning they slept in, deciding to have a coffee and cereal breakfast with an early lunch to follow.

'We could walk to Reading by the river, Mum,' Stephanie suggested as they sat on the patio with their afternoon cup of tea.

'That would be nice, love,' Pam Driscoll said. 'We need to walk off all those extra calories and I could do with the exercise.'

'You'll get plenty when you go back to the shop. It was nice of them to let you have the Saturday off this week.'

'Won't be another chance with Christmas to prepare for. I suppose you get all the exercise you need at work?'

Stephanie laughed in agreement. 'I like the outdoors, though, when I get the opportunity, and I haven't had much of that recently. This weather is so perfect we should make the most of it—but I'll drive you back this evening, if you'd rather?'

'No, I like your first idea. I don't want to be late back as the evenings get dark quickly now, so we'll walk to Reading by the river and have a cup of tea, or better still a cream tea, somewhere before I catch my bus.'

'I thought you were the calorie-conscious one?' Stephanie joked.

'Lucky you—no need to worry about such things,

but at my age I have to be careful,' Pam laughed. 'I'll be careful tomorrow! We don't get the chance to indulge too often, do we?'

Stephanie hugged her mother as they took their empty cups to the kitchen. 'It's been lovely to have you here for the weekend, Mum,' she said with genuine affection. 'Wish it could be for always. I can't persuade you . . .'

Pam Driscoll rounded on Stephanie. 'No, you cannot.' She looked at her daughter curiously. 'You must be overtired, my girl, if you're getting emotional. Independence is what your dad wanted for you and it's what I know he would expect of me. Do you think I haven't spent many lonely hours wishing we were somewhere together, darling?' she said in a softer, husky voice.

Tears pricked savagely at the back of Stephanie's eyes. 'Mum, you should have said. Stay on now, you know you can.'

'Two days? Three? Then for ever? And what happens to me when you decide to get married?'

'Mum—I haven't even met anyone . . .'

'You've met plenty, Stephanie. Perhaps losing your dad made you wax cold for a while, but I want you to be married. I want you to find a good, kind, caring man who'll look after you like your dad wanted. Graham seemed to be all of those things, I thought.'

Stephanie rinsed the crockery without looking at her mother. They were too close for this conversation.

'You didn't tell me the whole truth and nothing

but the truth,' Pam Driscoll accused, but with a grin.

'I told you all you needed to know and I didn't lie to you, Mum.'

'But there was a big fight between you and Graham because he thought it was time you moved in together?'

'Mum!' Stephanie reproached.

'It's true though, isn't it? Graham didn't keep anything back, believe me.'

'And you didn't tell me that you'd met him in Reading.'

'Because I hoped you'd tell me your version all in your own good time.'

'Girls don't usually tell their mothers all the intimate details. Their sisters or friends, maybe.'

'I thought we pledged to be more like two sisters—that's how your dad saw us.'

'That was only a joke, and you know it. Anyway, Graham and I are good friends now, but nothing more. He did me a favour by wanting to share my bed because he made me realise that it wasn't what I wanted.'

'Perhaps we set our standards too high for you, Stephanie,' her mother said with a troubled expression. 'Values of today are so different, it can't be easy for you.'

Stephanie was thoughtful for several minutes, then she said, 'It *is* easy because I haven't met the man I could really go overboard for.'

'Well, you'd best get your skates on. Having babies is best done before you're thirty.'

'As Dad would have said, there's no besting you today, is there?'

Pam Driscoll put on her jacket and a pair of lightweight gloves to match the smart, navy blue suit she was wearing. She stood before the mirror in Stephanie's lounge and checked that the pleated chiffon scarf was covering her burn scars.

'I'll carry that,' Stephanie insisted, picking up the overnight bag, and putting her own shoulder-bag over one arm.

'It's light,' her mother said. 'Good job I can keep a set of things here for when I visit, though when you get that super-perfect husband he'll want to see the back of me and my belongings.'

'Then he won't fit in here,' Stephanie snapped adamantly.

They soon reached the tow-path along by the river and strolled leisurely in the direction of Reading, though it was all of two miles away. Pam tucked her arm through Stephanie's in her usual motherly way but no one in the world would have guessed that they were mother and daughter.

The sun was really warm on their backs, but a cool breeze blew off the River Thames and Stephanie was glad she was wearing a pleated skirt with a matching short waistcoat made in a wool material in soft pinks and mauves. Her jumper was a pink angora one and she'd had packed her cagoule in her black leather shoulder-bag.

'Gran would say this was St Luke's summer,' Pam said.

'Don't you mean an Indian summer?'

'I'm not sure whether they're all one and the same thing. I believe in America an Indian summer is the same as a St Martin's summer which comes at the end of the autumn. St Luke's summer is mid-October, like now—as if it matters! It's lovely and we're lucky, and so are those folk with their boats.'

'Idle rich,' Stephanie said.

'One of the things your dad would have liked and never had.'

'He should have had what he wanted and not given me the car on my twenty-first.'

'It wasn't that he didn't have the money, Stephanie, and he'd have bought you the car for your seventeenth birthday if I'd agreed.'

'As it was he gave me your old banger,' she laughed, 'but I'm glad he had a brand new one. Well—I think I'm glad,' she said, remembering the tragedy which killed him.

'Like most men he was car-mad, and the accident wasn't his fault.'

They stood silently at the riverside, the water gently lapping against the side of a splendid cabin cruiser. After a bit Pam said, 'This is really something.'

'Then come aboard.'

Stephanie looked up in disbelief. A figure wearing a black track suit with thick white stripes accentuating the length of him, was cleaning the windows of the cabin. His dark hair was windblown and his eyes were covered by dark glasses, but there was no mistaking the familiar voice.

'Oh, no,' Stephanie groaned in an undertone.

Pam, not really aware of the fact that Stephanie knew the boat's owner, glanced from him to Stephanie.

'Is that an invitation we can't afford to turn down?'

'I only wish we could,' Stephanie muttered in her mother's ear as she urged her forward to meet the tall, ambling figure who came up the gangplank to meet them. He nodded, then held out his hand to Pam to help her step aboard.

'This is my mother, Mr Atherstone,' Stephanie introduced her. Guy held her arm as she climbed aboard and she felt his grip tighten.

'Your mother?' He smiled lazily, with almost a hint of contempt, looking from one to the other.

'The name is Pam,' Stephanie's mother said.

'Mr Atherstone is a consultant surgeon, Mum,' Stephanie explained.

'And the name is Guy, even though your daughter means that I am *the* consultant surgeon at Thames Vale hospital.'

Arrogant pig, Stephanie thought, biting back the ready retort.

'Isn't that right, Stephanie? The consultant surgeon who blights your every working day and keeps you on your toes?'

Stephanie blinked against the glare of the lowering sun. 'If that's how you see yourself,' she mocked.

Guy studied her without response and Pam eased into the conversation with, 'We were admiring your boat.'

'Then you're my instant friend,' Guy said with charm. Taking Pam's arm he led her into the wheelhouse and below to the cabin.

Stephanie drew in her breath in preparation for whatever was to come. Seeing the petite figure of her mother beside Guy Atherstone she realised how she must look when she had to accompany him on his rounds. True, she did have a cap which gave the impression of extra height and she did wear slightly higher heels than her mother, but she'd still look tiny.

She followed at a discreet distance as Guy showed Pam over the boat, obviously revelling in her enthusiasm for *Thames Jewel*. Trust him to think he had the only priceless jewel on the river, Stephanie thought, and as she watched him devoting his attention to her mother she felt an awful unrest creep over her. He wouldn't—not even *he* would make a pass at her mother! But, obliged as she was to watch him displaying his effusive passion for his boat, and the way Pam was responding to his charm, Stephanie finally admitted that he had whatever it took to bewitch every female who came in contact with him.

Except for herself, she resolved. She had so far managed to keep a cool, calculated distance between them—well, almost. There was that kiss which had embarrassed and devastated her. There were those unguarded moments when he touched her in a familiar but not quite intimate way . . . But she shrugged those taunting memories off. She must be alert today on her mother's behalf.

Guy propelled Pam back to the cabin and indicated that she should sit down.

'You evidently aren't impressed by boats, Stephanie,' he said, flashing her an aggrieved look.

She nodded in a conciliatory way. 'No one could fail to be impressed by a super boat like this,' she said.

'Feel free to wander through and investigate all my mod cons. All on a small scale, but everything's here, even to afternoon tea.' He smiled in his most beguiling way and before Stephanie could explain that they were on their way to Reading, Pam said, 'Just what I could do with.'

'I was going to brew up, anyway.' He came to the small galley where Stephanie was propped up against the door and from the draining-board he picked up a damp chamois leather. He tossed it to Stephanie. 'Be an angel and just finish off my windows while I make the tea.'

Stephanie felt an icy chill of indignation flood through her veins, but at least she could get outside and away from the claustrophobic cabin, though not before she met his wicked, taunting eyes with a withering stare.

As she polished the windows she kept one eye on her mother, whose voice she could hear explaining that she was returning to Windsor by bus. When she heard her mention her father and the accident, Stephanie purposely moved further on round until she was absorbed in polishing all the windows—or were they officially portholes? she wondered.

'Trying to prove you can do the job better than me?' Guy called from the doorway.

The gentle breeze from the water and the invigorating fresh air had tempered Stephanie's indifference and she returned to where Guy was standing with a smile.

'I didn't know how much you had done, so I've polished them all,' she said. 'I suppose you're getting ready to bring it in for the winter—or do you moor it on the river permanently?'

Guy looked down into her upturned face with an amused grin. 'Not just a pretty face after all! Quite knowledgeable, I see.' He took the chamois but deliberately tangled his long, slender fingers with hers as he pulled her inside. 'Actually, Stephanie, I was going to get her up this weekend, but if this weather continues I shall postpone it for a week or two.'

'Do you have to do a lot of work on it through the winter?' She wasn't really interested, but it seemed courteous to acknowledge his obvious first love.

He turned, and in a low voice over his shoulder said, 'Are you offering help?'

'No!' she answered with vehemence.

'Stephanie's never been one for the water. Maybe your dad should have had his boat after all.'

Stephanie found it difficult to meet her mother's self-satisfied look. What could she be making of all this? For some reason over this weekend Stephanie had found herself deliberately avoiding making any mention of the tyrant of Thames Vale hospital, but that didn't mean she hadn't thought about him, and now here was her mother, flattered beyond belief over his attention.

'No, my dear,' Guy said resting his hand on her shoulder, '*Thames Jewel* is only a year old so there won't be a lot to do. I shall have to assess her condition when I get her out.'

'A bit like doing surgery, Guy,' Pam said. 'You can't really know what you're going to find until you get to the root of the trouble.'

'Quite right, though in medicine today we have a considerable number of efficient aids to help our investigations. Now—how do you like your tea? Milk, sugar?' Stephanie sat on the opposite side of the cabin to her mother and Guy passed round sandwiches and cakes.

'I'm sure you weren't expecting to entertain,' Stephanie said in appreciation of all that he had prepared.

'I'm always prepared, Stephanie. Besides, I have to feed myself and I've spent the whole weekend cruising on the river. Your mother tells me that she's on her way back to Windsor, so you're both in for a river trip. Much more pleasant than sitting on a crowded bus.'

'But we shouldn't take up your time,' Stephanie began.

'No you shouldn't, not by arguing.'

Stephanie noticed the conspiratorial glances exchanged between Guy and her mother. He'd won her over all right, she thought with dismay, and if Guy had intended to silence her with his words he succeeded. Stephanie decided to opt out. Her mother had got them into this situation now she must take the consequences.

Pam Driscoll was obviously enjoying this un-expected treat and she was evidently impressed by Guy Atherstone. Stephanie studied her mother closely as Pam gave her full attention to the hand-some doctor. His slightly rugged features and snip-pets of grey hair probably made him appear older than he was. Thirty-six, if rumour could be relied upon, and her mother was forty-six. Lots of women did marry younger men. Stephanie turned away in disgust—but self-disgust at such thoughts. They'd only just met, she reproached herself, and it was good to see her mother enjoying herself. Who was she to cast a blight on the afternoon? And wasn't a trip down the river appealing?

Guy steered the *Thames Jewel* from the small but well-equipped wheel-house and insisted that Stephanie and Pam remained in the cabin, out of the wind. There were locks to pass through, quite an exciting experience, but on the whole it was a pleasant and uneventful journey.

As Guy negotiated the precarious job of mooring at Windsor it occurred to Stephanie that she might now have to return to Reading by bus. It would then be dark, so she would need to take a taxi home. As if reading her thoughts, Guy laughingly said to Pam, 'Do you trust me to see your daughter safely home?'

'If I can't trust her with you then I probably can't trust her with anyone, but she is quite able to take care of herself, you know.'

Guy inclined his head with a nod of agreement. 'I can believe that. How far away do you live, Pam?'

'About five minutes behind the shops. I'll be fine—and thanks for a delightful trip.'

'I'll walk up with you, Mum,' Stephanie interrupted their relaxed conversation.

'I know I'm not dressed suitably to escort young ladies through the town but, if you don't object, I'd like to come too.'

It was inevitable that Guy, being the nosey-parker he was, would want to see what kind of home Stephanie had come from, and while she showed him the garden and then over the house Pam made coffee and a light supper, evidently loving every minute of the occasion. Stephanie felt a terrible pang of heartache for her mother as she watched her fussing. Please don't, Mum, she pleaded silently. Think of Dad and how sad you'd make him. Don't be taken in by this idiot of a man who's ready to break every weak heart he can locate. It was almost rewarding to see her mother so bright and effervescent but tomorrow, or the next day, or whenever the big let-down came, she was going to suffer such misery.

CHAPTER NINE

'I DON'T like having to hurry you, darling,' Guy said suddenly to Stephanie, 'but it'll take us a while to get back and I may need your help on the locks if it's dark.'

The thought struck Stephanie that he'd been the fool to offer to take her mother back to Windsor. If he hadn't, she would have been home anyway by now and Stephanie would be relaxing on her own settee, watching the Sunday film. Serves him right if he gets stuck on a mud-bank or whatever, she thought savagely. That'll teach him to chat up older women! But if he got stuck somewhere Stephanie was going to be stuck too. She just prayed for a quick and easy trip back to Reading.

They said their goodbyes, Stephanie arguing mentally with herself as to whether she oughtn't to stay the night with her mother in an effort to play down her infatuation for Guy. Pam's eyes were alight with admiration for him, making her appear several years younger than forty-six, and Stephanie was consumed with guilt. She ought to have acted more responsibly, taken decisive action against going on board the *Thames Jewel*. But the damage was done and soon she was tripping along by Guy's side, trying to keep up with his long, purposeful strides.

'If you knew you were going to get caught out by darkness you shouldn't have insisted on bringing Mum home,' Stephanie ventured to suggest.

He glared down at her. 'Never waste your breath talking when you're hurrying.' Then with a rare warm smile he added, 'I can always pick you up and carry you.'

He grasped her hand and she felt ridiculous, just like a schoolgirl again, but she refused to be goaded into that kind of conversation and she renewed her efforts to keep up with him.

It was much cooler now and Stephanie put on her cagoule as she stood beside Guy in the wheel-house. The river looked quite romantic as lights flickered from houses on the banks and passing boats, everyone making their way to their home mooring before night fell.

Stephanie was impressed by Guy's expertise in making a U-turn on the river and heading back the way they had come, observing the navigation channels which he pointed out to her as they cut through the water. They passed through the last lock safely, much to Stephanie's relief, and were going at a fair speed when, without warning, Guy began to slow down. There were only distant lights now, the banks high and overgrown except for an occasional clearing, and to Stephanie's annoyance Guy did another U-turn, coming to rest by an old white-painted building.

'Painted white,' Guy explained, 'so that I know when I'm home. It's the old forge next to the mill. I'd have liked to buy both, but the mill really is too far gone—and I couldn't afford it.'

Stephanie was surprised. She knew such old buildings were all part of a decaying countryside but somehow she hadn't imagined that Guy Atherstone would have a feeling for such nostalgia.

He cast his rope to the mooring-post and pulled up by a wooden landing-stage, securing the *Thames Jewel* fast. Then, with both hands on Stephanie's shoulders, he gently pushed her backwards into the cabin.

'Now I have you all to myself at last,' he said in a different tone of voice from any he had used before. 'Let's establish first of all when you have to be in bed, or what time you're next on duty?'

Stephanie hesitated. He was a clever swine, making her think he was sweet on her mother in order to set a trap which she was well and truly caught in.

'I'm not abducting you, for heaven's sake,' Guy said laughing devilishly. 'But I don't want to keep you up if you have to be on duty early in the morning. I'm on holiday for a few days for the purpose of getting my lady-love out of the water, but I'm loath to do that too soon. As you've probably noticed, some trees are beginning to turn early and there's no better way of admiring the autumn countryside than from lazing down the peaceful river.'

'I'm on late shift tomorrow,' she said in a small, rather shaky voice.

'Shall we have supper on board? There's still a little activity on the river at this hour—after all it's still quite early, not yet ten o'clock. Then we can go inside.'

Stephanie's heart plummetted, but recovered speedily. She was sure he was just being genuinely friendly, as he had been on the night he had followed her home. She was quite confident that she could handle him, and maybe the opportunity would arise to discover more about Guy Atherstone, the man. The man who had a wife somewhere; the man who had a bevy of girlfriends, especially one called Andrea . . .

All Stephanie's doubts came flooding back with terrifying force and she joined Guy in the small galley saying hurriedly, 'Just a coffee would be fine. We had a huge lunch and I think it was supposed to be supper that Mum provided.'

'There's a lot more of me to fill,' Guy said grinning. 'Being on the river always makes me ravenous and I'm sure you'll be able to manage something. You can work it off on the ward tomorrow.'

Stephanie watched the coffee while Guy grilled steaks, and in spite of her previous doubts she found a hearty appetite. He was an agreeable companion and in the solitude of the riverside, with only the light flip-flop of the water outside when some other craft went by, Stephanie found it easy to talk about her parents.

'Your mother is a very courageous woman,' Guy said, 'and you've weathered the storm with a degree of spirit. I admire you both for keeping your independence. It can't have been easy. Pam is anxious to see you married and I know you're cynical about it, but it is only natural for her to be concerned about you living alone. You mustn't blame her for that.'

'But I don't,' Stephanie said, 'and I'm not really cynical about marriage. I just don't want to make any mistakes.'

Guy popped the cork of a bottle of sparkling wine and filled her glass.

'Here's to finding the perfect partner,' he said, and she raised her glass to that. It was ironical that such a man should be making the toast. He had evidently made a mistake, yet he had an irresistible charm which made it difficult for her to believe he was totally to blame for a failed marriage. There was Andrea too, and from all that Stephanie had witnessed, that affair didn't always run smoothly.

Tonight though—well, tonight he had chosen Stephanie to be his guest, and she was flattered, even though she had decided to warn her mother against him. He was a man who spread his influence far and wide.

Gradually Stephanie's doubts faded, though she learned nothing about Guy as he cleverly extracted all her background details. They laughed together over incidents and embarrassing moments in her training-days, her school-days, holidays with grandparents—but never a word about *his* private life.

After they had finished eating they washed up and then Stephanie went out onto the deck to gaze up at the moon. She stood at the railing feeling slightly light-headed but very carefree, and when the giant of a man came up behind her, drawing her back against himself, holding her hands in his across her waist, she made no protest.

'A beautiful harvest moon,' Guy whispered into her hair.

'The end of a perfect day,' she whispered back.

'Not the end, darling,' he crooned, 'this is just the beginning.'

She giggled helplessly as he nibbled her ear and Guy chuckled as she wriggled sensuously against him. His response was immediate. She felt his grip tighten on her wrists and his body ceased to be flexible. She had the feeling that he didn't really want to make love to her, that it was against his better judgment to release his passion in kisses in the fold of her neck, which rendered her powerless. She closed her eyes in sheer enthralment and with some aggression he swung her round, pulled her violently into his arms and kissed her lips hungrily. When he broke away Stephanie laughed nervously.

'That must *really* be the end of a perfect day,' she said.

'We'll lock up the boat,' he said in a low, uncertain voice. 'I invited myself in to see your house, now I'll show you mine.'

She couldn't argue with that. She wasn't too familiar with these strange feelings. Was it the wine going to her head? Or was it the gentle roll of the river lulling her into a state of abandonment?

He steadied her as she walked unsurely off the

Thames Jewel and along a gravel pathway up to the back of the old forge.

'Just wait here,' he said, 'I'll put some lights on.'

He left her for a moment, then a brilliant bulb illuminated an outside staircase. More fluorescent tubes lit up the huge space beneath the house, evidently used as a workshop by the look of the accumulation of things stored there.

'We'll go in the back way,' he said and urged her forward up the solid oak staircase.

He unlocked a glass-panelled door, which led into a spacious kitchen, but didn't give her time to take in all the modern equipment in the American-styled room before he showed her into a medium-sized, open-plan living area.

A rough, red-brick fireplace was the centre-piece of one wall. It had a carved over-mantel on which stood a pair of silver candlesticks. Several cosy winged armchairs covered in floral tapestry to match the curtains at the latticed windows gave a homely, country-cottage look and the deep-piled, plain oatmeal carpet added warm luxury.

Flames quickly ignited the logs in the grate. 'It's a bit late to light a fire,' she said.

'But we've got all night, so we may as well be comfortable.'

'I ought to be—'She got no further as he held her gently, his large hands spanning her waist. He stooped to kiss her then with a devilish twinkle. 'I hope you aren't going to give me any trouble. How do you suppose you're going to get home?'

She knew he was teasing her. 'I assumed you

would drop me off where you picked us up,' she said.

'And let you walk home by the river in the dark? Darling, I'm not that insensitive.' Then, squeezing her roughly he joked, 'I can always toss you in the river and let you swim home—if you're going to be a nuisance.'

'But, you . . . I am intruding,' she protested lamely.

He kissed her sweetly on her lips. 'And what a delectable intruder. Stephanie,' he added seriously, 'I'm not a worthy companion, having been messing about on the boat all day. Would you excuse me if I take a quick shower and get out of this track suit? I can't have made a good impression on Pam.' He went to the fire and poked about with long brass poker and fire-tongs. It all seemed so welcoming. Soft melodies came from a music centre and on dark built-in units near the television stood all his video equipment.

'I'll only be ten minutes. Have a wander, explore my domain, help yourself to a drink of any sort,' and he went across the hall. She heard him whistling. What the hell was he up to? She knew about his reputation and she'd walked right into his net—and there was no way out. It wasn't safe to walk the streets alone, especially in an area she wasn't familiar with.

She idly took a magazine from a nest of tables but she didn't see what was on the centre pages. Instead she absorbed her surroundings, trying to find something hideous, something she could dislike about

Guy Atherstone's home. But like the man who had created this aura of homeliness, it drew her into its familiarity.

In an alcove at one side of the fireplace were several built-in shelves and on one of them a bust of a woman. It had a lifelike quality that demanded her attention and was, Stephanie felt sure, taken from a real live model.

She felt a slight shiver run through her so she got up and went to the fire, rubbing her hands lightly over the flames, inhaling the scent of pinewood crackling in the iron-grilled grate. Guy came up behind her, a pleasant smell of cologne or after-shave pervading her senses.

She half turned. 'It's . . . it's lovely,' she said, pointing to the bust. 'A real piece of art, and beautifully sculpted.'

'Thank you.'

Stephanie looked up into his eyes quizzically, but she didn't need to ask the question, she knew by the tender blue pleasure she saw there that he had created this figure. There was a subdued pause while he seemed lost in some world of his own.

'Doctor, sculptor, what else?' she asked.

His sensuous lips parted with an almost coy smile of self-satisfaction, then he transferred his gaze to her.

'A very poor host,' he said. 'Forgive me, Stephanie, but at least I feel more human now. Are you interested in art? Would you like to see more of my work?'

'Of course,' she felt urged to reply, and Guy led

the way through from the ultra-modern dining area leading off from the kitchen, up a flight of open wooden stairs to an attic room above, which spanned the whole building. Not all of it was accessible for Guy on account of his height, but there were benches and stools, an easel with a partly finished painting on it and numerous cupboards beneath the dormer windows.

A big yellow moon clamoured for attention through the roof windows, which were there to allow the daylight in and afford Guy the best conditions for his work, and Stephanie was fascinated by all that she saw.

'You're terribly clever,' she said, glancing up at him with a mixture of envy and admiration. It hadn't passed her notice that many of his paintings were of women.

He shook his head. 'No, darling, there's cold calculation in sculpting, even though you may mould with a measure of affection. It'll never love you back—and that's what I want from a woman.'

It happened so easily. Stephanie slipped into the snugness of his protective arms. All her defences faded into nothing as he tilted her chin with one finger and with his other hand etched the outline of her face as if to remember each and every detail.

His eyebrows were smooth, his forehead unlined, blue eyes smiling as he held his loving kiss in check while he discerned her eagerness for that kiss. By the time his mouth reached hers the blood was racing through her veins, and she could feel the pound of his heart against her breast. The kiss was

deliciously sweet as he crushed her small body
against him. His caresses were manipulative,
arousing a fierce desire in her, and her body seemed
to melt into the contours of his.

'This is ridiculous,' he murmured, and edged his
way to the door, snapping off the lights. With a
significant glance up at the moon he prised her lips
apart with his tongue compelling her to respond
with heat-ridden passion.

She felt giddy with happiness as they went down
the stairs and, by the light from the flames leaping
from new logs, Guy began to unbutton her waistcoat. She wanted to assist him but it seemed important to be provocative, to cast a spell, to maintain
this unexpected togetherness. Gently, he removed
the waistcoat, eased up her jumper and explored
the softness of her breasts. She fondled his broad
neck, rousing him more by tantalising the nerves
behind his ears.

Her body glowed, his fingertips exciting her until
with frustration he growled, 'You've got too many
damned clothes on! You're staying, aren't you?'

Suddenly she went cold. 'No, it's late, Guy, I
should never have come. I must go home.' He'd
taken it all so much for granted, just like Graham.

'Why?' His voice was edged with anger.

'Well—Mum might ring. And I don't stay out all
night,' she excused herself, feebly.

'I should have kept you on the boat,' he said.
'I've got no intention of getting my car out at this
hour, or waking your neighbours up.'

'But they'll wonder where I am.'

Guy laughed cynically. 'Your car must be in the drive, they'll think you're there—and you will be, in time for duty.' He swept her up in his arms and carried her to the most luxurious bedroom she had ever seen. He placed her on the bed gently. Subdued lighting and colourings blended with white wardrobes and cupboards, deep fluffy carpet with deeper wool rugs, and while she took it all in Guy bent to kiss her lightly.

'Sweet dreams, sweet Stephanie,' he whispered and she watched him go to the wardrobe and take out a velour robe in red and black. He turned and saw her covetting every inch of him and his smile was intimate, but he moved towards the door, running his tongue around his lips before switching off the light. Then she heard the door close softly and he was gone.

Stephanie lay on her back listening. Was he going to return? She had never wanted anything as much as she wanted him now, but she guessed he had changed his mind. She had seen it in his face. When the house seemed still and Guy's influence less apparent, Stephanie rolled off the bed and undressed, then she slipped beneath the duvet.

After several minutes she passed her hand lightly over her forehead. 'You're Stephanie Driscoll,' she told herself, 'and you don't sleep in other people's beds.' But she didn't have much alternative. She really was too deliciously sleepy and comfortable to make an aggressive stand tonight.

Against what, she wondered? He was being the perfect gentleman—well, almost. She snuggled into a little ball, relishing the feel of her naked flesh primed by his tender caresses. She ought to be hating him. Did he treat all his women this way? Or had he cried off at the last minute because he had met and liked her mother? Or was she just a small, insignificant piece of womanhood, too delicate to be—oh, God, how desperately she wanted him!

Drowsiness enveloped her and she lost consciousness, disappointed that Guy had not returned to his bed. She was not physically fulfilled but she was mentally satisfied that at last she recognised the deeper meaning of love. It left her with a gnawing ache in the pit of her stomach but also an upsurge of hope for the future.

She had stretched in a feline sort of way, realising that it was morning, while her mind untangled confusing thoughts, when the door opened and she was aware of long, straight, bare legs and feet approaching her bedside.

Stephanie closed her eyes. She wasn't sure that she could trust herself. Had her deeper emotions levelled out to more normal proportions today? Was it just a flight of fancy that a few hours ago beneath a harvest moon she had willingly fallen into Guy Atherstone's arms? Was it love or just infatuation? The response to his charm?

'Good morning, Stephanie,' he said gently, and the very sexiness in his tone made her tingle all over. She was in love! She did love this great hulk of a man, and she was really mad with herself for doing so.

She rolled on to her back and displayed a neat bare arm.

'Good morning,' she answered. 'What am I doing here, I ask myself?'

'Tempting me, seducing me, behaving most promiscuously,' he said as he came to stand by the bed. He picked up her hand and sat heavily next to her, caressing her wrist with his thumb and then using both hands to fondle her arm, hand and fingers until she was laughing as she struggled to get free. He tousled her hair and, pushing her well down in the bed, leaned over to kiss her awake.

'Fortunately,' he said, 'you have no cause for regrets. I slept in the spare room.' With expert fingers he felt her body. 'You're not cold, I hope?'

She fluttered her eyelashes shamelessly at him thinking, I'd have rather you'd kept me warm! Such erring thoughts brought a bright flush to her cheeks.

'I'm sorry I turned you out of your bed,' she said.

Guy paused, his expression changed, and he smiled intimately at Stephanie. She looked up expectantly from lazy, trembling lids fringed with golden-brown lashes and noticed without embarrassment that his robe had fallen loose, the belt trailing. Surely he had come to her for one reason only, yet at this moment he was in full control. She wished they could reverse roles so that she could explore all the intrigue of his masculinity. He lingered a moment as if he were conjuring up some wicked prank, then went to the door.

'I'll dress, then get the breakfast. Make sure

you're up and dressed in twenty minutes or I won't be responsible for my actions.'

Was he ever? Stephanie didn't say as much, but doubted it. Of course he could remain in control—he was a past master at entertaining women. And there was that wife as well as Andrea. He'd lost Meg to Jason it seemed, so that was probably the reason he was trying her out. What a stupid fool she was to be taken in by him. Later, as the warm water of a luxurious bath soothed and extinguished the fire in her, she almost hated herself for such self-indulgence.

She looked at the clock as she entered the kitchen and dining area and saw that it was a little after ten. Thank goodness there were still nearly two hours in which to revive herself—and coffee would help. But coffee, she was informed, was bad for her, so she was detailed to pour out the tea while Guy dished up scrambled eggs on toast.

The dining-room chairs were made of chrome with cane seats, the table-top smoked glass on chrome legs, and now in the daylight she observed that although the old forge was furnished comfortably, there was a distinctive maleness about it.

She felt cheated. Her mind raced on, visualising this same cosy scene enacted countless times before with a variety of women. Mostly more sophisticated than her, women with whom he would be totally satisfied. He had just played with her, making a fool of her.

Suddenly he leaned across and placed his hand over hers. 'I'd like to sculpt you.'

Stephanie pulled her hand away sharply. 'Is that how you get cheap thrills?'

'Stephanie!' There was real pain in his voice but she didn't pay heed to it.

'Is that what you've gained a reputation for?' she went on heatedly. 'Women by the score? You lure them here, make advances to give you ideas for your—your hobby!'

To her surprise he calmly went on eating, although she suspected he was burning with contempt. His complacency riled her.

'No wonder your wife went off and left you,' she continued. 'I suppose she was only necessary for a bed companion, and posing?'

'I had better get you home before you accuse me of rape! Grow up, Stephanie. You don't have to have a guilt complex because you were actually leading me on!' With an angry sigh he pushed away his plate and stormed out of the room . . .

CHAPTER TEN

AFTER that she couldn't look at him. To her chagrin he was right about her guilt complex; her only excuse being that she did genuinely love him—so much that it hurt. Otherwise she would never have been party to this, this dumb-show. The more she thought about it the harder it was to bear, but she knew she must hide her wounds. As far as she was aware, Guy Atherstone loved no one but himself . . .

They moved about his home in starched obstinacy and Stephanie was glad when they finally started off for her house. But now in the stony silence she could see signs of his anger. His knuckles were taut as he gripped the steering wheel fiercely, and several times he had to brake hard to avoid a collision. She clung to the side of her seat, thankful that she was strapped in, but wondering what the outcome would be if, *when* they finally hit some other vehicle!

Tears began to materialise. If only she could get out! She closed her eyes in the end and tried not to think of her father. Was she going to be scarred for the rest of her life by these memories? Life! Did she have much left?

The squeal of skidding tyres forced her to open her eyes only to find they were outside her house.

She released her belt quickly and hurried up to the front door without a word. Tears of anguish rolled unhindered down her cheeks. She almost fell inside, with Guy immediately behind her. Why didn't he just go away? She never wanted to see him again—oh, but she did, she did!

'Stephanie—I'm terribly sorry. That was unfeeling of me.'

'Kill yourself if you must,' she managed to yell, 'but next time let me walk!' There was a significant silence while she sniffed and found a tissue.

'I . . . I'm sorry,' she mumbled, 'I shouldn't have said all those dreadful things to you, especially as you were kind enough to take Mum home.'

'I'm sorry, Stephanie, that you have such poor regard for me. Maybe it's time I stopped trying to hide the truth. Evidently when people don't know the facts, they invent fiction—thankfully it's my reputation which is in question, not yours. Hurry up and make yourself presentable, and I'll run you to the hospital.'

But Stephanie waved this suggestion aside and seconds later Guy Atherstone left. She watched him go from behind the kitchen blind. She thought his shoulders drooped with dejection, but then she turned away doubting very much that anything she said would affect him.

In her quiet, lonely moments, Stephanie couldn't visualise future meetings with Guy. They were bound to have to speak to discuss patients and she knew it was going to be a ghastly experience, but Guy remained off duty for the first half of the week and Pete Burnley, his registrar, took over his theatre list and dealt with all the problems.

Stephanie looked in at the rehearsal for the pantomime before she went home on Monday evening and watched the dance routines, which were looking quite professional. She didn't stay long as she felt miserable and weary. A good night's rest was what she needed to help her cope with a busy theatre schedule the following day. No matter how much sleep she had, her heartache would remain. She longed to see Guy again, if only to observe him from a distance, but she knew that just the merest glimpse would intensify her love for him. She could never forgive herself for the unwarranted attack she had made on him and she realised that he wasn't the forgiving kind.

She was on late shift again next day in order to see the surgical cases through until the night staff arrived. Everything had gone smoothly and while she was writing up her report she heard dainty footsteps hurrying along the corridor. She glanced at her watch. It was too early for the night staff so it must be Matron, Stephanie concluded. She glanced up expectantly, but it was Andrea de Souza who flew breathlessly into her office.

'Andrea!' Stephanie greeted her, noticing at once the older girl's cheerful expression, her expensive outfit and chic hair-do.

'Hullo, darling,' Andrea gushed. 'Can't stop, got a fabulous date with a fabulous guy—oh, Guy!— How funny—get it? He asked me to return this; you left it at the forge. See you soon at rehearsal. It's all coming together beautifully but we need you now to understudy for Meg. Better be prepared, hadn't we?' She put Stephanie's kagoul down on the nearest chair and swept away, leaving behind her a cold draught lingering with a sweet fragrance of perfume.

Stephanie stared into space, then at her cagoule, feeling as if someone had punched her on the chin. Two days ago she had slept in Guy's bed. Had Andrea just come from there? And was she just returning to him? She felt sick, not with envy or jealousy, but with self-reproach. Even if she did feel that Andrea was not suitable for Guy, that was no excuse for her responding to his love-making so readily. She had cheated Andrea, and it only added to her feeling of desolation.

Andrea wasn't at the next rehearsal but Graham was and he seemed only mildly pleased to see her.

'We're going through most of it except the solo spots which Andrea is coaching, so if you've come ready to sing your heart out—'

'I can't do it, Graham,' she said flatly. 'I don't want to do it.'

'Well, you're a fine one!' He looked as if he might explode. 'You suit the part and you've learnt the songs! We'll never find anyone else to do it at this late hour.' He peered into her face. 'What's up? Cold feet? Not well? You can't let us down *now*, Stevie, you can't!'

'I'm sorry, Graham, but the whole thing—I mean, well, I don't have as much time as I used to.'

'Oh? Why's that?' he asked sharply.

'The ward, it's not the same as men's medical.'

'It wouldn't be, it's women's surgical—and that's not the reason. Andrea tells me you've been entertained by Guy Atherstone. I warned you about him. Don't come running to me if you've bitten off more than you can chew.'

'It's got nothing to do with him—or you. As a matter of fact, Guy offered to take Mum home on his boat.'

'Oh yes?' Graham's face wore a thunderous expression. 'So where did he take you afterwards? At midnight when I got in, your Mum telephoned me because you hadn't answered the phone and she wondered where you were.'

'Having a harmless supper on his boat before he brought me home.' It sounded innocent enough and it was what she planned to tell her mother when she phoned. Her pink cheeks gave her away, though.

'You've got plenty of helpers with this show,' she gabbled on, hating the deceit and the guilt. 'You don't need me at all, but if you can't find another understudy for Meg I'll do one rehearsal. But Meg shouldn't let you down.'

'I just hope she doesn't. I never would have believed this of you, Stevie. I'm disappointed in you.'

'Oh, big deal,' Stephanie said sarcastically and went on her way.

She tried not to think of what all the cast might think. She couldn't continue working with Andrea, who seemed not the slightest bit perturbed at having to return the cagoule, but must be hating her all the same.

Fancy Guy giving it to Andrea! Didn't the man have any discretion? She continued to torture herself with images of Andrea draping herself in her self-centred way around the forge. Now she suddenly remembered those sculptures and paintings—they must be Andrea, even though she hadn't recognised Andrea in them at the time. How could she have been so blind? Stupid fool, blinded by passion, she rebuked herself. She didn't know what had come over her these past few days—she was going out of her mind. But although she tried hard to pull herself together, nothing could change her melancholy because she felt keenly her inability to please Guy.

Stephanie was on early shift the following day and she was just getting into her car when she went off duty at four-thirty when Andrea drove up and blocked her path. She got out of the car and came to Stephanie's window.

'Just caught you,' she said. 'Hope you're not in a hurry, I want to talk to you.'

Stephanie pursed her lips but knew that excuses would be futile—she might as well take courage in both hands and get it over with.

'I'm sorry, Andrea, really I am—' she began.

'Oh, come on, let's go and have a cup of tea somewhere. There's that nice little tea-shop just along the road, with plenty of parking space at the back. Follow me.'

She didn't sound too outraged, Stephanie decided, and talking in a public place might be easier, so she started up her engine and followed Andrea away from the hospital to a shopping suburb where the tea-shop was situated. They parked the cars side by side and Andrea placed her hand on Stephanie's shoulder as they went up the back stairs to the warm, friendly restaurant.

'Darling, you look awfully pale! I'm so sorry about you giving up the show. Is it because you're ill?'

Stephanie couldn't meet the other girl's eyes, which were brimming with sympathy. She kept her gaze directed towards the dainty embroidered table-cloth, a rare luxury in restaurants these days, she thought. Now it was going to be harder than ever because she realised Andrea was here to talk about the show.

'Andrea,' she said, 'can we forget about the show? I have a confession to make, and you're going to be very displeased with me.'

Andrea inclined her head with curiosity. 'Forget the show! You mean you really are opting out?'

Stephanie shook her head. This was getting her nowhere, she'd just have to be blunt.

'I mean I don't want to talk about the show now. I want to talk about us—well, you and Guy. Nothing happened at the forge, honestly. He hasn't been unfaithful to you—well not with me, anyhow.'

Andrea stared, adding to Stephanie's discomfort, but she went into a lengthy explanation about how her mother had visited and on the way to Reading . . .

'Oh, that! Guy told me all about that and said you stayed overnight at the forge. Super place he's got there, isn't it? He said enough to make me realise that you couldn't really love Graham as I'd been led to believe when I was a patient, which is why I wanted to talk to you—because he and I,' she shrugged, 'get on very well together, Stevie. I can call you that can't I? Graham always does. He's still very fond of you, but you aren't of him or you wouldn't have—well, shall we say been willing to spend the night with Guy?'

Stephanie blinked. Her head was beginning to ache. Suddenly the tangle of worries opened up and, looking across at Andrea, she laughed. Andrea laughed in response.

'Let's get this straight,' Andrea deliberated. '*I* want Graham, *you* want Guy.'

'No!' Oh, what was the use of hiding it from her now? Stephanie let out a long, deep sigh. 'I'm crazy about him,' she said, 'but what's the use? He's got a wife, and I must confess I thought that you and he—'

Andrea looked crestfallen for the first time. 'Ooh—dear,' she muttered. 'What an idiot that man is.'

'Why?' Stephanie asked, rushing to his defence.

The tea arrived with the Welsh rarebit which they had ordered, and Andrea looked long and hard at it while Stephanie poured.

'I never thought that he'd manage to do it,' Andrea said. 'In a hospital the size of Thames Vale, it's incredible! He'll kill me for telling you, but I'm going to.' She took a deep breath and looked directly at Stephanie with a mixture of pain and relief. 'Claudine, my sister, was Guy's wife. He's my brother-in-law, nothing more.'

'Claudine?' Stephanie echoed, 'but she's—'

'Dead.' Andrea had gone white and she began to put small pieces of toast into her mouth. She must have been a very devoted sister, Stephanie thought as she watched memories etch the shadows of pain across her face.

'I didn't know,' Stephanie murmured, the shock of this revelation causing her pain too. 'Am I just a blind fool or didn't anyone know?'

'No one is supposed to know, but I sensed that you and Guy were beginning to be aware of each other as people rather than doctor and nurse. If he seems short-tempered it's because he won't allow himself to feel sexually attracted to a woman again.'

'I don't understand why he would want people to think that he was separated from his wife if in fact he's a widower.'

'Poor darling,' Andrea said with feeling. 'Even though Claudine was my sister she was a bitch. They met and married years ago at university. The first couple of years were fine, but then Claudine's interest in music and singing increased and really came between them when Guy was houseman, then a registrar. He had so little spare time. Claudine, as I told you, became a star in her own right, so I managed her. I'm not that mature—I'm three years younger than her. But by being there I hoped I could prevent her from making a fool of herself.' She shrugged in despair. 'She just got caught up totally in the showbiz world, wanted a divorce which Guy wouldn't agree to and then, just like the sword of judgment, she was stricken down with this dreadful disease. Where could we go? Our parents had split up and gone their separate ways years ago, so Claudine came home to Guy.'

'And they were reconciled?' Stephanie asked. 'I remember seeing him with a woman at a Christmas service when I first came here.'

Andrea laughed with scorn. 'Not reconciled as husband and wife. Guy isn't that forgiving and no one can blame him for that. He was embittered. After all, Claudine probably wouldn't have come home to him if he hadn't been a doctor. She was convinced he could cure her.'

'Poor Guy,' Stephanie mused sympathetically.

'My flat, the one I live in now,' Andrea went on as if it was a relief to talk, 'was their home really, but Guy moved out to the forge. He'd bought it as a place to be alone and no woman except me ever stayed there to my knowledge—or hadn't done until you did. No, Stephanie, there was never anything between Guy and me, but not for want of trying. I'm sure I always loved him more than Claudine ever did, only now I know that it was more as my protector. He is a super man, he did so much for Claudine, moved heaven and earth for her to see the best people and she had every imaginable treatment, but I just watched her fading away.'

'I'm afraid some diseases are terminal and we have to face that, Andrea.'

'I did blame Guy sometimes. I accused him of being hard and not a husband to Claudine when that might have given her the will to live, but he knew her so well. Oh, Stephanie, he must never know I've told you, he'd be so angry! You won't let on, will you—please?' Andrea was almost weeping with entreaty.

'Of course I won't tell a soul, Andrea. I'm glad you have told me, though I'm sorry I can't go to him and beg forgiveness for the nasty things I said to him. I really thought he was a ladies' man, luring women to the forge, getting them to sit for his paintings. I love him desperately. In my subconscious I've tried to hate him, having learnt of his reputation. How can he live with that, Andrea? What an impossible situation!'

'I know. I've begged him to let me drop a hint or two but he's a proud man. He didn't want sympathy for Claudine's death when she really meant nothing to him. He blamed himself for their marriage. He insists he persuaded her into it when they were both too young and should have allowed their careers to mature first. His love for her had long since died and he refused to live a lie just because she was dying, but that doesn't mean he was cruel. Don't get the wrong idea about him, Stephanie. He did everything to help her, everything to keep her going. And he tried anything to make her happy—except live with her, and even she couldn't change his mind about that.'

Stephanie gazed across at Andrea with pity.
'You've had to live with all this? For how long?' she
asked gently.

Andrea fluttered her long, curling eyelashes
which now glistened with moisture.

'I couldn't even tell Mr Perry or the psychiatrist,
I just had to bottle it all up, knowing that Guy was
taking the rap for Claudine. Gosh!' She sighed and
let out a rush of air. 'I can't tell you how much
easier I feel now that I've talked. And it is all true,
Stevie, honestly.'

'Guy should never have expected you to hide it
all. He's a doctor, he should have known better,
but then his suffering made him blind to his own
needs. Here we are, all candidates for love, and
I've no way of expressing my love for him or trying
to win his.' Stephanie felt hopeless.

'One reason for allowing this rumour of his
broken marriage to continue, and for letting people
think I was one of his many girlfriends, was to
prevent other women chasing him.' Andrea
laughed. 'Of course, he's only human, so when his
defences are down he just has to treat an attractive
woman as he really wants to. I know there were
times when the theatre sister, Meg Welford, could
have won him over—but I don't suppose he did
really love her. I've always been convinced that the
right woman would come along and change everything. I wish I could give you some hope, Stevie,
but I know how stubborn Guy is. You're young and
he probably imagines you'd behave like Claudine
did. I suspect he also thinks, as I did, that you and

Graham will eventually get back together.'

Stephanie managed a nervous laugh. 'I thought so too, once. But when he started to get over-possessive I knew it wasn't right.'

'But he is still very fond of you, Stevie. If it weren't for you I'm pretty sure I could get him easily. Guess there's a lot of Claudine in me. I know what I want, but I like you too much to take Graham if you want him.' Andrea watched her reaction carefully.

'Things that are right have a way of coming together in the end, Andrea. I'm fond of Graham in that he helped me over a difficult patch after my dad was killed. I came here knowing no one, trying to adjust to a new job, coming to terms with grief as well as feeling I had a duty to care for my mother. It's taken ages to get it all in perspective.'

'And now you've found a man you could really love, if he let you?'

'Isn't that just one of the complexities of life? I'll just have to be extra nice to him, though I realise I threw away every chance when I behaved so utterly selfishly. Somehow I always felt he couldn't be as black as everyone painted him—yet you see, for all that, everyone really adores him,' Stephanie said quietly.

'Because he can't successfully hide the real him, I suppose.' Andrea leaned across the table. 'You've been such a friend to me, Stevie, giving me the chance to help with the show, even though Guy doesn't seem to approve. And I know now I can start a new life away from Guy.'

'Away from Guy?' Stephanie tried to hide her surprise and curiosity.

'Yes, with Graham's help. I want to release Guy from any responsibility he may feel he has towards me for Claudine's sake. He must be free to live his own life, and so must I. Oh, it'll be nice to know that he's around if I need him, but one day I mean to leave his flat and cut loose from the ties that inevitably sprang up when I was nursing Claudine. Graham tells me that physically I'm fine, so now it's up to me. I told Graham all this, by the way. I had to, or I wouldn't have got anywhere with him because everyone thought I was Guy's girlfriend. Silly, wasn't I? I did actually believe that if only Guy would marry me I could make up to him for Claudine's mistakes. I'm glad he put me down ruthlessly. I only wish I could persuade him to tell people the truth, then he could start afresh too.'

'Well, I won't betray your confidence, and I'm sure Graham won't. Good luck to you both.' Stephanie stood up. 'Now I must go.'

'Please, Stevie, not before you've promised to carry on with the show? It'll fill in those spare moments when you have nothing else to do but brood.'

'I thought I was supposed to be the nurse!' Stephanie laughed.

'A very special one you are too, but none of us sees our emotions objectively. I wish I could offer to talk to Guy, but he's no fool and if I tried he'd accuse me of trying to run his life. He hoped I wouldn't fit in with the hospital staff. I must be an awful menace to him because I can be stubborn too, and I expect he suspects I'll talk too much. This is a hospital show and I'm an outsider so you must carry on, Stevie, for my sake—or I'll be accused of pushing you out.'

'Mm—all right then. I suppose I do really want to do it, as long as you stick with us to the end.'

'Try kicking me out—my reward will be winning Graham!'

'That shouldn't be too difficult,' Stephanie said as she led the way back to the car park. 'I'll leave you to tell him I'll be at the next rehearsal.'

She was glad to get home. There she could be alone to think on all that Andrea had said. The fact that Guy was a free man and completely the opposite of what everyone had thought didn't help her quell feelings for him—they just became stronger. In consequence the pain tore her apart.

Later in the evening her mother telephoned and Stephanie was tempted to pour out all her despondencies to her, but Pam sounded excited and probed more intrusively about how she had spent the time with Guy.

'We had supper on the boat to round off the evening,' Stephanie said evasively, 'but I was glad to get home to bed. I slept late and then had to go on duty. Now all my spare time is taken up with the show. We're putting it on in less than a month.' She prayed forgiveness for the lie. She'd never kept things from her mother, or been deceitful, but this new desperate longing for a man who didn't love her was making her behave irrationally.

She promised to get her mother a ticket for the show and invited her to stay over for the Saturday night and Sunday when it was to be performed. Secretly Stephanie longed for it to be all over, but the panto was improving all the time and she dutifully understudied for Meg at the following day's rehearsal. On her way to the rehearsal room she almost bumped into Guy, and to make matters more embarrassing he was in earnest conversation with Graham of all people. Perhaps they were discussing Andrea, she thought. Would Guy approve of Andrea and Graham's relationship? What did it matter now that she knew the truth?

Their first meeting was when Guy did his next round. He came with his usual retinue of registrar, houseman and students, which made it easier to bear. She'd harboured a secret hope that he would come to the ward alone one day and somehow she'd find a way of being extra sweet to him. This, she knew, would be foolish and wrong. He wanted to keep his life very private and no way could she betray Andrea's trust.

He was a stubborn, blind idiot, she thought, after he had hurriedly and rather pointedly left the ward. Once everyone knew the truth it would all quickly be forgotten——but then all his admirers in the hospital would start paying homage. She could see his reasoning behind such a decision, but she still felt he had made a ghastly mistake by not revealing to the world the fact that he was a widower. He didn't want pity and sympathy but he was a strong enough character to make that obvious and dissuade any-one who attempted to chase after him.

Each time he visited his patients Stephanie found it became more difficult rather than easier to be with him. She tried to behave normally but some-how her voice always seemed to desert her. She tried to meet his gaze but one glimpse of his pen-etrating, condemning eyes and she was reduced to jelly.

Just before the final dress rehearsal when all the members of staff taking part were beginning to show signs of nerves, Stephanie had to send for Guy and Pete to attend a patient who had col-lapsed. Stephanie drew the screens round Mrs Wiltshire's bed, isolating her from the rest of the occupants in that bay, and she watched Guy's expert ability to deal calmly in such an incident. She saw him as a professional surgeon, rather than Guy Atherstone, the man she loved.

One of the junior nurses popped her head round the screen.

'You're wanted on the telephone, Sister. It's urgent.'

Stephanie looked up. 'Who is it? Ask them to leave a message or ring back in fifteen minutes.'

A few moments later the nurse returned. 'It was Graham Porter, Sister. Will you please ring him as soon as you can?'

Stephanie nodded her acknowledgement, wishing that Graham had chosen some other time to demand her attention. When the patient was resting more comfortably Guy escorted Stephanie back to her office, and while he was preparing to leave the telephone rang.

'Sister Driscoll speaking,' Stephanie said quietly.

'Stevie, Graham here. We need you at once, Meg's gone down with flu and we must do a dress rehearsal.'

'I'm on duty, Graham. I can't come now. I can't leave the ward at present.' Graham pleaded, then argued, obviously unaware that this was quite the wrong moment to expect her to put the show first.

'I can't be bothered with the show at the moment,' she barked impatiently, and slammed the receiver down on its rest. She made to stand up but a hand came down heavily on her shoulder.

'It's all right,' Guy said gently, 'Pete and Liz can cope, Stephanie. Mrs Wiltshire will be fine now.'

Stephanie looked up at him helplessly, and fell in love with him all over again at the soft tenderness in his eyes.

'The show must go on,' he said with a smile and hurried away.

CHAPTER ELEVEN

ALTERATIONS had to be made to Meg's costume so that Stephanie could wear it. She grumbled a great deal and her solo spots had to be rehearsed several times, for the heartache which had consumed her made the singing of love songs seem impossible.

'Oh for heaven's sake, Stevie,' Graham yelled at her, 'you're not going to have hysterics, are you?'

'Her own remedy for that is a smack across the face,' Andrea said smugly, 'only I haven't got the heart.'

Eventually, very late that night Stephanie calmed down enough to get through a final dress rehearsal. What was fate doing to her? How could she go on stage and face an audience of two hundred people? The mayor, councillors, local GP's and their families, all the consultants and their families—oh it just wasn't fair! But she couldn't let her colleagues down, especially as she knew that the performance of everyone apart from herself was splendid, thanks to the coaching by Andrea and Graham, among others.

There was great excitement next day. Patients were equally as enthusiastic as the staff about the pantomime and all those taking part went off duty at four o'clock for a rest and last minute preparations. Stephanie drove into Reading to pick her mother up and she was glad of Pam's calming influence.

At last the curtain rose. No longer was she Stephanie Driscoll, sister of women's surgical ward, but Little Red Riding Hood about to be devoured by the wolf—only this story had to have a happy ending, so the wolf transformed himself into a handsome young man who wanted to marry her.

The whole show was well received and there was applause and laughter for the send-ups as well as warm appreciation of the singing and dancing. But Stephanie's heart ached more than ever, knowing that the words of love she had sung to Jason were meant for Guy. Was he there? Did he know? Could he tell that she was pouring out so much of her own emotion in the love-song?

Thankfully she hadn't had any inclination to search for familiar faces among the audience. She was too nervous. From behind the foot-lights it was like looking at a big screen of bobbing, dark heads. Of course he wouldn't be there. He didn't approve of hospital theatricals and even less of Andrea being involved.

Stephanie felt too emotionally drained to stay for the party afterwards. The damp December air chilled her as she slipped out of a side-door to the car park. She ran to her car where she sat inside and rested her head on her hands on the steering-wheel. Rain started to beat noisily against the windscreen and with it Stephanie's tears began to flow.

She thought longingly of Guy's lovely home by

the river and the blazing log fire. Poor darling, she thought, he'd been through so much and borne the pain of it all alone. If only there was some way of making it up to him. But Andrea had suggested that he considered Stephanie too young and likely to behave as Claudine had done. If he got to hear about her being the leading lady in the pantomime he would have every right to think that.

She heard a door bang, then footsteps running. She'd have to go back to find her mother eventually. A draught of cold air as the passenger door opened made her look up, startled. Graham's bulky frame rocked the car as he got in beside her.

'What are you doing out here for goodness's sake? Everyone's been asking for you,' he said. Then with rough fingers he pulled her face round so that he could examine her tear-stained cheeks. 'Oh, Stevie, you've fallen at last. Hook, line and sinker for a man—' Graham stopped short. 'It's no good, I can only think badly of him because he's managed to succeed where I failed.'

Stephanie sniffed into her hanky, pulling her face out of Graham's grasp.

'I . . . I can't help how I feel about him,' she stammered. 'It's useless, of course.'

'He's a free man,' Graham said cryptically.

'He'll never be free from his memories,' Stephanie said. 'It's understandable if he's wary of women. He's too proud to run the risk of being hurt a second time.'

'Then isn't it up to you to prove that you wouldn't hurt him?'

'If I ever got the chance,' she said miserably.

'That's up to you, too,' Graham said positively.

'How? If he won't allow himself to let his feelings run free there's nothing I can do.'

'Just keep on being your sweet, lovely self, my dear, and he won't be able to ignore you,' Graham advised.

'I don't feel sweet or lovely,' Stephanie snapped, 'and I hope Meg's better for the next performance at the weekend.'

'She'll do the show on the wards, she says, if you'll do the other official performance.'

'But that's not fair, Graham! I only agreed to understudy in case of emergency, and Meg's far prettier than me. Besides, she's done all the hard work rehearsing.'

'And haven't you more or less rehearsed everyone's part? You have to know it all inside out and back to front to be a good director or producer. Tonight's performance was the best we've ever done, Stevie,' Graham enthused. 'You were superb—honestly! Meg realised that you were better on stage than her and you're also—well, tiny and sweet—just like Red Riding Hood was meant to be.'

Stephanie turned on him aggressively. 'Are you telling me . . . You aren't telling me that she deliberately faked this illness?'

Graham raised his eyebrows and Stephanie looked round for something to hit him with. 'You rotten—' she raged.

'Stevie, be reasonable—you did it better than

Meg, everyone says so,' he pleaded.

'But I didn't *want* to do it. I didn't audition for it. That wasn't fair,' Stephanie protested.

'Grow up, Stevie—you know you've got talent as a performer! You're wasted directing.'

'Don't say that!' she cried with venom, and once again tears of misery fell down her cheeks.

Graham was patient. 'Crying isn't going to cure your heartache, Stevie,' he consoled. 'Come on, cheer up and come on back to the party.'

'I suppose I'll have to go and find Mum.'

'She's OK—Guy's entertaining her.'

Stephanie groaned. 'I can't go back in there then, can I?'

'Why not? Don't think I'm going to do your dirty work for you.'

'Oh Graham, please?' she implored, but he shook his head adamantly. 'Dry your tears, put on your sunniest smile and make sure he notices you,' he told her. 'I've got a date with a pretty nice girl myself. Mind you . . .' He smiled wistfully. 'Oh, never mind. Just be at your best next Saturday,' he warned, and left her.

Stephanie switched the interior light on and pulled down her sun visor on which was a large mirror. She rubbed her face with a tissue but it made little impact until she opened the window and soaked it with rain water. After a few minutes of intense cleansing to get rid of the remains of the grease-paint, she decided to go inside to find her mother.

So Guy *had* been at the performance tonight,

and now he'd be pretty disgusted with her for taking over from Meg. It wouldn't be much use her trying to tell him that she only intended to be understudy because whatever she did to help on the entertainments committee it must brand her in his eyes. He didn't approve of hospital theatricals, she reminded herself, so what hope was there of them ever being compatible? It was all a lost cause, a fairty-tale dream which she would have to try to put out of her mind.

She was shivering with the cold as she cautiously returned to the hall where the party was in full swing. Guy would have attended the pantomime just to show willing and do his duty, and now her mother would be all starry-eyed again, she supposed.

Someone pushed a drink into Stephanie's hand and before she knew it she was in the centre of things, even though she refused to acknowledge that she had become the star of the Thames Vale hospital pantomime overnight. Eventually she managed to break away when she spotted her mother sitting in a corner with Guy Atherstone, who had his back to Stephanie.

She hurried over. 'We ought to be going, Mum,' she said.

At the sound of her voice Guy stood up at once and turned with a mocking, lopsided grin on his face.

'Little Red Riding Hood!' he said and Stephanie went tense at the sarcasm in his tone. 'Your mother was worried, where have you been?'

'I just popped out,' Stephanie said lamely.

'In the rain?' He was towering over her, his eyes like sharp needles of steel piercing her defences. 'I came out to look for you and saw you with Graham.'

There was no mistaking the condemnation in his voice, but Stephanie was too unhappy and too weary to fathom out the reason.

'The star has the world at her feet tonight,' he added, and then with a complete change of mood towards Pam he said, 'Thanks for your company, Pam. This kind of thing isn't usually of much interest to me, but it was made much more pleasant by having the star's mother as my companion. You must be very proud of Stephanie.'

'I am.' Pam beamed at him, and Stephanie knew her mother was captivated.

If only it were all over, she thought. But there wasn't long to go now, and then she had the whole Christmas period off to go to Oxford with her mother to visit her father's ageing parents. She'd hate being away from the hospital and she'd spend every minute wishing she were back where she might glimpse Guy, even if he did treat her with disdain.

Pam didn't say much until they reached Stephanie's house—then she busied herself in the kitchen preparing hot drinks.

'You look worn out, my girl, and why the tears?'

Stephanie opened her mouth to deny that she had been crying, but a glance at her mother and she knew it was no use hiding anything.

'I *hate* him!' she said vehemently, 'but I love him as well.'

'That much was pretty obvious to me weeks ago, so why the tears? Shouldn't you be overjoyed?'

'He doesn't love me—he's been married before and—'

'I know the full story, he told me himself. This Andrea you spoke of is his late wife's sister. And now Graham—'

'Oh, you *are* well informed,' Stephanie exploded.

Pam was silent for a while as she divided the milk between two mugs.

'Is it because Andrea's taken Graham?'

'No, Mum. I know you'd have liked me and Graham . . . but I'm glad he's got Andrea and is off my back. I suppose Guy thinks I'm trying to get Graham back now because he saw us in the car together. It wasn't like that at all, but what does it matter to Guy? He hates hospital theatricals, he was angry because Andrea got involved and he assumes I can't do my job properly on the ward if I have an outside interest. Anyway, he doesn't like me very much as it is, so there's no pleasing him.'

'Whatever he says, my dear, I can tell you this— he enjoyed every minute of that show tonight. He thought the comedy sketches hilarious, he appreciated all the send-ups and he was most impressed with your performance.'

'Mum, how can you be taken in so?' Stephanie pleaded. 'That's only for the look of the thing. In his position he has to be seen to take an interest, but after all the hassle he had with his wife he must hate anything to do with the stage.'

'I think he's much more over his wife than people think,' Pam said thoughtfully. 'He probably created a barrier at first and now it's too difficult to break down. I understand how he feels. Sympathy and pity come in such large doses at the time that it's almost a necessity after a while. He's a really nice man and it'll be a lucky girl who gets him.'

Stephanie took her drink upstairs with her. She couldn't go on talking about the man she loved when she knew there was no hope for her. Before duty next day she took her mother to the bus station in Reading and saw her off, putting on a generous smile as she waved the bus on its way.

As it was getting near to Christmas only emergency cases were being admitted and the ward had lost some of its urgent bustle. Stephanie got away early and was thankful to have her house to herself. She was packed and ready to go away, even though there was a week still to go, for she knew that with all the hospital activities she'd never have time for preparation at the last minute.

Just a relaxing evening in front of the television, she'd promised herself, yet she couldn't settle, so she went into the kitchen and listened to a carol concert on the radio. The chimes of the doorbell made her start. Before she opened it she peeped out from underneath the blind and could hardly contain her surprise. A familiar TR7 stood outside. She hurried to open the door. There was so much to explain to Guy, even if he hated her for the things she'd said, for the things she did. She needed to try to explain . . .

'Is this where Red Riding Hood lives?' he asked as she flung open the door. Then, as he stepped inside he waved a long, accusing finger at her. 'You haven't a chain on the door, and you didn't ask who it was.'

'But I knew,' she said confidently. 'No one but you has a TR7—no one, that is, who's likely to visit me.' She led the way into the lounge. 'Actually I was busy in the kitchen listening to some carols. Would you like coffee?'

He grinned. 'Why else do you think I've come? Is your mother here?'

Stephanie felt as if he'd punched her below the belt. She felt sick inside and presumed the huge, flat parcel he was carrying was for Pam. She explained that Pam had to work right up to Christmas Eve, so had returned to Windsor, then she made for the kitchen in a hurry. What was he up to? Maybe it was just as well she and her mother were going to Oxford for Christmas.

Stephanie took ages to make the coffee. It was as if she'd been winded and at every slight sound she jumped nervously, but finally reasonable-looking coffee filled two of her best china cups and saucers, which she used just to prove that she had them rather than mugs. She took them to the lounge, when Guy was stretching up over the fireplace.

'You took so long I unwrapped your present for you,' he said.

'Present?' she queried.

He stood back and she saw that he had hung an oil painting on the wall.

'I felt you needed a picture here when I visited you before.' He looked down at her and smiled. Her heart fluttered at the warmth in his eyes, a warmth she hadn't ever expected to see again. 'I hope you don't think I'm taking a liberty?'

She shook her head solemnly. 'It's really lovely,' she breathed in a whisper. How could he have known that she loved wild and stormy seas crashing over rocks? He took the tray and set it down on the coffee-table.

'I know you so well, darling,' he said huskily, 'that I felt this would be your choice.'

They stood gazing at one another, then Guy laughed.

'Little Red Riding Hood. The only thing that pantomime lacked was me as the wolf—lucky Jason to have you singing that song to him at the end!'

'I wasn't singing it to him,' she said simply. 'I was singing it to you, only I didn't know you were there.' She looked down at her hands, wishing she could find some way to occupy them, but then Guy was holding them tenderly between his fingers.

'I believe you,' he said gently. 'I thought there was too much between you and Graham and I didn't want Andrea to need psychiatric help again. I tried not to get involved, but you tempted me with every glance.'

'I did *not!*' she denied sharply, pulling away.

'I prefer to think you did.' She knew it was useless to argue with him. 'I had a lecture from

Andrea and Graham after the show,' he went on. 'I'm sorry you cried on my account.'

'I . . . I don't cry often,' she said wistfully. 'Only when something hurts more than I can bear.'

'Come here.' It was a low, gutteral sound, barely audible, but she obeyed willingly.

'I know you don't like hospital theatricals,' she said as he held her close to him. 'I didn't want to take part, they tricked me into it. It's Meg's part really.'

'I'm glad they did. Everyone needs an outside interest, and you fitted the part better than Meg.'

'But you said—'

He kissed her forcibly to silence her. 'Never mind what I said, from now on the only outside interest you'll have is me.'

'Oh, Guy—I do love you,' she managed between his hungry kisses, 'and thank you for the picture.'

'It was too big to take all the way to Oxford.'

'Oxford?' she echoed.

He leaned back and smiled a devious smile. 'I've been invited to a real family Christmas. Mind you, that mother of yours has something to answer for. She gave me to understand she'd be here this evening.'

'That's not like Mum.'

Guy kissed the tip of her nose. 'It's her way of telling us to get on with it. I'm old-fashioned enough to believe it's right to ask permission of a parent to marry her daughter, so I got that formality over with the other evening.'

'Can you forgive me for the things I said?' she

Mills & Boon

4 Doctor Nurse Romances
FREE

Coping with the daily tragedies and ordeals of a busy hospital, and sharing the satisfaction of a difficult job well done, people find themselves unexpectedly drawn together. Mills & Boon Doctor Nurse Romances capture perfectly the excitement, the intrigue and the emotions of modern medicine, that so often lead to overwhelming and blissful love. By becoming a regular reader of Mills & Boon Doctor Nurse Romances you can enjoy EIGHT superb new titles every two months plus a whole range of special benefits: your very own personal membership card, a free newsletter packed with recipes, competitions, bargain book offers, plus big cash savings.

**AND an Introductory FREE GIFT for YOU.
Turn over the page for details.**

**Fill in and send this coupon back today
and we'll send you
4 Introductory
Doctor Nurse Romances yours to keep
FREE**

At the same time we will reserve a
subscription to Mills & Boon
Doctor Nurse Romances for you. Every
two months you will receive the latest
8 new titles, delivered direct to your door.
You don't pay extra for delivery. Postage and
packing is always completely Free.
There is no obligation or commitment –
you receive books only for
as long as you want to.

It's easy! Fill in the coupon below and return it to
**MILLS & BOON READER SERVICE, FREEPOST, P.O. BOX 236,
CROYDON, SURREY CR9 9EL.**

Please note: **READERS IN SOUTH AFRICA write to
Mills & Boon Ltd., Postbag X3010,
Randburg 2125, S. Africa.**

- -

FREE BOOKS CERTIFICATE

**To: Mills & Boon Reader Service, FREEPOST, P.O. Box 236,
Croydon, Surrey CR9 9EL.**

Please send me, free and without obligation, four Dr. Nurse Romances, and reserve a
Reader Service Subscription for me. If I decide to subscribe I shall receive, following my free
parcel of books, eight new Dr. Nurse Romances every two months for £8.00, post and
packing free. If I decide not to subscribe, I shall write to you within 10 days. The free books
are mine to keep in any case. I understand that I may cancel my subscription at any time
simply by writing to you. I am over 18 years of age.
Please write in BLOCK CAPITALS.

Name _____

Address _____

_____

_____ Postcode _____

SEND NO MONEY — TAKE NO RISKS

Remember, postcodes speed delivery. Offer applies in UK only and is not valid to
present subscribers. Mills & Boon reserve the right to exercise discretion
in granting membership. If price changes are necessary you will be noti-
fied. Offer expires 31st December 1984.

8DN

EP11

DREAMS

In the depths of despair with her love-
life and her work, Nurse Fleur Hamilton
finds herself pouring out her troubles
on the sympathetic shoulders of Dr
Antoine Devos. Next morning, filled
with embarrassment, her only comfort
is that at least she'll never have to see
him again . . . or will she?

*Books you will enjoy
in our Doctor Nurse series*

SURGEON'S CHOICE by Hazel Fisher
NURSE AT TWIN VALLEYS by Lilian Darcy
DOCTOR'S DIAGNOSIS by Grace Read
THE END OF THE RAINBOW by Betty Neels
A NAVAL ENGAGEMENT by Elspeth O'Brien
MATCHMAKER NURSE by Betty Beaty
STAFF NURSE ON GLANELLY WARD by Janet Ferguson
DR PILGRIM'S PROGRESS by Anne Vinton
HEARTACHE IN HARLEY STREET by Sonia Deane
DOCTOR ON THE NIGHT TRAIN by Elizabeth Petty
LOVE ME AGAIN by Alexandra Scott
A MODEL NURSE by Sarah Franklin
NURSE ON THE SCENE by Lindsay Hicks
ISLAND DOCTOR by Clare Lavenham
TABITHA IN MOONLIGHT by Betty Neels
MARINA'S SISTER by Barbara Perkins
EXAMINE MY HEART, DOCTOR by Lisa Cooper
INTENSIVE AFFAIR by Ann Jennings
NURSE IN DOUBT by Denise Robertson
ITALIAN NURSE by Lydia Balmain
PRODIGAL DOCTOR by Lynne Collins
THE HEALING PROCESS by Grace Read
LIFE LINES by Meg Wisgate

DREAMS ARE
FOR TOMORROW

BY

FRANCES CROWNE

MILLS & BOON LIMITED
London · Sydney · Toronto

First published in Great Britain 1984
by Mills & Boon Limited, 15–16 Brook's Mews,
London W1A 1DR

© Frances Crowne 1984

Australian copyright 1984
Philippine copyright 1984

ISBN 0 263 74814 6

Set in 11 on 12 pt Linotron Times
03/0884

Photoset by Rowland Phototypesetting Ltd
Bury St Edmunds, Suffolk
Made and printed in Great Britain by
Richard Clay (The Chaucer Press) Ltd
Bungay, Suffolk

CHAPTER ONE

A FRESH, early autumn breeze tugged at Fleur Hamilton's dark cloak as she crossed the grounds of the Hilldown General Hospital towards her flat.

It had been one hell of a day on Fraser ward, and if Sister Morton found any more faults with her work, she seethed murderously, someone was going to discover that wretched woman's hat floating in the river . . . Well, she amended her thoughts quickly, maybe it wouldn't be as bad as that, but things were certainly going that way. Particularly when you were tired out and felt a hundred and four, instead of twenty-four. Life was rotten . . .

'Hey, hang on, Fleur! Wait for me! You in a daze or something?'

Katy Ashford's pretty, if slightly plump, figure appeared at her side panting for breath.

Fleur swung round with an apologetic grin. 'Sorry, Katy, love. I honestly didn't hear you.'

Katy put an affectionate arm around Fleur's slender shoulders. 'Now listen. I've got something to tell you that's going to cheer you up and put a great big smile back into those cheeks.'

'Don't tell me Sister Morton's getting married!' Fleur said hopefully, as they went inside the building and waited for the lift. 'That would really be the answer to my prayers!'

'No. Forget her,' Katy said, when they walked

along the quiet corridor and into their two-roomed flat. She kicked her shoes off as soon as they had closed the door. 'Don't let her get at you. What I have to say is heaps better. Put the kettle on while I get the coffee and I'll give you the low-down.'

Fleur did as she was told. 'Oh, come on, Katy, what is it?' she laughed, flinging down her white cap on to the bed and running her hands through her short, brown, shining hair.

Katy busied herself with the biscuit tin and then put two mugs of steaming coffee on a tray and remained stubbornly silent until they were both comfortably sprawled in armchairs beside their glowing electric fire. 'You know those trendy doctors who've been wandering all over the hospital as part of that big international conference they're attending, watching how we work and all that stuff?'

Fleur nodded. 'Only too well. Wish we had some like that at Hilldown.'

'Well, guess what?'

'Oh, Katy!' Fleur tossed a well-aimed shoe at her friend, fortunately missing the coffee. 'Get on with it!'

Katy's round face was bright with excitement. 'Listen, they've invited some of the doctors on our staff to a slap-up party next week at a splazzy hotel in the West End of London as a kind of thank-you. And guess whose names were drawn out of the hat? Our favourite housemen! My Bill, and your pal Ken Martin. They're taking us, and all expenses paid!'

It was Fleur's lovely eyes that were shining now,

large and brown, fair cheeks flushed. 'Oh, I don't believe it!'

Katy nodded. 'And that's not all! We're being put up for the night if we choose, so that there's no problems with driving home.'

'Wow! That sounds terrific!'

Katy looked at her friend's animated face, thinking how small a thing it took to cheer Fleur up when she was still fighting the heartache of being jilted. 'Yes, and what's more,' she went on, 'do you remember that snooty-faced Professor? Can't think of his name . . . Oh, yes, Antoine Devos, the one I said kept looking at you when we were on theatre duty last week. You remember . . .' she urged.

Fleur wrinkled her smooth brow. 'Vaguely. What about him?' She sipped her coffee thoughtfully.

'Well nothing much. Except that he'll be at the party and who knows?'

Fleur stared into the fire smiling. 'Oh, Katy, your imagination! He won't know me from a bar of soap once we're away from the hospital environment.'

They talked on for a while about what they might wear, but it wasn't until they had showered and gone to bed that night that Fleur murmured drowsily, 'I think I'm steadily going off nursing all together, Katy.'

Katy shot up in bed like a rocket. 'Fleur Hamilton, you can just stop that line of talk! Just because you had a rough time last year being let down by Tom, that's no reason why you should give up the thing you love best in all the world.'

Fleur was sitting up by now, hugging her knees. 'I'm wondering whether Morton has a point and I'm not working as well as I should,' she said quietly. 'She's not the only one who's been getting at me. Night Sister was as sarcastic as only she knows how last month. I haven't forgotten that yet.'

Katy climbed from her bed to cross the room and sit on her friend's. 'Fleur, love, you've got to stop this defeatist talk. I'm twenty-seven, I know what I'm talking about. I haven't gone through what you have, but one day Bill and I hope to marry when he's no longer a penniless houseman, and I can imagine the bitterness you feel. So far, you've coped marvellously. Most of us here know what happened, but we're trying to make things appear normal as time passes. They know also that you don't want their pity. You had it in the beginning, but it can't last forever.' Her kindly grey eyes looked hard into Fleur's. 'What you desperately need is a change. You've had to fight through the shock and misery and it's now, when you're beginning to emerge from the numbness, that you want things to happen.'

'I know you're right, Katy,' Fleur sighed. 'In fact I was thinking the other day about writing to Ann Morley in Brussels—you know, the girl who started her training with us.'

'Yes,' Katy said slowly. 'She works in a private clinic over there doesn't she? Why not write and see if she has any ideas?'

'I think I will.'

'Well, it's something new isn't it? You've passed

your Finals, but it's no earthly use your contemplating Midders with me, or anything else at this stage.'

'I just couldn't face it. I'll write to Ann tomorrow.'

For the whole of the following week, having written to Brussels without much hope, Fleur forced herself to work on Fraser with as much goodwill as she could muster. She had always been happy there. It was a mixed surgical ward, male and female divided by the corridor on the third floor of the very modern hospital block. Small, glass-partitioned bays of two or four beds dominated, and a few single areas prettily curtained off for the more serious cases were situated near the office and the nurses' station. Bright with pastel bedcovers and Swedish wood furniture, alive with pot plants and flowers, Fleur was convinced there wasn't a nicer place anywhere else in London.

By the time she had got through ops days on Tuesday and Thursday of that particular week without any kind of altercation with Sister Morton, she began to hope things might be improving. But on Friday, whilst she was alone on duty with only one junior nurse, there had been two admissions. One, a straightforward appendicitis; the other, the result of a road accident, an amputation. In the ensuing emergency, and afterwards dealing with relatives and preparing a post-op bed with the junior who seemed scared out of her life, Fleur disappeared into the sluice room to make some order out of chaos. She thought she heard one of the doctors speaking and, turning off the tap water in the huge sink, went out to investigate.

Her heart sank as she saw the disappearing shoulders of the senior surgical registrar. 'It's OK, Staff,' the junior said brightly. 'He said not to bother, he'd come back later.'

That would have been fine if Sister Morton had not chosen to return to duty a few minutes early and overheard the conversation.

Fleur's heart sank, and in the office Sister proceeded to wipe the floor with her. 'Haven't I told you before, Hamilton? Whether you are the only trained nurse on duty or not, you are supposed to be aware of a senior doctor's presence!' she exploded. 'That young junior has only you for an example. You are to blame. *She* should have been in the sluice and *you* outside.' She paused only to take breath. 'How you passed your exams I'll never know. Your mind lately isn't on anything for more than two seconds. What's the matter with you girl, been crossed in love or something?'

Her words were like a dash of ice-cold water in Fleur's white face. Sister Morton was a comparative newcomer to the hospital, and knew nothing of the jilting.

Fleur kept a rigidly tight expression as she said, 'No, Sister.'

'There's something lacking in your intellect. God knows what it is. At the moment you seem to be of little use to me . . .'

'Yes, Sister.'

'Are you being insolent?' she said, suddenly moving closer to Fleur. 'Because if you are, I intend putting in a report to Matron about you which you will not like one little bit.' She sighed as though she'd run out of steam. 'Well, what have you to say for yourself?'

'I'm sorry, Sister. May I go now?'

'Oh, get out of my sight, Hamilton! And you'd better come back from your weekend off in a better frame of mind.'

Feeling shattered but trying to look bright when she said goodnight to the patients, Fleur made her way to the tea bar in the main reception area, which was nearer than going up to the canteen. A cup of coffee might revive me, she thought miserably as she queued amidst the usual mêlée of visitors, staff and patients, still smarting at Sister Morton's words. She must be forty if she was a day, unmarried, dedicated, and probably heading for the kind of future that Fleur herself was trying desperately hard to avoid.

She collected her beaker of coffee and looked around for a chair, and as she did so she collided with someone who cried out angrily, '*Mon Dieu!* What is this?'

Horrified, Fleur looked up into the face of the tall Professor Antoine Devos, one of the visiting surgeons. Dark brown hair flopped over his brow as he endeavoured to mop up the brown liquid now sprinkled down the front of his immaculate silver-grey suit.

'I'm terribly sorry, sir, I didn't see you. I . . .' Mortified, she realised that without thinking she too was mopping up his jacket with a handful of fresh tissues. She drew away hurriedly as he indicated that she should.

The dark blue eyes were cold as they bore into hers, yet the deep voice was not unreasonable considering what had happened. 'Please do not worry, Nurse,' he murmured rapidly, the French accent more pronounced in his agitation. 'I, too, should have been looking where I had to go.'

Fleur was still covered in confusion, her soft cheeks burning. 'Please forgive me. Will you let me pay the cleaning bill?'

He shook his head disdainfully. '*Non, non*. It is all right. I will attend to it.'

Still trembling, Fleur watched the tall, athletic figure disappear, broad shoulders way above everyone else. He chatted with a colleague, who seemed more excited about the whole thing than he was, as they went out to their car.

Collapsing into a chair, Fleur drank her remaining coffee, which now tasted like mud, and got back to the flat as soon as she could. By the time she had relaxed in a bath and changed into jeans and shirt, Katy had come in. After telling her all about the unfortunate mishap, she didn't feel quite so bad, especially when Katy assured her,

'He probably thought you did it to gain his attention. You know what these Frenchmen are!'

'He's Belgian I think . . .'

'Well, a lot of them speak French. I don't know the difference. Anyway, when I last saw him, he didn't look too upset. He was laughing and chatting up two of the nurses.'

Fleur had busied herself making scrambled egg

on toast. 'Thank heaven for that! The way he looked at me at first, I could only pray for the earth to open and swallow me up!'

Katy giggled. 'I know the feeling. You won't think that though, when you're the belle of the ball tomorrow night!'

'Flattery will not get you my fur wrap my girl!' Fleur paused at the look of dismay on her friend's face. 'Don't look so worried, Katy, you know the fur wrap suits you much better than it does me! I'll be quite happy with my mohair cape.'

Over their scrambled eggs they decided on outfits for them both and, as if on cue, the minute they had finished there was a light tap on the door and Ken Martin, a tall, gangling, fair-haired house-man, grinned at them.

'Come on you two! It's badminton night.'

'We know, that's why we didn't go down to dinner,' Katy said. 'Not that we'd have missed much. Come on Fleur.'

'OK!' she called, collecting their sports bag from the bedroom. 'We've been talking about clothes for tomorrow.'

'I should have known!' he said with a disarming grin and flung an arm around Fleur's shoulders. 'Let's go.'

'Is Bill joining us?' Katy asked anxiously.

'In half-an-hour's time if he's lucky,' Ken told her with fiendish delight. 'He's gone to maternity!'

Next evening there was a deep and concentrated silence in the girls' flat as they put finishing touches to their appearance for the special night out. It had been madly hectic because Katy had not come off duty until four that afternoon, but as Fleur had the whole weekend off she was able to shower, lay her clothes out and prepare something to eat for them long before Katy came rushing in. Now, as Katy appeared at the bedroom door, she looked far from the limp creature she had declared herself to be two hours earlier.

Fleur smiled at her. 'You look lovely in that gorgeous kaftan, Katy! I don't know what Bill's going to say when he sees you.'

'Listen to who's talking! There you are, looking like something out of *Vogue* in that ravishing little jade number. Some people have all the luck. I'd given anything for your figure!'

Fleur was clipping on large hoop earrings to match the gold necklace her uncle and aunt had bought her for her last birthday. She secured the clasp carefully, thinking of the two people who loved her and had brought her up on their Yorkshire farm after her parents were killed in an air crash. Finishing off with a spray of Patou's Joy, which a grateful patient had given her, she checked that the halter-neck strap of the chiffon dress was right, smoothed down the gathers of the floor-length skirt, secured the buckles of her gold, high-heeled sandals . . . and she was ready.

Meantime, Katy had been excitedly pouring them both a glass of sherry. 'Dutch courage before the boys come, Fleur!' she grinned, as they took up their glasses. 'Here's to our super evening!'

'Fingers crossed!' Fleur smiled back, her small, pert nose wrinkling in excitement. 'What time are Bill and Ken picking us up?'

Katy's long hair fell forward as she glanced at her wrist-watch. 'Two minutes time, I hope.'

The large and imposing hotel was just off Sloane Square. When they had parked the car, Fleur felt her first thrill of anticipation on entering the deeply carpeted vestibule banked high with flowers. After signing in at reception and leaving their things in the sumptuous rooms assigned to them, they then went up to the twelfth floor in the lift, which decanted them into a crowded reception room where the group of doctors who had been at Hilldown waited to welcome them.

Ten minutes later Fleur's heart was banging like a sledge-hammer when she realised that Antoine Devos, elegantly handsome in evening dress, was enjoying a jovial word with Bill and Ken—and it would be her turn next. Katy was already being greeted warmly by some of the others and Fleur wished it had been her. But no such luck. The Professor's hard gaze was already upon her as he moved nearer, his smile enigmatic as he raised her outstretched hand to his lips, his deep blue eyes slightly questioning, while she almost held her breath.

'*Bon soir, mademoiselle*,' he murmured in a low, seductive tone that told her nothing except that he was a flirt *par excellence*.

'*Bon soir, monsieur*,' Fleur said breathlessly, imploring him not to recognise her as the clumsy nurse who spilt coffee all over him.

'I think we have met on,' he paused, one sleek eyebrow raised as he pondered, 'Fraser ward. Am I right?'

'Yes, Professor,' she said, breathing normally again. 'You have a good memory!'

'Always, for a beautiful woman,' he returned, quick as a flash. But he was already conferring an equally heart-stopping smile on the girl behind her as Fleur joined Katy and the others.

'What was he saying to you, Fleur?' Katy whispered excitedly. 'Do let's hear!'

Fleur hoped her cheeks were not burning. 'Oh, just that he remembered me on Fraser ward.'

'So he didn't mention the coffee episode—the crafty Casanova!'

When they entered the Mezzanine Room where the evening was to be spent, low lights replaced the glistening chandeliers of the reception room. Small tables were set in a horseshoe shape, leaving space for the cabaret and dancing that was to follow. A pop group of international repute was already setting the pace for the evening and once they were shown to their table, the two girls found a pink carnation corsage beside their plate and cigars for each of the men.

'Ah, this is the life!' Bill said with a grin, his good-natured face taking on a wistful expression as they all studied the menus. 'Do you know, chaps, we're quite definitely in the wrong job!'

'Why don't we kidnap the chef and press-gang him into service at the hospital canteen?' Fleur laughed above the chatter and music two hours later, after one of the most delicious meals she had ever eaten in her life.

'Trouble is, some of those cabaret turns are enough to put a man off the most delectable food,'

Ken sighed, having just ogled four lovelies in as few sequins and feathers as they could get away with.

'You men!' Katy grinned. 'There's nothing to choose between any of you!'

It was whilst the good-natured banter was going on that dancing had begun and Fleur had seen Professor Antoine Devos making his way towards their table. To her utter astonishment he fixed Ken with a charming smile, saying briefly, 'May I?' and extending a hand to Fleur.

Ken nodded, too bemused with good food and drink to do more. 'Be my guest,' he mumbled, smiling at Fleur who was having great difficulty in appearing outwardly calm and composed as this tall, charismatic man placed a hand beneath her elbow and they descended the few shallow steps to the dance floor.

In his arms Fleur tried to stop trembling with excitement as they moved to a romantically dreamy tune. Antoine Devos' face in such close proximity to hers was making her heart thud in a most alarming fashion. Thankfully there was little likelihood of it being heard above the general revelries all around them. His lips were against her ear. 'You know my name; it is only fair that you remind me again of yours.' He smiled down at her admiringly.

She couldn't help herself doing the same. The lean, angular face with high cheek-bones was lightened by small laughter lines around the deep-set eyes fringed by long lashes. His lips moulded over perfect teeth. The square chin with a deep cleft in the centre enhanced the long line of his jaw. He was too good to be true and thought too highly of himself, she decided briskly.

'If you do not tell me your name, I will make it my business to find out before we leave for home on Monday,' he was murmuring.

She knew he had been drinking enough to make any statement of that kind rather dubious. In a sudden wave of laughter and with a wicked glint of devilment in her eye, she said, 'Don't go to any trouble, Professor, it's Sally Hall.' The name was as good as any she could think up on the spur of the moment!

He held her very tightly. 'Sallee Hull . . .'

'*Hall*,' she corrected, as the dance came to an end.

When he escorted her back to her table and re-joined his friends, Katy was looking worried. 'Typical isn't it? Bill's taken Ken up to his room. He's out to the world. Too much drink and not enough rest, I suppose. I'm sorry, Fleur, this would have to happen.'

Fleur sipped a liqueur. 'Don't apologise, love, I'm having a wonderful time. So is poor old Ken, I'm quite sure. Just being here is a tonic.' Bill was making his way back to their table. 'Look, you two go off and enjoy yourselves. Please, Katy, I insist.'

When Katy eventually took her at her word, Fleur went to the powder room to tidy up and was amazed, when she saw her reflection in the mirror, at the difference an evening like this could make. The shiny page-boy bob that curved perfectly around her small features, huge brown eyes looking as wonderous as a small child in front of a Christmas tree—everything about her seemed to sparkle. Perhaps she was riding for a fall, she told herself sternly. This often happened when everything was going right. It had been so on the night Tom had told her they were through . . . She left the powder room quickly, banishing the unpleasant thought and lifting her small chin high.

'At last! I have been searching everywhere for you.' Antoine Devos was giving her a broad grin, putting a possessive arm around her and leading her back to where the dancing was in full swing.

From then on Fleur recalled only a succession of dances, some with Antoine's friends but mostly with Antoine. Interludes of laughter, sipping unfamiliar drinks—and all the while getting more and more on an easier footing with this man, until at last Fleur realised her legs no longer seemed to hold her up. 'I'm so sleepy, Antoine,' she murmured, her head upon his shoulder while they were outside on a balcony overlooking the twinkling lights of London.

He smiled down at her. 'Now don't say that, *ma chérie*. The night is young! Come, you must allow me to kiss those beautiful lips . . .'

She lifted her full, rosebud mouth to his and when contact was made the most delightful sensation she had ever known flooded through her. Quite suddenly all her tiredness fled. She felt radiantly alive and ready to do any mad thing that came into her head—or Antoine's. Then he was kissing her again and she wanted it to go on for ever. The pressure of his mouth was firm enough to be satisfying, but gentle enough to be polite. It was all rather lovely. Tom had never made her feel this way . . . Antoine was running a long, slim forefinger across her brow, down her nose and very slowly across her lips and on, over the curve of her throat.

'You are so very attractive, Sally Hull. Many men must have told you thees?' His lips brushed hers as he spoke, holding her very close.

'Oh, Antoine! You are such a flatterer. Did you know I was engaged once?'

'I am not at all surprised,' he whispered, running his fingers through her soft hair, lifting the fringe and planting tiny kisses across her brow. 'Why did 'e not marry you? 'e was a fool . . .' Antoine's voice sounded thicker, his diction just a little slurred.

She giggled. 'He didn't want me any more.' She burst into louder giggles. 'What do you think of that, Antoine Devos? He actually jilted me two weeks before our wedding day!' She began to laugh hilariously, uncontrollably.

'Come. We shall go to your room. You have had enough of this party,' she heard him say.

She seemed to crumple up against him. 'I don't want to, Antoine! I want to—I want to stay where all the action is,' she said petulantly.

Despite her feeble protests, he took her arm, checked on her room number and collected the key at reception. Once upstairs he unlocked the door and without a word swung her up in his arms and placed her gently on the wide bed.

She smiled up at him blissfully. 'Oh, Antoine, this is perfect. Kiss me . . .' She reached out her arms to him, his virile length against her pliantly supple body giving her the impression she had bubbly champagne rushing through her veins. She was floating, drifting. Nothing else mattered. He was kissing her now with a new kind of intensity that seemed to inflame her . . .

Then, quite suddenly, he wrenched himself away, saying unsteadily, 'I will make us some coffee.' He glanced around the room for the prepared tray.

Through her eyelashes, Fleur lay and admired him. He was so devastatingly handsome. All she wanted was to feel him near her again. To hell with the coffee! She stretched her lovely body luxuriously on the silken bedcover. Everything was luxurious. Antoine especially. When he had stopped playing with the coffee, she would tell him all about Tom and how he only wanted her to be a farmer's wife. She was glad now that she wasn't going to be one! She suddenly erupted into hysterical laughter again. 'Do you know why I'm not going to be a farmer's wife now, Antoine?'

'No, I don't,' he murmured in a low voice, stirring the coffee into two beakers.

'Well, because, it's because,' her voice was serious, then she burst into peals of mirth, 'I don't, I don't like mice!' Then she enjoyed the joke so much that tears began to fill her eyes until she was sobbing. 'It's really very funny isn't it, Antoine?' she gulped, as he stood the coffees on the bedside table. 'I really did love him you know. But he didn't want me. There was someone else . . . Kiss me again, Antoine.'

CHAPTER TWO

FLEUR groaned slightly as she stirred in the extremely comfortable bed. Opening one eye only, she was surprised not to see the familiar striped, no-nonsense folkweave curtains of her flat.

Two eyes revealed gold, floor-length drapes, covering far more space than she and Katy ever had in their bedroom. She sat bolt upright, giving another groan. What a headache! She was still in the London hotel, and it was morning. While fumbling for aspirin in her handbag, she noticed that it was nine o'clock, which was unimportant because breakfast was quite definitely out.

Flopping back on her pillows, she forced her mind to go over the events of the night before. Something wasn't quite right . . . It was after Ken left that things became rather hazy. She wrinkled her brow a little, trying to recall what had happened.

He had gone to his room quite early. It was then—while Katy and Bill were dancing—she came out of the powder room and met Antoine Devos again . . .

My God! Suddenly her head throbbed even harder. Certain recollections were flooding back. She had been feeling woozy; she had danced a lot and talked a lot, far more than she should have, if she remembered rightly . . .

Afterwards, Antoine had taken her up to her room. Her heart was beating madly now as her thoughts raced ahead. She vaguely recalled him mentioning coffee, and now she could not go back any further than that.

She looked down at herself suddenly. She hadn't a nightgown on, yet she had put one of her prettiest in her overnight bag. Had she? Had he? Her cheeks blazed with the implications. Then something made her turn her head quickly.

Pinned to the pillow at her side was a note which read: *Au revoir, Sally Hull. Thank you for a wonderful night, A.D.*

Fleur knew she had turned pale as she stared at the piece of paper and read it through a dozen times. Eventually she thrust it impatiently into her handbag and went to take a cold shower to pull herself together and think more clearly. She was just struggling into jeans and sweater when there was a tap on the door and Katy came breezing in.

'Hi, love! What a night! What a party! I gather you're not bothering with breakfast. Bill and I managed to stagger down. We passed Ken on the stairs, so he's just about in the land of the living!' She stopped in mid-flow suddenly and said, 'Hey, Fleur. You all right?'

Fleur was busily brushing her hair in the mirror, but suddenly swung round. 'I . . . I can't remember what happened last night, Katy!' she said quickly.

Katy burst into a peal of laughter. 'Who can?'

Fleur started stuffing things into her toilet bag. 'No, seriously. Look, this note was pinned to my pillow.'

Her friend read it and collapsed on to the bed, her face a picture. 'Hey, that must have been some night!' she said with a low whistle, her bright eyes twinkling.

Fleur threw her an impatient look. 'Katy, you don't understand! I honestly mean what I said. I don't remember much after Antoine brought me up to this room. Then he said he was going to make coffee. Look, there are the used beakers.'

Katy raised her eyebrows. 'What you're really saying is, you don't know if he slept with you or not?'

Fleur stared at the carpet. 'That's about it. If it were true, I'd be thoroughly ashamed of myself.'

Katy stood up and crossed the room briskly to draw back the curtains. 'Oh, for heaven's sake, love. It probably did you good.' She grinned, but quickly looked concerned when she saw Fleur's face. 'If it was the case, he's the one who took advantage. You were probably quite incapable of knowing what you were doing. He's nothing but a nasty, self-opinionated opportunist,' she exploded, outraged now. Then shrugged her shoulders and said quietly, 'On the other hand, it could have just been a doctor's prank, and we all know what they are!'

Fleur finished her packing. 'I always feel better when I've talked to you, love.' She gave Katy a wan smile. 'Anyway, you've got to get back on duty, I mustn't make you late. We'll leave now, shall we?'

In the car on the way home, Ken and Bill were looking a little the worse for wear, but they all agreed about the terrific evening, although Fleur and Katy said nothing of the thing that was uppermost in their minds. Ken seemed to imagine that Fleur had a tremendous time without him. He must be more keenly perceptive than Bill, she thought wryly as he said, 'Next time we go to a dance like that, Fleur, I'll make damn sure I have enough sleep and gallons of orange juice!'

'You just do that, Dr Martin . . .' she joked as they turned into the car park.

Once back in their flat, Katy bustled around. 'What are you doing with the rest of your day, Fleur?'

'I'll probably ring home this afternoon and then write some letters to far-flung places.'

Katy was taking her uniform from the cupboard as she answered from the bedroom. 'I shouldn't bother. My guess is that you're going to hear from Ann sooner than you think.'

'Wish you were right.'

'Well, you never know,' Katy said, with all the wisdom of an old sage. 'I'm going down for twelve o'clock lunch. Can you face it?'

'Might as well . . .'

On Monday morning, after the usual rush of baths and bedmaking, treatments given and medicines dispensed, Fleur remembered the letter that crackled tantalisingly in her apron pocket. The Brussels postmark had sent her hopes soaring and even driven thoughts of Antoine Devos from her mind temporarily.

Sister Morton seemed in better spirits that morning when they had their coffee-break together, but was determined to talk. 'How did your weekend go? You went to the big dance didn't you?'

Fleur secured one of the white cap-pins more firmly into her freshly washed hair. 'Yes, it was terrific,' she enthused for Sister's benefit. 'The food and drink were out of this world.'

Sister sniffed. 'Quite a generous thing for those doctors to do I suppose.' The telephone interrupted the rest of the conversation. After a few curt remarks she replaced the receiver and said briskly, 'Matron wants to see me. The police are in her office about that road accident patient of ours.'

'OK, Sister. I see his temp's down this morning.'

'Yes, thank God. But he's had a bad time this weekend. By the way, his fiancée's no longer sleeping in the side ward now he's out of danger,' she called as she hurried away.

Once she had disappeared, Fleur checked that the junior nurses were occupied busily and there were no doctors around before she withdrew the envelope and quickly scanned Ann's letter. She had barely stuffed it in her pocket and resumed checking a new parcel of drugs when Sister Morton returned, muttering about wasting her time. It seemed she had been speedily despatched by the arm of the law and was slightly put out that it hadn't been more interesting. She glanced at the duty sheet. 'Can you get me some stamps if you're going anywhere near the shop at lunchtime?'

'Yes, of course,' Fleur said vaguely, her mind reeling with the contents of Ann's letter.

In the dining-room amid the usual chatter, mostly shop, she hardly realised what she was eating. One of her junior nurses on Fraser was giving her a wide grin. 'The shepherds pie's not as bad as all that is it, Staff?' she said brightly.

'Oh no, Wendy. It's just me today! You make sure you eat yours though. You'll need the energy. I happen to know that Sister Morton's got a heavy job lined up for you this afternoon!'

'Oh, yes. What's that then?' The girl's eyes were placid as she continued eating.

'Turning the linen cupboard out!'

'Hells bells, I only did it last week!'

Fleur stood up to leave. 'Ah well, that's just to keep you on your toes, in a manner of speaking!' She grinned at the disgust on the young girl's face.

On the way back, Fleur happened to run into one of the nurses from Fleming ward where Katy was a staff nurse. 'Do you happen to know what time Katy's off tonight, Nurse?'

'Late, I should think. There's been a coach accident on the motorway and she's been sent down to Casualty to replace the staff nurse whose gone off sick.'

'Thanks very much.' Damn! Fleur thought as she carried on to Fraser, she was longing to tell Katy the contents of Ann's letter, but it couldn't be helped.

As Sister Morton was off for the afternoon, Fleur was in charge and they seemed to be madly busy. All the beds were occupied.

When she went into the office, Ken Martin had parked himself on her desk, his white coat somehow making his nice, friendly face almost good-looking. 'Hi, beautiful! I'll move in a minute. I've just been down to see old Mrs Morris, I think we'd better have her in X-ray tomorrow at ten sharp, OK?'

'Sure. Anything else?'

'What's on offer?' he grinned cheekily.

'Certainly not what you're thinking! Goodbye, I can hear visitors arriving!'

He made for the door. 'Right, nothing like feeling wanted! See you, love!'

Fleur spent most of visiting time attending to the mass of clerical work that seemed to get worse. She could hardly believe it when she next looked up and saw the time. There was always an atmosphere once the visitors had gone. Some days it was for the better, others, not so. This particular afternoon it was not so. Making her way around the ward she was satisfied that most of her patients were settling as comfortably as possible. One young man of no more than twenty was depressed after having two of his fingers amputated in an accident. She spent some time talking to him about his girlfriend and the job he hoped to regain, until she felt he seemed relaxed and more composed. She lingered for a word or two with most of the patients, always considering it part of the recovery process, as she knew most of her nursing colleagues did. The trouble was, thought Fleur as she went back to the office, everyone seemed to need sympathy that afternoon and it took time . . .

Writing up her report later, she marvelled at the amount of work they got through in one day. Pushing aside the book, now in readiness for the next shift, she stood up with a long stretch, then wandered over to glance from the uncurtained window. Although they were in the suburbs, thirty miles from London, there was a quiet about the semi-rural atmosphere that felt comforting. As she stared out, she thought about the changes she was contemplating. At twenty-four years old, she seemed to have been studying for exams most of the time since grammar school. Getting engaged to Tom, the most exciting thing that had happened to her, she had never questioned that he expected her to give up her job. Being so head over heels in love, she was sure it was all she would ever need. Now she realised it was because it was the only deeply emotional experience she had ever known.

She sighed, moving back to the table. Was the rest of her life to be spent caring for other people until her own emotions had been wrung dry? To be a dedicated nurse was to be prepared for a disciplined existence. The unsociable hours were difficult to fit in with others. There was loneliness, too, in off-duty time. Katy was really her only good friend. If she did not make some drastic move now, was she to live the next thirty years or so doing the same work? Living with the same routine of hospital life until she was too old to have any plans other than living in a cottage, growing roses and making jam for the local church fêtes?

She shrugged, giving a wry smile at her downbeat thoughts, as she heard footsteps and laughter coming along the corridor. It was the next shift, and hearing their cheery greetings and gossip, she immediately felt better and carried on with the procedure of handing over.

Katy was all agog once they eventually met after a late evening meal and were relaxing in their room at last. 'I just don't believe it, Fleur,' Katy said, wide-eyed. 'Although I had a feeling something was going to zoom out of the blue like this. It's as though the whole plan were ready made for you!'

'Well,' Fleur said thoughtfully, 'it certainly seems that way on the surface, but . . .' She thrust the letter at her friend. 'Read it out aloud, Katy. Perhaps I've missed something.'

'OK,' she said, curling up on the floor in front of the fire. 'We'll bypass all the social niceties. Here goes . . . "I shall be leaving my job at the clinic just two weeks from now—hang on to your hats—to get married! He's an American airline pilot who wants us to be based in California. I took a chance and mentioned to matron that a friend of mine, with whom I'd done part of my training, wanted a job over here. She lost no time in assuring me that as we were from the same stable, so to speak, she'd have no qualms in offering you first refusal. I rent a smashing furnished flat in the city, which you could take over, or you could become resident at the clinic, whichever you prefer. If you like to ring me as soon as possible I'll make an arrangement for the interview. If you come soon, we can meet."'

Katy dropped the letter on her lap. 'Well, honestly, Fleur, it sounds great! From what she mentions of working conditions and pay, about four times as much as we get, it sounds fantastic!'

The two girls went over the possibilities until Katy said thoughtfully, 'Quite honestly, Fleur, much as I hate the thought of your going, I can't see that this move would be wrong. After all, if you hated every minute of it you could always come back here and pick up the threads. Your aunt and uncle—what do you think they'd feel about the move?'

'I mentioned it when I rang, and Aunt Jean said she thought it was just the answer, Uncle Bob too, apparently. They thought it would shake off the jilting business quicker than anything at this stage.'

'My feelings exactly,' Katy said briskly.

'I think I'll ring Ann tomorrow evening and find out more about the place before I start thinking of interviews. In any event, I don't imagine that our chief nursing officer will be exactly surprised.'

She stood up, stretching her arms above her tousled head. 'Wow! I'm bushed! I don't think even Antoine Devos will come into my mind tonight, and that's really saying something.'

The telephone call to Ann was timed for her to have returned to her flat in Brussels the following Tuesday evening. As soon as they were connected, Ann was still adamant that the job was ideal for Fleur.

'I'm sure you'd fit in well. The staff are of mixed nationalities, but there is a girl from Scotland. Everyone's very nice to work with as you'll see when you come over. The clinic's lavishly fitted with all the most modern equipment. You don't have to work as hard as you do at home, there's plenty of off-duty time, and, well, everything's flexible. Matron's German, but very nice. She likes

English nurses. Apparently she thinks they can be trusted!'

There were still a hundred and one things Fleur wanted to ask, but she felt reasonably satisfied enough to tell Ann that she would start things moving from her end. As Fleur had hoped, the chief nursing officer was extremely understanding when she knew why Fleur wanted the move and gave her three days off, which would give her time enough to travel to Brussels and back without too much hassle.

'I do hope for your sake the trip is successful, Hamilton. You are a good nurse and although I don't want to see you go, in this case I think it might well be the answer,' she smiled warmly.

It was surprising how swiftly events began to take place once Fleur had made up her mind to seriously consider leaving Hilldown. Another phone call to Ann established that Fleur would leave Heathrow on Monday of the coming week, have her interview on Tuesday, and return home by Wednesday. This was later confirmed between them and Fleur received her plane ticket and an assurance that all expenses would be met.

She found it difficult to concentrate on her work for the remainder of the week. She had been given Sunday off which surprised her because of the Saturday evening that went with it. 'It will give you more time to arrange things. I don't blame you for aiming to make a fresh start. Matron told me of all the trouble you've had,' Sister Morton told her.

It ran through Fleur's mind that Morton wasn't

such a bad old stick after all. She looked quite human when she wasn't shouting at her.

For the rest of the week things went fairly smoothly. There were several discharges on Fraser and only one admission, a straightforward hernia. But the patient, Mr Butler, who was a bachelor in his seventies and had never been in hospital before, had come round from the anaesthetic refusing to have a female nurse attend him. As Fleur went off duty at five o'clock Saturday evening, a large grin spread across her face as she heard Sister Morton giving the poor old boy the sharp end of her tongue—but at the same time sending for a male nurse.

At ten a.m. next Monday morning, Fleur, dressed elegantly in a brown suede coat and long leather boots, hair freshly shampooed and a light make-up, turned several heads as she checked through Customs and boarded the eleven o'clock flight for Brussels. Once seated in a no-smoking section against a window, Fleur gave a small sigh of relief, loosening the silk scarf of misty blues and greens that matched her shirt, smoothed down the brown pleated skirt and settled back to enjoy the journey. Soon she caught a brief glimpse of Brussels gleaming in the autumn sunlight and before long they were back in an almost identical airport, this time on the other side of the Channel.

Ann was waiting for her at the exit barrier and as Fleur waved excitedly to the tall, willowy girl with the long dark hair, she thought how little she had changed since the days when they had been raw students and their one aim in life was to pass current exams. 'Ann! It's good to see you!'

They hugged each other warmly. 'You too, Fleur! You look gorgeous, as usual. How do you do it? Have a good journey?'

Still talking, they hired a taxi and were soon rushing along the flat motorways until they reached the city that was bustling with life and colour. Ornamental ironwork, tubs and window boxes were spilling over with masses of autumn blooms, and when they entered the Grand Place, with its cobble-stones and ornate gold scrolled façades making an irregular skyline of guildhouses, it was like theatre scenery.

A short distance away they turned into one of the quieter side streets and stopped outside a tall, narrow, balconied house. Once having stepped into the wide, lofty entrance hall and been welcomed by a petite woman, Madame Guiot, the owner of the house, Ann took Fleur for a lightning tour over her flat—which only registered vaguely. They were talking at such a rate that the evening was upon them almost before they realised it, and after eating out at one of the many small cafés in the locality, with Ann chattering excitedly about her wedding plans, they were soon too exhausted to do any more than fall fast asleep the minute their heads touched the pillow.

At ten o'clock next morning, Fleur and Ann arrived at the Van der Meulebroeck Clinic on the Avenue Winston Churchill. It was a large, rambling, pleasant-looking building in white stone, but red and bronze tinted climbers obscured most of the gracefully curved contours, all but the hugely ornate oak door. Set well back in its own grounds, 'Meulebroeck' exuded a contented look of understated opulence.

Fleur's heart pounded as they walked up the short flight of marble steps to the front entrance. But once inside and with the maid gone to inform matron of their presence, Fleur calmed down and decided she liked the look of the few members of staff she had seen so far.

Matron Lisa Hauptmann was a large, big-boned woman with short, brown curly hair and an almost Junoesque figure. Her smile of welcome was sincere, and after Ann had made the introductions and they had all exchanged greetings and polite enquiries about Fleur's journey, Ann left them to start one of her three remaining days on duty.

'Come into my office, Miss Hamilton.' Matron conducted her to an oak-panelled room in which stood a large desk, several comfortable leather chairs and a very professional flower arrangement of scarlet chrysanthemums in a *jardinière* against long french windows overlooking the lawns.

'Do sit down, please,' the woman said in very good English, as she seated herself at the desk opposite Fleur. She smiled at her. 'I cannot tell you how delighted I am that Ann suggested you come to work for us here.' She glanced quickly at Fleur's qualifications and the letter from the chief nursing officer at Hilldown. Her grey eyes as she looked up again were shrewd but kindly. 'You think that,' she searched for the correct words, 'you will be happy to stay away from your home for a long while? A year at least?'

Fleur smiled. 'That is what I should like to do, Matron.'

'Good, good.'

They discussed details of salary, times of duty, living in or out, leave, uniform and the type of service necessary in such an establishment.

'Patients who come here pay a great deal of money, Miss Hamilton, and therefore they expect more time and consideration than perhaps you are able to give with your National Health Service. We have visiting specialists and consultants. The senior consultant, and owner of the clinic, is not available today but is in complete agreement with any decision I may make regarding my staff. Nonetheless, I am quite sure he will wish to meet you once he knows you have accepted a job here with us.'

She stood up with a smile. 'Come, Fräulein. I'm sure you could do with some coffee. I will get Ann to show you over the clinic, and if I am not available before you leave, I hope that you will write and tell me that our offer—which I now make to you—will be acceptable.'

'Thank you, Matron. You are very kind.'

In the staff restaurant, which looked more like one of the elegant rooms of the London hotel where she and Katy had stayed recently, Ann had met her and was now eager to know how the interview went.

'She offered me the post, so I presume she was satisfied,' Fleur smiled, more relaxed now.

'Great. She's a sweetie to work for.'

Later, with Ann looking most attractive in a white princess-style, side-buttoning dress and pleated cap, Fleur was conducted over the entire building as far as possible, with its expensive air of a luxury hotel rather than a hospital.

Fleur asked Ann what had been on the tip of her tongue for a half an hour. 'What's the senior consultant like? Matron said he's also the owner.'

'I haven't seen much of him. His father used to own this place. He apparently has a swish heart clinic in Paris also, but found coming over here too much for him. The son struts around with his nose in the air when he is here. Very good at his job, but the rest of us are way down at his ankles as far as he's concerned. Some of the girls think he's good-looking, but I don't go for those tall, dark and silent types.'

Fleur swallowed hard as they finished their tour, and Ann seemed to have lost interest in the subject. Even so, he sounded formidable.

'Now, look, Fleur, you can take a tram from outside here to anywhere in the city. It's worth doing. Buy a booklet of tickets which gives you six trips on the bus, tram or metro. There's plenty of places that give out information, no need to worry. You have to telephone on the street if you need a taxi. It's expensive but the tip's included!'

As they walked down the very ornate staircase that swept gracefully to the front reception area, Ann said, 'I forgot to mention there's an indoor and outdoor swimming-pool here that staff are allowed to use. But on the whole I usually like to get back to my flat, away from it all!'

Fleur nodded, her head so crammed full of new sights, sounds and knowledge, she wondered just how much she had really taken in. She glanced at the door of the room where she had been interviewed earlier.

'Hadn't I better say goodbye if she's there?'

'I think she's had to go out,' Ann said, tapping lightly on the door, then peeped inside. 'No, she's gone. I'll ring for a taxi for you.' She laughed. 'I don't think you'd better go on the trams yet! I should be back at the flat by about six. I thought we could have a quick dash round the city tonight if you're not too shredded. I've invited Moura, the Scottish girl, to come over. She's looking forward to meeting you, but had to go to the dentist this morning. But we can get together later.'

'OK. Fine. Are you sure I'm not taking up too much of your time?'

'Oh, Fleur, I'm loving every minute of it! I'm going to miss everyone so much when I'm living in California. Excuse me while I get them to ring for a taxi from here at the desk. Anything's possible in this place!'

Within minutes the vehicle had arrived, and as Ann gave the driver his instructions Fleur stepped into the taxi. As she did so there was a sudden skidding of tyres on loose gravel.

Fleur, glancing from the rear window to where a grey Rolls Royce had slid to a halt, subconsciously assumed another rich patient had arrived. A door was flung open; the tall, elegant figure of a man stepped out. He slammed the door shut behind the driving wheel as he gave a cursory glance at the taxi. As he did so, Fleur's heart turned over and almost stopped . . .

The expensively cut swathe of dark brown hair fell exactly right over the tanned forehead. The angular jaw was thrust out at a recognisable angle. It could only be Antoine Devos, Fleur thought wildly as the taxi started up, and she watched him disappear swiftly inside the clinic . . .

CHAPTER THREE

FIVE weeks later, despite her earlier misgivings, Fleur was hurrying along the corridors of the Clinique Meulebroeck as if she had been established there far longer than just seven days. She headed towards one of the rooms to which she had been assigned and entered the wide spaciousness of it, where lay a frail little old lady surrounded by a bower of expensive flower arrangements.

Madame Sophie Conrad, her bandaged eyes not preventing her from turning her elegant white *coiffure* warily in Fleur's direction, snapped in rapid French, 'I am not comfortable, Nurse. You English have no idea how to make my bed. My back is aching and I must have more pillows,' she finished petulantly.

Blessing her painful mastery of French at school, Fleur managed to answer her patient.

'Come, Madame! That is very naughty of you. Matron has told me that on no account must you do anything but lie flat for the first twenty-four hours after your operation.' Fleur smiled, straightening the eighty-year-old's bedcovers. She touched the gnarled old hands gently. 'I cannot read French too well from your newspapers, but perhaps you would like me to read to you from an English one?'

The hand tightened upon hers. 'I have not seen you yet, young lady,' she murmured in perfectly good English, 'but I like your voice. Yes!' she commanded. 'You may read to me.'

It was at least another half hour before Fleur could leave Madame Conrad and make her way downstairs to the nurses' common-room. As she went to the small dressing-room where members of staff each had a cupboard in which they kept fresh items of uniform, her thoughts reverted again to her decision to accept this job—even though she was riddled with doubt once she had seen Antoine Devos. She had told no one, certainly not Katy, of the man she had seen as she left the clinic. But after giving careful thought to all the advantages the job held, and the totally new environment she was being offered, she handed in her notice, and any doubts or reservations she had later were quickly thrust to the back of her mind.

Now, as she slipped into a fresh, white side-buttoned dress and set another pleated cap upon her gleaming hair, Fleur wondered, as she had a million times already, if the man she thought to be Antoine Devos was merely a figment of her imagination. However, her main worry at this moment, she admonished herself as she smoothed the dress down over slim hips, was the imminent appointment that morning with her new employer, whom she had not met since her arrival. Matron had informed her the day before that he had expressed a desire to meet her and, taking one last brief glimpse into the mirror, Fleur purposely forgot Ann Morley's guarded words about the man and went swifty to the reception area. With some trepidation she tapped lightly on the door.

'Come!' Matron looked up from her desk as she entered. 'Sit down, Nurse.' The older woman broke off, suddenly glancing at the still open door where a tall, impeccably dressed man wearing thick, dark-framed spectacles had followed Fleur into the room.

He gave a perfunctory greeting to Matron and took her place at the desk, immediately scanning the papers she indicated to him.

But Fleur did not see Matron's smile, or catch her murmured words of introduction before she left the room. Her eyes were riveted upon the handsome features, the stern, rigid jawline and cold, deep-blue eyes of the man now sitting opposite her. Her face paled and her heart raced as she stared at the senior consultant and owner of the Van der Meulebroeck Clinique. It *was* Professor Antoine Devos. Faintly, she realised he was addressing her. He rose from his seat momentarily as they shook hands.

'*Bonjour, mademoiselle*. My apologies for not having seen you earlier.' He glanced down at the papers before him. 'You are Miss Fleur Hamilton?'

'Yes, sir,' she murmured, wondering where her voice had gone, and her newly acquired confidence of the last few days.

'I see you were at Hilldown Hospital.' He lifted his head, the cold gaze meeting hers abruptly, but with no apparent sign of recognition. 'Matron tells me you appear to have settled in well. Do you think you will be happy with us?'

Fleur managed to dredge up a few words. 'I do hope so.'

The faintest glimmer of a smile played about the firm, mobile lips. 'At least you are being honest, Nurse. A short time ago I attended an international conference in Britain which included a visit to Hilldown. One of many, but I do remember it well. The staff were extremely helpful and friendly.' He glanced at the papers again. 'Fraser Ward, yes. Wasn't it Sister Morton in charge?' The smooth, dark eyebrows were raised quizzically.

'That's right,' she murmured, bracing herself for what was to follow.

'A very efficiently run ward, if my memory serves me right.'

He paused to study the papers again as if casting his mind back, and Fleur found her eyes drawn to the long, slender fingers immaculately manicured, a gold signet ring on the little finger of his left hand glinting in a sudden shaft of sunlight that filtered through the open french windows. 'There were many things to see,' his deep voice continued. 'So many people one met.' The thick black lashes lifted unexpectedly to stare as hard at her as politeness would allow.

Fleur knew instinctively he was searching his brain, wondering if he actually recognised her, but could not be sure. Neither could she decide if she were glad or sorry that before leaving England she had made an entirely new start in more ways than one. It had included buying new clothes and giving her old ones to Oxfam. She had splashed out on a totally different hair-style. Soft curls now feathered her brow and sprung attractively to the nape of her neck. According to an excited Katy she looked 'absolutely another person'.

Remembering this, Fleur's confusion began to wane gradually as she said with a smile, 'It must have been a most interesting trip, Professor, although I imagine rather rushed.'

Tension eased as far as she was concerned, and for a while they conversed on various aspects of Hilldown in comparison to certain work at the clinic. Then he glanced at the clock on the wall suddenly. His expression suddenly closed as he stood up. 'Forgive me. There is much to be done, I must go, I'm afraid. I have been away from the clinic far too long lately. Matron may have told you my father runs our Paris clinic. He is a heart man and very well known in his field but, alas, he is not getting any younger. I find myself compelled to visit him more frequently of late, although he will not admit to the fact that it is time he concentrated more on growing his beloved orchids.' A soft light came into his eyes, and left just as swiftly. 'I shall be in the theatre tomorrow morning. I should like you to be there. One of your patients requires hand surgery. Have a word with theatre sister, will you?'

'Yes, of course.'

He held the door open for her, and as Fleur watched him stride away she moistened her dry lips with her tongue, relieved the encounter was over, yet convinced there were troubles ahead. Then she killed the thought immediately. No good meeting problems half-way, that was one of Aunt Jean's favourite sayings, and Fleur knew she was right.

In the small coffee bar overlooking the lake, where weeping willows were still green despite

autumn tints upon the lofty trees, Fleur got herself
a drink and slumped down at a table by an open
window. Almost immediately, a bright Scottish lilt
sung out. 'Hi, Fleur! How did it go?'

Moura McLean, her round, intelligent face in a
cloud of red hair, grinned at her as she joined Fleur
and banged down her own coffee. She was large-
boned and tall, clumsy in her enthusiasm for life,
but as gentle as a baby when it came to handling
patients. She leaned forward eagerly to Fleur.
'What did you think of him then?'

Fleur sipped the delicious coffee, her brown eyes
rather guarded as she smiled at her friend. 'Everything you said. High, wide and handsome; cool,
calm and icy!'

Moura lit up a cigarette. 'You can say that again,
love! It's been great without him for a few weeks, I
can tell you. Long may it continue!'

'I have news for you!'

'Yes?'

'He's spending more time here now.'

Moura let out a howl, making one or two other
members of staff grin broadly, obviously knowing
her well. 'Just our blessed luck with Christmas
nudging the horizon. God! We had a whale of a
time last year! He went off on a skiing holiday with
his wife for a month.'

She drew shallowly on her cigarette, the smoke
hardly given time to settle anywhere before she
exhaled it again. 'The parties and shenanigans we
got up to would make your hair curl. The only fly in
the ointment was Senior Sister Feraud. We never
dreamed she'd be that way. I'd always got on quite

well with her until we started our Christmas all-night sessions in the nurses' rooms. Talk about Victorian, I don't know where she's been all her life! Anyway, she shopped us to Matron but it didn't get her anywhere. Matron's broadminded. Her principle's live and let live, that's why she runs a good ship here.'

While Moura was still mixing her metaphors, Fleur had inwardly digested the fact that Antoine Devos was married. Stupidly—not that it mattered—it had never occurred to her that this might be the case. She had imagined his work came first and any affairs he had were just small areas of his life that occasionally relieved his otherwise complete dedication to a semi-monastic existence.

Realising that Moura had paused for breath, she said quickly, 'That's really interesting, Moura. I liked Matron from the beginning. I wonder how she gets on with the Prof?'

'Very well, as far as I know.'

'What's his wife like?' she asked casually, having brought the conversation back to where she wanted it.

'Quite honestly, I don't know. He's always kept her under wraps, so to speak. Was crazy about her apparently. Now he's a woman-hater.'

'Really. How come?'

'She plays around. I suppose that's what makes him the way he is. From what I heard, even Matron began to feel the icy lash of his tongue, and that's saying something. As we all know, she can be as cutting as the next one if necessary.'

'Does his wife live with him?'

Moura was gazing from the window, obviously rapidly tiring of the subject. 'Separated as far as I know. I'll tell you one thing, though,' she grinned, looking back at Moura impishly. 'There are a few housemen here wanting to know who *you* are. Honestly, I wonder they didn't prepare a question-naire to give me so that you could fill it in!'

Fleur laughed and glanced at the watch pinned to her dress. 'Plenty of time for that! I must go, I'm afraid. I've got an evening off and I thought I'd make a moussaka. Come over to the flat and help me eat it if you like.'

'Great, love. Thanks. I might just do that. Hang on, I'm coming.' Moura finished her coffee in one gulp, and they made their way back to the hospital area where, behind white doors with ornately gilded handles and flower arrangements set in alcoves along wide corridors, patients lay with much the same apprehension as the less fortunate people at Hilldown.

Fleur left Moura to carry on ascending in the lift to the sixth floor where she worked, and Fleur alighted at the third. She reported back at the office to the pleasant, Belgian sister in charge, who could only have been a year or two older than herself. Sister Thérèse, who was leaving to get married in a few weeks, gave her a smile.

'Will you check that the two junior nurses who have replaced my last two, know how to set up the drugs trolley under your supervision, Staff, please.' She wrinkled her brow as she glanced at some notes on her table. 'I almost forgot, I'd like you to have an early lunch. Professor Devos will be coming round some time this afternoon while I'm off duty to see young Jacques Hein again before he operates tomorrow.'

'Yes, Sister. He mentioned it briefly to me this morning.'

'Good. I hope he treated you politely?' She smiled, her dark hair and eyes an attractive foil for a very fair skin.

Fleur nodded briskly, 'Oh, fine, thanks.'

'I know he can be rather overbearing.'

By the time Fleur had given the two young student nurses a mini-lecture on the layout of a drugs trolley, it was with some surprise she realised she was due to go to first lunch. In the dining-room she saw no one whom she knew and, although still feeling slightly self-conscious until she found a vacant table, she did not mind eating alone. There seemed to be so little time to stop and think of anything more than hurrying back and forth across the city to the clinic.

She liked Ann's flat very much and had taken it willingly, but so far there had been no chance to enjoy it. But sister had given her two days off next week when she hoped to make the most of settling in. The revelation of Antoine Devos being her employer had also not fully impressed itself upon her brain yet, and so far she felt it best to try and forget the entire encounter at the London hotel as though it just hadn't happened.

That afternoon, Fleur was returning to the sluice after attending to an elderly patient's pressure points with Drapolene cream when she heard footsteps and male voices. Remembering a similar situation at home when Sister Morton had battered her verbally, Fleur was on hand almost as soon as the visitors emerged from the lift.

Professor Devos gave her a thin smile and glanced at the young man beside him in a white coat. 'Afternoon, Staff. This is Dr Raoul Millaise. We just want to take a look at Monsieur Hein.'

The two junior nurses stood back respectfully as the retinue approached the boy's room and went inside. The good-looking young rugger enthusiast gave them a nervous smile and stood up.

'Right now, Jacques. Sit down on your bed will you?'

Fleur unbandaged the afflicted hand and the Professor studied it intently for a second or two, then turned to the houseman. 'These sort of extensor tendon injuries are difficult to examine in relation to their function.' He looked at the patient and questioned him again closely on the details of the accident on the rugger field. 'As you can see,' he said, turning back to Dr Millaise, who had been looking at Fleur's legs, 'there were only minor lacerations when he was first admitted to casualty, but from the X-rays it seems the distal interphalangeal joint has been ruptured by impact from the ball.'

When the examination was concluded and they had left Jacques Hein's room, Fleur glanced up at the Professor as they walked along the quiet corridor.

'Would you like a cup of coffee, sir?' she asked, as they drew near the office and went inside.

'No thank you, Staff.' His eyes swept hers like an

icy blast. 'Just remember to have that boy in the
theatre in good time will you? I have a heavy
schedule in the morning.'

He stalked out, leaving Raoul Millaise to give
Fleur an apologetic smile, as if for his master's
behaviour. Or at least, that's how it seemed to her,
Fleur thought two hours later during the sudden
flurry of teas and general odd jobs before she went
off duty. She'd had the suggestion of a headache
ever since Antoine Devos had left the third floor,
but tried to tell herself that his attitude had nothing
to do with it. And by the time she went out into the
chilly evening and waited for the tram, she still
wasn't sure.

After covering the short distance from the terminus and along the Avenue Louise, which was
already brilliantly lit with a hint of Christmas, she
was inordinately glad to enter the pleasant tranquil-
lity of her flat. Two flights of stairs took her through
a long, narrow hallway which was furnished by a
gilt-legged escritoire with a baize-covered board
above it, upon which Madame Guiot displayed
the tenants' post. To her delight there were two
letters from Aunt Jean and Uncle Bob and one from
Katy.

Fleur let herself into the large, lofty living-room,
carpeted and curtained in an almost Victorian
fashion, with a wide, open fireplace filled with
artificial flowers and a circular mahogany table
covered with a dark silk cloth edged with pom-
poms. Another door led out to a small, immaculate
kitchenette, which in turn backed on to a mini
bathroom. An added bonus in the main room were

the long windows that opened out on to a small balcony overlooking the quiet street.

Putting away her jacket in the capacious, old-fashioned wardrobe near her divan bed, Fleur threw off her clothes and took a quick shower before getting into jeans and sweater, and at last felt that she was off duty. For the next hour or so she busied herself in the kitchen and was happily humming a pop tune to the accompaniment of music from a London radio station when the buzzer of her flat rang. Pushing a still-damp curl behind one ear, she spoke into the grill, knowing she would hear Moura's voice.

'Hi, Fleur! I've brought company. Can we come up?'

'Sure,' Fleur said immediately, quelling a moment of panic and wondering if the moussaka would stretch. She pressed the front door buzzer and in seconds Moura stood grinning at her. Beside her was Dr Raoul Millaise, a slightly shy smile on his round, pleasant face, topped by a veritable halo of brown corkscrew curls.

'How nice! Come in,' Fleur smiled. 'Great to see you both.'

'You've met Raoul, I think, Fleur,' Moura said easily. 'I had to bring him. He says he has an apology to make to you.'

Whilst the two discarded their coats, Fleur was pouring three Martinis. 'Apologise, what on earth for?'

'Because, Fleur,' Raoul Millaise said quietly, 'Professor Devos was very impolite to you this afternoon. *We* all know him, but it is, um, so

different with a person who is new.' His halting
English made his announcement all the more pro-
found, and the serious expression in his clever,
brown eyes made Fleur convinced it was something
about which he felt deeply.

'It's most kind of you to be concerned, Raoul.
But honestly, I was so busy myself I hardly had time
to notice,' she said untruthfully.

The young man raised his shoulders in a Gallic
shrug. 'That is not the point. He can be rude to us,
but not,' he smiled, 'to pretty girls from England.'

Moura was tucking into some olives Fleur had
bought on one of her quick trips into a local supermarket. 'I told you, didn't I, love? He just needed
an excuse to come and see you!'

They all laughed hilariously and from then on it
seemed to set the tone for the evening. While the
girls were serving food, another young doctor-
friend of Raoul's 'just happened' to be passing
and was invited by Fleur to join them. The newcomer was named Guy and obviously just as curious
to see the new member of staff and if she could
cook!

When the food seemed to disappear like magic,
Fleur laughed happily. 'Do you know, I was thinking of having a house-warming, but I wasn't sure if
you'd think I had a cheek suggesting it as I only
really knew Moura.'

Moura and Raoul burst into loud mirth. 'She
doesn't know us, does she Moura?' Raoul grinned.
'Whenever there's a hint of a party, we will come
there. Ask old Guy, he thought it was hairy when
he first came to Meulebroeck last year!'

The thick-set young man with a large, slow smile, nodded agreement. 'It is better, much better, now!'

'I think it's great,' Fleur said with genuine feeling. 'The work's so interesting, and I must admit I don't feel so tired here that I'm not interested in some kind of social life.'

'You can say that again,' Moura said darkly. 'I used to feel a hundred years old when I worked in Edinburgh.'

They talked on long into the night, and when at last they had to leave it was not before they decided to get together again for an evening out as soon as they could arrange it. When Fleur went to bed she realised, as she drifted into sleep, that it was the first time for ages she had done so without worrying about her problems.

Next morning at the clinic, Fleur prepared Jacques Hein for his operation and by the time she and the porters had taken him downstairs to the ante-theatre in the lift, much of his nervous chatter had been overtaken by drowsiness from his pre-med. When the unconscious patient was wheeled into the operating area, Professor Devos glanced at Fleur with a brief, 'Good-morning.' Clad in green gown and cap, mask dangling beneath his square chin, he was scrubbing up at the wall basin and talking to Theatre Sister.

Fleur stood by, awaiting Sister's orders, and it was only when the operation was about to be performed that she noticed at least four young medical students were in the observation gallery, and two housemen were attending the Professor at the patient's side. One of them, Raoul Millaise, gave Fleur a small wink above his mask and the work proceeded.

Antoine Devos' voice was deep, calm and almost hypnotic. 'In this case, tendons of the hand need repairing, as you will see here. This will involve suturing and applying a plaster-back slab up to the elbow. The hand must be nursed upright in a suspension sling to prevent swelling.'

Fleur watched the long, slim hands of the Professor work with calm precision. As always, fascinated by what she saw, she quite forgot the people around her. The voice droned on. 'The hand must be kept immobilised in moderate extension during healing, which usually takes three or more weeks.'

'Staff! Swab the Professor's forehead,' Theatre Sister was hissing at her, as she handed the Professor the suture he required.

Fleur jumped slightly, realising the warmth of the surroundings had made her drowsy, particularly after her very late night. She did as she was asked, her hand trembling, and Antoine Devos' ice-blue eyes met hers over their masks. 'Too many late nights, *Mademoiselle*?'

She blushed a fiery red, hating the sarcasm in his voice and the scorn in his eyes. What had she done to deserve it? All the way back to Jacques Hein's room the question played around at the back of her mind as the patient was put back to bed, and Sister Thérèse left Fleur to keep an eye on him until he showed signs of regaining consciousness. Once he was round, Sister and Fleur suspended the limb gently in a sling from a drip-stand as ordered by the Professor, and soon he called in to see his patient.

Satisfied that all was well, Fleur accompanied him out in place of Thérèse, who was at lunch.

Only brief instructions had been exchanged between them until the tall figure beside her stopped suddenly in the corridor by the lift. 'Nurse Hamilton, I'm aware that Matron thinks you are settling down well here, but I prefer that you do not come to the theatre again unless you are fully alert.'

He flung the cruel words at her as he stepped into the lift, leaving her too stunned to reply.

CHAPTER FOUR

FOR THE next two weeks, Fleur threw herself into the work of the clinic with a grim determination to give Professor Antoine Devos no cause whatever to make any further remarks of the kind he had on the morning they were in the operating-theatre.

She had not been asked to attend again, and although she did not want to ask Sister Thérèse the reason, the unpleasant thought niggled at the back of her mind that it might have been at the Professor's express request. Well, even if he didn't rate her very highly, Jacques Hein *did* when he wished them all an emotional goodbye that morning. And his parents left an enormous iced cake to be divided between the staff for their care and attention!

In the office she had coffee with Thérèse, who handed her a cup and said with a smile, 'How very kind and grateful people are. I shall miss all this so much, Fleur. It does not seem possible I am leaving in two weeks. Now the time is near, I am reluctant . . .'

Fleur dispensed with the discipline of status when on duty, and put her hand on the girl's shoulder.

'Thérèse, you'll love the new life! Just imagine being your husband's nurse/secretary for a while at home. That's going to be a very cushy number!'

The girl laughed happily although her eyes

57

were misty. 'I know you are right Fleur. But,' she shrugged, 'soon I think there will be more engagements also. I have seen Raoul Millaise and the way he looks at you. Rather a lot just lately. *Oui?*'

Fleur thought again of those words when she was shopping in the city centre that lunch-time and being beguiled by the beautiful shops and arcades on the Place Rogier. She, too, had been aware of Raoul's attentions, but she simply liked him as a friend and usually tried to go out only in a crowd with him. They had all been to a disco several times in the city, but apparently their goodnight kisses had meant more to him than to her. Hurriedly she put these thoughts from her mind as she tried to concentrate on her shopping.

She intended sending Ann Morley a belated wedding present to California and buying a small gift for Thérèse. Fleur had always appreciated the young sister's friendliness towards her. They had got on well together despite language barriers.

In the large Bon Marché store, Fleur felt quite at home and quickly purchased a pretty, circular table-cloth with matching napkins for Ann and a more personal present of a small piece of pottery for Thérèse. After remembering she needed more white tights for duty, she bought those, and left the store still complimenting herself on noting she had been given one Belgian franc short in her change—to the chagrin of the assistant!

Outside a light rain was beginning to fall. It would be a wet walk to the Gare Du Midi, from where she had to take the tram to the clinic. Automatically, she headed for a tram stop, then changed her mind on spotting a small café.

It was at that moment she imagined she saw Antoine Devos approaching in her direction amidst the shoppers. Her heart began to pound. Surely it couldn't be!

But why not? How could anyone fail to recognise the imperious bearing, the proud lift of the dark head as he walked along, apparently lost in a private reverie of his own? There was no mistake, she could see that now. He was the last person in the world she had expected to meet at this time of day. Why, she had no idea. Feeling she needed to run for cover if her afternoon was not to be spoilt, it was with relief she made for the café. Walking inside quickly, she found a small vacant table, priding herself on her quick thinking.

'Do you normally dash away from your friends with such unflattering haste, Miss Hamilton?' The deep timbre of the voice removed any shred of doubt she might have had.

She lifted her eyes to where Antoine Devos was seating himself opposite her. 'No, not my friends,' she said hesitantly, hoping he'd caught the true meaning in her words. 'But please join me, by all means.'

The waiter appeared and the Professor ordered coffee for them both. His deep-set eyes met hers as he leaned across the table. 'Once outside the clinic, the rigid protocol of hospital life ceases to exist, as far as I'm concerned,' he said lightly.

'I'm glad to hear it,' she said, matching his easy manner to her own, but wondering how on earth they could sustain a reasonable conversation. 'That's how it was at Hilldown.'

He loosened the belt of his soft, black leather jacket, a blue cashmere slip-on over a matching check shirt giving him a younger, more casual appearance. 'Ah, Hilldown, yes. You still find it strange here?'

'In some respects.'

'Such as?'

She took a deep breath. 'Being reprimanded rather unfairly and without explanation.'

He paused, then a half-smile flitted across his angular features. 'You know, Miss Hamilton, we all have to endure injustices. Sometimes it is our unfortunate lot to be on the receiving end of a—shall we say, small tirade—when in actual fact it has been set in motion by another factor entirely.'

'I see,' she said quietly, feeling she had learned as much as she was going to. She moved off the topic. 'Working abroad is a very good way of comparing work methods as you know, Professor. It's proving it for oneself that is so interesting.' She took the cream jug he offered her when their coffee was served. 'I miss my friends though.'

'But you are making new ones?'

'Yes, of course. Everyone is very kind.'

'I am glad. I do not like to think that members of my staff are unhappy.' He leaned back in his chair with a smile. 'Putting work aside for a while, what do you do in your leisure time? Apart from going out with Raoul Millaise, that is.' His voice held thinly disguised censure with its lightly mocking laugh.

Her cheeks flamed. She thrust her small chin out defiantly as she said, 'As you yourself have just reminded me, Professor, we are outside hospital protocol now, and therefore I see no reason why I should answer that. Furthermore, I resent the question.'

'*Touché* . . .' he smiled maddeningly. 'Please forgive me, Miss Hamilton. You have not yet had time to see much of our beautiful city, I presume?'

They talked a little about tourism and places of interest to visit until he suddenly glanced at his gold wrist-watch. 'I can give you a lift back?'

She shook her head, preferring to be independent. 'Thank you, no. I still have one or two more shops to go to.'

'Very well,' he said brusquely, and stood up. After paying the bill, he gave her a remote smile. '*Au revoir, mademoiselle.*'

Fleur had quite forgotten it had been raining when she had made her quick dash into the café, and now, as she emerged in the darkness onto the brightly lit boulevard, the previously light shower had turned to a heavy downpour.

Swiftly, she ran to the nearest tram stop to take her to the terminus, cursing under her breath when she realised she was now in the thick of the lunchtime crowds, and the shelter did not stretch to her end of the queue. Within minutes she was soaked to the skin. Wet and dejected, she took no notice of the large car that glided to a stop at the kerbside, until a stern voice commanded, 'Miss Hamilton, jump in quickly. I'm not allowed to stop here!'

In a reflex action she did as she was told. As she sank back into the upholstered luxury, Antoine Devos smiled at her laconically, concentrating on joining the mainstream of traffic at the same time.

'Would it not have been more, er,' his eyes raked the wet, bedraggled ringlets of her hair, '. . . *comfortable* if you had accepted my offer in the first place?'

She clenched her fists tightly to prevent herself from lashing out at that suave face, but retained her dignity. 'I'm perfectly OK, thank you, I . . .' She stopped in mid-sentence, her face pale as she looked down at her lap. Her handbag was there, but not her parcels! She must have left them in the café, her mind still on Antoine Devos and the clever way she thought she had scored a point over him when turning down his offer of a lift. Now, her whole lunch break had been wasted.

'Something wrong?' The cool voice asked.

'No . . . I . . . it's nothing.' How could she tell him what had happened? She had ample proof of his thinking she was an incompetent already. Once she got back to the clinic, she consoled herself, she would ring the café. There was just a faint chance the proprietor had spotted her purchases. Neither of them spoke again as the car purred its effortless way through the rush. Then suddenly she realised certain landmarks were familiar to her from the tram each day. And they now appeared to be back on the outskirts of the city.

'I'm sorry, Professor, but I think we're going in the wrong direction for the clinic.'

He threw her a casual glance, his face impassive.

'No, Miss Hamilton, not if you want your shopping back.' His eyes were fixed firmly ahead. 'Fortunately I happened to notice your parcels when we were having coffee, and it did not take much deduction to see you no longer had them. Besides,' the faintest glimmer of a smile played about the corners of his mouth, 'I'm sure you're not the sort of girl who would usually look so agitated as you did, apropos of nothing.'

Why did he always make her feel so stupid? She straightened herself up on the rich beige upholstery, always wishing at a time like this that she was as tall as a beanpole. 'OK, it can happen to anyone, and I certainly did not want to trouble you to return to the café. I intended getting in touch with them by phone.'

The car slid to a stop outside the café. He leaned across with one arm, a drift of aftershave reaching her as he opened the door, his eyes in the shadow meeting hers. 'You have a touching belief in the trustworthiness of humanity, Miss Hamilton.'

'I never give up hope, Professor,' she said tartly, and stepped out.

The café was busy and her heart sank when she saw no sign of her parcels at the table where she had sat. The proprietor listened to her halting explanation, and then with a large beam dived beneath his counter and produced her bags, giving her an expansive, *'Voila!'* After expressing her thanks and promising she would call again, she left the place.

Greatly relieved, Fleur ran back to the car and slipped inside the already opened door before they headed once more for the clinic. 'Thank you, Professor,' she gasped in relief.

'It must be your lucky day,' Antoine Devos said quietly, after she had described the kindness of the owner. 'Or the fact that you are British, and he wishes to make a good impression.'

'Does he have to have a reason for being honest?'

'These days it seems to be mostly that way.'

'I don't agree. I think there are still some very good and kind people about.' She decided to be bold. 'After all, you yourself performed an act of kindness in taking me back to the café.'

He gave a harsh laugh. 'Oh, that's just because I happen to know you are due back on duty. Purely for selfish reasons, I assure you.'

Little more was said, and once they pulled up outside the main clinic entrance, Fleur thanked him once more and was about to leave the car when he said curtly, 'When I was visiting your old hospital I met a nurse called—Sally Hull, I think it was. She was on Fraser Ward. Did you know her?' In the mellow light from the building outside, his face was turned to her, his eyes enquiring.

Surely he would hear her heart thumping as she searched her mind for a suitable reply? 'No,' she said briskly. 'I've an idea she was on night duty. In that case I may not have met her.'

'I see,' he said laconically. 'Hard work at the conference and hard drinking at a subsequent party made me somewhat vague. I hoped I could get in touch with her through you. From what I recall she was a very nice girl, and I don't think I treated her as well as I should have.'

'I'm sorry, I can't help you. I must go now, I'm on duty in a half an hour,' she stammered, leaving the car quickly before he could think of anything else.

In the nurses' common-room Fleur washed and changed as fast as she could, relieved that her hair was now almost dry and her reflection in the mirror not too harassed, although she still felt flustered and ill at ease at the time she had spent in Antoine Devos' company.

On the third floor, Sister Thérèse discussed the day report book with her, and they remembered to add two extra names to the diet-sheet list. It was with a smile of relief that Thérèse stood up from her desk with a discreet yawn.

'It has been a very prolonged day,' she sighed, her English grammar flagging a little at the end of her tiring spell of duty. 'Did you have a good morning off?'

'Lovely, thank you,' Fleur said, rather too hastily. 'The shops are so exciting this time of year.'

Thérèse smiled, opening the office door to leave. '*Mon Dieu*! But they are expensive also!' She drew an envelope from her dress pocket suddenly. 'I almost forgot to give you this, Fleur. Goodnight!'

The phone rang, and Fleur thrust the missive into her holdall. From then on she proceeded to allay Madame Conrad's daughter's fear that her mother might not be making an excellent recovery from her eye operation because of her age. 'She needs only rest now,' Fleur assured the woman. 'The operation was a complete success.'

'Thank you. Thank you. You will not tell her I

have contacted you this way, Nurse, please? Otherwise my mother will be cross and think I am fussing. I shall be visiting her later this evening.'

After putting the phone down, and for the next few hours, Fleur's mind was wholly taken up with the well-being of her patients. Nothing dramatic had happened during the morning, nor were there any new admissions, for which she was thankful. Nevertheless, if she were truthful, she was not in the least sorry to hand over to the night staff when they came on that evening. It had been the sort of emotionally wearing day that she would prefer not to experience too often.

She was glad that she had declined an invitation to go to the cinema with Raoul that evening. Instead, when she got home she soaked in a good hot bath and lay back thankfully in the perfumed foam. She didn't always indulge this way, but she had quite a lot of thinking to do and needed to feel as relaxed as possible. The contact she'd had that day with Antoine Devos had been totally unexpected and fragments of their conversation kept returning to her. It would have been reasonable, but for his bombshell—asking after Sally Hull. Why had she been such a fool to dream up that name for herself? It might have been better had he known in the beginning and none of this subterfuge need have happened. She'd no idea at the time there would be such far-reaching repercussions. It was obvious that Antoine Devos suspected nothing with regard to her part in it and was simply trying to ease his own conscience about an incident that might dent his precious ego.

If only she herself could recall exactly what had happened that night! But try as she might, she seemed to get no further than the fact that he was in her room making coffee, and she could think of nothing more after that. The only other detail that bothered her was why her nightgown remained in her overnight bag.

Realising the bath water had gone cold, she scrambled out quickly and towelled dry. Pulling on pyjamas and housecoat, she curled up in front of the electric fire and wrote to Katy. It helped to get some of this whole business over the Professor off her mind. She realised how much she missed Katy's sound common sense approach to life and appreciated her regular letters. She managed a short note to her aunt and uncle, but when her eyes became drowsy she gave up.

About to get into bed, she remembered the envelope Thérèse had given her. Mystified as to what it might be, she drew out the white and silver card with a little whoop of joy. A wedding invitation to Thérèse and Pierre's marriage! And the mere thought of their kindness at including her in their celebrations made her feel a whole lot better as, at last, she fell asleep that night.

The following Friday morning, the day before Thérèse's wedding, Antoine Devos rang Fleur from Matron's office, asking her to go along immediately. When she arrived, having first applied a dash of lipstick and smoothed her hair beneath a fresh cap, she was not sorry. Antoine Devos was waiting to introduce her to a dark, rather vivacious looking woman. 'This is Miss Betty Kenstein,

Nurse. She'll be our replacement for · Sister Thérèse.'

'How do you do,' Fleur smiled, but immediately decided she could not imagine herself enjoying the same relationship she'd had with Thérèse.

'So nice to meet you, Nurse.'

'Miss Kenstein has worked in some of the largest training hospitals in California,' Antoine Devos explained. 'I'm sure much will be gained from your respective experience. Miss Hamilton is from England of course. She is a fully trained SRN and has been with us now for nearly two months.'

Miss Kenstein gave the Professor a flash of her perfect teeth as she smiled at him. 'That's very interesting. Just so long as our patients benefit, that's the main thing, wouldn't you say, Professor?'

In the coffee bar an hour later, Fleur was telling Moura of the latest development. 'I don't know how we're going to get on, Moura. She may be all right, but I'm really going to miss Thérèse.'

Moura's usually bright face nodded morosely. 'I know the feeling. One unpleasant person in this sort of set-up puts us all out. Everyone's so nice here.'

'I know it's not fair of me to judge, but there's something about that woman. You know, I'll tell you something, Moura. When there's a man around she doesn't want to notice another female. Oh well, I suppose it'll sort itself out. You probably all thought the same when I came!'

'We did,' Moura teased with a deceptively straight face. 'We thought the place would never be the same again, once we saw you!'

Fleur grinned. 'By the way, I'll meet you in the cathedral tomorrow in good time for the service. It's quite near my flat so there'll be no problem with transport.'

'Raoul's bringing a crowd of us in. The weather had better be good for Thérèse's wedding. Did you know that Matron and the Prof had been invited? Hope they'll come.'

Fleur finished her coffee suddenly, her spirits plummeting like a stone. 'Why not, if they've been invited?' she said weakly, wondering if *she* wanted to go now.

Moura flopped back in her seat staring into space. 'I remember one of the other girls doing the same, and the Professor made some excuse. Matron went, but . . . well, he's different. So damned haughty. He passed me in the corridor this morning as if he didn't know me.'

Saturday morning, pale sunlight filtered through the huge stained-glass windows of the cathedral of Saint Michael as Thérèse, radiantly beautiful in her grandmother's bridal gown of Brussels lace, stood at the altar and amid all the impressive pomp and ceremony was married to her Pierre.

In the large congregation, tears stabbed at the back of Fleur's eyes as she watched the heart-wrenching service, trying not to think of her own dreams which had been so cruelly ended. She focused her eyes on the unusual pulpit, carved from a single tree-trunk with lifesize figures of Adam and Eve—strangely enough, fully clothed! But at the sight of the bride and groom so confident and happy as they returned triumphantly down the aisle, her moment of emotion soon left her.

The reception was being held at one of the luxury hotels in the city, and in the milling crowd outside the church after the bride and groom had gone ahead, Fleur found herself detached from Moura.

'Have you got a lift, Miss Hamilton?' Antoine Devos, poised and smiling on the cathedral steps came towards her.

'Well, I did have, but . . .' she broke off, embarrassed.

'And you have now,' he grinned. 'Come on!'

Immediately she was struck by the change in him, so relaxed and friendly as they sped in his car across the city. His whole demeanour conveyed the festive air of wedding celebrations and he quickly drew the same response from her.

Still laughing at something he'd said about the staff from the clinic and what an interesting assortment of guests they made, they were soon part of the crowd in the banqueting room, where flowing champagne was making everyone very talkative as the bride and groom welcomed them.

Raoul suddenly appeared at Fleur's side, two nurses hanging on his arm. They seemed not to matter, for he said to her in a loud voice, 'You look utterly captivating, Fleur! Doesn't she, sir?'

Fleur was glad of the noisy babble of conversation going on around them. She prayed Antoine Devos had not heard the remark. But he had. His small talk with Matron ended suddenly, and he turned slowly, his eyes going over her, noting the coffee-brown silk suit and frill-necked shirt, small round hat with its sweeping ostrich feather and pale, high-heeled shoes—the outfit she had bought for her own honeymoon.

He gave an impish smile suddenly at Raoul, his silver-grey morning suit enhancing the lean, devilish attractiveness of him. 'Raoul, my lad, so far I've never given you much credit for good taste when it comes to the fair sex. But,' his gaze went back to Fleur, 'I certainly intend to from now on.'

'So I should think!' Raoul grinned, taking off unsteadily with the two girls.

Fleur had felt swift pink colour rush to her cheeks at the words from Antoine Devos. He was still looking at her now.

'Thank you for the compliment,' she murmured shyly, then realised his eyes were holding hers. Quite suddenly the noise and laughter died away, and for one brief moment Fleur almost stopped breathing. It was as if a veil had been pulled aside, revealing something tantalisingly unattainable by the fleeting expression in the depths of that dark blue scrutiny. And when the world steadied itself once more and silence was being called for the cake-cutting ceremony, she realised she was still trembling.

'Weddings can be something of an anti-climax, don't you think, Miss Hamilton?'

They had just returned to the hotel foyer after waving their goodbyes to the young couple, and Antoine Devos had tucked a hand beneath Fleur's elbow to propel her through the crowd to where they were trying to join their friends from the clinic. Fleur nodded agreement at his words.

'Yes, I always think these events would be better held in the evening. As they are in Egypt.'

But there was no time for further discussion. Another colleague claimed their attention and the party continued until, eventually, some of the guests began drifting away. Moura appeared to be getting more and more jolly. 'Hey, Fleur!' she squeaked excitably, 'A whole gang of us are getting together later tonight. Will you come?'

'Nice of you, Moura,' Fleur said, not too keen on extending the drinking session. 'I'll let you know later.'

But Moura was already in gales of giggles at a guest's remark and seemed not to hear her reply one way or the other. Fleur was chatting to several other nurses and Matron, when she noticed that Antoine Devos had ended his animated conversation with Thérèse's parents and was making his way towards them.

'Can I have a word with you, Miss Hamilton?' he murmured quietly, and promptly led her to a smaller lounge off the main foyer. 'I had to rescue you from all that noise. It is difficult to hear ourselves. Now, have you made arrangements for the rest of the day?'

Fleur's heart sank. Although this was her day off, he was probably going to ask her to go back on duty, as so many of the staff here looked incapable. Certainly those who had not been invited to the wedding would not be too keen to see them. 'Why, no, I . . .'

He broke in quickly and said with a rush, 'As you are virtually a visitor to our city, I wondered if you would care to do a little sight-seeing in Brussels before dark, and then perhaps we could have dinner?'

Her smile of relief and pleasure burst out before she could stop it. 'I'd like that very much!'

'Fine. Now, I suggest that we use first names for the rest of the day, Fleur. I'm sure Thérèse would want us to!'

Fleur smiled up at him. This man could really be quite nice when he tried. 'If you put it like that, Antoine, yes I agree!'

Still laughing, they walked across the wide frontage of the hotel to the grey Rolls. As Antoine unlocked the passenger door for her, out of the blue, one of the white Landrovers from the clinic skidded to a halt. A young houseman leapt out and rushed up to them.

'Thank God I've reached you, sir! Couldn't get you on the phone.'

'What's wrong?'

'There's been a bad car accident. I think you should come straightaway!'

CHAPTER FIVE

ANTOINE Devos glowered angrily at the house-man's worried face. 'Good God, man, isn't there someone competent enough at the clinic to deal with a car accident, instead of bothering me now?'

Embarrassed, the man shook his head. 'I'm very sorry, sir. But the accident . . .' He hesitated fractionally, then said, 'It is your wife.'

The effect of the man's words were electric.

'My wife! Why the hell didn't you say so in the first place!' Antoine Devos glanced at Fleur in the passenger seat beside him. 'You must come also, Miss Hamilton. We shall probably need extra help.'

'Yes, sir,' she murmured, all previous informality gone as the car glided forward followed by the Landrover. The Professor's face in profile was almost that of a graven image, only a small nerve working at the temple betrayed the shock of the news he had just received as they sped along the road and away from the city.

Nevertheless, the atmosphere in the car became increasingly tense with anxiety as they neared the clinic. Fortunately the journey was not hampered by weekday traffic and already they were in sight of the graceful white stone building between the trees.

'I thought it best to say nothing to anyone at the

hotel,' Antoine Devos muttered in a low voice. 'In any event they would not have been much use.' He looked across at her suddenly. 'I am sorry to have dragged you away like this.'

She shook her head. 'Please don't apologise. I only hope things are not as bad as they sound.'

But they were. Much worse in fact. As soon as they stepped inside casualty, the registrar surgeon, Emile Vaumont, left one of the curtained cubicles, his usually genial face serious. 'It's your wife, Jeanne.' The man looked anguished. 'Little Marie-Claire also, I'm afraid.'

At these words, Antoine Devos—so far in command of himself—seemed to blanch. He accompanied his colleague to where the victims of the car crash had been brought in. Casualty Sister Schultz appeared at that moment giving Fleur an odd look, for she was standing there in all her finery. 'You must have been to the wedding also,' she announced rather disapprovingly. 'You must get changed, I think.'

Like an automaton, Fleur hurried to the common-room. In a daze she scrambled into uniform, unable to erase from her mind the sight of Antoine Devos' face when he learned of the double tragedy that had hit him. Ten minutes later when she returned to casualty, it was in time to see a trolley being wheeled away. Fleur glanced at the still figure of a woman lying on it. Long, silver-blonde hair, a pale, arrestingly beautiful face, bruised and swollen eyes closed. And on the other side of the room, Antoine Devos, white coat thrown over his morning suit, standing immobile, observing the progress of the trolley until it disappeared into the lift and out of sight.

'How bad is it?' Fleur asked quickly, going to his side.

He ran a hand over his broad forehead. 'Apparently my wife had been drinking as usual—she conceded the fact when confronted by my housekeeper on the wisdom of taking Marie-Claire for a drive. But it did not stop her. We live apart, but she has a right to see the child,' he added flatly. 'They crashed into a tree. Jeanne's injuries appear to be superficial. But Marie-Claire!' his voice shook slightly. 'Just six years old and now having a brain scan for head injuries!' he said bitterly, tensing his hands behind him to prevent the trembling she had seen. 'I was no use to them in there just now. I could not help.' His voice shook. 'I am devastated.'

'There's little you can do at the moment, Professor,' Fleur said gently, a great rush of sympathy overwhelming her. 'I think you should sit for a while in the doctors' private rest-room over here. I'll fetch you some tea, and as soon as they have finished the scan I'll send the registrar to you.'

Like a man in a dream he did as she suggested. In the quiet of the room he slumped down into a chair, staring glassily ahead of him.

As Fleur hurried away towards the small canteen for visitors, by sheer chance she saw Sister Kenstein.

'Hi, Staff, we have the Professor's wife on third. By the look of her it's sure gonna take her a few days to dry out. She's damned lucky to have got away with only a few superficial cuts and bruises. Have you heard how the little girl is yet?'

'No,' Fleur said quickly. 'Any time now I should think.' She took the tray from a waitress. 'Excuse me now, Sister.'

When she returned to the doctors' rest-room, the registrar and another houseman were already there, talking in low tones with Antoine Devos over some X-rays they were examining. She left the tray of tea and went back to casualty just as Sister Schultz emerged from the lift.

'Marie-Claire, Sister. How is she?'

The older woman shrugged philosophically. 'It is uncertain. A hairline fracture of the skull maybe. A broken right tibia and unconscious for . . . how long we do not know. She is with the ortho-paedic surgeon now. You are on the third floor, yes?'

'Yes, Sister.'

'Then perhaps you will go up and see Sister Kenstein about the child's room. She will be in plaster.'

When Fleur went into Sister Kenstein's office she waited until the American woman looked up from where she was writing the day report, then said quietly, 'On duty, Sister.'

'Why is that, Staff? When I saw you in the canteen, I wondered why you were there.'

Fleur seethed at the woman's deprecating manner. 'Professor Devos said he would need help with his two relatives, Sister. As you know, we are short-staffed because of the wedding.'

'I'm aware of that aspect, Nurse Hamilton, yes.'

She sighed heavily. 'I shall have more to say about this later.'

'Yes, Sister.' Still shocked with the afternoon's events and furious at this new member of staff's attitude, Fleur bit back the retort that rose to her lips.

Kenstein looked at her coldly. 'Mrs Devos is in room 28, opposite Madame Conrad. Keep an eye on her, she's sleeping at the moment, but once she's told of her daughter's injuries she's likely to become overwrought.'

'And the room for the little girl?'

'She must be near at hand. Room four, I think.'

With the help of a junior nurse, Fleur busied herself about the pleasant room with its large windows overlooking the ornamental lake.

'Nurse, go to the linen cupboard,' she instructed the shy young Belgian, 'and fetch a cradle to keep the bedclothes from the patient's injured leg, and extra pillows please.' Briskly, Fleur rolled the bedclothes to the side of the bed for post-op reception. She checked that fracture boards, hot-water bottles and blankets were in place, and made sure that a tray containing bowls, swabs, tongue depressor and forceps stood on the locker. Should an emergency arise, oxygen cylinders and a tracheotomy set were near at hand.

At that moment one of the patients rang for attention, and Fleur had just identified the room from the number indicator in the corridor and despatched the junior to see what was needed, when the lift arrived and the porters brought the small, still body of Marie-Claire into the room on the theatre trolley.

The Professor and two other surgeons followed, with Sister Kenstein bringing up the rear. From the rigid expression on Antoine Devos' face, all trace of his earlier emotion was well under control.

Sister Kenstein and Fleur transferred the unconscious child to the bed after removing the hot-water bottles, gently settling Marie-Claire down, her face to one side and a towel beneath her chin. Once pulse and blood pressure were checked, covers smoothed and bed-sides pulled up and secured, the rest of the retinue left, leaving only the Professor with Sister Kenstein and Fleur.

For several moments he stood staring down at the inert little body and pale, delicate features, saying nothing. At length he said tonelessly, 'As far as we can tell there is no hairline fracture of the skull as we had at first thought, Sister.' He indicated the bulge of the plaster cast. 'They've done a good job on the leg. As it's a green-stick I don't think we have any worries there. But the one thing we don't know is how long she's likely to remain unconscious. I want Staff Nurse Hamilton here, to special her. Perhaps you'll make arrangements accordingly. I shall, of course, be here a great deal of the time myself. In fact I intend asking your hospitality for a room nearby so that I can snatch a couple of hours sleep.'

Fleur wondered if it was imagination when she saw a look of near-jealousy pass over Sister Kenstein's face, but it was quickly replaced by a dazzling smile with the Professor's next words. 'This state of affairs may last only for a day or two—we hope. I'd like *you* to give my wife all the necessary attention. Draw extra staff from elsewhere if you have to.'

'Yes, sir. Thank you,' she said, filling in Marie-Claire's headboard.

Antoine Devos moved away from the bed suddenly, his tall, athletic body seeming to sag as if with the burden he carried, his features etched with tiredness and the aftermath of shock. He glanced at Fleur, the long-lashed eyes heavy with fatigue. 'Go downstairs and get yourself a meal, Staff, I'm sure you need something. Just give me a moment to go and change now, will you?'

'Yes, of course,' Fleur murmured, wondering why her fickle senses should choose that moment to visualise the lean, muscular frame of this man as he threw off the clothes in which he had looked so rakishly attractive such a few short hours ago.

When he left the room accompanied by the Sister, Fleur remained at the child's bedside. She could hear Sister Kenstein's strident voice, no doubt already complaining of the injustice to nurses in general when one agreed to return to duty on her day off!

An almost imperceptible movement of Marie-Claire's head brought Fleur's attention back swiftly. Fascinated, she stood looking down at the daughter of the man who was such an enigma to her.

Fair curls tumbled over the pillow as the closed eyes quivered slightly, silky lashes brushed the rounded cheeks, one of which bore a dull red mark which would be a livid bruise in a day or so.

Summer freckles sprinkled the small, snub nose. On the turned-down sheet a chubby hand lay, dimpled and soft, making Fleur's heart contract with pity when she thought of the six-year-olds she knew, boisterous and so full of life. And yet this little girl could easily have been killed by a drunken, thoughtless mother who professed to love her child.

Taking the pulse on the radial artery and counting respirations for a full minute, Fleur recorded the rates on the chart. In less than ten minutes the Professor had returned. He glanced up at the headboard, nodding. 'Pulse rate a hundred and ten. So far, so good.'

'You wanted her on a quarter-hourly check?'

'Yes, that's fine. You get along.' Clad in sober grey now, he stood over the bed, looking down at the still figure upon it, hands thrust deep into the pockets of his white coat. 'My God, I can hardly believe any of this,' he said bitterly.

Fleur made some inadequate reply as she left the room, but he didn't hear. His eyes were riveted again to that small, precious form.

In the dining-room, Fleur found it difficult to eat. Eventually she gave up and took a cup of coffee to an easy chair near the windows. It was there that Moura found her. Moura, not yet changed from her wedding clothes, was looking worried and obviously dealing with a lingering hangover.

'We've only just got back,' she said anxiously. 'What a terrible thing to happen! I see the Professor roped you in to help. What's the gen now?'

Fleur gave her the details, then looked at her

watch. 'Sorry, Moura, I'll have to be getting back. This whole thing could have been much worse I suppose. But once Marie-Claire has regained consciousness we'll all feel better.'

'You're specialling, is that right?'

'Yes.'

Moura raised her eyebrows. 'Why you, I wonder?'

Fleur felt herself blush. 'Simply because I happened to be on hand at the time, I should think.'

Moura grinned fiendishly. 'I bet old Kenstein's nose has been put out of joint.'

'I don't think so. She's looking after Mrs Devos.'

'I see. Well,' she said, as Fleur stood up to leave, 'the whole clinic's buzzing with the news. So the eyes of the world are on you!' She sang out with a pseudo-American accent.

Moura's particular brand of humour set Fleur's teeth on edge at times, she thought as she hurried back to third. When she arrived at room four, Matron was there with the Professor. Fleur hesitated on the threshold.

Matron glanced round. 'Come in, Staff. I was saying to the Professor, you had better have a room here instead of going back to your flat to sleep. Just while this emergency lasts, of course.'

'Very well, Matron.'

The kindly woman gave another anxious survey of the small patient, placed a comforting hand on Antoine Devos' arm, and left the room.

'I'll go in and see my wife now that you're back,' he said, almost reluctantly, to Fleur.

'How is she?'

'Under sedation at the moment. According to Sister Kenstein she frequently becomes restless and then starts throwing herself about the bed. I didn't want to drug her too much with the alcohol she still has in her body. But she'll recover, no doubt about that.'

When he had gone, Fleur took up her position by the child again, at the same time speculating on what it was that had really broken up this small family, and sighing deeply at the unhappiness love seemed to bring.

A constant twenty-four hour vigil was kept on Marie-Claire. The strain was telling. Everyone was waiting to hear that the VIP patient had emerged safely from the coma she was in. Professor Devos was at her side continuously, hardly taking any of the two hour allocation of rest that Sister Kenstein decided was a reasonable enough rota to which the nursing staff could adhere.

At least the pressure of caring for Mrs Devos had eased somewhat. But she was giving rise to concern and the Professor and Emile Vaumont had called in a heart specialist, who had recommended she be moved to another hospital for stringent tests. The patient herself opposed it roundly.

Fleur, although tired with anxiety over Marie-Claire, which seemed to grow rather than diminish, was relieved not to have been nursing the selfish young woman. From all accounts she had been pampered since birth and was very unpleasant because of it.

Relief came on the fourth evening after the accident. The night staff had just come on duty and

Fleur had finished making Marie-Claire as comfortable as possible. She was replacing the bed-sides when suddenly the child's eyes appeared to flutter.

Fleur's heart hammered with hope and excitement. Instantly she rang the buzzer that in turn activated the bleeper Antoine Devos carried. Within seconds he rushed through the door. 'Yes?' he said, going straight to the child.

'Her eyes, sir! I'm sure she almost opened them. There, you see!'

Again the lids moved from the eyes, as though heavy with sleep . . .

With a smothered gasp, Antoine Devos bent swiftly over the child, letting down the bed-side and smoothing her brow. 'Marie-Claire! Marie-Claire!' he murmured softly, *'Ma belle chérie, mon petit . . .'* The endearments were repeated over and over again until at last the silky lashes lifted from the pansy-blue eyes briefly, and almost on a sigh the child's lips moved. 'Papa?'

Antoine Devos stared at the child as if in a dream, then moved slightly when Fleur replaced the bed-side. For a few moments he buried his face in his hands and when he looked up, the lines of pain mixed with emotion revealed the true man to Fleur as he whispered brokenly, 'I think . . . I think she is going to recover, after all.'

'I'm sure she is, sir,' Fleur whispered gently. 'This is only the beginning, tomorrow she will be even better.'

The tall, proud man whom she thought to be so unfeeling and hard, the woman-hater, embittered because of a wife who had let him down, momentarily cast off the role as he looked down at her. The expression in his eyes seemed as though he had been to hell and back.

'Thank you, Miss Hamilton,' he murmured softly, taking her hand and pressing his firm lips to it, sending her nerve ends racing. As he raised his head, the dark swathe of hair falling to his brow enhanced the blue depths of the eyes, at last no longer like raging, turbulent seas. A calm had settled, if only temporarily, as he gazed at the rose blush on her cheeks, the tremulous mouth.

It was then that Sister Kenstein chose to enter. Being female she had sensed, if not seen, the incident—but said nothing when the Professor turned to her joyfully with the good news. She listened, making all the right responses, but Fleur had the feeling that this woman was stoking up resentment against her by the bucket-load.

Nevertheless, nothing could prevent Fleur's lightness of heart as she went downstairs to dinner that night. She was convinced that this was the beginning of Marie-Claire's recovery. There was something different about the way she was sleeping when she left her, and Antoine Devos had said the same. Her heart missed a beat or two when she recalled the way he had kissed her hand. In seconds it had completely renewed the deep attraction she had felt for him at the hotel party. Again the words of his note, *Thank you for that wonderful night*, burned into her brain. Frustration and guilt swamped her at the prospect of never really knowing all the facts of that occasion. Try as she might, it was a near impossibility to imagine the Professor actually planning to spend the night with a strange girl. Then she chided herself for such naivety and decided that this man, with whom she seemed to be so inextricably linked, remained as much a mystery as ever.

Marie-Claire was now beginning to sleep more restfully and continued to make progress. Each time she awoke there was some positive improvement in her awareness. A week later she was no longer on intravenous feeding, and one afternoon gave her father a sweet smile and asked for 'Danielle'—which according to the Professor indicated that she was now well on the road to recovery.

'Who is Danielle?' Fleur asked, as they drank tea, which Sister Kenstein had taken to serving them each day. Only, Fleur thought darkly, to keep an eye on them!

'It's a favourite rag doll she's had ever since she was a baby. I've asked my housekeeper to send it from home, but she tells me it's gone missing. Which isn't surprising, since Marie-Claire had it with her on the day of the accident.'

'I suppose nothing else will do?'

'No, 'fraid not,' Antoine Devos smiled as the door opened and Sister Kenstein appeared, face chalk-white. 'Mr Vaumont's on the phone, sir!' she said quickly. 'It's bad news from the hospital, I'm afraid.'

Ten minutes later, when the Professor had left the building, a shocked Sister Kenstein announced that Jeanne Devos had died of a sudden heart attack. She was visibly shaken.

'My God, I don't believe it! That poor guy just looked like stone. He's gone racing off like a bat out of hell. Apparently Mrs Devos had been her regular petulant, sulky self and insisting upon getting up. She went against advice; ten minutes later they found her dead! Delayed shock from the accident. It does happen.'

'Oh, no,' Fleur whispered, appalled, her thoughts immediately going to Antoine Devos. After all, the woman had been his wife.

The news rocked the clinic. But a day later the Professor returned, hard-faced, to work and gave instructions that his daughter was not to be told of recent events by anyone. He appeared to pick up the threads of his life at the clinic with admirable control, and apart from sympathetic felicitations from the staff, carried on as before.

On his return he addressed Fleur in a flat monotone. 'I suggest you return to normal hours of duty now, Nurse. I still want you to special Marie-Claire by day. Leave the rest to the night staff.'

It was quite an experience going home, Fleur thought contentedly as she let herself into her flat at last. She had done some shopping on the way and for the first time in days felt relaxed enough to resume her existence as it was before the accident.

Yet, although she enjoyed the leisure, Fleur felt strangely restless, as if she had no right to be in the flat, but should be watching over Marie-Claire. Or even helping Antoine Devos in some way. Despite trying to harden her heart against him, as a nurse she knew that reaction to the extra shock he had sustained could not be delayed indefinitely. His icy composure was unnatural and already she had overheard him enquiring after some of his patients and trying to catch up with the backlog of work, which would not help.

That evening she attempted some letter-writing, but still the six-year-old's bright little face asking for Danielle came between her and the notepaper. In the end, Fleur decided to set to work on a vague idea she'd had for the child, one which might help until something better caught her attention.

Busying herself with two thick white linen tea-towels, she attacked them boldly with scissors, pins and thread. She stuffed the pieces with washable filling she had bought while shopping and soon had a reasonable basic shape about thirty centimetres long. Donating one of her large silk scarves to the cause, one hour later 'Antoinette' was reclining on the corner of a chair. Her embroidered face, large black eyes and curling lashes were positively coquettish. With two bunches of bright yellow woollen ringlets and a smiling rosebud mouth, she seemed quite happy. A vision in lilac and gold, even Fleur felt the effort was worth the trouble.

Reporting next morning for duty, a business-like air of bustle on third indicated that the staff had endured a bad night. There had been admissions from two car accidents, plus the fact that it was Thursday, and one of the Professor's operating days.

'Staff, I want you to go to the theatre this morning,' Sister Kenstein said, as they went over the night report. 'There's a man coming up from casualty with a fractured pelvis, and a boy with broken ribs. There's also a straightforward appendicectomy. I'm off duty this morning. Leave Marie-Claire to the other nurses now and concentrate on these theatre cases.'

'Yes, Sister.' She hesitated, then said quickly, 'Don't you think one of the juniors should go down to the theatre instead of me?'

'Good Lord, no! I'm telling you to go, Hamilton. Isn't that clear?'

By eleven o'clock that morning, Fleur had prepared all three patients for their operation, and collected X-rays and papers. She glanced at the corridor clock hurriedly. Just time to slip in and see Marie-Claire. The child's face lit up when she entered the room.

'*Bonjour, mademoiselle*,' she lisped shyly, enchantingly pretty in a pink-frilled, long-sleeved nightie.

'*Bonjour*, Marie-Claire! You are looking very well today. What a lovely book you have there!'

She nodded solemnly. 'Papa bought it for me,' her quiet, grave little voice whispered. 'But,' she added sadly, 'I do not like the new doll. It was in a big box. Her face is not . . . nice.'

Fleur had noticed the abandoned wrappings containing the expensive Parisian doll dressed in satins and lace. In comparison, how could Antoinette ever hope to see the light of day?

'That is a pity, Marie-Claire,' she said brightly, 'but perhaps you will get used to her. I must go now. I'll come and see you again as soon as I can.' She disappeared through the door, at the same time noticing that the child had looked down-hearted. But with the morning's work still facing her, those thoughts had to be diverted to other things.

In the ante-theatre the porters left Fleur with the first of her patients. She was about to wheel the trolley forward when Antoine Devos appeared, still gowned and masked, peeling off a pair of rubber gloves and discarding them as he glowered at her. 'And why are you here, Staff?'

Fleur's heart sank. So he hadn't forgotten her last appearance in the operating-theatre after all, when he'd hinted she was unfit to be there.

'I . . . Sister Kenstein instructed me to do so,' she stammered, embarrassingly aware of Theatre Sister and Raoul Millaise listening through the open doors of the theatre.

Antoine Devos yanked the mask from his face. The hard, stony features were more chiselled than ever, all previous softness gone. Menacingly he stood over her. 'I take it you are capable of accepting orders and carrying them out?' he thundered.

Her face burned at the cutting sarcasm in his voice. Why did he unnerve her this way? She swallowed the sudden dryness in her throat. He was like an enraged lion playing with its victim before delivering the last stunning blow. 'Why, yes.' Her eyes flashed back into his, signalling her own fury at his attack.

'In that case, kindly return to third and send another nurse down here to take your place.'

She found her tongue and heard herself say, 'But Sister Kenstein's off duty, she . . .'

'Exactly!' he broke in, crashing his fist down onto

a side table.' And you are in charge, so what the hell are you doing in theatre?'

'I'm sorry, I don't understand!' she retorted hotly. 'I took my orders from Sister, and there are four other reasonably competent nurses on third. What am I supposed to do?' Her voice rose on a note of near hysteria; tears of frustration trembled on her lashes, making her eyes brilliant as diamonds. Her lovely breasts heaved at the injustice of his accusation and she clenched her fists to her sides while awaiting this arrogant male's next broadside.

But instead there remained just one long, terrible moment of complete silence. Fleur could hear her own ragged breathing while the cold man before her, whose powerful chest beneath the green gown was as steady as a king of the jungle, still waiting his moment to spring. The blue-black eyes glittered, mesmerising Fleur. Her heart thudded like a drum. Then, quite suddenly, he put up a hand to his eyes with a groan, muttering hoarsely, 'This is no time for such a discussion. Very well, Staff, we'll carry on. But I shall want to see you later.'

Fleur would never forget that morning. The leaden atmosphere of disapproval seemed to invade the theatre. Of the assembled staff, Raoul and Theatre Sister came in for the sharpest edge of the Professor's tongue. The anaesthetist and Raoul had exchanged guarded glances throughout the operations and feelings ran high at the iniquitous remarks being flung about by the Professor.

Although he worked smoothly with his usual calm, methodical skill, words fell like acid from his lips. The appendicectomy turned out to be more complicated than at first supposed, and when at length Fleur returned with her last patient to third and was able to take her break for lunch, the entire unreality of that terrible morning seemed set to stretch endlessly on.

CHAPTER SIX

WHEN Fleur returned from lunch Sister Kenstein was busy with the young teenage appendicectomy patient, Nicole LeClerque. Having come round from the anaesthetic she was now vomiting badly, and at the same time being scolded by Sister for not avoiding this particular state of affairs. One of the junior nurses had been despatched for fresh bed-linen, and Fleur seized the chance to slip into room four to see Marie-Claire again, determinedly closing her mind to the threatened confrontation with Antoine Devos.

To her surprise, the child was lying propped up by pillows, cheeks flushed and traces of tears on her face. As soon as she saw Fleur her weeping began anew and she said plaintively, 'Nurse Fleur, I did not think you were ever coming back to see me!'

Fleur felt a stab of anxiety at the child's obvious distress. 'You must not think that, *chérie*. I've been very busy this morning. I am here now and you must not upset yourself.'

'Sister told me that you could not come.'

Realising there was more to that statement than met the eye, Fleur tried to take the child's mind off the subject, tidying the bed and endeavouring to revive her interest in the bevy of gaily-coloured books she had on her locker. But Marie-Claire turned her face away. '*Non*.' She shook her head, lips quivering again. 'I want Danielle.'

'I'm not too sure where she is at the moment,' Fleur said truthfully. 'But if you are a good girl and promise not to cry any more, I'll come back again in a few minutes.'

'Do not be long, please!'

Fleur left the room with the express intention of first collecting Antoinette from the cloakroom to give to Marie-Claire, and then of mentioning the child's unease to Sister Kenstein. She had only just entered the office when Professor Devos came striding in also. His face made Fleur quake. Even Sister Kenstein looked taken aback at his sudden appearance, with the black brow and scowling countenance menacing, but to her credit she managed a smile. 'Professor?'

'Leave us a moment please, Staff,' he snapped curtly.

Fleur left, and her heart was pounding. Perhaps it was just as well that one of the patient's buzzers went at that moment. By the time she had returned from the sluice and helped Madame Conrad to the patients' sitting-room where she held court each day, looking formidable in dark glasses, Fleur had lost the first shock of nervousness at the sight of the Professor.

She knew, too, that he would want to see her shortly and the sooner the better to get it over with. Again she was needed by one of the patients, and it must have been about a half an hour later she was passing room four and, to her astonishment through the open door heard Marie-Claire sobbing.

Fleur rushed in, but stopped in her tracks to see Antoine Devos, the bed-side down, holding his small daughter tightly in his arms as she tried to tell him she wanted Nurse Fleur. The Professor left the child and drew himself up to his full height, looking at her with the cold, ice-blue gaze she was coming to know so well.

'Here you are, Staff. As you know, I wanted to see you,' he said shortly. 'I have told Sister Kenstein in no uncertain terms that I did not wish her to put you on theatre duty away from caring for Marie-Claire during the day. Maybe I did not make myself quite clear at the time, but I think I have now. This child is no ordinary patient, she is my daughter,' he said pompously. 'And as such I intend seeing that she has every attention and consideration I can give her.'

He shrugged. 'She has become used to you. I do not wish her to be spoilt, but she needs reassurance—especially now that circumstances have changed.' He lowered his voice but Marie-Claire was already reaching for a book, looking as if all her problems were over. 'From now on, Staff, you continue on duty here only, unless I say otherwise. Is that understood?'

'Yes, Professor.'

When he had gone, Sister appeared in the doorway. 'I won't have my staffing arrangements disrupted in this way,' she said tight-lipped. 'I'll be seeing Matron pretty shortly.'

Fleur said nothing except to acknowledge the words addressed to her, and she wondered how much longer this impossible situation could last.

Before she went off duty that afternoon, Fleur placed a large paper bag on Marie-Claire's bed, saying, unthinkingly in English, 'Close your eyes and open them when I tell you!'

The child responded immediately with an excited laugh.

'Clever girl!' Fleur said, mentally complimenting the small, exclusive *lycée* that Marie-Claire attended. 'You understand English very well.' She lifted Antoinette out and sat her on the bedcovers. 'Now, you may look!'

Marie-Claire's large, violet-blue eyes flew wide when she saw the doll. She stared at it soulfully for several seconds and Fleur's heart sank. Then, with a small, ecstatic clap of her hands, she snatched Antoinette up to her, hugging and kissing her out of all proportion to her value, which Fleur knew was the least important thing of all. And to her relief the doll was obviously a good enough substitute for Danielle. '*Merci, mademoiselle! C'est très jolie!* Oh, thank you, Nurse Fleur!'

'No more tears now, *chérie.* I will see you at tea-time.'

Feeling weak with relief that Antoine Devos had more or less explained his rage in the theatre that morning, Fleur spent part of her afternoon off in the heated swimming-pool. On several occasions she had gazed longingly at the glass-domed area, where green palms around the pool made it reminiscent of a jungle clearing.

Moura had often suggested they went, but this particular afternoon the last thing Fleur wanted was to talk. She needed to be alone with her thoughts. There were several members of staff in the water, and as soon as she slipped into the inviting blue depths, her troubles seemed to fall away like an abandoned cloak. One or two of the young housemen gave her an appreciative smile as they soared off the high diving-boards, but apart from that, Fleur was left entirely alone and it was heaven.

Half an hour later, climbing from the water and standing on the side adjusting a shoulder strap of her yellow bikini, someone came up from behind and a familiar voice said, 'Don't tell me you're just leaving?'

Fleur swung round with a laugh. It was Raoul, clad in black briefs—and his eyes were going over her from top to toe. 'Afraid so, Raoul, I'm on duty again.'

'Can you spare half an hour?' he pleaded, resting his hand on her shoulder. 'Just for a cup of coffee, perhaps?'

There was a small coffee bar for swimmers across a short corridor. Fleur flung a towelling jacket around her shoulders. 'OK then. It'll have to be a cool one!'

He put his arm round her as he held the swing-door open to allow her to pass through. She did not know what made her glance upwards suddenly. The wide glass observation panel was part of a restaurant where one could eat and overlook the pool at the same time. There was no one else there, just one dark, arrogant face looking down at her and Raoul.

Antoine Devos turned and walked quickly away.

For some ridiculous reason the incident caused a vague pang of guilt to run through Fleur, but she forgot it as soon as she returned to duty.

Sister Kenstein was in a terrible mood and lashing out all round. When Fleur arrived, she pointed to the clock. 'Five minutes late, Staff. Don't forget to make it up before you leave tonight.'

In the rush of tea and bed-making and with drugs to be given out and bed-pans collected, the Frenchman with the fractured pelvis was complaining of pain and kept bursting into hysterical tears. In his room, Fleur bustled about the bed, putting on a professional face as she returned the thermometer to its holder. 'Come now, *monsieur*. Your wife will be visiting you quite soon this evening. You do not want her to see you this way. I will ask Sister for some pain-killers, and then you will smile for me, yes?' She adjusted his pillows and gave him a sympathetic grin of encouragement.

He nodded, smiling weakly. '*Merci, merci . . .*'

By the time Fleur got home that evening she again blessed Ann Morley for letting her have the flat. It was such a relief to get right away from the clinic. The telephone cut across her thoughts. Hoping it was not Raoul she picked up the receiver. 'Hello.'

'Miss Hamilton?'

Fleur's heart lurched. It was Antoine Devos. 'Yes. Good evening, sir.'

'We are off duty, Miss Hamilton, no formality please. I should like to come and speak to you if I may?'

'Here?' she croaked. 'In my flat?'

'Well, that's where you are, isn't it?'

'Yes, but . . .'

'Miss Hamilton, it is important that I speak to you.'

'Very well.'

'In about a half an hour then. It is Rue De La Grosse Tour, I think?'

'Yes,' she said faintly, 'that's right.'

She put the instrument back on its base, realising she was trembling. Half an hour, he'd said. Wildly she looked around the flat, but the moment of panic quickly subsided. It was a question of dividing half the time exactly between herself and the sitting-room. Twenty-five minutes later, things looked reasonably presentable.

As for herself, how could she know? In the mirror she saw only a stranger with wide, nervous brown eyes, shining brown hair, and cheeks already warm with trepidation. Her black woollen polo-necked sweater and scarlet corduroy skirt, were the first thing she could think of to team with black low-heeled pumps and cream lacy tights. She'd brushed her hair into shape, used a dash of lip gloss and a spray of perfume, but as for knowing if she looked presentable? The question had to remain unanswered.

In her hurry she had at least remembered to switch on the coffee-pot, and as the buzzer rang and she told Antoine Devos to come up, she realised with heart-plumetting desperation she'd had no time to work out what it might be that he could possibly want to see her about so urgently that evening.

She waited for him at her open front door. When he appeared at the top of the stairs he looked as informally handsome in the soft leather jacket and grey slacks with blue cashmere sweater, as he had the afternoon he rescued her from the rain. With a small, slightly self-conscious grin he shook her hand. 'Forgive me for this, Miss Hamilton, but it was the only way.'

'Do come in,' she said breathlessly, wondering why she was such a fool that he should affect her in this manner. 'Let me take your jacket.'

His bigness seemed to fill the room. She had switched on only the large, old-fashioned standard lamp, but with two fireside chairs drawn up before the electric fire it looked quite welcoming.

Seeming to relax suddenly, he said, 'Coffee smells good.'

'Would you like some now?' she asked, hoping it would ease her embarrassment.

He followed her out to the kitchen, watching her every movement, but gradually her heart rate slowed down. He carried the tray to the sitting-room and when they were both settled, and there was only the odd flurry of rain against the windows, he sat back in his chair and said reflectively, 'It is about my daughter.'

'Marie-Claire? Nothing's happened has it?' she said anxiously.

He gave a small laugh. 'No, thank God. She is doing very well. So well, in fact, that I do not wish her to stay in the clinic any longer. The surroundings are not right when my child is recovering.' He raised a dark eyebrow, looking at her thoughtfully. 'Sister Kenstein is a good nurse, but she is the kind who has not a very big heart—non-medically speaking, that is!' He smiled. 'She does not understand how much Marie-Claire means to me. Since my wife died she needs more care than ever.' He stared morosely into the fire. 'And I do not wish to tell her of Jeanne's death yet. I want her recovery to be nearer completion.'

'Your wife loved the child though?'

He took a deep and bitter sigh before answering. 'I had come to the unhappy decision long ago that Jeanne was far too selfish to love anyone but herself. Since Marie-Claire outgrew babyhood and became a pretty child, it flattered Jeanne to have her at her side as an ornament and reflection of her own beauty. But what is beauty when it is ice-cold? I think even my daughter in her childish way was already beginning to see that the love she craved was not there.' He broke off suddenly, as if distracted at the truth of his words. Again, Fleur felt a great surge of sympathy go out to him as he sat, long legs straddled, blue woollen tie loosened at the collar of his check shirt.

A woman would have had to be made of stone to reject the love this man offered. Fleur remembered again the touch of his lips that night in the London hotel. He looked now as he did then, a dark wing of hair across the brow, blue eyes deep with shadows, long lashes almost feminine against the angular masculinity of his face. Only the strong cleft in his chin emphasised the slight cragginess of the features.

She pulled her glance away from him, thrusting a hand through her hair restlessly. Wasn't she still getting over her own love affair? Yet, being so aware of this man and the magnetism of his attraction for her, she pondered as she had several times lately. Had she had ever really been as much in love with Tom as she'd once imagined?

'Marie-Claire is a lovable child,' Fleur said quickly, realising his eyes had been upon her while awaiting her reply. 'And . . . and most of them at her age adapt to new circumstances with almost indecent haste.' She smiled, trying to lighten his abstracted expression.

'Too true. Later she will have to learn that thngs have changed,' he said flatly. 'Fortunately, Madame Leon, my housekeeper, and her husband, have been with us for some years, they are two excellent people. Marie-Claire is very fond of them and . . .' he shrugged expressively. 'It has to be that way.' He straightened up in his chair, laughing into her eyes suddenly. 'But I imagine you think I have strayed from the point. Perhaps you realise by now I have something I wish to ask you, Fleur?'

She blushed at his use of her name. 'If I can help?'

'I wonder if you will spend say, a few weeks looking after Marie-Claire at my home in Chaumont-Gistoux, outside the city. It is about half an hour's drive. Normally, of course, I take Marie-Claire into the *lycée* each day, or a neighbour does, if necessary. Unfortunately that will not be yet, but I ask nothing of you except that you nurse her there, although there will be little needed once she has a walking plaster. Nevertheless, I want her convalescence to be as pleasant as possible and I know that she is happy with you and will make a quicker recovery. Of course, I shall arrange for the radiographer to attend, and those sort of things.' He paused, his face earnest and serious, then added quietly, 'It would help me a great deal, Fleur, if you would do this for the child.'

Fleur's mind was reeling. A hundred and one things tumbled through her brain all at once. 'But,' she stammered, 'how could I leave the clinic just like that? It would be inconvenient for the rest of the staff!' She floundered, as he allowed a slow grin to spread across his face.

'Fleur, you may have forgotten. I happen to be the owner of that particular clinic. I think you could safely leave those details to me.'

'But Matron . . .' she persisted.

'Ah, the dreaded Matron-complex all you nurses have! So far, I have spoken to no one about this. I wanted to know your feelings on the matter. If you are willing to take on this duty for me, I will see Matron tomorrow.' He leaned forward suddenly, touching her hand. 'Do not look so worried! You must understand that I can arrange everything.'

He glanced at his wrist-watch. '*Mon Dieu!* I have the feeling you have not had time to eat since you got home from the clinic! What an insensitive fool I am.' His face was so worried suddenly, it was Fleur's turn to break into a smile.

'I'm quite certain the same applies to you,' she said. 'But it was better to discuss business first, and we . . . I . . . need a little time to think about it.'

He stood up. 'Of course. I understand. Let me take you to a café?' He said simply.

Fleur had the feeling it was not what he really wanted. Nothing had been resolved about his amazing proposition, and a crowded eating place at this time of night might not be conducive to such decisions.

'It is kind of you, Professor, if you prefer that. But I have bread and pâté here. Salad too, I believe.' She laughed, as again he followed her out to the kitchen while she opened the fridge door. 'Even a half-bottle of wine. Would that be OK?'

As she stooped down to the shelves, she glanced over her shoulder at him. His eyes were unfathomable as he watched, and when she withdrew the bottle he put out an arm to help her up. The sudden closeness of him, the faint tang of expensive cologne and leather, stunned her senses. His breath fanned her cheek as he held her for one brief, yet endless moment. The smouldering in his gaze was back again and seemed to reduce her to a state of weightlessness as his arms held her like steel. Then they fell from her.

'It sounds a feast fit for a king!' he said abruptly.

With legs still shaking, Fleur laughed and closed the fridge door. The heart-stopping moment was an exact repetition of the one she had known with him on Thérèse's wedding-day. Why was she such a fool?

During the meal their conversation reverted to hospital affairs, but when Fleur had made fresh coffee and they were sitting once more in the pleasant intimacy of the fireside, Antoine Devos resumed the topic obviously uppermost in his mind. 'If you would come to the house, Fleur, I do not think you would be unhappy.'

She had the feeling of being drawn down into a vortex from which there was no escape. It was as though, when he looked at her, the pleading she saw there was more than she could deny. Hesitantly she looked down at her coffee-cup. 'Well, if Matron agrees, perhaps I'll think about it.'

'Good! I'm sure you will not be sorry, and I shall not be ungenerous with time off.'

'Thank you.' Her velvety brown gaze met his steadfastly. 'But I have not said I would agree to it yet.'

'That is understood,' he said, yet his face seemed released from the strain it had shown when he first arrived. 'One other thing. Your boy-friend, the one with whom you swim?'

'You mean Raoul,' she supplied non-committally. 'But haven't you just said there will be time off? So I imagine that side of it will be satisfactory.'

'I see. Yes, of course,' he said curtly.

It irritated her that he should have mentioned Raoul. Surely it was hardly worth mentioning, unless he only wanted to let her know he had seen her in the pool with him? 'I presume my off-duty time would be my own affair?' she asked coolly.

'Indeed. I only wanted to ensure that you were not deprived in any way.'

The icy sarcasm that had returned to his voice was more normal to her. It was not difficult to see that now he imagined her to be on the brink of accepting his offer, all the dashing charm had been switched off. Before she could think of a suitably sharp reply, there was a sudden officious tap on the flat door. With a polite, 'Excuse me,' Fleur hurried to see who it was.

When she opened the door, Madame Guiot stood there, her small body bristling, bright bird-like eyes darting over Fleur's shoulder to receive confirmation of her suspicious gaze.

'*Mademoiselle*,' she snapped, 'my guests cannot leave until your : . . *friend* removes his car.'

The abrupt appearance of Antoine Devos quite took Madame Guiot's breath away as he gave her a dazzling smile. 'My sincere apologies, Madame. I am Professor Antoine Devos. It was necessary that I discuss something of great importance with Staff Nurse Hamilton, rather than waiting until she arrives at my clinic tomorrow.'

The effect created a complete transformation of Madame Guiot's face as she smiled up at him. 'Forgive me, monsieur. Of course, I understand perfectly. I will tell my friends you will be but a few moments.'

Antoine Devos turned to Fleur with a con-spiratorial smile. 'She was going to be awkward.'

'You are very diplomatic,' she murmured, hand-ing him his jacket.

He made a small grimace, then shook hands with her. 'Goodnight, mademoiselle. Thank you for your hospitality.' His eyes remained cool, despite the firmness of his grip before he let her hand go. 'I shall see you tomorrow when I have had further discussions on this matter.'

Bemused, she nodded. 'Yes,' she said vaguely, then had a sudden rush of blood to the head. 'Professor! Why did you want me in particular to look after Marie-Claire? It could have been any of the other nurses.'

A faint warmth touched his expression as he said with slow deliberation, 'Because, Miss Hamilton, it is very strange, but at times there is something about you—just a little something—that reminds me of your friend, Sally Hull. *Au revoir.*'

CHAPTER SEVEN

NEXT morning Fleur was in the office with Sister Kenstein. Everywhere shone with cleanliness, fresh flowers and late autumn sunshine as if in readiness for the consultants' rounds. As Fleur listened to the American drawl discussing post-operative patients from the day before, only the voice seemed to strike a discordant note against the beauty of the surroundings.

'The young girl, Nicole, who had the appendicectomy. She's causing one hell of a fuss. To make our task even more dandy she has boyfriend trouble and apparently no longer wants to live. I'm just putting you in the picture on this, Staff. Night Sister Feraud said she's been threatening to kill herself, so let's make sure she doesn't put on a performance here. Be firm with her. None of that soft, prissy talk, otherwise we're gonna have trouble on our hands.'

'And the two other operation cases?'

'The Frenchman had a quieter night,' she said, turning a page of the report book.

'The boy with the broken ribs will probably be up and about in a few days. No problem there.'

She glanced at Fleur suddenly. 'Despite Professor Devos' instructions, I'll be needing your help watching over Nicole. Leave Marie-Claire to me.'

'But, Sister, he . . .'

Sister Kenstein held up her hand. 'Whilst I am in charge of third, I'll give the orders, Staff. I've had a word with Matron and told her my feelings on this. I like Professor Devos, he's a very nice guy, but I do not approve of his daughter receiving so much extra attention. Obviously I know why, but I still don't agree with it, and I shall tell him so again.' Her eyes softened. 'We had quite a long talk yesterday, and I'm pretty sure he saw it my way in the end.'

Fleur kept quiet, wondering how this tied up with the Professor thinking he had made himself quite clear to Sister Kenstein! One of them was definitely labouring under the wrong impression and, thought Fleur with a small wave of panic, she had no desire to be around when they realised it. For the rest of the morning it was almost restful conducting the consultants around and taking Marie-Claire to the X-ray department. Just lately she felt that she was living on the edge of a volcano.

At lunch-time, Fleur sat with Moura at a table for two. She couldn't help confiding her fears about Sister Kenstein, but did not intend mentioning Antoine Devos' plans for her to nurse Marie-Claire at his home. In fact, in the brilliant light of this rather fantastic November day, she found it hard to believe the events of the previous evening had actually happened at all. Moura's eyes nearly popped out of her head at the news.

'You mean she's really going against the Prof's wishes for his daughter?'

'That's how I read it.'

Moura attacked her food with gusto. 'God, she's a crazy woman, I'm telling you! The Prof won't stand for that. You remember saying she was different when there were males around? Well, you were dead right! Even old Raoul and Guy have found her eyes focused on them like laser beams! They're scared stiff of her!' she laughed, pushing aside her empty plate.

'I'm not surprised,' Fleur said, toying with a delicious boeuf bourguignon.

'Coming to the disco tonight, Fleur? You said you've got an evening off, didn't you?'

'Yes, but . . .'

'Oh, come on lassie,' Moura said, breaking into her homely Scottish lilt. 'Stop worrying, will you, and have some fun!'

Fleur tried to get out of the invitation in case Antoine Devos endeavoured to contact her. 'Thursday's not a very good night there, is it?'

'Och, of course it is! Any night's a good one when you're in the mood! I'll round up some of the gang.'

Back on third, the afternoon exuded a pleasant somnolence that often developed, especially when Sister Kenstein was off duty. Everywhere was so quiet; most of the patients had visitors and in the patients' sitting-room Fleur found Madame Conrad sitting in her usual place, but quite alone. She looked up expectantly through her large, dark, fashion glasses, upon which she had insisted at great expense, to comply with medical approval. She smiled at Fleur. They always addressed each other in English these days, and Fleur had grown quite fond of her.

'Hello, Staff. Have you come to see me?' she

said, elegant as ever and sitting straight as a ramrod in a high-backed chair.

'Yes, I have, Madame. I had a feeling you were not having any visitors this afternoon. But my goodness, you are looking fine!'

'You beautiful young girls!' she shrugged. 'How easy it is for you to say that! But I must not get depressed—at least that is what my consultant says. But what does he know of a woman's feelings when she loses her looks? Still,' she brightened, 'I have to tell you, my dear, that I am going home with my daughter very shortly now that her town house has been completed. I had no intention of staying here so long, but I was persuaded. Now she stells me she is taking me away for a long holiday on the Côte d'Azure.'

'That is just what you need, Madame! You have a very good daughter.'

'I do not deny it. But my son!' the old lady turned down her mouth. 'He is a good man, but has many worries with his wife. He is getting a divorce soon. Did you know that Jeanne Devos was a friend of hers?' she said with a deprecating snort. 'I know I shouldn't speak ill of the dead, but a fine couple they were. Neither of them deserved good husbands. Clothes, parties and men, that was the all-important thing!'

Fleur sighed. 'The world is not perfect, Madame.'

The woman's direct gaze met hers. 'Professor Devos should have someone better. If I were fifty years younger I would hurl myself at his feet!'

Fleur laughed. 'No woman should do that, Madame. He is only a man!'

'Ah, there you are you see! You are sensible as well as beautiful, Nurse. The young have everything these days!'

After sending her nurses to tea, Fleur looked in on Nicole LeClerque. She was resting and appeared to be asleep, her long dark hair spread dramatically over her pillow—but the white face was stained with tears. Fleur closed the door softly with a small sigh. Why did love cause such heartache? With no ready answer, she withdrew to the office in case any of the departing visitors should wish to speak to her. Marie-Claire was sleeping also, and Fleur welcomed the chance to settle at the desk and write up some notes before going off duty.

It was as Sister Kenstein returned to the office that Fleur heard the whine of the lift again. Brisk footsteps approached, then came a curt rap on the door as the Professor flung it open, his face the usual inpenetrable mask, no doubt concealing his thoughts about the plan he was going to put to Sister Kenstein.

'Good-evening,' he said, with formal curtness. 'Which of you is going off duty now?'

'I am, sir,' Fleur said quickly.

'Very well, carry on.'

With a feeling akin to escape, Fleur murmured a faint goodnight in the direction of Sister Kenstein's implacable features and hastened away with all speed from the low buzz of voices which had already begun in the office.

In the nurses' common-room, Fleur washed,

changed her uniform for street clothes, and was leaving when she literally bumped into Moura in the doorway. 'Hi, Moura,' she said without much enthusiasm.

'Fleur! I was hoping to meet you down here. Look, I'm on duty tonight after all, but we'll call for you about eight thirty, OK?'

'I'm still not sure, Moura. I wanted to wash some smalls tonight . . .' Fleur trailed off, feeling that her excuse was weak.

So did Moura, apparently. 'Look, I'll give you a final ring once we get into town tonight, Fleur. The others are looking forward to seeing you. I know Raoul is.'

Fleur grinned at her friend's enthusiasm. 'OK, I'll let you know for sure later.'

Once out in the city, Fleur did some shopping in one of the *galeries* near her flat. The shops were bulging with merchandise, and again she remembered that Christmas was now only weeks away. She wandered around some of the fascinating antique shops, looking at old maps, engravings, silver and crystal.

Reluctantly, at length she made her way to the supermarket for provisions, after which she lingered over coffee in one of the many terraced cafés and watched the glistening lights over the city before walking home. On arrival she was stunned to see the familiar sight of Antoine Devos' grey Rolls Royce parked outside her flat.

With rapidly beating heart, she opened the street door. In the entrance hall, Madame Guiot appeared, face flushed with pleasure as she said, 'I thought I would offer the Professor a glass of wine while he was waiting, Miss Hamilton.'

Antoine Devos strolled into sight, his eyes looking over the older woman's head at Fleur. 'I should like to speak to you now if possible.' He turned to Madame Guiot, saying with delightful, old-world charm, 'Thank you so much, Madame. You have been most kind.'

Once inside Fleur's flat, Antoine rounded on her instantly. 'Where have you been?' he demanded angrily, his captivating manner completely abandoned.

'Professor,' she said coldly, furious at his domineering attitude, 'shopping, if you must know! It's the only time I get.'

He snatched the basket from her and dumped it on the table. 'You knew I'd be contacting you again . . .' He trailed off, giving a small, contrite, sideways grin, running a hand through his hair. 'Of course, I'm sorry. May I sit down?'

He still wore the immaculate silver-grey pin-stripe suit he had worn at the clinic earlier that day and his blue-striped shirt and tie looked a little awry around the neckline. There were lines of tiredness on his face and near-desperation in his eyes. Despite her annoyance, Fleur could not help a brief pang of sympathy for this man who seemed to have everything, yet nothing . . .

She indicated one of the chairs, then busied herself switching on lights and the fire and drawing curtains. 'You must think me inhospitable, but I really wasn't expecting visitors,' she said, throwing off her fur jacket. 'Would you like coffee?'

He rubbed a hand over his lean jaw where already a dark shadow of stubble was beginning to appear. 'No, thank you.' He paused as if to gather his thoughts. 'No, really.'

She sat opposite him, waiting.

'Women!' he suddenly exploded. 'Women are the very devil!'

His words were so unexpected that Fleur broke into a gale of laughter. Then, realising her mistake at the seriousness of his face, immediately apologised.

'Forgive me, Professor . . . I . . . I wasn't assuming that to be the cause of your visit here,' she said, still unable to keep the amusement from her eyes.

Fortunately she saw a matching light of mirth in his own. 'No, not entirely.' He gave a wry smile. 'I think you must be good for me! I know I'm taking everything rather seriously at the moment. But Sister Kenstein and Matron seemed to have conspired against me as far as I can see. Do you feel the same way, Fleur?'

Her name had slipped again from his lips, and she felt the give-away colour rush to her cheeks. Although she could guess, she said calmly, 'About what?'

'Removing Marie-Claire from the clinic and having you nurse her at my home.'

Fleur glanced down at her soft, slim hands. 'I haven't had a lot of time to give it a great deal of thought. What I do know is that Marie-Claire does not appear to be all that happy, even though she knows nothing of her mother's death. She seems to be fretting over something.'

He leapt from his chair and prowled about the room as he spoke. 'That's exactly it! The child is eating her heart out for the background she knows, the home and security she needs at this particular time. Surely, even though she is having every attention in the clinic, for a small girl it is too much to ask that she endure the shock of the accident without some severe reaction sooner or later! This is why I am so worried.' He stopped suddenly, swinging round to her. 'Will you come out with me for a drink?'

She remembered Moura's invitation.

'Well, yes, if you'll excuse me while I make a phone call?'

'Of course. I'll go down and wait in the car.'

Strangely calm, Fleur rang Moura and said she was unable to join them that evening after all. Thankfully her friend said little, except to hint darkly that she would discover why, later.

With a few seconds to herself, Fleur quickly brushed her already shining hair and applied eye make-up, and peach gloss to her lips. Drawing on high-heeled leather boots, which blended with the full peasant skirt and cream polo-necked sweater she was already wearing, she felt confident enough to deal with Antoine Devos' changing moods.

In ten minutes they were seated in a bistro just off the Grand Place, and by the stuffed deers' heads gazing down at them from oak panelled walls, it was not difficult to guess why it was named 'Le Cerf'. Antoine Devos had ordered wine from the welcoming waiter who seemed to know him. Considering their late arrival in the crowded place, they were more than lucky to be seated in a secluded corner.

'Hope you like the local brew,' he smiled. 'It is not possible to get anything stronger here unless one becomes a member of the *club privé*, then for a nominal fee you are entitled to your well-earned drink!'

Fleur shook her head. 'Thank you, it doesn't worry me.' She put the glass to her lips. 'This is fine.'

They talked politely for a while about the local characters in the bistro, who occasionally burst into song to the accompaniment of accordions. The noise allowed them to converse easily without being overheard, and it was not long before Antoine looked serious again. 'I asked you to come out with me this way, partly so that you should not be worried by Madame Guiot and what she may be thinking.'

Fleur's lovely eyes looked a warm gold in the softly mellow light. She lifted her lashes, her gaze meeting his. 'Thank you, but my conscience is clear so why should I worry?'

He lit a cheroot, waving the smoke from her, his eyes almost languid suddenly. 'That is one of the reasons I admire you English nurses, Fleur. You are so practical.' His eyes swept over her with a discernment she was quick to notice. 'As well as attractive.'

Paying compliments to a woman was as natural as eating and drinking to him, she thought fiercely, glancing away from his gaze to the gingham-covered table. 'I imagine it's the practical side of things we're here to discuss,' she said pointedly, but with a smile. 'I gather then, that Matron and Sister Kenstein did not particularly like your idea for Marie-Claire?'

'They didn't say it outright, but it wasn't hard to know what they were thinking. They had quite obviously discussed the matter beforehand. I am surprised that Matron was lured to Sister Kenstein's train of thought. She wasn't too happy about you leaving a gap in her staff for a while, either. But, of course, she could hardly refuse.' He leaned across the table towards her. 'The main point is now, what *you* think about it. Not Marie-Claire. I'm convinced home is best for her, but for yourself? Do you think you could cope for a few weeks in this way?'

Fleur knew then the true purpose of his visit. She stared at him. He evidently expected her to say yes. His eyes already conveyed self-confidence, bordering on arrogance. Some impishness within her wanted to hold back. A weak acceptance was going to make him all the more sure of himself. The ridiculous thought had even struck her that the whole thing was a plan to get her on her own, especially when he had said out of the blue that she reminded him of Sally Hull. Was he playing a cat-and-mouse game?

'*If* I accepted,' she prevaricated, 'I would, of course, need to know more about the whole thing.'

'I can take it then that this is not a refusal?'

His low, almost caressing, voice made her cheeks burn and pulses race. 'Not entirely.'

'I can explain anything further you need to know. Go ahead, ask anything you wish.'

She played idly with the stem of her glass. 'Marie-Claire is of the greatest importance. Would she be quite happy with this arrangement?'

'I'm absolutely sure of it.'

'When should I have to take up the job?'

'On Monday. That gives you the weekend to organise your own affairs. I'll see to it that Matron and Sister are made aware of the plan tomorrow morning. Take the weekend off. Monday morning be ready with your suitcase for someone from the clinic to collect you. I shall have an ambulance ready to transfer Marie-Claire with you. Emile Vaumont has promised to visit my daughter regularly. I'm also arranging X-rays, special treatment and so on. Madame Leon, the housekeeper, will look after you and I think anything else you may need you have only to ask. That includes usual time off each day and one day a week.'

He paused suddenly, as if he had an inkling he was assuming too much, then went on. 'I should be so relieved to know that you will accept this temporary transfer.'

Fleur kept her eyes averted from the man who seemed to dominate her when she was with him. He attracted her and yet she detested the haughty image he was so quick to convey. He was still awaiting her answer, and quite suddenly she thought of Katy at Hilldown and how they had laughed about Fleur setting off on her adventures.

'First stop, Brussels!' Katy had giggled. And wasn't it just that? An adventure from which she could move on if it didn't work? She had more than enough money these days with her clinic salary, and the bank account which had been added to regularly for when she and Tom set up home.

And it was at that moment, with a sudden burst of revelation, she fully realised the astounding fact. She was released at last from the dreaded word— jilted! Tom meant absolutely nothing to her any more!

The thought gave her immense satisfaction as she glanced up quickly and met the eyes of the man opposite her. She didn't care, her thoughts were joyous. She no longer felt that having been jilted, no one else wanted her. Although she had never voiced it, the thought had haunted her.

Now she said coolly, surprising herself, 'Very well, I'll nurse Marie-Claire and trust that Matron will approve my leaving for a while.'

A small nerve jerked in his temple as he closed his firm hand over hers. 'I can't tell you how grateful I am, Fleur.'

'It is my job,' she murmured, embarrassed that just the fleeting touch of his fingers could make her blood race so easily.

He ordered coffee for them. By now the bistro had become hot and noisy, yet Fleur had the feeling it had been easier to talk here. Antoine Devos almost took the thoughts from her head.

'I don't think we could have talked as we have anywhere else but a place like this. Nobody knows us, nobody cares. The best possible background for serious discussions.' He smiled, looking pleased.

When one of the huge clocks in the Grand Place

struck eleven they left, and once in the car were back outside her flat in minutes. In the half-light he left the engine running as he turned to look at her. 'I'm sure you won't regret this break in your time at the clinic, Staff. All good experience, wouldn't you say?'

She noticed how formality had crept in again. 'I agree,' she said curtly.

'Just one other thing, bring your uniform. I think children are impressed by them.'

Or was it simply to remind her of her place in the family home? He helped her from the car and they said their polite goodnights, shook hands and, with a hint that he might ring if necessary, parted company.

Upstairs, while showering and undressing for bed, Fleur was determined not to lie awake into the small hours pondering on the rights or wrongs of her decision. Her revelation over Tom had given her an entirely different outlook on things, as well as herself, she thought as she drifted into sleep.

Next morning she rang Moura and made an arrangement for the four of them to have an evening out. She gave no further explanations as she would have done normally, and Moura did not ask for any. Maybe even she had realised Fleur sounded more confident, more self-possessed than usual. She hoped so.

The rest of the day was spent tidying the flat until it shone. Madame Guiot had a young Moroccan girl living in with her who did all the basic cleaning, but Fleur wanted to be sure that everything was in its place before leaving.

In the car that evening, Moura let it be known that everyone already seemed to know about her transfer. 'I wouldn't be in your shoes for anything, love!' she said with a shudder. 'Just imagine being closeted in some barn of a place with *him* for days on end!'

'Moura, I'm going there to do a job, not wander about the house.'

'I do not think you will be happy,' Raoul said soulfully over his shoulder.

'It's only for a few weeks, what are you all making such a fuss about?' Guy said abruptly. And it was quite the most sensible remark of the evening, Fleur thought, as they went into a Chinese restaurant. Later they danced at the disco, then returned to Fleur's flat for coffee. One hour later when they left, Raoul hung back while Moura and Guy went out to the car. He took Fleur in his arms. 'I shall be jealous of Antoine Devos,' he murmured, kissing her passionately, and Fleur drew away quickly.

'Raoul, please! I must go.'

'I shall ring you, wherever you are,' he muttered flatly. 'I am very attracted to you, Fleur, you know that, don't you?'

Eventually, pleading tiredness, she was alone at last and flopped into bed, falling asleep immediately.

Sunday evening she received a short, business-like call from Antoine Devos, saying he would meet her at the clinic at noon on Monday, and Matron would want to see her before she left.

*   *   *

By Monday morning Fleur had attended to everything. After telling Madame Guiot of her change of plan and that she would be calling at the flat weekly, Fleur picked up her suitcase and went down to her waiting taxi, which she had decided on instead of the tram.

In the reception hall no one was about. Leaving her hospital cape on a chair and smoothing down the sleek, white uniform dress and cap, Fleur knocked and entered Matron's office in answer to her call. Lisa Hauptmann smiled. 'Good-morning, Miss Hamilton. Do sit down.' The grey eyes seemed to penetrate Fleur's calm demeanour, but the words were kindly.

'Now, how do you feel about nursing Marie-Claire? I'm sure you are competent enough for the job, but are you quite happy about it? You have not been with us very long.'

'Yes, I should like to take it on, Matron.'

'Good. I realise it is a difficult situation. Professor Devos has expressed the wish that you do so, and it makes things a little complicated if you were not in agreement. Had you been genuinely disinclined, of course, I should take the matter further.'

Fleur could sense the admirable control with which Matron was displaying the iron fist in the velvet glove technique. In every word it was just possible to detect the hint of disapproval. 'Thank you, Matron. I shall do my best for Marie-Claire, and return to third when necessary.'

Matron looked reasonably satisfied. 'I shall, of course, be replacing you if possible, but once the

Professor's daughter has recovered sufficiently I will get in touch with you.'

A brisk tap on the door curtailed any further discussion and Antoine Devos entered, giving them an impatient glance. 'Shall we go, Miss Hamilton? If everything is satisfactory with Matron, that is?'

'Indeed, Professor,' came the unsmiling reply.

CHAPTER EIGHT

TWO HOURS later, the ambulance conveying Marie-Claire and Fleur, with Antoine Devos driving ahead, arrived at the house in Chaumont-Gistoux.

The journey had been comparatively short, but Marie-Claire was fretful one minute and over-excited the next, and by the time they had turned into the long drive between tall pine trees, her little face was quite flushed.

Two male orderlies from the clinic took the child gently from the vehicle under the supervision of her father, and it was not until they entered the interior of the house that Fleur realised several people waited to welcome them.

'Madame Leon! Nurse Fleur is coming to stay with us. Look, here she is!' The small girl, eyes bright with happiness, was obviously overjoyed at being home.

Madame Leon, a plump, comfortable-looking woman whom Fleur had seen once or twice during visiting times, was aware of Marie-Claire's over-emotional state and said softly. 'Yes, yes, *mon petit*. All in good time you will tell us everything.'

A small, bald-headed, dapper man at her side was introduced as her husband, and two other young girls as Madame Leon's domestic help.

Fleur was only conscious of going through a large, square hall, ascending a wide staircase and going on to an upper landing that was on three sides of the hall like a minstrel's gallery. As they stopped at one of the bedrooms where the door stood open, Marie-Claire clapped her hands. 'This is my room! My very own room, Nurse Fleur!'

Mr Vaumont had already arrived at the house and now he and the Professor, with Fleur's help, soon had Marie-Claire comfortably settled in her perfectly prepared bed. Antoine Devos was checking that everything he'd ordered to be brought from the Clinic was at hand, and by the time they had finished, the afternoon light was fast fading.

Marie-Claire was soon drowsy with excitement now that she was actually home. While the Professor stayed with his daughter, Emile Vaumont said to Fleur outside the room, 'She'll be fine, Staff. But tomorrow I think we should have another X-ray of that leg, just to make sure. We have portable equipment erected in the bedroom next door, it can be wheeled in when it's wanted.'

Antoine Devos joined them just then, his face pleased. 'She dropped off to sleep, in sheer relief, I should think.' He smiled at them both. 'Do come down to the study, I believe Madame Leon has organised tea.'

An hour later when Fleur returned to her charge, she was already wide awake again and talking as if she'd never stop. 'Can I show you all my toys, Nurse Fleur, please?'

Fleur was sponging the child's hands and face before dinner and smoothing the bedcovers. 'Tomorrow we shall do all kinds of things, Marie-

Claire, but you have to go to sleep early tonight. It has been a very exciting day for you.'

'Did Papa say that?'

Fleur smiled. 'Yes, he did . . .'

'Did what?' The Professor stood framed in the doorway as though he could not believe Marie-Claire was actually there.

'Did you say I have to go to sleep early tonight, Papa?'

He crossed the room, and sat gently on the side of the bed. 'I certainly did. And when I go to the clinic tomorrow, you must be very good and do everything Nurse Fleur tells you.' He glanced at the doll clutched in Marie-Claire's arms. 'Hello, and who is this young lady?'

Marie-Claire planted a large kiss on Antoinette's vermilion cheeks, handing her over to her father. 'She is Antoinette, Papa. She is my very own now that Danielle has gone away.' The child settled the doll with a motherly air into the crook of the Professor's arm. 'I love her. Nurse Fleur made her for me.'

Antoine Devos turned his head to look at Fleur, his blue eyes amused and yet deeply appreciative as he said with studied thoughtfulness, 'Nurse Fleur is very surprising.' He looked back at his daughter with a large grin. 'Do you think she would make one for me?'

Marie-Claire burst into a peal of childish laughter. 'Oh, Papa! You do not want a doll! You are so silly!' They hugged each other lovingly, and after a little more teasing Antoinette was returned to share the invalid bed. During this exchange

Madame Leon had arranged a light meal for the child on her bed-table, and Antoine Devos suggested he show Fleur her room, which had a connecting door with Marie-Claire's.

As they entered, Fleur could not resist an exclamation of sheer delight at what she saw. The dominant feature was the bed, a small four-poster topped by a white lace canopy and below, a matching bedspread. Drapes of white organdie graced the windows, and the fitted carpet of apple-green was repeated in a paler shade by the silk wallpaper. White brocade boudoir chairs and couch held apple-green satin cushions, and the rest of the furniture blended with mirrors and gold leaf detail.

'You approve?'

Fleur almost jumped at the deep voice beside her, she had been so entranced with the sheer, unadulterated luxury confronting her. 'It's absolutely charming,' she murmured, slightly breathless at the close proximity of Antoine Devos in the privacy of his home.

'I hope you will be comfortable here.' He nodded to another door beyond one entire wall fitted with mirrored wardrobes. 'The bathroom is in there. You will see later.' Through the open door Madame Leon was encouraging Marie-Claire to eat, and he smiled.

'I think I shall see that dinner is served a little later tonight. It will give you time to unpack. Would eight o'clock be suitable?'

'Thank you.'

Once Marie-Claire had eaten, it did not take long before she was sound asleep and settled for the night. Fleur was glad to relax in the comfort of her room. But the appeal of the rambling old house made her eager to see the rest and the grounds in which it stood. Only recently she had learned that it was known as the Mill House, and had a great water-wheel that sent a crystal clear stream gushing through the garden. From the little she had seen so far of the house and estate it was a sumptuous blend of old and new.

When the dinner gong rang, Fleur went downstairs wondering if Mr Vaumont would still be there. But apparently not, for Antoine Devos was already in the dining-room when she entered and the meal was set for two. 'Do come in, Staff,' he smiled, pulling out a high-backed chair for her.

'Thank you.' She was very conscious of her uniform and his renewed formality. The meal bristled with his excessive politeness, which served only to increase her unease.

Once Madame Leon brought in their coffee, she was relieved to hear him say, 'There will be some evenings I shall not be here. I'm sure Madame Leon would be delighted then with your company, or if you wish, you may dine earlier upstairs with Marie-Claire.'

She sipped her coffee, trying to appear as she should in her professional role. 'That will be fine. I'll let Madame Leon know. Perhaps you would tell me the off-duty time you wish me to take during the day?'

His eyes were in shadow from the soft illumination over the portraits hung around the room, and she recognised his face had a strong family resemblance. 'Tell her exactly what you want. She is expecting to help in any way she can.' He lit a cheroot, his casual dress of woollen shirt and silk cravat giving him a slightly informal air. She wondered if he had chosen to dress this way because of her uniform.

'I gather Matron did not deal with you too harshly this morning?'

'No. She was very kind. Sister Kenstein was off duty, so I wasn't able to see her.'

He gave a languid shrug which said more than words. 'So long as you keep Marie-Claire happy, there is nothing else for you to worry about, Miss Hamilton.'

He glanced at the clock, pushing back his chair and rising to his feet. 'I'm sure you'll want an early night yourself. I'll be having breakfast in the morning-room tomorrow. Join me for coffee if there are any points to clear up.'

She stood up and he held the door open for her. 'Sleep well,' he said curtly, and went in the direction of his study, leaving her to return upstairs.

Fleur went into Marie-Claire's room trying not to think of her casual dismissal. The little girl appeared to be sleeping soundly, and it was with relief that she went into her own room, leaving the communicating door ajar. Eventually she went to bed pondering on how this whole assignment was going to work, but fortunately the problem did not keep her awake.

Some time later Fleur struggled through the mists of sleep thinking she heard the noise of a small cry. She threw on her blue silk dressing-gown and hurried into Marie-Claire's room, noticing that it was two-thirty in the morning.

'I cannot sleep, Nurse Fleur,' the child mumbled sleepily, no doubt having been awake only a matter of seconds. 'I had a nasty dream. I couldn't run with this nasty thing on my leg.'

Fleur stroked back the fair, curly hair from the child's forehead. Her head was cool enough and pulse normal. She checked also that the leg plaster was not causing any swelling of the toes and they were a good natural colour.

'Look, *chérie*,' Fleur said softly, 'I'll go downstairs and get you a drink of nice warm milk. How would that be?'

'*Oui, merci, mademoiselle*,' she murmured drowsily, her voice already fading into sleep.

Nevertheless, just as well to get the drink, Fleur thought, as she padded barefoot through the silent house and downstairs to the kitchen. Whilst waiting for the milk to heat she gazed around the room at the sturdy French white-wood furniture, the row of iron cooking pots hanging from one shelf, gleaming copper from another. Herbs and dried flowers, and strings of onions hung to dry from a ceiling beam and a stoneware jug of bronze, mop-head chrysanthemums filled the air with a softly pungent aroma. The huge, scrubbed centre table with its rush place-mats all gave a homely air to an otherwise luxuriantly appointed work room.

Pouring the warmed milk into a beaker and standing it on a small tray, Fleur put out the lights and went through the door. She had not bothered with the light in the short corridor that led to the main front hall. There was moonlight enough from the garden and . . .

A short scream burst from her as she collided with someone. Strong arms steadied her, and she found herself looking up into the eyes of Antoine Devos.

'I'm so sorry!' she gasped in dismay as his hold dropped from her and she only just prevented the beaker from toppling over on to the tray. But not before it had already splashed milk on his silk Paisley dressing-gown. 'I just didn't realise . . .'

She broke off, mortified, as he stared at his spattered robe with a frown of annoyance on his face. '*Mon Dieu!* What is this?' he cried angrily.

It was like a bolt from the past. In that same instant she recalled those very same words on the awful day Sister Morton had raved at her and she had first collided with the Professor. Now, it had happened again! She began to tremble. Would he, too, remember the incident? She prayed that the anger still smouldering in his eyes was not going to erupt. Her soft brown curls were awry and eyes wide with nervousness as she said, 'I didn't hear you I'm afraid.' She awaited his tirade.

But it didn't come. His eyes were suddenly staring into hers, moonlight softening his face, seemingly all anger dispelled as he said, 'And neither did I hear you just then.' His quizzical note and wry, thoughtful smile, made her heart pound again. 'Come,' he said suddenly. 'I will carry the milk for Marie-Claire. I presume it is she who wants it?'

'Yes. Thank you,' Fleur whispered, sure that he

hadn't finished with her yet. Upstairs, Marie-Claire was fast asleep again. Antoine Devos smiled tenderly at the tousled head and the small, chubby arm clutching Antoinette.

'Everything is peaceful,' he pronounced, again giving Fleur a strange look as he closed the child's door softly, and they stood together on the upper landing. Fleur had been trying desperately to get herself together, not least her dressing-gown which persisted in slipping lose from its tie. She blushed as she said, 'I . . . I'll take the beaker back downstairs.'

But he stood in front of her, blocking her path. His masculine form was almost overpowering as he placed the palm of his hand on the door above her shoulder. The brown hair dropped elegantly over his brow, the lips curved into a familiar twist. 'Now, I remember,' he murmured under his breath so that she had to strain her ears to catch his words. 'I think this little scene has happened before!'

Her heart nearly stopped beating as she whispered with dry lips, 'I don't understand.'

'Well you see, I have learned that you English nurses may be very practical but you are not very good at balancing cups of liquid. But it has brought it back to me. One of those foolish incidents one instantly dismisses from the mind at the time. At Hilldown I recall another young nurse colliding with me; she tipped the contents of her coffee-cup onto my suit. It seems to be a national trait!' He smiled, his eyes twinkling.

Fleur nearly fell to the floor with relief. Again, he seemed not to recognise her as the culprit. She gave a light laugh. 'That is not a very good impression to have. I must apologise for the whole of our nursing fraternity, and perhaps you will not think badly of us.'

He dropped his hand from the door suddenly, and in doing so his fingers skimmed her cheek. The contact was like an electric shock going through her. She was devastatingly aware of his powerful chest where a gold chain hung. The lapels of his robe revealed the tanned, muscled torso, as he said softly, 'You remind me of Sally Hull, Miss Hamilton. I do not understand it.'

He moved a little from her, smiling a little. 'No,' he said thoughtfully. 'It cannot be.'

Fleur seemed incapable of speech, but gave a nervous laugh. 'It must be the uniform.'

'Perhaps,' he murmured, then his eyes took in her slight figure in the flimsy robe. 'I suggest you now return to bed to avoid a chill. I awoke thinking we had been disturbed by burglars, but this . . .' he lifted an eyebrow as he smiled, 'was much less unpleasant.'

Before she had time to answer him, he put a hand on her neck, spanning his fingers beneath her chin and kissing her as softly as a summer breeze. 'That is a thank-you for giving Antoinette to Marie-Claire and making her so happy. Goodnight, Miss Hamilton,' he said with sudden abruptness, in exactly the same dismissive tone he had used some hours earlier. But this time he left her mind in a state of tumult . . .

Next morning, wishing she could stay longer in the delightful green and gold bathroom with its white shag-pile floor covering, Fleur showered and dressed after peeping into Marie-Claire's room to find her still sleeping. She intended going to the morning-room to see Antoine Devos and tell him Marie-Claire had a good night. And that she needed her friends to visit her. Anything to obliterate the night before from her mind, and the memory of the turmoil it wrought within her.

She adjusted her cap carefully, taking a final glance in the mirror before finding her way downstairs. In the morning-room, Antoine Devos, immaculately dressed, rose to his feet when she entered, giving her a pleasant smile.

'Good-morning. I hope you slept . . . for what little remained of the night,' he said briskly, pouring her a cup of coffee and passing it to her.

'Thank you, yes. The patient also.' She smiled back as if they were addressing each other on third.

'Excellent.' He put his newspaper aside. 'Do you drive, Nurse?'

'Yes,' Fleur said, somewhat startled at the question.

'Good. There's a Mini here you can use. Leon will make all the necessary arrangements. Just let him know what you need.'

They talked over details of Marie-Claire's daily care, and as he left the table he said briefly, 'Any problems, ring me at the clinic.'

Fleur watched the grey Rolls disappear swiftly into the white mist that shrouded the gardens, and quite suddenly found herself looking forward to the day ahead.

Madame Leon turned out to be a kindly and

helpful companion. Through her, Fleur learned that Mill House at one time was alive with parties and visitors, but since his marriage *Monsieur* was not the same man 'He lives only for the little one,' Madame said sadly. 'Madame Devos broke his heart with her goings-on.'

Fleur thought it best not to have too many conversations on this topic. 'I see. How beautiful the house is, and very large, especially for a small girl.' She smiled. 'Has Marie-Claire many young friends?'

'Oh, yes. They will come to see her now she is back. Her father encourages it.'

'Good,' Fleur breathed a sigh of relief.

From then on the pattern of the days ran smoothly and easily. Fleur met Antoine Devos occasionally at breakfast, but not at dinner unless she wished to discuss something with him. She filled in her charts and progress reports, which she left on a small writing-desk in the corner of Marie-Claire's room for the Professor to inspect at his leisure. There was an easy, relaxed feeling about the house, as if each member of the household felt responsible for the smooth-running of it.

On the day that Emile Vaumont and the radiographer came, when they pronounced the fractured limb progressing satisfactorily, the Professor invited them and two other medical colleagues from the clinic to dinner. But apart from that one evening he seemed to spend most of the time at the clinic, or working until late into the night in his study.

Marie-Claire's friends arrived in an endless

stream and the house was usually alive during the day with the bright chatter of children or their mothers. Fortunately, Madame Leon was well able to control the situation.

Marie-Claire always took a nap during the afternoon, and each evening before she slept, Fleur had made a habit of reading Hans Christian Andersen stories to her, or *The Wind in the Willows*. 'I love it when you are here, Fleur,' she said suddenly one evening as she was being tucked down for the night. 'I don't want you *ever* to go back to the clinic.'

Fleur smiled at the beguiling little face. 'But what about all those other people who need looking after, Marie-Claire?' she said briskly, knowing that she was becoming too fond of the child.

'It does not matter,' she said grumpily. 'I do not want you to go.'

'Well, it's my day off tomorrow and you must be very good with Madame Leon.'

The bright, pansy eyes were suddenly alert.

'When will you come back?'

'After you are asleep in the evening.'

This conversation returned to Fleur's mind next evening when she drove the Mini carefully along the drive of Mill House and took the right fork to the large garage complex that housed four cars. Cutting the engine, she sat in the star-spangled darkness, thinking of the day she had just spent in the city.

She had gone first to the flat and had coffee with Madame Guiot, who listened with rapt attention to anything about the Professor. Later she collected more clothes that she needed, had lunch out and her hair washed and shaped at one of the exclusive salons that abounded in the *galeries*. After an early dinner she rang Moura, and lastly Raoul. He sounded rather surly.

'You did not telephone me earlier. I have missed you, Fleur. Had you let me know you had this day off I could have taken you out.'

Fleur smothered a sigh. 'Perhaps I'll get round to it next time, Raoul, but I'm very busy at Mill House, you must understand. Remember also, we are just friends.'

'It is not so with me.'

'I'm afraid it will have to be.'

Fleur shrugged the recollection away as she got out of the car, leaving it for Leon to garage.

Indoors Madame Leon greeted her warmly.

'Nurse! Have you had anything to eat?'

'Thank you, yes,' she smiled. 'Is Marie-Claire quite happy?'

The woman raised her hands. '*Mon Dieu!* She has been so high-spirited today! She also kept asking what time you would be back! But she is fast asleep now.'

After looking in at the rosy-faced young patient, Fleur threw off her coat in her own room, glancing at the hyacinth blue dress she was wearing, with its fitted bodice and tailor-pleated skirt; it was such a change to be out of uniform and the dress even seemed to enhance her hairdo. The hairdresser had been very adroit with shaping the curls to her neck, and a softly feathered fringe slid attractively forward on her forehead.

A gentle tap on the door interrupted her thoughts.

Madame Leon entered in answer to her call. 'I'm going to my flat, Nurse. Leon and I have our daughter and her husband visiting us for supper. Is there anything else you need?'

'No, thank you, Madame Leon. You enjoy your evening,' Fleur smiled. 'I shall probably have an early night myself.' Less than a half an hour later, when Fleur was writing letters home to Yorkshire and to Katy, the house phone rang.

It was Antoine Devos. 'I should like to see you in the long room, please, Miss Hamilton.'

Fleur replaced the receiver slowly, her heart beginning to pound. Was something wrong? Quickly she put the thought from her. It was probably just something to do with Marie-Claire.

Absently she checked her appearance in the mirror, applying a faint smudge of blue shadow to her eyes, which matched the dress, and a dash of rose pink gloss to her lips. After all, it was still her day off, she thought with a smile of bravado.

But as she walked gracefully down the thickly carpeted stairs, she wished that she felt as composed as she looked.

CHAPTER NINE

THE LONG room was exactly what its name conveyed, a beautifully proportioned salon that ran the width of the house. It was richly furnished in cream brocaded upholstery, with delicate china figurines set in shell-pink illuminated alcoves. Flemish oil paintings graced the pale silk walls, and the cream and white decor was a perfect foil for several crimson button-back chairs which gave a touch of gaiety to the cool opulence.

A pine-log fire blazed in the huge, natural stone fireplace. Sprawled full length on the Aubusson rug was Prince, the Great Dane. He opened one superior eye as Fleur entered the room, then closed it again with a contented sigh.

Antoine Devos, dressed in a wine velvet dinner-jacket, had been standing gazing into the leaping flames until he saw her reflection in the massive gilt-framed mirror above the mantel. He turned, giving her an effusive smile.

'Do come in!' he said, his eyes going over her. And she remembered she was no longer in uniform.

She glanced down at her petite figure. 'I'm sorry. There was no time to change.'

He indicated one of the couches by the fire. 'Why should you, you look enchanting! Can I pour you a drink?'

140

'A dry sherry, please,' she said as she sat down, wondering what this was all about. There was something different about the man tonight.

He placed her drink and his whisky on a low table before them, giving her a long, studied glance as he sat beside her. 'I thought it to be time we discussed how you are feeling here.'

That was one thing Fleur had learned about Antoine Devos. When he was tense his mastery of English was no longer impeccable!

'I am very happy looking after Marie-Claire,' she said carefully.

'And Madame Leon is good?'

'Yes,' she smiled. 'She is very helpful.'

He tossed his drink back in one gulp. 'That is fine.' He stood the crystal glass down thoughtfully. 'We are suddenly very busy at the clinic and I have had little time to know these things.'

'I understand. Has Sister Kenstein a replacement for me?'

'Yes, I believe Matron has arranged it.'

'I'm glad.'

'And what about your day off? Leon said you had used the Mini.'

'Yes, I was very grateful. I went shopping in such a short time, I think I should buy a car of my own to travel to the clinic later on!' She laughed, not realising how the mellow light from the outsize reading-lamps sprinkled gold across her hair and brilliance in her eyes. 'Wildly impractical no doubt!'

'Perhaps,' Antoine Devos said curtly. He sat forward suddenly to fondle the dog, and she was mesmerised by the width of his shoulders and the way his hair curved thickly behind his ears, just skimming the collar of his white evening shirt. He stroked the dog's head, saying casually over his shoulder, 'And what about Raoul?' He returned to his position against one corner of the couch, long legs outstretched, arms resting nonchalantly, waiting for her answer.

His overbearing stance and the sarcastic gleam in his eyes irritated her suddenly. 'And what about him?' she said crisply, her face taut with a slow, burning anger for allowing herself to be lulled into thinking that this man was far nicer than she gave him credit for.

'Come now, Miss Hamilton.' His smile was thin. 'The grapevine in the doctors' common-room is always flourishing.'

She jumped up, almost knocking over her sherry in doing so. 'That is entirely unnecessary, Professor! Whatever you've heard is of no interest to me. Neither should it be to you!' she said, her voice shaking with the unfairness of the suggestion. 'If this is all you called me down here for, perhaps you will excuse me?'

She knew she was on her high-horse, as Katy used to say. But she didn't care as she made to leave, head held high, cheeks blazing. But it wasn't going to be as easy as that. Antoine Devos waylaid her, gripping her arm like a vice, preventing her from going any further. Another hand was clamped on her shoulder and he spun her round to face him.

'I will *not* excuse you! My conversation is not yet

finished. You will listen to what I have to say, *ma belle!*' His eyes glittered and his mouth curved into a lazy smile that had cruelty in it.

'And I would add that it is not all I called you down here for. Firstly, we'll prove that you are no better than other women!' His arms tightened on her, his mouth fastened on hers with such ferocity it was impossible to cry out. She was only conscious now of the faint smell of whisky about him, realising too late that he had probably been drinking long before he had telephoned her. With a sharp intake of breath she tried to wrench her lips from his.

Yet even at such a moment she could not deplore the nearness of his hard, lean body against her own. The mass of conflicting emotions racing through her like liquid fire, were dominated completely by a primeval instinct, sweeping every other consideration aside. Still she could not move, although his hold had loosened slightly to rake through the silky mass of her hair with one hand. Then he tugged back her head until she was powerless to protect the quivering beauty of her mouth from his next onslaught . . .

His lips muttered hoarsely against hers. 'As I told you before, women are the very devil! This is all they are fit for!' His kisses seared her, and when his touch met the soft vulnerability of her breast, causing every nerve of her traitorous body to respond to him, it was like a shock wave knocking all sanity from her.

But quite suddenly it receded. He was staring like a man emerging from a terrible brainstorm. He pushed her from him onto the couch, where she fell against the cushions. With lips bruised and senses reeling she could only gaze with shocked disbelief at the outburst from this stranger—for that was what he seemed.

A fearful groan of anguish came from Antoine Devos as he slumped down on to the couch opposite her, burying his face in his hands. The room was so heavily charged with emotion, yet nothing could be said in that long silence of shocked incredulity.

Then he raised his head, his eyes almost as darkly violet as Marie-Claire's, the sultry expression through the thick eyelashes bemused with self-recrimination as he stared at her. '*Mon Dieu!* What the hell is happening to me?'

Fleur pressed her hands up to her cheeks in sudden consternation at the complete collapse of this man before her. His entire body seemed to sag momentarily. There was nothing she could say—or do.

He suddenly drew himself up with his usual military bearing and got to his feet, saying quietly, 'Make some coffee, Fleur, please. This damn fool needs a cold tap run over his head.'

It was some ten minutes later, while she set the coffee tray and prepared the black, fragrant liquid, that Antoine Devos returned, hair damply gleaming, face hard as granite. She carried the tray back into the long room, and he slumped down, saying nothing as he drank three cups right off.

Fleur's trembling limbs were at last beginning to feel her own again and her steady hands no longer betrayed the depth of feeling she had experienced with Antoine Devos. As she drank her own coffee, she tried to throw off the emotional storm he had set up within her. Yet as she looked at the man at her side, she knew he needed far more help and attention than she herself.

At length he placed his cup down slowly and carefully, giving her a long, discerning look. 'Firstly, will you accept my deepest apologies for the lapse, Fleur?' he said hesitatingly. 'It was unforgivable of me, and if you decide to walk out now I couldn't blame you.'

'I accept your apologies,' she murmured with difficulty because of a rapid swelling forming on her lower lip. 'And if you still wish me to stay with Marie-Claire, I will,' she heard herself say.

He nodded slowly, staring into the glowing red firelight, with Prince still asleep on the rug. Antoine Devos took a deep breath and some of the tension seemed to go from him. 'As you know, I've been under great stress. No doubt the reaction had to come. In a way I suppose I was a fool to invite you here so soon. But I thought of nothing but my daughter. Your presence seems to have brought things to a head.'

'But how?'

He skimmed long, beautifully manicured fingers through his hair. 'I suppose the quickest explanation is that since my wife gradually dissolved all the love I had for her with her numerous affairs, I have felt like this. In a strange kind of way all my dealings with women since then have highlighted aspects of those very things with which Jeanne taunted me. Women are made up of basically selfish characteristics. They lure a man to his doom, it is only later he sees what scheming creatures they really are!' He stared into some middle distance, as if he'd forgotten Fleur's presence.

'For example,' he went on. 'I mentioned Matron and Sister Kenstein, both of them revealing in their way. Matron obviously deplores weakness. She sees me as a weak male wanting my daughter at home. She only admires strength in all its guises. Sister Kenstein represents the vanity of females, and expects me to fall for her American brashness. For a start, she cannot leave an unattached male alone.' He lifted his eyes to meet hers. 'Vanity and weakness personified. Do you want me to go on?'

Fleur was rapidly recovering, as he seemed to be. 'Do, please. Tell me where I fit into this rogue's gallery?'

He gave a scornful twist of the lips as he looked at her. 'Yours is the most dangerous type of all. It represents everything that is the feminine allure, the fatal mixture of all that a man could desire in a woman. Yet, could he ever really be sure of her?' He lit a cheroot, taking his time to attend to it. 'When I have mentioned Dr Raoul Millaise and yourself, I'm sure you have misinterpreted my interest.' He shrugged. 'Maybe even thinking that I was jealous; how do I know? But it is not that. Dr Millaise is a young man who will go far in the medical world and I do not wish to see his career ruined, or even diverted, at this stage. I fell in and out of love during my training, but I possessed a streak of caution that warned me when to stop.' He sat back, blowing a smoke ring up to a crystal chandelier. 'I don't know if Raoul has the same sagacity.'

Fleur knew now he was recovering very quickly indeed from his lapse, and her previous feelings of sympathy began to wane. 'Nevertheless, your . . . caution was not enough to prevent you marrying someone who did not measure up to your estimation,' she said coolly.

'No,' he replied honestly. 'It was mistaken judgment.'

Fleur suddenly felt she had lived through a lifetime in the long room that evening, particularly when she heard the clock chime midnight. 'Do you perhaps feel purged now of your grievance against the world; the existence of women, especially?'

He gave a short laugh, his eyes softened.

'Thanks to you, yes. I find it good talking to you, as I have said before.'

Fleur smiled. There was a typical male naivety and frankness about him that would so easily bring out the maternal instinct in some women. Then she banished the thought hurriedly, realising she was following his example in categorising the dreaded female species! 'I'm so glad I please you, at least on a superficial level,' she said, allowing herself to relax slightly in the comfortable aftermath of past danger.

Antoine Devos looked the same way. As if he had battled his way through, and out of, some onrush of mental torment. 'There is no doubt about it. I hope you will put some of my ravings from your mind after tonight, Fleur,' he said seriously. 'But there is just one other thing I wish to discuss with you.' He sighed, rubbing the side of his chin as if unsure where to start.

'Yes . . . ?'

'Sally Hull at Hilldown. I think you will be returning home on holiday in a few months or so and perhaps will see her? Or even make a point of seeing her for me if she is still on night duty?'

Fleur was quite taken off guard at this sudden switch. Her heart, which had only recently calmed down, began to beat out messages of alarm again.

'I'd rather not, if you don't mind. Why not write to her if there's something worrying you?' She could feel his eyes upon her, knowing she did not sound too convincing.

'Something is worrying me. The fact that you are here reminds me of Hilldown and in turn, of her. Talking to you confidentially tonight has made me determined to mention it. You see,' he said, ignoring her reluctance, 'this pretty girl attracted me. As we were later to discover, we were both very unhappy and therefore had something in common. At the hotel that night we had both drunk enough to make us slightly irresponsible. I know she hadn't had much, but when people are desperately unhappy the chemical reaction can be very dramatic. She became rather hysterical and I took her to her room.' He paused as though expecting Fleur to speak, but how could he know it was a physical impossibility?

'She told me that she had been jilted. I heard about the man who had so callously tossed her aside just days before the wedding. She needed consolation, she said. But I was not so insensible that I could not see how she would have felt next morning. I made coffee for us both. Then as happens, she had a moment of clear-headedness and said she was going to get undressed. While she was doing this I went into her bathroom to get her a glass of water. She had been chattering to me from the bedroom but suddenly there was an ominous silence. As I thought, she had gone out cold across the bed. I covered her, for she had no nightgown. Then, after making sure she was OK, wrote her a note which I left on the pillow.

'This has worried me ever since, because in my own unsteady state, my English could have easily been misinterpreted.' His smooth eyebrows drew together suddenly as he said, 'I believe I thanked her for a wonderful night. But of course I meant evening. The difference between the two words to an English girl would have a very different connotation altogether.' He drew in a deep breath, as though relieved of yet another burden. 'So I should be glad if you could see her and put her mind at rest.'

Fleur's eyes had been cast down, and her cheeks had bloomed like poppies during his explanation. But had he given her two pins she would have burst into tears, or kissed him, despite all that had happened. She did neither of these things but sat just long enough to say calmly, 'I'll certainly try and see her, Antoine. Thank you. Any girl would want such a misunderstanding cleared up.' She stood up shakily, stepping over Prince who gave a little groan in his sleep.

Antoine Devos was at her side. He crossed the room with her and at the door took her hand, putting it to his lips with the elegance only a European possesses. 'Goodnight, Fleur. I hope I am forgiven and we can resume as before?' His eyes were anxious and held a tinge of sadness as he retained her hand in his.

'There's little to forgive, Antoine,' she said, trying desperately hard to fight down the unrelenting magnetism this man continued to have over her, particularly now that he had cleared up a problem that had given her so much anxiety. She raised her eyes to his and said simply, 'It is really part of my job to listen. Isn't that exactly what you did for Sally Hull? Goodnight, Antoine.'

Once upstairs she stood gazing at Marie-Claire's sleeping form for some minutes. Then, with a soft sigh, took a warm bath before going to bed. Between the sheets, gazing up at the pale apple-green lining to the canopy of her white, lace-covered bed, a persuasive lethargy claimed her. She was far too tired to go over the events of the evening, and fell off to sleep immediately.

Next morning after breakfast, Marie-Claire started calling out excitedly to Fleur, her eyes brilliant with excitement. 'Nurse Fleur! Papa says I can be taken downstairs! I can have my friends in and we can play better games than up here, and I can . . .'

Antoine Devos arrived just then, holding up his

hand to curb the little girl's outpourings. 'Good-morning, Nurse Hamilton.'

Their eyes met, and Fleur tried to steel herself against the immediate appeal of this tall, handsome man clad in his usual grey attire, enhanced this morning by a cream rosebud in the lapel of his jacket. She gave him a polite smile. 'Good-morning, Professor. It seems that Marie-Claire has good news!' she said, beaming at the child wriggling about in the bed, rosy cheeks brimming with renewed good health.

'Well, I had a word with Emile yesterday and he saw no reason why we couldn't get her down to the morning-room, which is fairly central. She could have a day-bed in there and when her friends come in it will be much less of a problem.'

'I think it's a marvellous idea, sir. What about morning and night?'

'We have a stretcher here that Leon and I can use. If at any time I am not here, Leon and Madame could, under your supervision, manage adequately.'

'Yes, that sounds workable.'

He picked up his brief-case and kissed Marie-Claire goodbye.

'We'll get it all arranged tonight, *ma chérie!*' he promised as he extricated himself from a huge bear-hug.

Outside the room he said to Fleur, 'We hope in another two weeks or so to remove that plaster for one that allows her to walk. But not a word to her, she would never sit still from then on!'

Once the transition was made, Marie-Claire was

much happier being at the hub of things in the house. Moreover, when Fleur's day off came around the following week, she felt quite happy as she drove away on that frosty morning.

A huge red disc of sun was just appearing over the fir woods and tinting the twelfth century church spire that stood on the outskirts of the village. It had been a relatively mild autumn, but early winter now seemed to be establishing itself with heavy frost that coated the farmsteads along the way as she headed for the city. Fleur was meeting Raoul Millaise that evening, whether in stubborn defiance of Antoine Devos she did not know. But at some stage she had to convince Raoul there could be nothing between them.

After going to the flat she did all the usual things that required attention. But her main job that day was to buy materials for Christmas decorations of the kind that Marie-Claire and her friends could help to make, and hang in a place of honour. Fleur and Madame Leon had plans to complete the Christmas preparations before she renewed duty at the clinic. The thought sent a small pang through her each time it crossed her mind.

Near the Grand Place she shopped locally at the glass-domed Galeries Saint Hubert. The arcade, with its long shop windows flanked by flat brown and white marble columns and walls, held a plaque stating it was opened in the year eighteen forty-six. A wintry sun shone through the glass roofing, casting chequer-board patterns on the flagged doorways and making the windows glisten like gems. It picked out the delicacy of handmade lace, succulent chocolates and eye-popping fashions, but Fleur managed to keep her mind firmly on the Christmas decorations.

They were not difficult to find—only the choice caused consternation! She had never seen such a dazzling array. Once out again on the Grand Place the sun had gilded the flamboyant buildings with gold and the flower market, set on cobble-stones, was like a giant's palette of colour. She went to a boulevard café for a snack lunch and then returned to the flat.

That evening in a restaurant near the imposing facade of the Guildhall, Raoul sat opposite Fleur as they talked over a delicious lobster fricassée, followed by chocolate cake and black coffee.

'I shall give up food for another week,' Fleur grinned as the waiter provided fresh coffee.

Raoul eyed her steadily. 'Are you having good food at the Mill House?'

'Marvellous,' she said quickly, suspecting that Raoul was waiting for her to complain in some way.

'When are you returning to the clinic?'

'Before Christmas I should think,' she replied casually.

His grey eyes devoured her, making her uncomfortable. 'You know I'm in love with you, don't you?'

She shook her head. 'Don't say that, please, Raoul. Just let's keep it on a friendly basis. I'm honestly not wanting a serious affair. I'm . . . I, well, love isn't my scene at the moment,' she stammered.

He stretched out and touched her face. 'Whatever you say, I shall not change my mind.'

'Oh, yes you will, Dr Millaise! You have a great deal of studying to do yet and that comes first!' She was staggered to hear herself reeling off Antoine Devos' words. They just came out. It seemed that everything he said stored itself away in the computer of her mind.

He gave a wry grin. 'I can cope with that, don't worry. Old Guy, my room-mate, keeps me at it.'

When they arrived at her flat she was glad she had the Mini parked there—it allowed her to decline his offer of a lift to Mill House. Accompanying her to the front door, his face was serious in the white moonlight.

'I'll be waiting for your return.'

She evaded the comment. 'Take care, Raoul. Work hard. Thanks for the lovely dinner.'

They kissed and he gripped her hand, saying no more. Then he got back into the car and gave her a final wave before shooting from the kerb. As she let herself into the flat to collect her bags, Fleur was relieved that there had been no harsh words between them. Raoul was too nice for that.

At about midnight she arrived back at Chaumont-Gistoux with the usual sense of homecoming. Contentedly, she turned into the drive. But on rounding the sweeping curve she was mystified to see the house ablaze with lights from the uncurtained windows. Something was wrong!

Leaving everything in the car, she ran to the front entrance where Antoine's Rolls stood. And that in itself was significant . . .

CHAPTER TEN

As FLEUR entered the front hall of Mill House, Antoine Devos, his face gaunt and preoccupied, was taking a packed overnight bag from Madame Leon. His casual polo-necked sweater and beige cords indicating an emergency of some kind.

Catching sight of her, he said urgently, 'I have to drive to my father's home in Paris, Nurse. The news is not good. He has suffered a severe coronary thrombosis, and I must be with him.'

'I'm so sorry,' Fleur said quickly. 'Is there anything I can do?'

He was hurrying past her through the open front door. 'Just continue with what you are doing for Marie-Claire. I shall ring when I have assessed this present situation for myself.' He went then, leaving a shocked and bewildered household behind him.

As they heard the car sweep down the gravel drive, Leon muttered something to the effect that the Professor should have allowed him to go too, to share the driving. 'But,' he grumbled as he made off for the kitchen, 'he is so stubborn, just like his father. They are two of a kind, and it will break his heart if anything happens to the old man.'

Despite her pleasant day, Fleur went to bed that night with a black sense of foreboding and next morning, she had to tell Marie-Claire that grand-père was ill and her father had gone to visit him.

'He was coming to see me soon,' she said, her lips trembling. 'Can he not come now, Fleur?'

'Maybe not for a little while, *chérie*. You had a big parcel of books and games from him last week didn't you? Well now,' Fleur said briskly, removing a breakfast tray, 'why not write him a letter on some of your new Disneyland notepaper?'

Marie-Claire's golden curls bobbed enthusiastically. 'Yes! When I go downstairs this morning I will do it then. I will draw him a picture also, shall I?'

That evening, Antoine Devos rang, his voice flat but controlled. 'My father is very ill. I think there is hope, but who knows. Please ring me here only if it is of great urgency.'

For the next three days, their conversation was much the same. Then news came of an overall improvement and a stabilising of his father's condition. Antoine Devos' voice on the phone was quietly jubilant. 'I shall, of course, remain in Paris for at least another week, but I'd be grateful if you would only make contact should it be really urgent.'

The following day, in a mood of light-hearted relief, Fleur had made Marie-Claire comfortable in the morning-room where she sat, excitedly watching the first snowfall of the year, when the telephone rang in the study. Fleur answered it, but failed to recognise the female voice.

'Miss Hamilton? Matron here, Meulebroeck Clinic.'

A small frown crossed Fleur's brow. 'Good-morning, Matron. You must have heard the good news?' she said, thinking this to be the reason for the call.

'Yes, indeed. That is why I'm ringing you, I did not want to trouble the Professor.'

'If I can help?'

'I think you can, Staff.'

Was there a sudden frostiness in the formal mode of address? 'Yes?' Fleur said quickly.

'We seem to have been hit by a short, sharp outbreak of a particularly virulent type of flu among the staff. I know that you have been told to remain at Mill House, but nevertheless, you are badly needed here. We must have another fully trained staff nurse. Sister Kenstein's nurses have been particularly badly affected, but I understand that with suitable treatment and precautions, the whole thing should pass in about a fortnight. So what I propose is that you report for duty tomorrow morning.'

Fleur made a face at the phone. 'I can't do that Matron! Who is going to look after Marie-Claire?'

'I intend sending another nurse over for a daily visit, say for two or three hours. Madame Leon is very capable with general care. There will, of course, also be Mr Vaumont's continued visits and instructions. The leg is healing well, I understand. Obviously we do not wish to trouble the Professor over the next few days, but I'm sure he'll see it my way once he hears of the difficulties. There was a slight pause, then the voice said firmly, 'We shall see you tomorrow then, Staff. Nine o'clock will be acceptable as you have a journey to make.'

Over coffee that morning with Madame Leon, Fleur tried to get her to see what Matron wanted. 'I can do nothing about it, but I really don't know what the Professor will say,' Fleur said worriedly as she looked into the outraged eyes of the house-keeper.

'But she cannot do that! Little Marie-Claire will be so upset I shall not know how I am to console her!'

Fleur sipped her coffee thoughtfully. 'Well, Matron has ordered me to return, and this I must do until the Professor is able to deal with it.'

The rest of the day was spent in a welter of instructions to Madame Leon about the small things that kept Marie-Claire happy during her recovery. The sort of details, Fleur thought sadly, that a mother would do. Like reading to the child, or playing games. But it was hard to imagine Jeanne Devos ever having been in the role. Fleur had grown to love Marie-Claire, and hated the thought of leaving her. On the other hand, she knew that she must not become closely involved. This was the very thing sister tutor had always warned them against at PTS.

After agonising all day as to how she should break the news of her going to Marie-Claire, Fleur waited until she was brushing the child's hair prior to her bed-time story, then made it as matter of fact as she could. 'I have to go back to the clinic for a few days tomorrow, Marie-Claire. Matron needs me there,' she added almost guiltily.

The child looked solemn, then opened *The Wind in the Willows*, saying with artless logic, 'I do not want you to go, Nurse Fleur. But I think you will come back with Papa in time for Christmas.'

Fleur's heart contracted. The child's instinct had warned her that things were different without her father. But her faith in an ultimate return to normality once he returned was implicit.

Nevertheless, reading about the antics of Mr Toad and his red car had never been so hard before. Fleur's mind seemed permanently fixed on Antoine Devos, his continued absence causing her far more heart-searching than she cared to admit to.

Next morning in Matron's office, Fleur was told of all the difficulties under which they were working. 'I'm sure Sister Kenstein will be very relieved to see you,' Matron smiled, dismissing her.

But by the time Fleur had arrived on third and entered Sister's office, she very much doubted that statement. Sister Kenstein's dark eyes looked up from her desk suspiciously.

'Oh, there you are, Staff.' Her tone implied that Fleur had been playing truant. 'We have no operations so far this week,' she said, plunging straight into work, pulling the report book towards her. 'Some of the patients you knew have now been discharged. Madame Conrad went at last, and the boy with broken ribs. Oh, yes, and the Frenchman. We've had twelve admissions in the last two weeks, four of whom are teenagers. Three with broken legs would you believe, through motor bike accidents!' She glanced up at Fleur suddenly. 'You remember Nicole LeClerque?'

'The girl who threatened to commit suicide? Had an appendicectomy.'

'You've got it. Well, we have her here again. She took an overdose of aspirin, but she survived. She's allowed up so that she can mix with the other patients. I don't see any problems now, but we're keeping her in for another week or so for observation.'

Fleur was quickly drawn back into the day to day routine of the clinic, and apart from Sister Kenstein's cold attitude, and missing Marie-Claire, she quite enjoyed being back. During her off-duty time she rang Moura and one or two other of her friends who were off sick with flu, having been warned by Sister not to go visiting any of them whilst they were still infectious.

On the eve of her day off, Fleur was at home in the flat when she made a sudden decision to visit Marie-Claire and Madame Leon at Mill House next day. She had rung earlier in the week and Madame had told her that all was going fairly well with the daily nurse calling. No one knew when the Professor would be returning. Now, she rang but could get no reply, as often happened with Madame Leon being slightly deaf. But she would make the visit nevertheless.

She made contact the following morning from the call-box in Chaumont-Gistoux, and was welcomed at Mill House in a flurry of excitement. The day-nurse had come and gone and Marie-Claire was already downstairs in the morning-room, her little face pink with happiness when Fleur hugged her.

With Madame Leon, they all had lunch together, and it was while Marie-Claire was telling Fleur about one of Antoinette's escapades—her imagination was incredible for a six-year-old—that she broke off suddenly, and said in wonder, 'Here is Papa! It is! I heard his car!'

Fleur's heart nearly turned over when a few minutes later, sure enough, Antoine Devos came striding into the room, looking slightly drawn but no less handsome than usual. He smiled a big welcome at Marie-Claire, the signs of strain on his features easing as he embraced her.

'*Mon petit!* How good it is to see you! And you are very well I think, those eyes are as bright as stars. Grandpère is on the mend too, and sends you all his love.'

Marie-Claire was breathless with kissing him. 'It is good! It is good! And you have come at the same time as Nurse Fleur. I missed *her* so as well, Papa!'

A great blackness seemed to descend upon the Professor's brow as he stood up and turned to look at Fleur. 'Missed her? Does Marie-Claire mean during your day off?' His eyes flitted over her brown tweed suit.

Fleur glanced anxiously at Marie-Claire. 'No, Professor. May I speak to you in the study, please?'

They crossed the hall and entered the small, oak-panelled room, where they stood facing each other. 'Well?' His expression was slightly impatient.

'I had to return to the clinic last week . . .' She rushed on before he could interrupt, his face already beginning to show signs of a gathering storm. 'There is a flu outbreak and Matron rang to say she needed me.'

'But this is outrageous! How dare she do such a thing!' He seemed to tower over her, his eyes sparking with fury. 'And how dare you contravene my orders! What right have you to leave Marie-Claire!'

Fleur trembled under the lash of his words. Whatever she tried to say now was obviously going to do nothing to placate him. 'I had little choice,' she said quickly. 'Matron did not wish to concern you with such matters whilst you were in Paris.'

He growled a reply she could not catch, flung off his expensive-looking overcoat, and snatched up the telephone. 'Leave me, will you, Nurse?' he snapped.

The whole tension-fraught afternoon passed before she saw Antoine Devos again. Fleur had had tea and played games with Marie-Claire, all the while her mind in a turmoil of apprehension. Quite suddenly the child looked up from her space-ship game, saying plaintively, 'My leg hurts, Fleur!' Her lovely blue eyes with the hint of violet, so beguiling. Fleur laughed as she put her arms round her. 'Oh, darling, I think you're pretending, you know!'

Nevertheless, she removed the small, wrinkled pillow from beneath the injured limb, patted and smoothed it before replacing it again. 'There we are!' she said, as brightly as she could, tidying the bed in general. 'That's much better isn't it?'

Marie-Claire nodded, already deeply engrossed in the next move of the game. Fleur knew the child was aware of tension since her father arrived and decided she needed a little extra attention. Later on, once Marie-Claire was tucked down for the night, and Fleur had promised to come back again soon, she went downstairs slowly. One more confrontation had to be endured with Antoine Devos before returning to the clinic that night.

As if he was waiting for her, the study door opened and the Professor called her. 'Just a minute, Miss Hamilton!' His face looked desperately tired as he collected up his brief-case and overcoat.

'I have talked to Matron. I realise she has done her best in difficult circumstances. I have told her to leave things as they are for the present until I can return. My father's business affairs are by no means updated yet, but I had a great need to see my daughter . . .' His eyes held hers. 'I am very glad I did, but I can see you were only doing your duty. I will go up to say goodbye to Marie-Claire now. I have to return to Paris tonight, so I shall drop you at the clinic first.'

Thanking Madame Leon for her day with them, Fleur sat beside Antoine Devos when they set off, and at first very little was said between them. Then he began to talk about his father—haltingly at first, but gradually stories came out of when he was a boy and what a friend his father had always been. There was nothing she needed to say. It was enough that he was talking in this way.

At the gates of the clinic he drew into the kerbside. 'My apologies for not taking you to the entrance, Nurse. I do not want to be delayed by Matron, I've a long drive ahead of me.' He turned to look at her, eyes deep with shadows. 'A great deal has happened since that night I was fool enough to have too much to drink, Fleur. I hope it has not worried you since?'

In the half-light of the car's interior, there was a faint aroma of flowers tinged with cigars and cologne. Fleur was overwhelmingly aware of her feelings for Antoine Devos. His closeness was causing a vibrant sensation of madness within her. His physical presence seemed to reach out to her, as she said quietly, 'No, of course not. Please don't worry.' She made an almost superhuman effort to open the car door.

'Fleur!' The name seemed to fall upon the charged atmosphere in a hoarse whisper.

She turned her head quickly. His face was close to hers, her heart thudding as his lips brushed her mouth, tenderly, delicately, as if they were as fragile as a butterfly's wing. Yet the contact was enough to set her trembling like a blossom too heavy for its stem.

'Thank you,' he murmured. 'Thank you for all the help that you've given to Marie-Claire and myself.'

Fleur thought she made some sort of barely audible reply as she stepped from the car. And as it sped swiftly away she gazed after its gradually disappearing lights until the road was empty, before going into the Meulebroeck.

For the next three days Fleur was in a daze of varying emotions. Because of it she worked like an automaton. Taking a beribboned bouquet of flowers to a convalescent patient in the sitting-room one morning, Fleur was surprised to see Nicole LeClerque there executing some very soft, but professional piano-playing in the corner of the room. The girl's face was happy and calmly tranquil. 'You play beautifully, Nicole. You must have had many hours of practice.'

The girl looked pleased. 'Thank you, Staff. My father says it's the only thing I can do well. But he is wrong,' she laughed gaily. 'I can fall in love!' And Fleur felt a subconscious relief that although the recipient of Nicole's love had abandoned her, she was recovering enough to joke about it.

By now, the hospital staff were gradually returning from their flu attacks. One junior nurse was back on third, yet the patients seemed fretful and required more than usual attention. Fleur had just returned from only one hour off duty, which was all that could be spared, and Sister Kenstein had none. Tempers were frayed, and by the time most visitors had gone that evening Fleur had glanced at the corridor clock hurriedly, amazed to see it was almost time for the night staff.

As she was on her way to the office Nicole floated past her in a gauzy negligee, carrying flowers and with a look of serenity on her face. Which certainly boded well for the future, Fleur thought as she joined Sister Kenstein where she was writing at her desk. While waiting for her to finish, Fleur pondered on what she had just seen. Sometimes suicide cases were very cunning if they still intended to take their life . . .

After discussing the day's work behind them, Fleur voiced her fears. Sister Kenstein snorted with derision.

'Good God, Staff, if she sees we're fussing over

her she's bound to stage another performance. She's an exhibitionist. I've told her to arrange her own flowers, it'll give her something to do. Best to leave her alone now. Concentrate on the more serious cases, Staff,' she said with heavy sarcasm as the night staff arrived. 'You go off duty now, I'll be a few minutes yet.'

When Fleur got home that evening she was too tired to do any more than bath and wash her hair before having an early night. But she could not sleep. She was filled with a terrible sense of unease; her only consolation being that it stopped her thinking of Antoine Devos and the devastating effect he continued to have on her.

She thought of Sister Kenstein, still wondering why she could not get on with the woman. There had been a wariness about her from the beginning, even though Fleur had tried to make their working relationship smooth. But it took two, and a one-way effort had proved unproductive. She had apparently resisted attempts from other members of staff to meet her socially—except the males. But in that particular area she had not been too successful according to rumour. Eventually Fleur settled down to sleep, but still with a subconscious anxiety nagging at her brain.

Next day it was not long before she knew why. The minute she arrived at the Clinique Meulebroeck in the morning, she sensed that something was wrong. This was confirmed when the receptionist told her that Matron wished to see her as soon as she arrived.

In the office, Fleur was surprised to see Senior

Night Sister Feraud seated beside Matron behind her desk, her face as accusing as a member of the Spanish Inquisition.

'Sit down, Staff,' Matron said curtly, her usually pleasant face set in hard lines. She leaned forward, hands clasped together on her blotter, one eyebrow slightly raised. 'It is my unpleasant duty to tell you that through your apparent gross incompetence, a young woman here is fighting for her life this morning.' She paused, knowing from her long experience the impact her scorching words would have.

She was right, Fleur was nearly speechless with shock. She moistened her lips. 'I don't understand!'

Matron took a very deep sigh. 'Last night, only minutes after the night staff came on, Nicole LeClerque was found bleeding from heavily slashed wrists. She had inflicted this upon herself by using a knife she had been given to cut the thread around her flowers. Had it not been for the swift attention of Sisters Kenstein and Feraud, the girl would by now be dead.

'It appears that Sister Kenstein had warned you several times to keep an eye on this girl. Certainly to make sure she went nowhere near the kitchen where she might have had access to knives. I understand you were given a further reprimand about the girl handling her own flowers. You actually passed her in the corridor carrying some. Yet, in your laxity you omitted to check she had nothing with which she could cause injury to herself.'

Fleur opened her mouth to speak, although her heart was racing so rapidly she wasn't even sure she could manage it. But Matron had held up her hand not wanting any interruptions.

'I do not wish to go into detail at this stage. Sister Feraud witnessed the entire thing. We did not think—in fairness to you—that Sister Kenstein should be here at this first hearing. What have you to say?'

Fleur was very cold suddenly. She was trembling, and clasped her hands together until the knuckles showed white, not wanting these women to see any sign of weakness. 'If I cannot go into detail now, Matron,' she said as calmly as she could, 'I prefer to say nothing until I am able to do so.'

'Very well, Staff.' The two women stood up. Fleur did the same. 'You realise of course that you cannot return to duty until a meeting of the clinic tribunal can be held. Professor Devos must be informed. Until you hear from us again you are temporarily suspended.'

'Yes, Matron.'

'And, Staff. You realise the very serious consequences should this patient die?'

Fleur lifted her chin. 'I do, Matron.'

CHAPTER ELEVEN

FLEUR did not remember the tram journey back to her flat after Matron's hostile accusations and summary dismissal that morning. She only knew that snow was falling and the grey, leaden sky above held a prospect of more to come.

Once indoors she threw off her coat, and stood, staring down from the long windows, watching people scurrying by in the street like a toy snow-scene paperweight she had as a child; snow falling constantly, whichever way she twisted it. Her life was like that. Fate intervened remorselessly, whichever way she twisted and turned to try and deal with the problem.

Still trembling, she made herself a hot drink in the hope of throwing off the chilled numbness that invaded her body. She switched on the electric fire, drawing up a chair as close as she could and slumping into it, wondering if the morning's events were true or if she was in some terrible nightmare from which she might awake.

But she didn't. Stark reality was all around her. The only thing her brain seemed to comprehend was that she was utterly alone, and in complete isolation.

During those lost hours it was the treachery of Sister Kenstein's lies with which Fleur found it so hard to come to terms. What had the woman got against her that would drive her to bring about the downfall of a colleague, and the disgrace?

No doubt the tribunal would give Fleur a chance to tell her side of the story, but would they believe her? Sister Kenstein was her superior. She was older and had far greater experience. And what of Antoine Devos, once he heard? If he believed her guilty would he want her ever again to see Marie-Claire? The loyalty she thought she had built up between herself and the Devos family would be swept completely away.

Even in this, one of the blackest moments of her whole life, her heart cried out at the thought of Antoine Devos and those cold, ice-blue eyes looking at her accusingly. He would hate her, he had no time for inefficiency of any kind. She knew it mattered to her, mattered more than she would care to admit even now. And it was just one more blow to her shattered pride.

Afternoon shadows had crept insidiously about the room when Fleur became aware of the jangling of the telephone. She ignored it. She was in no fit state to talk to anyone. Perhaps tomorrow she could get herself together. Or maybe the day after . . .

But still the ringing persisted. With a low moan she dragged herself across the room to the telephone table, switching on the reading-lamp and clumsily picking up the receiver. 'Hello.'

'Antoine Devos here. I'm just back from Paris. Matron has told me about Nicole LeClerque. What is your side of the story?'

For one moment Fleur could not bring herself to

think, let alone reply. She had descended to such an abyss of despair that to hear a perfectly normal and non-accusatory voice addressing her pulled her together miraculously with a jerk. 'It's not true,' she faltered.

'Go on.'

As briefly as she could she told him the details—from when she saw Nicole playing the piano to Sister Kenstein telling her she should concentrate on the more serious cases. 'That's about it.'

'I see. I shall be in touch with you again as soon as possible.'

The phone went dead, and with it the one remaining tinge of normality. The only thing sustaining Fleur throughout that sleepless night was the fact that Antoine Devos had said he would be in touch again. But by morning even that hope floundered. She convinced herself that after talking to Matron, Sister Feraud and Sister Kenstein, her case would be damned.

She took a shower and dressed, afterwards made coffee and drank three cups. The flat by then had become hopelessly oppressive and she began to realise how poor Nicole must have felt. By the time she made the decision to go out, and had reached the Grand Place, the festive season burst upon her. Huge Christmas trees glistening with decorations were placed every few steps, it seemed. Coloured lights strung like necklaces moved gently in a cold breeze as snow began to drift down upon fur-coated shoppers. In one of the brilliantly lit arcades, Fleur forced herself to think of something to take her mind off her thoughts, and Christmas presents were the obvious thing. She bought lace-edged handkerchieves and cigars for her aunt and uncle, a Hans Andersen book of fairytales for Marie-Claire and a small gift for Madame Leon and her husband—by which time all she wanted to do was escape people.

Back in her flat she threw the purchases aside, deep depression swamping her again as she looked round the room. She could eat nothing but she heated some soup for something to do. She had just tasted a little when the phone rang. This time her heart pounded in such a suffocating manner her voice came out in a whisper. 'Yes?'

'Antoine Devos. I should like you to come over to the clinic. I will come now and pick you up.'

'Right.' This was it. He had lost no time.

She was trembling uncontrollably as she tried to replace the receiver. It was seconds before she accomplished it. Glad now that she had already been out, she thanked heaven she had at least dressed in her decent suede suit and long leather boots. Yet even an angora polo-necked sweater did not prevent her from shivering. Minutes later it seemed, there came a tap at the door. Madame Guiot must have opened the street door to him, she realised.

Antoine Devos stood filling the doorway, informally dressed in sheepskin coat and white Arran sweater, hair slightly awry from the drifting snow, the expression on his face impossible to define. Without any preliminaries he murmured quickly, 'Matron's waiting for us. You are ready? There's no rush if you are not!'

She flung her jacket around her shoulders, picking up her handbag and locking the door as they left.

In the car, Fleur sat rigid with nervousness. She heard Antoine Devos say easily, 'Don't look so worried! The end of the world has not come.'

Not even his words helped. As they turned into the drive of the clinic the thoughts she had long ago, that she was steadily going off nursing, were more reinforced than ever as they entered the reception area and went into Matron's office.

Fleur's first surprise was to see Matron seated at her desk alone. She indicated chairs to them both. Fleur sat stiffly, hardly able to breathe. Antoine Devos took her jacket and, with his own, handed them to a maid who had come in at Matron's behest. She ordered coffee and biscuits, but Fleur could not think why she bothered, because nothing would pass her own lips in that room. All she wanted now was to get the whole thing over and make her escape.

Matron's eyes were upon her. 'It's good news, Miss Hamilton. Nicole is out of danger and is being moved to another hospital more suited to her needs. Now, the Professor has expressed a preference that I tell you what has happened. When he confronted Sister Kenstein he was quickly of the same opinion as I. She appeared to say one thing at one moment, only to contradict it minutes later. I had already heard about certain troubles on her ward. And with regard to Nicole, there were—as you say in England—loopholes. The Professor has investigated the matter and has decided that on this particular occasion you bear no responsibility for Nicole's actions. Sister Kenstein has given her notice and will be leaving within the week.' Matron gave a long sigh, her eyes smiling at Fleur, the warmth back in them. 'We hope that you will continue with us, Miss Hamilton, after this unfortunate happening. I feel regret that you have had to suffer this way, but I do hope you understand that misjudgments cannot always be avoided when taking on staff.'

Fleur felt new life flowing through her. She swayed lightly at Matron's words and heard herself saying, 'Yes, of course I understand, Matron.' At the same time she wondered what else could she say? Neither Sister Kenstein nor Matron could ever make up for the hours of anguish she had spent. That was simply something that wasn't included in the package deal.

The voice went on. 'The Professor and I thought that you might like to take a fortnight's leave—which would include the Christmas period—and then return here afterwards, when I do hope all will be forgotten,' she said, with typically German thoroughness.

Antoine Devos looked across at her as coffee was brought in, and Matron poured. 'Do you feel all right, Miss Hamilton?'

'Yes, I'm fine,' Fleur said, attempting a thin smile in Antoine Devos' direction. But his face blurred, and to her intense annoyance there was a terrible pounding in her head that wouldn't stop, and suddenly she was falling down, down into blackness . . .

A low murmur of voices troubled her. Matron's face swum into vision, stony and accusing; then Sister Kenstein's. She shot up, crying out . . .

A cool hand brushed her face. 'It's perfectly all right, Miss Hamilton. You've nothing more to worry about,' Matron's voice soothed. Fleur felt the sting of brandy on her lips, and soft cushions at her head. Antoine Devos was seated at her side on the settee where she lay in Matron's sitting-room. Relief came like a full tide rolling in as she looked up into Antoine Devos' anxious face. 'I'm sorry about this.' She began to move.

His hands gently urged her back. 'No need for apologies. As soon as you feel like it I'm taking you home.' They said their goodbyes to Matron and arrived back outside her flat in no time. Fleur was still in a daze and once they were inside the street door, Antoine Devos suddenly swept her off her feet, into his arms and carried her up the stairs. She didn't protest but just dropped her head on his broad chest for two blissful moments before he stood her down while she found her door-key. She gave it to him and he took it with a grin. 'I can vouch that you are definitely not drunk if you think Madame Guiot is lurking behind one of her pot plants!' he smiled, opening the door.

She opened her mouth to speak, but he placed a forefinger upon her lips. 'No talking. You are going to rest under the duvet on your bed, while I go into the kitchen and make you a cup of your English tea. I shall give you a sedative, and at eight o'clock this evening I shall take you out to dinner!' He looked down at her, all teasing gone, just deep concern in his eyes. 'After what you must have been through it's the least I can do,' he said softly. 'Now, I'll get to work in the kitchen. I think I know where everything is.'

He did exactly as he said, and when the flat door closed on him she only vaguely remembered hearing his whispered farewell as she floated off into sweet oblivion.

On waking a few hours later, she was surprised to hear it was on the insistence of her travelling alarm clock. With a grin she thought how ingenious Antoine Devos was. She had not realised to what extent until she switched on her lamp and saw the note propped up, addressed to her. Her hand shook as she picked it up.

Dear Sally Hull . . . The words danced in front of her eyes as she threw up a hand to her mouth. So he knew! *From the above you will see that my memory has not played me false, as I once thought. We shall talk tonight. AD.*

He really knew it was her, after all this time! She didn't know whether to laugh or cry—to be furious with him or relieved that at last he'd admitted to knowing that she and 'Sally Hull' were one and the same girl.

In a different kind of daze now, she bathed and shampooed her hair. All the time her thoughts raced as to what she would tell him about her silly spur-of-the-moment joke. And someday, when she was nursing up the Amazon or some similarly remote spot, perhaps she would feel nothing more than faint amusement at the recollection. For she had decided that despite Matron's suggestion about staying on at the clinic, her feelings towards Antoine Devos were too deep for her to continue working this way. She would have to leave Brussels.

She dressed that evening in a black velvet mid-calf skirt, its controlled fullness just right for her white cotton broderie anglaise blouse, with its deep-frilled, off-the-shoulder line. Black pumps and a two-string pearl choker completed the outfit, because this evening she needed all the confidence she could muster.

Looking at herself in the mirror, she showed little sign of the strain she had undergone that day. She added a touch of lip and cheek colour, wondering if the girl reflected before her could ever start life afresh, for now she really knew what love was, she had to relinquish it so soon. Strange that in coming to work in a foreign country she had also found what life was all about. Rather like peeping into Pandora's box and having to close down the lid again.

She turned from the mirror hastily. For the next few hours she must simply be practical Staff Nurse Hamilton who was being taken out to dinner, maybe as a kindly attempt to appease her feelings.

When she opened the door to Antoine Devos, she caught her breath on seeing him in evening dress.

'Come in,' she smiled.

His admiring glance swept over her. 'You are quite recovered now?' he asked in a low voice. 'You look so chic.'

The phone rang just then and he did not see the

swift wave of colour that rushed to her face. He wandered over to stare from the window as she picked up the receiver.

'Hi, Raoul! Yes, I'm certainly relieved, too,' she said, as she was showered with messages from everyone at the clinic.

His voice was light-hearted as he said eagerly, 'Now can we all meet for a celebration?'

'Not tonight, Raoul, sorry. I'll call you tomorrow. Yes, I promise.' As she put the phone down, she could see disapproval in the set of Antoine Devos' shoulders. 'My apologies,' she said as he turned to face her. 'They were all pleased for me.'

A smile barely touched his lips, but he made no answer, except to pick up her jacket and hold the door open for her. They drove out to a restaurant known as Le Bon Accueil, a small but pleasant manor house in a park on the old Roman road to Strombeek. Fleur knew as much because Raoul had once told her this was the place he would take her when he was rich. They sat in a secluded alcove, and Antoine Devos picked up the outsize menu with a smile. She would not broach the subject of his note addressed to Sally Hull, it was for him to do so.

'You must have the speciality of the house. Tender Brussels chicken treated with champagne-brandy. It is definitely the thing to have when you come here!'

The attentive waiter came and went between courses while soft music played and the atmosphere became more and more relaxed. By the time they had reached coffee and liqueurs, all the earlier events of the day seemed to have faded to an unreal blur in her mind.

Fleur put the large scarlet napkin to her lips. 'That was the most perfect dinner I've ever tasted,' she said, sitting back in her chair with a smile.

He blew a smoke ring away, as he lit a cheroot, his deep-set eyes meeting hers as he leaned forward on his elbows. 'Now, Sally Hull! Don't tell me that you hadn't some idea that I knew all the time?'

She blushed and grinned. 'Sally *Hall* if you re-member! Yes, I knew more or less on the day I came for my interview. I saw you briefly in the car.'

'And yet, you still came?'

'Why not? You could have been a patient. I wasn't to know then that you worked there, and I was desperately wanting to get away from my old life.'

'Away from the unhappiness of the jilting?'

'Yes, I didn't realise at the hotel in London just how much I'd talked. I was stupid. I've had the feeling all along that you knew, and despised me for my behaviour.'

He shook his head. 'No, I understood once I realised why you were so unhappy. How could you be in control of your inner feelings? When you let go, that was the first thing that tumbled out.'

'I was very lucky to meet someone like you that night. I shudder to think of other possibilities.'

His lips turned upwards and his eyes crinkled attractively at the sides. 'You know, it was not until I came home here that I linked you with the lovely young nurse who tipped her coffee down me. When it happened again at Mill House . . .' He laughed teasingly. 'Well, how could I be mistaken? But on that first morning when you came into Matron's office—although I knew she had appointed someone from Hilldown—at first sight I thought little of it. Maybe,' he shrugged, 'I thought I might have recognised you, but you looked different. From then on I decided I was giving it all too much thought, and later I was not proud of the way I treated you. But there was resistance in me to acknowledging you.

'Yet, after Marie-Claire's accident things began to change. I knew who you were, and I was going through a bad time hating all women. As playthings, yes; but anything else, never . . .' He broke off suddenly, watching her guardedly as if the recollection of the night he was drunk in the long room was still painful.

She gave a small, wry smile, performing the Gallic shrug like a native. 'It's life. What can we do but deal with it as we feel is right for us?'

He pursed his lips, nodding agreement and saying quietly, 'Marie-Claire keeps asking after you.'

'How is she?'

'She knows about Jeanne, and has accepted it extremely well. Her resilience is marvellous. She now has a walking plaster! We kept her in bed for forty-eight hours to make sure it dried out thoroughly and as a special treat she's going to the party of one of Emile Vaumont's daughters tomorrow. She is so excited.'

'That's wonderful news!' Fleur smiled happily, then more soberly. 'The day-nurse still attends?'

'No longer,' he replied dismissively. 'When you return after Christmas you must visit Mill House.'

She smoothed a sleek eyebrow with her finger. 'I shall not be returning to my job, Antoine.' She used the name easily, formality now rather futile.

He scowled in surprise. 'What the devil do you mean?'

She drew a deep breath and said, 'I shall go home as Matron suggested, and then set about finding another job abroad.'

His face was angry. 'You can't do that!'

Fleur ran a slim forefinger over the red and gold Christmas centre-piece between them. 'I didn't sign a contract. I always understood only a month's notice was required. There are many reasons I must go . . .' How could she tell him the real one; that seeing him from now on each day would be torture?

He chose to ignore her words. 'Will you come out to see Marie-Claire tomorrow after the party?'

'Well . . .' She hesitated, then said, 'Yes, perhaps, as I'm leaving.'

He seized on her hesitancy. 'I'll pick you up on my way home from the clinic. I shall tell Madame Leon you will be staying to dinner.'

'No, I . . . but I'm not sure.' She was blabbering like an idiot at his insistence. She resented his old tactics of pushing her around. 'I'll think about it.'

He called for the bill suddenly. When they left, he said very little on the drive back to the flat. In the starlit night he escorted her to the front door and saw her safely inside. 'I shall be along about four tomorrow afternoon.' He was gone before she could reply.

There was so much on her mind that she slept heavily out of sheer exhaustion. Next day she spent time packing together things she had collected in Brussels, all the while thinking of the man who, despite their stormy relationship, she had come to see as the one person in the world to whom she had given her heart. What a damn fool she was. Of all the arrogant males in the world she had to fall for one of the worst of them!

By four she was dressed and ready in a cream woollen suit and honey silk shirt. She was happy at the thought of seeing Marie-Claire, but the rest would be an endurance test. She gift-wrapped the presents she was taking, at the same time making a resolution that Antoine Devos would not change her mind about leaving.

Later, in the car beside him, Fleur felt again the sweet torture of his nearness as they talked generally. She stole a look at the enigmatic profile. He had the formal trappings of a rich and very clever surgeon, yet he was still a man with sadness in his eyes.

'I was late, I'm afraid,' he was saying. 'There was a bad accident at the Place Rogier. Six people were brought in, but two died this morning.' She knew only too well how he felt when she saw a muscle in his face tighten. The needless loss of life and injury no doubt reminded him of the tragedy he had so recently had to bear himself.

Snow had begun to fall again as they drove through the gates of Mill House. Soft lights shone out from its as yet uncurtained windows, and Fleur had to quell a deep stab of heartache at the thought of never returning again. Antoine helped her from the car.

'Come, Fleur,' he said, 'Madame Leon can find us tea before Marie-Claire bursts upon us!' Nevertheless, he was smiling with pleasure at the thought.

'I hope she knows I'm coming,' Fleur said as they went inside. 'I don't want to overburden her.'

'No, but it has to be a surprise.' He took her coat and opened the long room door. A log fire burned brightly in the huge stone hearth, two large reading-lamps casting a golden glow over the brocaded couches. Holly and gilt fir cones, arranged over the oval mirror with long scarlet ribbons, fluttered gently as Antoine closed the door behind them.

Fleur stood before the fire, holding out her hands to the welcoming warmth, utter contentment going through her. 'This room is so beautiful, especially at Christmas-time,' she said, as Madame Leon entered with a tea-tray, her face suddenly wreathed in smiles.

'Nurse! What a lovely surprise! I must set a larger tray at once. Marie-Claire will be so happy!'

When the woman had performed all her duties, having drawn the curtains and finally closed the door, Antoine Devos crossed the room from where he had been putting the gifts out of sight and looked down at her.

'The room is beautiful yes. But there are days when its beauty fades, and there is nothing but greyness.' He looked drawn and tired, as if the road accident that morning had drained all energy from him, as he sat down.

She poured the tea. 'I understand,' she said softly. 'But unhappiness passes. At least through my troubles I've learned that I was never really in love with my fiancé. So something good comes out of these things.'

'Yes, I know you are right.' He placed his cup down on the low table between them. 'You have, I hope, changed your mind about leaving the clinic?'

'Of course not. I . . . I can't,' she stammered.

'It's Raoul who wants you to leave?'

'Definitely not. He is just a friend.'

'Well then, what is there to stop you returning after Christmas?' His expression was taut. 'We do not like losing a good nurse. I remember Matron saying you would be here a year at least. I thought you were a woman of your word.'

Anger rippled through her at his tone. 'Professor,' she said, with admirable control, 'I *am* a woman of my word. I've said I'm leaving with the appropriate notice, and this is what I am doing!'

He suddenly stood up, staring into the fire as if so furious he couldn't face her. Then he swung round saying, 'And what if I will not allow you to?'

Her answer never passed her lips for just then, above the sound of a car driving away, they heard a torrent of childish chatter and Marie-Claire burst into the room, Madame Leon behind her. The child looked entrancing in a long, blue velvet dress, and above her white lace collar, fair hair and pansy eyes sparked in the firelight. Her smile was ecstatic. 'Papa, I . . . Nurse Fleur! You are here . . . Oh! You are here!'

She came hobbling over the carpet, flinging herself into Fleur's arms, her lovely rosy face alive with happiness. 'Marie-Claire you look so pretty! Was it a good party?' Fleur asked tenderly.

'It was lovely. Look at all my things!' Party gifts tumbled to the floor and Antoine Devos seized the moment to drink his tea while Marie-Claire chattered on to Fleur, playing with balloons one minute and her other gifts the next. Then, like quicksilver, she disappeared. But suddenly a huge yellow balloon came floating over the back of the couch to settle between Fleur and Antoine.

She gave him a knowing smile. 'Now, I wonder where this balloon could have come from, Professor?'

He grinned. 'Very strange! *Mon Dieu!* Here is another one!'

There was a pause and Fleur said. 'No more? What a shame!' As she spoke, some inner perception alerted her. From behind them there was a low cry, a hoarse croak. They were no longer playing games.

Fleur jumped up and rushed to the back of the couch. Marie-Claire's little face was a terrible red, tinged with blue. She was fighting for her breath. The balloon now bobbing across the carpet, minus its mouthpiece, told its own story. Fleur pounced on the child, tipped her upside down, and gave her a decisive thump on the back, all in less than a second. A small plastic piece shot from her mouth.

Holding Marie-Claire tightly in her arms, Fleur waited for the little girl's breathing to regain normality, and at last, with relief, noted the cough reflex was established. Marie-Claire burst into great heaving sobs of shock, then tears. Antoine Devos, his face ashen, lifted Fleur from her knees on the floor, still holding the child, and moved them both to the couch. He knelt beside them, smoothing Marie-Claire's hair back from her hot face, murmuring over and over that she was perfectly all right now.

That was how Madame Leon found the tableau when she came in to clear the tea-tray. It had all happened so quickly, and suddenly everyone started to talk at once.

Two hours later when Marie-Claire, reviving quickly as children do, had been put to bed and Fleur had read her a story, she and Antoine Devos returned to the long room. Neither of them were able to think of dinner, as yet. Antoine poured sherries and they stood beneath the oval mirror, the room once again tranquil about them, Fleur's trembling reaction to the shock only now subsiding.

'She was over-excited of course,' Fleur murmured, unable to erase the child's face from her mind.

She was conscious of Antoine Devos' eyes upon her. 'She loves you, you know, Fleur,' he said softly, his eyes revealing such a depth of emotion as he brushed her cheek with his hand, that her heart leapt with a new hesitant joy. 'I love you also.'

Very carefully he took the glass from her, drawing her into his arms and kissing her with such sweet gentleness that Fleur felt tears on her lashes. 'I knew it was happening, Fleur. I tried to deny it because you had your new life to build. I invited

you here this afternoon because it was the first thing
I could think of when you said you were leaving.'
His arms tightened about her. 'Now, saving Marie-
Claire's life as you have, how can I restrain myself
any longer?'

Had he not been holding her, Fleur would have
slipped down to the floor in another faint, but this
time with the sheer, singing happiness that filled
her whole being. 'Antoine,' she whispered, still
disbelieving. 'You feel this way because . . . because it's shock reaction. Marie-Claire is your
daughter. You are . . .'

He interrupted impatiently. 'Will you stop running on, woman!' he bellowed in a voice that was
now beautifully normal. 'I love you, dammit! Don't
you understand?'

She was laughing now, laughing with all the
pent-up love she felt for this man, knowing that he
loved her, too; knowing he meant every word he
said! Then she looked at him seriously. 'Antoine, I
heard you!' she said shakily. 'I think I've loved you
for I don't know how long. My decision to leave the
clinic was simply that I couldn't bear to be so close
to you any more. It was . . .'

Her words were stilled by his kiss. One of such
demanding passion it lifted them to the stars, to a
world of their own for endless perfect moments.
At last he murmured against her lips, his voice
trembling.

'You must stay the night, *ma chère*. You will
marry me as soon as we can arrange everything?'

'Yes. Oh, yes . . . But Marie-Claire?' Fleur
stammered, her cheeks the colour of rose petals.

He ran a trail of tiny kisses down her throat to the edge of her shirt-collar. 'She will be the eldest of our children. Marie-Claire will be so happy. Both she and I need you so much.'

She traced his lips with her finger. 'I think I have loved you since we danced together in London.'

They kissed, and their bodies fused with such longing, neither of them noticed Madame Leon putting her head round the door and popping out again with a happy smile on her face. When they drew apart, he said softly, 'You will spend Christmas here, then I shall take you home to your family. Afterwards we shall have a long honeymoon.'

She nuzzled her forehead against his chin, then looked up at him, brown eyes twinkling. 'You are very bossy, Antoine. Before we go any further, remember we are to be partners in our work as well as our marriage.'

'Of course,' he smiled, kissing her lips teasingly. 'I am a very lucky man. You see I shall have Fleur Hamilton as my wife, and Sally Hull as my mistress. Could any man wish for more?'

And Fleur's eyes, as his lips met hers, left no doubt that he could not.

Doctor Nurse Romances

Amongst the intense emotional pressures of modern medical life, doctors and nurses often find romance. Read about their lives and loves in the other three Doctor Nurse titles available this month.

PRODIGAL DOCTOR
by Lynne Collins
All starch and no heart…That's Dr Eliot Hailey's verdict on his wife, Sister Claudia Hailey, when they're thrown together after a four-year separation. Having given up hopes of a home and husband, Claudia has dedicated herself to nursing — but will Eliot's sudden reappearance change her mind?

THE HEALING PROCESS
by Grace Read
'I'm quite capable of running my own life without advice from *you*,' Staff Nurse Nicky Pascall tells Dr Alex Baron. But if she is to recover from her broken heart, perhaps his tender loving care is the best way to start the healing process.

LIFE LINES
by Meg Wisgate
After the hectic routine of St Vincent's, life in the sick-bay of Leisure TV seems tame to Sister Penny Shepherd. Until, that is, she's asked to become medical adviser to a new series, *Life Lines*, and finds herself in constant battle with its autocratic presenter, Dr Justin Welles…

Mills & Boon
the rose of romance

4 Doctor Nurse Romances
FREE

Coping with the daily tragedies and ordeals of a busy hospital, and sharing the satisfaction of a difficult job well done, people find themselves unexpectedly drawn together. Mills & Boon Doctor Nurse Romances capture perfectly the excitement, the intrigue and the emotions of modern medicine, that so often lead to overwhelming and blissful love. By becoming a regular reader of Mills & Boon Doctor Nurse Romances you can enjoy EIGHT superb new titles every two months plus a whole range of special benefits: your very own personal membership card, a free newsletter packed with recipes, competitions, bargain book offers, plus big cash savings.

AND an Introductory FREE GIFT for YOU. Turn over the page for details.

**Fill in and send this coupon back today
and we'll send you
4 Introductory
Doctor Nurse Romances yours to keep**

FREE

At the same time we will reserve a
subscription to Mills & Boon
Doctor Nurse Romances for you. Every
two months you will receive the latest
8 new titles, delivered direct to your door.
You don't pay extra for delivery. Postage and
packing is always completely Free.
There is no obligation or commitment –
you receive books only for
as long as you want to.

**It's easy! Fill in the coupon below and return it to
MILLS & BOON READER SERVICE, FREEPOST, P.O. BOX 236,
CROYDON, SURREY CR9 9EL.**

**Please note: READERS IN SOUTH AFRICA write to
Mills & Boon Ltd., Postbag X3010,
Randburg 2125, S. Africa.**

- -

FREE BOOKS CERTIFICATE

**To: Mills & Boon Reader Service, FREEPOST, P.O. Box 236,
Croydon, Surrey CR9 9EL.**

Please send me, free and without obligation, four Dr. Nurse Romances, and reserve a
Reader Service Subscription for me. If I decide to subscribe I shall receive, following my free
parcel of books, eight new Dr. Nurse Romances every two months for £8.00, post and
packing free. If I decide not to subscribe, I shall write to you within 10 days. The free books
are mine to keep in any case. I understand that I may cancel my subscription at any time
simply by writing to you. I am over 18 years of age.
Please write in BLOCK CAPITALS.

Name _____

Address _____

_____

_____ Postcode _____

SEND NO MONEY — TAKE NO RISKS

8DN

EP11